ADVANCE PRAISE

"A page-turning thriller, a meditation on art, and a touching exploration of second chances, Peter Gooch's *Seren* is a novel that does all that."

— Adam Prince, author of *The Beautiful Wishes of Ugly Men*

"In this arresting novel, Peter Gooch uses his impressive talents as a writer and painter to craft a gripping mystery centered on a masterpiece by landscape painter Norris Bainbridge. . . . Gooch's hand with narrative and description is sure, and his knowledge of the milieu and characters carries the story along with satirical panache and absorbing suspense. *Seren* is at once a sharply comic satire of the art scene, a canny meditation on the nature of art, and an entirely absorbing murder mystery. Buy it. Read it. Enjoy."

— Arnold Johnston, novelist, playwright, poet, and author of *Swept Away, The Witching Voice* and *Where We're Going, Where We've Been*

"Peter Gooch's *Seren* is above all a good read, suspenseful, comic, and diverting. Drawing on his own career as a fine visual artist, Gooch constructs a puzzle centered on the life and death of a renowned and reclusive painter, Norris Bainbridge, the key to whose demise is Seren, his beautiful and enigmatic muse. This novel skewers the pretensions and infighting of the art world in the context of a thoroughly satisfying mystery that will make readers laugh and think."

— Deborah Ann Percy, fiction writer, playwright, and author of *Invisible Traffic* and *Dream Time* (Susan Smith Blackburn Award Finalist)

"*Seren* is a tour de force that dives into an artist's deepest desires—a glimpse of immortality, or his signature on the ceiling of the local bar beside other renowned artists. Peter Gooch offers a cast of lively, well-rounded characters in an affluent artists' world. The plot line quivers with energy and mystery as Fairchild Moss, a competent Midwest artist/art dealer, renews his singular talent for painting. Rooted in an archetypal battle between darkness and light, Moss is possessed by traces of the elusive and feral Seren, an artist's model. It appears that she has circled the death of three artists who displayed with their last brushstrokes across the broad canvas of life a luminous splash of creation. Is she the muse his vision requires, or is she nature's duende? Will a perfect fit with Seren's lithe body produce a work of genius? Or will the artist sell his soul in a Faustian bargain for his signature on the ceiling?"

— Phaedra Greenwood, author of *Beside the Rio Hondo* and coauthor of *Those Were the Days: Life and love in 1970s New Mexico*

SEREN

SEREN

a novel

Peter Gooch

Apprentice House Press
Loyola University Maryland

Seren is a work of fiction. Any similarity with living persons is purely coincidental.

First Edition

Casebound ISBN: 978-1-62720-563-4
Paperback ISBN: 978-1-62720-564-1
Ebook ISBN: 978-1-62720-565-8

Library of Congress Control Number: 2025931869

Design by Apprentice House Press
Promotional Development by Kate Tourison
Editorial Development by Becca Thompson

Cover background art by Peter Gooch, excerpted painting is "Elizabeth Winthrop Chandler" by John Singer Sargent, 1893

Author photo by Sharon A. Ransom, Lalibela Ethiopia

Published by Apprentice House Press

Apprentice
House Press
Loyola University Maryland

Loyola University Maryland
4501 N. Charles Street, Baltimore, MD 21210
410.617.5265
www.ApprenticeHouse.com
info@ApprenticeHouse.com

For my wife Sharon A. Ransom, M.D.

"The muse does not come without being called."
— Tchaikovsky

PROLOGUE

Detroit—January 1978

Cass Avenue. Wind rattles windowpanes in the old, redbrick ware-house, the clouded squares of glass loose in their wooden frames, caulk chipped and crumbling. Outside, snow is building up, obscuring the shapes of the stoops, the fire hydrants, the benches at bus stops. Rumors of the Nain Rouge abound. This blizzard has ambushed the Motor City—a place so derelict and impoverished since the 1967 riots it's unready for any sort of challenge, much less the snowstorm of the cen-tury. The plows have surrendered. The streets and highways lie under four-foot drifts. In the yellow glow of streetlights, flakes cascade relent-lessly from the heavens, signifying nothing less than the hand of God.

Inside the painting studio, electric heaters crackle, glowing orange and hot. The smell of turpentine, cigarette smoke, and urine saturates the air. There is no orthodox ventilation—chinks in the building's mortar do the trick.

Haller bends over the turntable and repositions the needle at the beginning of the track. Fauré's "Élégie for Cello" drones from speakers positioned around the room. Clouds of mauve, violet, and viridian fog the space. He has played the same piece all night. He'll listen until he is too exhausted or too drunk to lift the phonograph needle.

Seren no longer hears much of anything but the sound of her own breathing. Her job is to lie naked and let Haller look at her. Nothing more. Hours ago, she entered the dark tunnel of semiconsciousness. Her respiration is slow and shallow, heart pumping at a rate of fifty beats per minute. Inert on the filthy mattress, she's discarded all sense of time. The scene passing before her eyes flickers like an old film from the 1920s, images ratcheting through a cracked projector lens. Haller moves around the studio in a jerky motion of starts and stops. He's dressed in bib overalls, a soiled singlet, and yellow work boots with dangling laces, his bald head bent on a neck too skinny to bear its weight, heavy-lobed ears standing straight out and lending him the aspect of a startled baby elephant. A paint-stained rag hangs from a rear pocket.

As if from a great distance comes pounding on the metal door. Haller ignores the intrusive sound and tends instead to the mixing of a new color on a huge glass palette caked with decades of dried paint along its edges. The banging continues until he can stand it no more. He throws down his brushes and painting knives in disgust.

The heavy door screeches open on its balky track. A gust of freezing air carries voices into the room. At first Haller's tone is sharp, strident, complaining, then it levels out. Seren doesn't recognize the other voices, but few in Detroit matter to her aside from Haller, the man who pays her.

Figures appear, pushing past the makeshift curtain hung just inside the door to block the cold. Two old men enter, trailed by the diminutive artist who is looking peeved by the invasion. One of the men is enormously tall and gaunt, stooped at the waist from years of toil. The other man, wearing a dirty cap over wisps of white hair, glows with the aura of a saint. He is the American painter, Norris Bainbridge.

A rumble of conversation pierced by sarcastic laughter washes over her. She commences emerging into full consciousness. "That's Seren," Haller says to the men, waving his hand dismissively in her direction. "She's my best girl."

The tall man glances her way, nods slightly, and receives a glass filled with whisky from Haller. They collapse into armchairs. Music plays. Electric heaters snap and buzz. Outside, the wind wreaks havoc on the world. The saint approaches the dais, moving toward her like a wounded stork—each footfall seemingly rife with hazard. Grizzled beard, bushy eyebrows, furtive, unforgiving eyes. He bends to look at her, his gaze traveling over her naked body, up and down and back again, nostrils flaring when he picks up her scent. He mutters something in a voice too faint to hear.

The old man's thoughts take shape in her mind. Images gradually infiltrate the capillaries of her brain. She waits for him to recognize her. With agonizing slowness, she fills her lungs and widens her eyes, willing ordinary life back into her body. Bainbridge's weathered features cloud as if he's attempting to grasp the tail of something that remains just out of reach.

Then, nothing. His aging blue eyes glaze over and grow distant. His spirit has moved to another place—lost in the past. A picture of a battered, white chair surrounded by the dense green of vegetation in twilight floats before her eyes. The old painter's recollections wash through her like the first rush of heroin. The blush of new love.

Seren smells earth, rich with summer—the sweetness of honeysuckle. A weathered barn, shadowed under willow trees, a rain barrel, and a pair of sawhorses. She knows this place.

He brushes her cheek with the back of his hand. "Do yourself a favor, Mouse, don't fuck that limey bastard." His words carry the inflection of a benediction. The expression on his face tells her he knows it's already too late.

She doesn't respond to her childhood nickname. Instead, the vision dissolves and is replaced with the scene of an ice-rimmed river, a black pine forest under a brilliant yellow sky. At the edge of a tumbled deadfall, two crows pick at a rag of skin on frozen ground.

In the studio, there is more talk, more whisky, voices rising, shouting back and forth. The smell of bitterness and resignation permeates the room. Then Bainbridge—fool, saint, painter of land-scapes—pulls on his jacket and hobbles out.

Laughter. Haller brays like a donkey. Fauré plays over and over on the phonograph.

Seren snatches up her heavy wool coat and follows the old man into the blizzard. Whatever befalls him, she wants to be there—to lap up the remaining moments of his life with her wet, pink tongue.

PALIMPSEST

1

Detroit—June 1978

"Help me out here, buddy boy," Fairchild Moss said to the ghost of Norris Bainbridge. "How in fuck's name did you manage to pull off this magnificent beast? This crazy thing?"

The painter, now six months deceased, refused to answer. The artwork in question, a winter scene hanging in the gallery's private salon, was equally mute. Moss sighed with frustration, contemplating the turbulent yellow sky and the icy river. There was a wildness in the paint that pulled him outside himself, that made him want to genuflect—or flee.

Moss knew art. He'd sold enough of it. Over the years, he'd seen it all—the art world's hacks and charlatans, sad truths, half-truths, and dirty laundry. This painting was something else. This painting was good. Museum good. Its quality was evident when he first spied it in the artist's studio at the end of the big blizzard during January. Now it was June.

His eyes quartered and re-quartered the surface, trying to get a handle on the divine monster.

He had puzzled over the painting now for 103 workdays and 21 weekends. It nagged at him. After months of indecision, he could barely stand to look at it any longer. He needed to resolve the mystery—either that or sell the goddamn thing and forget about it. End of story.

He could feel the painting staring back at him. It might be the old man's spirit, but it seemed like something else. Completed the day prior to the artist's death, the big canvas was the last work the reclusive painter had touched.

Swiveling in his chair as if restless movement would somehow provide him with a clue, Moss searched for some key that would unlock the story of its origins. Seven feet wide by five feet high, the scale was imposing. The scene appeared to have been painted from a hill on the opposite bank that looked out on an arc of partially frozen river. A tangle of deadfall pierced the curve of shoreline like the tail of a Q then led to a swath of black pinewoods. Above the trees rose a huge expanse of winter sky, looming over the rest of the landscape in broadly brushed passages of tortured yellow.

Moss turned his attention to the upper portion. His eyes kept returning to a spot six inches in from the left-hand edge where a small circular depression indented the thick impasto of oil paint. Barely visible from a distance more than six feet was the imprint of a female nipple.

That tiny point wasn't the only anomaly concealed in the freshly dried pigment. Farther to the right lay the hint of a diminutive handprint. Lower down, gouged into the surface slightly above the treetops, were two deep and grimy fingerprints—the sort of brio gesture uncharacteristic of the artist, even in his later years. How those stray marks came into being was the question. Exhibited at Moss's gallery in February, only a month after the artist's death, critics attributed those peculiarities to artistic passion—a fusion of death and genius. The painter's coup de grace.

Some scattered evidence of underpainting also intrigued him. Peeking out from the impasto of white and yellow were vestigial flecks of alizarin crimson. At the transition from tree line to sky, where the overlying paint was thinnest, the red glowed through, imparting a rosy aura. Moss guessed that most of the alizarin had been scraped off before the heavy yellow of the sky was applied. Bainbridge had changed course radically in the end.

"Just what the fuck happened here? Clue me in, you old fart." Moss had lived in the art world for a long time. The idea of mystery and genius filled him with skepticism.

"I heard you invoking the dead, doll. It's not your usual practice." Kaye Richards—the gallery's assistant director—stood in the doorway. "By the way, Boo Tice just called."

"Oh?" Moss glanced in her direction with a wary eye. Beaufort Tice was Old South of a certain persuasion: he knew nothing about everything, and he knew it well. The industrialist embodied what Moss found most depressing about art, but somehow their friendship had lasted over two decades. Tice was a fixture in Detroit—a big-time art patron. Moss was the crown prince of Townsend Street; he owned the second-best gallery in the region. His next-door neighbor, Donald Morris Gallery, was the unchallenged king of high-end art.

"He's coming into town this morning," Kaye said. The skin of her face was stretched drum tight over Cherokee cheekbones. A plastic surgeon in Lausanne had done a good job, but it would take months before she could form a real expression. "He wants to see his painting." She nodded toward the Bainbridge.

"It's not *his* painting." Moss shook his head, already weary of Kaye's distraction.

"He loves it. He wants it. He has a check ready."

"He'll have to get in line, won't he?" Moss ran a finger under the curve of his handlebar mustache.

Boo Tice was a Tulane graduate, a charter member of ZBT fraternity—zillions, billions, and trillions. His family's company produced auto parts for General Motors—dashboard components and door panels and the like. He was an important supporter of the gallery. The two maintained a genteel détente. The tycoon bought art and required humoring; Moss sold art and did his best to humor him.

Simply put, the man's money paid the gallery's electric bill.

"Boo's not much for line-standing." Kaye shifted her weight, resting her shoulder against the doorjamb. Although the viewing room held two Eames leather lounge chairs with a small Noguchi table in between, it was understood she would not sit—her territory was the front of the gallery, upstairs. She waited silently for a few beats. "That painting has you hooked, lover."

"Not hooked," Moss said, more defensively than he felt. "Curious, that's all. We've dealt Bainbridge's work for years. Something about this painting doesn't add up. I just need some time to suss it out."

"You've been sussing for months."

He was, in fact, hooked.

"Well okay, what do you think? How does a good painter suddenly become a great painter at the very end?" Moss fixed her with a look of annoyance. He wasn't cranky with Kaye so much as he was with himself. He was a *dealer* for god's sake. Art dealers sold art. They didn't sit around mooning over it like lovestruck teenagers.

"I think he outdid himself—right at the end." Kaye shrugged. "Sometimes that happens."

"Something else is going on here," Moss said, swelling with irritation at having to explain a hunch he couldn't yet explain to himself. "This piece is too much of an outlier—the size, the color, the brushwork. There are elements that don't make sense, particularly the sky. I've carried his work for a long time. I know his style like I know my own face. Something here isn't kosher."

"Kosher?" Kaye asked carefully. "Does it matter?"

"Does to me." For years he'd been languishing in a deep swale of boredom. Sadness without reason. The Bainbridge gave him something new to think about. Lately, the puzzle pieces of his life seemed to fit together a bit too cleanly.

"What shall I do about Boo?" She glanced at the landscape, then back at Moss. As the owner, he was the guts of the gallery—the instinct. Kaye was the head and the hands.

"Distract him." He dismissed her with a wave. "I could have sold this piece twenty times by now. It's not for sale. Not until I get to the bottom of it."

"Boo will be here before noon," Kaye called back into the space she'd just vacated. She had been Moss's first hire when the gallery opened two decades ago—his first and his best. She knew the gallery business, and she knew Moss; managing his moods required the same deft touch she used to square the accounts.

"I'll be at lunch," Moss said. "Sell him something else—one of the small landscapes or, better yet, one of Gerome Nahni's sculptures. They're cluttering up the storage room." Nahni was a member of Bainbridge's cohort, a group of aging artists working in derelict studios lining Detroit's Cass Avenue. Along with a few compatriots, the bony sculptor's work enjoyed some renewed interest following Bainbridge's demise.

Moss settled back. The magnetic pull of the big painting absorbed the sound of Kaye's heels on the stairs. He let his eyes roam over the canvas again. The two fingerprints above the treetops reminded him of a pair of birds flying off into deep pictorial space.

From the rooms above came the muted sounds of commerce. A client. Unintelligible conversation. Inflection, innuendo, and snatches of sentence fragments drifted down to him like flakes of snow. He hoped the source of the voice wasn't the dreaded auto-parts magnate.

Sitting with the Bainbridge painting always made Moss a little dizzy. When he'd first caught sight of it in the artist's drafty studio right after the big blizzard, he'd guessed he was witnessing something rare—the first, fragile moments of a great work of art. The power of it had reduced him to silence back then. The piece humbled him.

Whoever was up on the main floor, he didn't want to see them. What he wanted was to puzzle out whose nipple had been pressed into the wet paint. Bainbridge worked alone—emphatically alone. Everyone knew that. Moss had never seen an assistant in the old fellow's studio.

The septuagenarian artist had been impossible to like. He was unwashed, bad tempered, and egocentric, so rigidly focused on his work no ordinary human could tolerate his company for long. So how did the imprint of a nipple suddenly appear on his final painting? By Moss's calculations, he had been the last person to see the painter alive. It was the day they crated the works for transport to the gallery—including the big one, still wet. The night before, when the last thick coats of brilliant yellow had been applied to the upper portion of the canvas, someone else must have been present in the studio. Unlikely, but there it was—the telltale tit. There was no other answer.

He opened his mouth to let Kaye know he was leaving but instead did an about-face. He would sneak out the back, through the labyrinthine storage rooms crowded with rack after rack of paintings, watercolors, and prints, then up the freight elevator and out through the loading dock that opened onto an alley he shared with six other galleries.

The brilliant sunlight felt good, but by the time he'd reached the street he was beginning to sweat. Turning a corner, Moss headed toward the Midtown Café. On his way, he passed the entrance to Donald Morris Gallery. Without thinking, he opened the door and poked his head inside. Sally Bright, the director and his long-time buddy, was pinning a label next to an expansive, wholly inarticulate abstract painting. When she noticed his shadow in the doorway, she looked up. "Hey, sweetie, it's a little early for you to be gallivanting around, isn't it?"

"I may be carrying a few too many pounds to gallivant these days," he said. "I'm evading a client." He scowled at the painting. "What in God's name are you doing with that mess?"

"Selling it." She gave him a smug nod. "A quarter mill . . ."

"No." He grimaced theatrically for her benefit. "Please tell me you're joking." It wasn't like Sally to bandy dollar figures about—there were price lists for that. Talk of money usually took place behind closed doors. Detroit wasn't Los Angeles, New York, or Tokyo. There was still some Midwestern discretion left.

"No joke. And there's more where this little lovely came from."

"Christ." Moss shook his head in grudging admiration. "Is Haller still in town?" he asked, naming the British figure painter who was one of the Morris Gallery's biggest stars.

Sally frowned, squinting to make certain that the painting's label was straight. "He's gone back to London. He's been tapped to take part in a group show at the Tate in September."

Moss's face must have revealed his disappointment.

"Why do you care about that smarmy little horn toad?"

"I'm trying to track down a hunch," Moss said. "I want to know who saw Bainbridge during the blizzard, the day before he died."

Now Sally looked interested. "Have you priced that landscape?"

"It's not for sale."

She gave a knowing chuckle. "Sweet pea, everything's for sale, whether it has a price tag on it or not. I know people who would buy it. You could retire—some quaint little villa in Italy, a leafy spot overlooking the Ligurian Sea."

"Not for sale. Not now. Not this one." Moss backed out of the doorway. "I'm heading over to the Midtown to see Claudine. Want to come along?"

"Love to but can't. Some of us are still in the business of selling art. Say hi for me."

Moss blew her a desultory air-kiss. He was feeling a little deflated. The number she'd mentioned was quadruple what he could get for landscapes these days. His business was good, but Donald Morris was drowning in cash. It didn't seem right.

2

Once he had made it as far as East Merrill Street, perspiring more than he cared to admit, he began to whistle the refrain from "Waltzing Matilda." Those bars of music seemed to pop into his head whenever circumstances forced him to ponder imponderables. He mulled over the question of Bainbridge's death. Alone in the dark with the snow piling up outside. Or maybe not alone? Moss whistled on until the disapproving looks from passersby silenced him.

Cutting his tune short, he arrived at the entrance to the Midtown Café, his favorite watering hole. Breezing through the etched-glass doors, he entered the cool and cloistered twilight of the restaurant's interior.

When he materialized on his customary stool at the end of the bar, Claudine Boatwright gave him a nod. The day was still young, but the Midtown was lively, thrumming with voices. The Townsend Hotel was located across the street, and its patrons had plenty of time to kill and money to spend.

"Claudine, my one and only," Moss crooned with enough irony in his voice to avoid sounding weird.

"Hello, pet," Claudine said, shooting him a touch of side-eye. "You're looking damp." She was in her customary work regalia—black skirt, high-heeled boots, and a broadcloth shirt of brilliant white. Slung low around her hips was a tooled leather belt adorned with an oval cowgirl buckle. Eyes the color of sand. Skin the color of a cinnamon stick.

"I'm off on a quest," Moss said, a little surprised he had uttered those words given the idea had barely coalesced in his mind. "But first I require liquid encouragement."

"Yellow Chartreuse on the rocks?" she asked. "Double? VEP?"

"Indeed." Celibate for a decade, he had become immune to the notion of romance. Life was so much easier that way. As far as sex was concerned, no option was by far the best option. Even so, he loved Claudine in his own fashion. She was always behind the bar, she knew his likes, and she was willing to talk to him.

Bracing both hands on the bar, she gave him a critical look. "One of seven, Moss."

"Come again?"

"The quest—one of seven possible plotlines, my friend. Not too original on your part."

"But it's *my* quest," he said, giving her a tight smile. "Try not to denigrate it before I even get started." He was disappointed at her reaction. "How do you know about this plotline shit?"

She shrugged, refusing to dignify his question with a response.

From far across the room rang a peal of laughter. Squinting, Moss failed to discover the culprit. His spirit struggled with the Bainbridge mystery. Why did it even matter if the old man's muse had pressed a boob into the wet paint? Ridiculous, yes, but so what?

"Double Chartreuse. That's for sure the way I like to begin all my quests," Claudine said, scanning the phalanx of gleaming bottles behind the bar. Like a crown of baby snakes, her short dreadlocks swayed rhythmically when she moved. From a certain angle she resembled a freshly hatched Medusa. She could turn you to stone with a look, but only if she felt you were worth the bother.

When not mixing drinks at the Midtown, Claudine modeled for artists and occasionally for magazines. In her teenaged years, she had graced the covers of *Ebony* and *Jet*. Claudine knew most of the Detroit art crew, but very few of them could claim to know her. Now, deep into her thirties, she remained a sphinx to the world—but not to Moss. Not entirely anyway.

Splashing a generous portion of yellow-green liquid into a rocks glass filled with ice, she set it in front of Moss, giving him a languorous up-and-down with heavy-lidded eyes. "So, what's going on with you, sugar?"

"My quest. I need to talk to Haller." Moss hesitated for a polite second before taking a long and satisfying drink.

"Gone back to England, last I heard." She began polishing wineglasses with a fresh towel. "What do you want with that tedious little fuck?"

"I need to figure out what was happening with Bainbridge right before he died." That was half of it. That declivity of the nipple imprint was the other half. Bainbridge never had much interest in the opposite sex—or in any human being for that matter. The artist's only love was a patch of ground on the Platte River in Nebraska, a locale that he painted with religious fervor across the decades of his career.

"I never met this Bainbridge guy," Claudine said. "I know the name, that's all. He had a studio down in the Cass Corridor, if I remember."

"There were mutterings floating around last winter. Something about one of Haller's models." Moss downed his drink and set the empty glass on the bar in front of Claudine. He nodded for another.

"I modeled for Haller years back. Like dozens of other girls. He's a creepy little weasel. But he does sport a magnificent schlong."

"So? Did you . . . ?"

"Sleep with him?" She made a face. "Don't be stupid, Moss. You know, I don't generally do dick." She expelled an exasperated sigh. "But he did show it to me once, just to see if I could be tempted."

"And?"

"No dice. It looked old and a little crooked to me."

Moss laughed. He'd missed Claudine. During the early months of the year, he had been distracted by the business of mounting the Bainbridge exhibition. "If I ever decide to try women again, you'll top my list."

She set the second drink in front of him. "And if I ever decide to switch teams, you'll *still* have to wait your turn at the back of the line."

They laughed at the same phrases they echoed back and forth over the years—their own private Greek chorus. Moss fell in love whenever they chatted. Claudine was smart, pretty, and, best of all, she tolerated him.

"What makes you think Haller can help you? Gerome Nahni was tight with Bainbridge—studios in the same building and whatnot."

"I'm grasping at straws." Moss brushed a stray lock of hair off his forehead. "Something weird must've happened with him during those last days."

Claudine said nothing.

A couple appeared at the far end of the bar, and she left to attend to them. Moss watched her go. She moved with a sensual grace. He couldn't help but admire the irony of it all.

Turning his attention to his fingernails—he needed a manicure—he experienced a surge of restlessness. Moss dreaded the long weeks before the advent of August. The month at the end of the summer was his salvation. It was his custom to close the gallery for six weeks and head up north to his hideaway on Lake Superior. He looked forward to a time absent from the whims of wealthy clients. These days trying to sell anything was a chore.

Inherited from his grandmother, the cottage sat at the end of the Keweenaw Peninsula—a spit of land jutting out into the cold, fractious lake. The original structure had been remodeled and enlarged over the years since his Gran's demise. One hundred forty acres of pine, hardwood, and boulder-strewn shoreline, the property was part of his hedge against old age. White plaster walls were hung with the best paintings he owned. The Bainbridge landscape was destined for center stage.

Claudine returned to his end of the bar. "Time for a haircut, Moss. You're looking a little too much like a cracker from the Confederate Cavalry for my taste."

"Image, my sweet. Image is all," Moss said, smoothing his ringlets. "Think General Custer."

"No, Moss, *you* think General Custer. As I recall, that whole Bighorn thing didn't work out so well for him. It's not the sixties anymore, kiddo. Get with it." She reached across the bar and grabbed a skein of gray-blond curl from his shoulder. "You should sell this. I know plenty of women who would give up a body part for hair like yours."

Moss winced at the idea of amputation. He frequently wore his hair tied back in a ponytail, but he'd been depressed lately. The Bainbridge question had put him off his feed. In the era of Abstract Expressionism, the old artist had persisted in painting landscapes, somehow managing to keep his mid-wattage career lit. Now that he was dead, his work was suddenly in demand. Artists, other dealers, and hangers-on all claimed a special kinship with the defunct curmudgeon.

That's how it worked. Legend was easier for ordinary people to handle once the subject was six feet under.

"Two thoughts." Claudine resumed polishing with a practiced economy. "One: ask around at Cranbrook, Wayne State, and CCS—all the colleges. Someone on the faculty might know something. Two: track down Gerome Nahni. He must have a clue about Bainbridge's doings right before he died."

Moss stared blankly at the ebony snakelets radiating around her face. "I hate those academic artists—so smug in their tenure, their ineptitude."

"As I recall, you carry the work of at least two dozen local luminaries."

Moss shrugged. He had never been averse to making a dollar off college poseurs, but he could barely stand to listen to their endless prattle about this theory or that movement. Christ, it was bad enough dealing with his Bloomfield Hills clients—at least they had access to ready cash.

He sat for a while, allowing the Chartreuse to smooth out his ragged nerve endings. The promising arc of Claudine's hip caught his eye when she turned to rearrange bottles shelved behind the bar. He wondered if the theory were true that one's first sexual glimmerings—gay or straight—came from following behind their mother's swaying hips. His gaze tagged along as she walked to the opposite end of the bar.

Swirling the remnants of ice in his drink, he contemplated the rest of his day. The prospect of dealing with Boo Tice was too much—the airy blather and pseudo-patrician attempts at camaraderie. The chances of quietly holing up in his own office for the duration seemed slim. Perhaps an expedition to the blighted corridors of Cass Avenue would yield up the attenuated figure of Gerome Nahni. With luck, the aging sculptor might shed some light on Bainbridge's last days.

"I guess I'll go downtown and see if I can scare up Nahni. Care to come with?"

"Some of us work, Moss. My shift doesn't end until four o'clock." She toyed with her belt buckle.

"What if I offer dinner downtown after you finish your shift? We'll have an adventure, brave the heart of the beast?"

Claudine's expression was skeptical. "You're asking me to be seen in my hometown, in company with a pudgy old white man? Shit, Moss, you've lost it. Think again."

The *old* part hurt a little. In his mid-forties, he was in his prime. Wasn't he?

"If you'll come with me, I'll drive Athena. Now that summer is upon us, I can safely unleash the bitch." Athena, the gray goddess, was the nom de guerre of his dove-colored, E-Type Jaguar—a gift to himself following a very good year of sales in 1972. The car was as much a part of Moss's signature as his wavy blond hair. Athena represented all that was good in his life.

A smile crossed Claudine's lips. "Out front. Four-thirty sharp. Don't be late, Moss," she warned. "You may be long in the tooth, a little too paunchy, and way too white—but you do have yourself one sweet ride. Top down?"

He emptied his glass. "Top down."

3

At 4:30 sharp, he eased Athena into a parking space outside the Midtown. The roadster drew envious looks wherever she went. People knew her, and people loved her—how could they not? The decadent burble of twelve cylinders echoed unmistakably from a brace of paired exhaust pipes. Feeling the fizz of self-satisfaction in his stomach, Moss leaned back against the tan leather of the driver's seat. He cast a surreptitious glance at his reflection in the restaurant's plate-glass windows—tiny round sunglasses perched on the bridge of a hawksbill nose, his hair tied back with a black velvet ribbon. It would do.

Aware of his friend's proclivity for finery, he had changed into a pair of white linen slacks, an Egyptian cotton shirt of blue and white stripes, and a navy and gold regimental striped bowtie. Bally driving moccasins in navy suede caressed Athena's pedals. He lit a Chesterfield to pass the time. Smoke from the first, glorious puff curled around his mustache.

When Claudine appeared, her work uniform swapped out for a multicolored print blouse, white shorts, and wedge-heeled sandals, the level of Moss's abdominal effervescence ratcheted upward.

"Oh, baby," she said, clearly pleased. "Don't we all look fine?" Fingertips skimmed the curve of Athena's fender.

Moss smiled to himself as she circled the elongated nose of the automobile and slid in beside him. "I booked something at the

Scarab Club at seven o'clock. Plenty of time to ferret out Gerome before dinner—pick his memory, get the lowdown."

"If you say so." She removed one of Moss's Chesterfields from a pack on the dash and lit it. "I'm just riding along to lend credibility. No hanky-panky, Moss."

"Hanky-panky? That's a phrase one doesn't hear much anymore."

He threw the car into gear and aimed the Jaguar south, down the long, sloping ramp of Woodward Avenue and into the heart of the city—the fabled Motown, the crumbling Day-twa. He had no idea what he might find, but he felt an urgency to find out anything that would shed light on Norris Bainbridge's final masterpiece.

At last, Moss had a quest.

• • •

Southbound the gray goddess swooped down the six-lane concrete ribbon, leaving behind the green eddies of the manicured suburban lawns of the B's: Birmingham, Bloomfield, Beverly, and Berkley. Descending the steep societal slope, they sped from the quiet acreage of wealth and privilege toward a wasteland of shattered neighborhoods where yards sat littered with burnt-out autos, rusted appliances, and worn-down tires. They motored past the modest cities of Royal Oak and Ferndale, sun gleaming on the windshield, arms hung on doorsills. At a stoplight Moss sailed the butt of his Chesterfield over the curb. Claudine closed her eyes and tilted her head back until there was nothing but sky reflected in the pink lenses of her sunglasses. Athena, oblivious, forever gray, nosed through the Woodward traffic like some implacable predator slicing through shoals of lesser creatures.

At the edge of Highland Park, a gaggle of small boys on bicycles hooted and whistled. Claudine flipped them a friendly bird, eliciting shrieks of derision—a choir of pubescent voices steeped in unquenchable desire.

"Does Gerome know you're venturing downtown?" Wind animated her serpent locks into a wriggling mass. One hand balanced her cigarette while the other drummed the chrome door molding with carefully tended nails.

"Nope," Moss said. "No phone in his place. We'll surprise him. He and Bainbridge were chums for a long time. He may know something, or he may not. Worst case, we'll still have a nice dinner."

Silence.

Flashing past them, the city parsed itself into rows of abandoned dark-brick houses, gas stations, shuttered grocery stores, and empty lots. Ten years after the riots of 1968, coyotes had returned to the city. They alone thrived.

"Seems to me you're going to a lot of trouble for a dead man," she said, pursing her lips. "I don't get what's in it for you."

Moss gently eased the shifter from fourth to second when the traffic slowed. He allowed himself a smile at the throaty grumble of the V12. "I don't know. Probably nothing at all." He patted the brown thigh near him. "It's a mythical quest, like in the old days. You know that grail thing?"

"Shit," Claudine snorted. "I never knew you to walk across a street but for some gain."

"Not this time."

"I guess we'll see." She jabbed a thumbnail to the right. "Get in the other lane. Cass Avenue is two blocks over."

• • •

It took some pounding before the heavy metal door slid open and the sculptor appeared in the entryway. Beside him was an ancient chow chow. The dog gave out a faint woof and fixed the pair of intruders with milky eyes.

"You remember Edna?" Nahni nodded toward the dog. "She's a fierce one—best mind your fingers."

Moss recalled that Edna had a well-developed palsy that made it difficult for her to stand for long. The poor dog looked a hundred years old. A black-mottled tongue lolled from one corner of her mouth, and fogged eyes stared vacantly in the general direction of the newcomers.

Gerome Nahni, an oily leather apron over his canvas coveralls, stood still as a sentinel. Welding goggles were pushed up on a sooty forehead, and three days' growth of white beard graced his cheeks. When his eyes focused on Moss, he said, "Did you, by any chance, bring me a check?"

Moss shook his head. "Kaye handles that sort of thing, Gerome. You know that." You could count on artists to think about cash—first, last, and middle. He found such avarice unseemly.

With a grunt of disappointment, Nahni shifted his attention to Moss's companion. "Claudine?" The gaunt man shifted from foot to foot, unable to make eye contact but also unable to look away. Seconds ticked by. Edna retreated to her pallet just inside the door.

"Gerome," Claudine said airily. "Long time."

Nahni appeared to struggle for words. "I never thought I'd see you here at the studio."

"Strange days afoot, Gerome." She took a subtle half step backward.

Artists and dealers shared a mutual distrust steeped in a grudging necessity. Growing impatient, Moss broke the impasse. "Let us in, Gerome. I have questions."

Another awkward moment expired before Nahni led them into the cavern-like studio, which was peopled with an army of gangly metal sculptures, some well over ten feet tall. The ominous steel figures reminded Moss of Giacometti, had the Italian ever turned his attentions from humans to arthropods.

A half-dozen heavy wooden worktables were arranged haphazardly in the huge space. Maquettes in varying stages of completion stood in a serried row like soldiers. The air bore the smell of machine oil and metal. Familiar with this sort of terrain, Claudine detached herself and wandered—looking, touching, humming to herself.

Moss followed Nahni toward a back corner. Here was a facsimile of a kitchen: a cluttered Formica table, an ancient hotplate, and an elegantly curved, mint-green Crosley Shelvador refrigerator that looked to be from the 1930s. Something tugged in Moss's chest when he surveyed the humble arrangement. He had grown up with stories from the Great Depression, a time he'd been too young to recall. Tales of want told by his Gran. The hardships, the acts of thrift, the ever-present scarcity—all had left their imprint on his psyche even if he himself had never experienced such trials. Deep down he harbored a secret kinship with the accouterments of privation despite his celebrated affection for luxury. More than forty years and a world war had passed since the days of the dust bowl. Gerome Nahni seemed a vestige from another era, now mostly lost.

The sculptor pulled a metal folding chair from under the table and gestured for Moss to sit. Rummaging in the fridge, he produced a rectangular chunk of orange cheese wrapped in waxed paper. He placed it in front of Moss.

"Velveeta?"

"We're heading to dinner at the Scarab Club after here." Moss eyed the symmetrical block with misgiving.

"Okay," Nahni said, casting a furtive glance toward Claudine, who was still poking around in the back recesses of the studio. "How about her?"

"I guess she'll abstain for the moment," Moss said.

"Sure?"

"I believe we'll both take a pass on the cheese, Gerome."

The lanky man collapsed into a chair and commenced unfolding the wrapping paper. Digging a heavy pocketknife from his leather apron, he sliced a quarter inch off one end and rested the newborn piece gently on the grimy surface of the table in front of him. Rewrapping the waxed paper, he returned the package to the fridge. "What do you want, Moss?"

Moss hemmed and hawed. The denizens of the Cass Corridor were a clannish lot. "Something about Bainbridge's death troubles me, Gerome."

"Yeah?"

"Yeah." He struggled to find the right words. Moss had known Bainbridge in a business sense, but Nahni had been a friend. He needed to tread with delicacy—these revenants were a different breed. They'd made it through three wars. Many had taken their art training under the GI Bill. They'd done things, seen things, that were beyond Moss. He hadn't fought. Not for a single thing. Not in the warm rains. Not ever.

Moss's gallery had handled Nahni's work for a decade, and yet Moss hardly knew the man. Over the years he'd made the sculptor a bit of money, but that's where it ended. He'd always felt like a greenhorn around the old guard. It was unnerving.

"So?" Nahni said, a crumb of orange cheese lodged in the corner of his mouth. Edna groaned in her sleep. Claudine wove in and out of the shadows. The sound of traffic filtered through an open window. Muffled voices floated in from adjacent studios.

He forced himself to begin. "Do you remember anything out

of the ordinary about the last couple of days before Bainbridge died?"

"Nope."

Suddenly he felt stupid. "Nothing at all?"

The sculptor shifted uneasily on his seat. "You were there, weren't you? Crating up the work for his exhibition? How did he seem to you?"

"I don't know. I wasn't paying attention. He seemed the same to me—tired, that's for sure. I'm at a loss, Gerome. There's something about that big Platte River landscape that doesn't sit quite right."

"How so?" Over the years, Nahni had made no secret of his views on painters. He considered them a frivolous lot who failed to possess the moral rectitude needed to deal with actual weight—stone, iron, steel.

A wave of frustration washed over Moss. "Was there anybody hanging around his studio? Right before he died?"

Nahni looked at him with evident disinterest. "He was up on the fourth floor, you know. I'm on the first. I didn't keep track. As far as I recall, he never had visitors up there."

"No women?"

Nahni laughed. "You're nuts. Noe was a decade older than me—mid-seventies. What're you thinking?"

Claudine rested a hand on Moss's shoulder. He watched as Nahni's eyes tracked the length of her. "What's up with you two geeks?" she asked.

Moss shrugged. "Trying to trace Bainbridge's movements at the end."

"Well . . ." Nahni stuttered. "Noe and I did take a hike over to Haller's place the night before, or maybe two nights before. It was snowing like a bitch."

"Yes?" Moss fought to keep his voice level.

"During the worst of the storm." Nahni glanced at Moss, then let his eyes linger in the vicinity of Claudine's Brancusi thighs. "He was dejected about the progress of the painting. I thought it would be a kindness to distract him a little. Haller usually has a bottle of decent whisky lying around."

Moss felt a fraction of the burden lifting from his spirit. "You went to Haller's place at the height of the Great Blizzard?"

Nahni lifted one massive hand then let it settle once more on his leather-covered knee. "I told you, Haller had drink. Reason enough."

"You ventured outside?"

"Yup."

"And?"

"And we all had a drink," Nahni said, looking at Moss like he was a dunce.

Moss was at the edge of his patience. "You, Bainbridge, and Haller had a drink?"

"There was a girl."

"I knew it." Moss half rose out of his chair, only to catch the impulse and resume his seat. "What about the girl?"

"Model." Nahni fidgeted. "Welsh, I was told. Older than Haller's usual. He likes them young."

Moss forced himself to breathe. He glanced around the dim space with its stilt-like, sepulchral figures. "This girl, did Bainbridge know her—this model?"

"Not that I could tell," Nahni said, shaking his head. "She was in a pose when we got there. Noe said something to her. I didn't hear. I was some distance away."

Claudine squeezed Moss's shoulder. He felt her warmth radiating behind him. Unthinking, he reached a hand behind and patted her knee. In a room filled with grotesque metal figures, he found himself reassured by the feel of living flesh.

"Can you tell me anything more, Gerome? It's important." It was, but Moss couldn't say how. He was stumbling down the uncharted path of his own discontent without a clue as to where he was headed or why he even bothered. "Do you remember anything else about this model?"

"No."

"Nothing?"

"Nope." The sculptor shifted uneasily in his chair. Edna raised her head. "Haller's models are mostly pretty. This one was too, but different."

"Yes?"

"She looked foreign. Thirties maybe? Forties?" He glanced at Claudine. "Noe went out after a drink or two. I stayed on to finish the bottle. She put on her coat and left a little while after he did. That's all I know."

"Good," Moss said, as much to the ether as to the others. "Anything else about this person?"

"Real pale . . . and small." Nahni fumbled a little, appearing to summon his thoughts. "Skin as white as I've ever seen. She had thick black hair on her head, but none anywhere else. That and the line."

"The line?"

"Yeah." Nahni's gaze flickered as if from one world to the next. "A tattooed line—as thin as an eyelash"

"And?"

"It went right down the middle of her face—hairline to chin."

Moss rocked back on his seat. "And you just now thought to remember this rather singular trait?"

Nahni shrugged.

Moss rose. "Good man, Gerome. You've been a help. Have you seen this model around since the blizzard?"

Nahni shook his head. "I don't get out much these days. Got to work."

"Okay." Moss reached out a hand to the tall man. "Thanks, Gerome. Did the model say anything to Bainbridge?"

"No, but he whispered something to her," Nahni said. "I wasn't close enough to hear what was said."

"I'll be in touch about those checks."

The tall man brightened. "Talk to Haller about the model. I got the sense he had knowledge of her."

Moss nodded.

Claudine waved a hand at Nahni, who, in return, shot her a look soaked in a longing that might have been endearing if it weren't so creepy.

Outside the weathered brick warehouse, Moss paused to inspect Athena. As a rule, he hated to leave the Jaguar unattended in the city. Much to his relief, she appeared unsullied by her brush with the ghetto—gloriously intact as only a virgin goddess could be.

He turned to Claudine. "So what's with you and Nahni? You never said you knew him."

"Nothing's with us. When I was a student at Wayne State, I modeled for a class he was teaching. That's all." She pursed her lips. "He's lonely, like a lot of these geezers."

He felt Claudine's eyes on him as he circled the car with agonizing slowness. His hands traced the sweep of the Jaguar's rear fender, lingering long enough for Claudine to twist her lips in impatience.

She tapped the toe of her strappy sandal. "I couldn't help but notice . . ." her voice trailed off.

Moss raised his head. "What?"

"You seem unusually *handsy* today."

It took Moss a second to grasp her point. "Oh?"

"Not your style."

Moss felt his face flush. "Sorry," he said, pausing a beat to examine his reaction. "I'm not myself."

"Not to worry," she said. "Something's got you spooked. Let's go eat."

4

At the Scarab Club, Moss let Claudine order their drinks while he went to the reception area to telephone the gallery. Kaye said Boo Tice had, in fact, shown up that morning. He had once more made an offer on the Bainbridge landscape. Moss detected a note of reproach in Kaye's voice when she relayed the amount of Tice's tender. The figure would enlarge the gallery's coffers in a significant way and, consequently, fortuitously impact Kaye's quarterly bonus.

Moss let the digits percolate in his brain for a moment, then said, "No."

"No?" Kaye's tone was incredulous.

"I can't," Moss said. "I just can't." He set the receiver on its cradle without signing off and instantly felt bad. He loved Kaye as a sister. They were almost like partners. Her great grandfather had been president of the giant university in Ann Arbor. Kaye's social passport was stamped a dozen times. Best of all, she was fluent in the language of discretionary cash. She knew people. He inwardly cursed himself for being rude. Something about the Bainbridge canvas had forced him out of character. He decided to greet Kaye with flowers the next day to make up for his lack of manners.

Still fretting when he returned to the table, Moss downed half his Chartreuse in a single draught. Setting the glass down, he said, "Fuck me."

"Maybe never." Claudine's eyes roamed over the squared-off wooden beams that spanned the dining room's ceiling. Signed by local and visiting luminaries of the art world since the late 1920s, the darkened wood was inscribed everywhere with names from days long past. In his youth, Moss had hoped his name might join those of the elect, but no—it was not his fate. He'd turned out to be far better at making money than making paintings. A generalist by temperament, he could talk any game in town, and on most days he could walk away with money in his pocket. He wasn't a man cut out for the solitary struggles of the studio. He liked good clothes, good cars. He liked Chartreuse.

"I can't find Bainbridge's name up there."

"He's in the back," Moss said. "I'll show you when we're done eating." He whistled a bar from "Waltzing Matilda" under his breath.

A waiter brought menus and filled Claudine's wineglass. A thousand miles from any ocean, Moss ordered crab cakes. Claudine ordered whitefish from nearby Lake Erie. When the food came, they ate mostly in silence. Moss pondered his own behavior of late. He felt unable to right his psychic ship. Truth be told, it was nice to be distracted from ordinary life. Having read medieval fantasies in his youth, he'd loved the idea of knight errantry—chivalric endeavor suited him, or so he thought.

"You're being weird, Moss." Claudine set down her wineglass, laced her fingers under her chin, and gave him a full-frontal stare. "Care to enlighten me?"

Moss folded his napkin and placed it next to his plate. "Boo Tice made another offer on the Bainbridge, but I can't do it."

"So?" she frowned. "What's the big deal? Sell it. Or don't. Lock it away. I don't see how this matters so much." Groups of diners filtered in, and the level of background noise escalated by a decibel or two. "I mean, do you even own the thing? What with Bainbridge being dead and all?"

"I think I may—I may own it." He ran a finger under the curve of his mustache. "Maybe not technically, but there might be a precedent somewhere."

"Oh God," Claudine gasped, leaning back in her chair and giving him the squint-eye. "You're going to steal it?"

"No. No. Not stealing." He fumbled for words. "I'm certain I have a reasonable claim on that piece."

"Moss! What's wrong with you?"

"I'm not sure I can explain." Moss raised two fingers to signal his desire for another drink. "It's bugging me that this last piece is so much better than all his other work. It seems like it was painted in—don't laugh—a . . . state of grace."

"Grace?" Claudine curled her lip. "No such thing."

"Okay," he said, arching his eyebrows. "How do you explain why this one's so good?"

"The guy got lucky. Maybe he realized he was on his last legs."

"Maybe." Moss sighed. "Maybe he had help?" he said, casting his gaze upward at the dense array of glyphs covering every beam. A part of him envied those guys. "What would you do if you were in my shoes?"

"Seriously?"

"Seriously."

Claudine took a long, thoughtful sip. "Are you ready?"

He felt himself growing a bit cranky. "Ready."

"If I were you, I'd sell that big fucking canvas—the one you may or may not actually own—and use the proceeds to take me to Paris." She paused, but not long enough for him to interrupt. "We could hole up near the Sorbonne, drink café au lait, eat good bread with butter and jam. We'd walk all over the city. Haunt the museums until evening, then sit in tiny bistros until it was time for bed." She drained her glass. "We would never once think about this wretched city," she said. "That's what I would do."

"You seem to have some pretty clearly delineated ideas about Paris for someone who's never been." He cocked an ironic eyebrow. Her version of the place smacked more of Hemingway and Stein than the modern Paris he'd known from his trips with Gran.

A cloud passed over her features. "I read a book." She dropped her napkin on her plate and pushed her chair back. "Satisfied? You know, you can be such an asshole sometimes."

By the time Moss reached the parking lot, Claudine was gone.

5

An hour later, twilight had turned to dark as Moss made it back to the northern suburbs and his town house on West Merrill Street. For years he'd lived kitty-corner to his gallery across Shain Park. It was a matter of convenience. Switching on the lights, he thought the place seemed emptier than usual. Surveying the interior, Moss decided he needed to rein in his organizing gene. The space looked like something from one of the dozens of décor magazines he kept stacked in a neat pile.

Claudine was right to be angry. He had no business scoffing at her dream of Paris, cliched as it might have been. He'd overstepped. True, he was a bit of an asshole—but then, wasn't that what he was known for? You had to be something of an asshole to succeed in his business. Everybody said so.

If that was the case, why did he suddenly feel like a shit?

Walking to the rear of the house, he opened a bottle of red wine he'd been saving for something he couldn't recall. In the light reflecting from the kitchen, his verdant bamboo garden glowed through the sheet of plate glass. He tended the garden plot obsessively, like a mother might keep watch over an only child. Nothing escaped his notice. Evenings spent pruning and fertilizing had yielded a perfect sanctuary. The greenery blocked all sight of his neighbors.

Sliding the door open, he dragged a Perriand swivel chair out onto the flagstone terrace and sat. The night was cool. He sipped, deep in revery.

As it did at such times, his mind turned to his Gran, long departed but never too far from his thoughts. Nell Regina Moss—N. R. Moss to her legion of fans—had plucked him out of a Catholic orphanage in Munising just shy of his third birthday. He had no memory of the nuns, only his Gran. Never married, she had money from her book sales to augment an inheritance drawn from timberland in Canada. Once the adoption papers were signed, she'd renamed him Fairchild simply because that's what he had been at the time—blond, rosy complexioned, and gentle natured. "I'm too old and too busy to be your mother, child. But I will happily be your grandmother. Let's leave it at that, shall we?" They did, and when the time came, Nell provided him with the best Michigan education money could buy—Birmingham Country Day, the University of Michigan for undergraduate studies in art and art history, and finally the fabled Cranbrook Academy, where he took an MFA in painting.

He seemed destined for big things. Everyone said so.

Nell Moss gave him everything he needed and most of what he wanted. In his early years, he sat blinking and bewildered next to the podium for her readings. The blond, quiet child invariably elicited questions. Whenever she was asked what the N. R. in her name stood for, she would glance down at her grandson and answer with a sunny smile, "No Relation." It was a long-running joke between her and her adoring readers.

Moss winced at the recollection.

Summers when he was growing up, the pair had trekked six hundred miles north to the Keweenaw Peninsula, a rocky, copper-rich spit of land that jutted like a knobby erection from the forested Upper Peninsula into the cold, grim wastes of Lake Superior.

It was at the cottage, a rehabilitated nineteenth-century fishing camp located on a deserted bit of coastline south of the town of Eagle River, that Nell donned the guise of author and wrote her cozy mystery novels. "Mystery is the fizz of life," she was wont to say. "Give me a good mystery over ordinary drudge any time."

Sitting in his bamboo sanctuary, the refrain from "Waltzing Matilda" escaped from under his breath. He hated the whole idea of mystery.

When the summer heat and humidity in Southeast Michigan became unbearable, Moss and his Gran left the sweltering urban sprawl. Once they'd crossed the big bridge, things changed. The Upper Peninsula—a day's drive from any population center—remained firmly lodged in a rural, postwar ethic. Things were kept simple; people leaned toward a pragmatic bluntness. Moss loved the rustic atmosphere—so long as it was understood his time up north was only temporary.

Nell Moss spent her days at the cottage writing or fly-fishing. Her grandson never joined her in either pursuit. In his early teens he'd fashioned a tiny painting studio from a long-disused storage shed set some two hundred feet off from the main house. There, he spent his days meticulously squeezing oil colors onto his palette, squishing the viscous paint here and there on one canvas or another, then, at the end of the day, scraping off the whole unsatisfactory mess and dumping the paint into the trash can. Over the years, he finished nothing.

His grandmother rarely inquired after his artistic progress. She pecked away religiously at her Underwood typewriter, and by summer's end she would invariably come up with a finished novel—one more installment in a long series of bestsellers. In every book, her protagonist was one Henrietta Bloodworth, a small, slightly daffy woman well into middle age. Gran's books sold out like clockwork.

She had been translated into a dozen languages.

One fall, when he was away at the University of Michigan, Nell showed a few of his scraped-down canvases to a friend who was visiting. A word here, another word there, and Moss found himself admitted to the prestigious Cranbrook Academy of Art in Bloomfield Hills. Having few alternatives after graduation, he packed up his paints and headed to the cloistered splendor of private school, fifty miles down the highway from Ann Arbor.

In graduate school, Moss continued to produce scraped-down canvases. They were a great success. Passages of eroded color and suggestive form fluttered in and out of the surface like shadows of passing clouds. Tantalizing, amorphous, enigmatic—the work wowed his professors. A cadre of graduate advisors agreed that his creative output appeared to be about something but was profoundly about nothing. Nihilist art. The resident art historian loved it. His paintings, she effused, toed a critical line between this world and the next—half-uttered promises dissolved by a capricious wind.

Moss's star was rising.

Faculty and fellow students assured him of his dawning splendor. In his daydreams, he conducted interviews with his later self, composing enigmatic responses to questions from imaginary biographers. In his musings, greatness was all but guaranteed. Despite the promise of future accolades, he was determined to remain gracious—his beatific magnificence would be bestowed on the low and high alike. Later in his phantom future, he would become an ascetic, living the life of a priestly recluse, turning his back on the material fruits of his genius. Moss spent hours and hours in his studio mapping out his own wonderfulness. Then, it all ceased.

One day, near the date of his graduate exhibition, he found himself psychologically unable to lift a brush. Surrounded by what he realized were blank, or close to blank, canvases, he broke down.

There was nothing there. He felt it deep in his core. All his efforts and imaginings had managed to amount to exactly nothing—his work was all intimation without a hint of actualization. He left the graduate painting studio that day, never to return. Despite his ignominious departure, he received his degree in the mail. The work from school was later shipped to Gran's cottage up north for storage.

His days of pretending to be a painter were over.

When he turned thirty and it became apparent to all that he would never produce another painting, Nell Moss bought a former yarn shop in the heart of Birmingham on Townsend Street, and Fairchild Moss Gallery was born. He invited a few of his school chums to exhibit their work. No one was more surprised than Moss when the gallery was a success. Five years after opening, he joined the other prestigious gallery on the street, Donald Morris Gallery, in bringing rising stars of the national art scene to town. It was almost too easy. Automobile money abounded in the northern suburbs. Houses designed by the hottest architects were becoming ever more expansive and increasingly modern. Companies vied with each other to establish the largest and best corporate art collections. Museums were hungry. As the end of the seventies neared, art was big in the Midwest. Moss found himself at the center of it all.

In those days he discovered his true vocation: that most banal of creatures, a successful merchant. A few years later he'd arrived at a place where he could work as much or as little as he chose.

In the dark wastes of Canada, acres of pine trees from his grandmother's trust were cut, stripped of their branches, and loaded onto giant trucks headed for faraway mills. It seemed the timber would never end.

Life was easy.

It was a problem.

6

On a Friday night in late June, Moss pushed through the door of the Donald Morris Gallery and entered into the brightly lit space. He adopted his signature smirk—customary psychic armor. In days past, he had loved exhibition openings. Nowadays, he wasn't so sure. Making an appearance at these festivities was an obligatory gesture. Sally expected him to show up, just as he expected her to make an appearance at his own openings. It was genteel business practice.

Packed shoulder to shoulder were colorfully dressed denizens of the metro-Detroit art world. Mavens from Birmingham, Grosse Pointe, and Bloomfield Hills—gray hair gelled or lacquered—mixed happily with dour downtown artists dressed in black denim and scowls. Willowy catering girls in tight skirts wove through the crowd carrying trays laden with flutes of golden champagne. In this exhibit, every canvas was coated with a dense and suffocating cadmium-red hue. Every single one. The homogeneity of the surfaces was broken only by a few subtle shifts in paint density, the hint of a brushstroke, or, in one case, an aimless line inscribed into wet paint. The effect sucked the light from his eyes.

In less than a minute, Moss had counted more than a dozen red dots signifying sales. He felt sick to his stomach. Beneath the happy buzz lurked the lubricious flow of lucre changing hands—checks deposited discreetly into cash drawers, nods of agreement, discounts negotiated. The rich getting richer. For a brief second his lips twisted into an ungenerous grimace. Somebody might as well make money on this dreck. He wondered why it couldn't be him.

He spotted Sally across the room, standing next to a young, bearded man wearing an expensive-looking kimono, jeans, and a pair of Birkenstock clogs. Both Sally and the beard were drinking from balloon goblets filled with red wine—the good stuff, reserved for VIPs. The artist was said to be part of the second wave of color-field painters centered in Washington, DC. Word had it that he'd been forced to reduce the accustomed scale of his work to fit through the Morris Gallery doors. Reduced in size for Midwest consumption, but not in price.

Moss hated the man on general principle.

The giant red canvases drained every iota of intellect from the room. He saw Sally attempt to shunt the beard toward lucrative knots of patrons, but the troll seemed intent on quaffing huge quantities of expensive wine and ignoring the crowd of would-be buyers. While Moss looked on, the artist's cheeks gradually bloomed into a ruddy color that nearly matched his vapid canvases.

Moss wound his way from the front door toward the drinks table. With a gratuitous grin, he liberated a flute from a passing tray, pleased to detect a smile and nod of recognition from the fresh-eyed young thing.

Back at his own gallery, only two doors down the sidewalk, the ever-reliable Kaye was minding shop. Ten days had elapsed since he'd ventured down to the Cass Corridor. Ten days since he'd seen or spoken to Claudine. Whenever he'd popped into the Midtown, she'd been absent. No one on staff was willing to vouch for her whereabouts.

Behind the drinks table was an invisible door built into the paneling. Here was where the real stuff was hidden. He slipped sinuously through the passage and found himself in a tiny cupboard-like room stacked high with cases of wine and dusty cardboard boxes imprinted with the names of famous distillers.

Moss rummaged until he found a bottle of Ardbeg 30 Year. Not Chartreuse, but perhaps the next best thing. He'd peeled the ring around the bottle's collar and was removing the cap when he heard a voice behind him.

"Naughty, naughty." Sally stood in the doorway. "Donald would not be happy." Having invoked the name of the Gallery's owner, she gave him a conspiratorial smile. "He usually saves that particular brand for people he likes."

Moss continued opening the bottle. "Nonsense," he said over his shoulder. "Donald likes me. He admires my taste—told me so once."

Sally took another step closer into the confines of the storage closet. "I doubt that was meant to include a taste for his favorite Scotch."

"I won't tell if you won't." Moss searched until he found two rocks glasses and poured three fingers of the amber liquid into each glass. Handing one to Sally, he said, "Cheers."

She gave him a frown but nonetheless took a healthy swallow. Closing her eyes in bliss, she said, "God that's good! I think I may have had a mini orgasm just now."

"Balm for body and soul," Moss said, raising his glass. "But please refrain from telling me if you have a second climax—that's just bragging." The whisky tasted like heaven.

"My God, Moss. You really are the devil, aren't you?" Sally sipped, a look of beatitude etched onto her features.

"Let's go out back and grab a smoke." He made as if to slip the bottle under his sports jacket.

"Okay, but leave the bottle or there'll be hell to pay."

Topping off both their glasses, Moss returned the bottle to its dusty carton. As surreptitiously as they were able, the two made their way through the back office to the loading dock. Moss unlimbered and lit a Chesterfield for each of them. "Seen Claudine around?" he asked, blowing twin funnels of blue smoke through his nostrils. He picked a speck of tobacco off the tip of his tongue.

Sally paused a beat. "She was here earlier. Gone now. She might be over at the Midtown tonight. I get the distinct impression she's mad at you."

"Mad at me? No, I don't think so—not really."

"That's what I hear." Sally ran her tongue across her upper lip. "You hurt her feelings."

Moss took a deep puff. Was there anything better in this world than a good whisky and a cigarette? "She wants to go to Paris. That's what she said."

Sally shrugged. "Who doesn't want to go to Paris?" She cocked an eyebrow. "You can be a bit oblivious sometimes, Moss. Maybe you don't realize?"

Intent on shifting the conversation back to himself, he interrupted her. "Sally, I think I've lost the plot. I don't know what I'm doing anymore." He gave her a helpless look. "I'm adrift—rudderless."

"Shit." She tossed her cigarette butt. "Don't mind my saying, but some people are never adrift. They just aren't."

"That's a mean thing to say." Maybe he deserved it. "I thought I had the glimmer of an actual quest a few days ago—the Bainbridge landscape. Now I'm not so sure."

"Is this still about Haller? The model?"

"Yeah," he said. "Haller seems to be the missing piece at the moment."

"He's in London."

"That's what they say." He finished off his drink, regretting not having brought the bottle.

"Why not call him?"

"He never answers his phone." Moss waved a hand. "Too important. You of all people should know that."

"He'll be at the Tate Gallery this September."

"I can't wait until September. I need to find out about a model of his."

Sally leaned against the loading-dock door, one arm hugging her waist, the other holding her glass. Moss could hear traffic on Woodward. The night was warm, freighted with the smell of new-mown grass and approaching rain.

"This Bainbridge thing, you must think I'm nuts." He paced three steps then back again. "Maybe I am."

"Why not check in with Marylou?" Sally said, naming one of the doyens at the university downtown. "She hires all the models at Wayne State. She might know something." Prying the door open and holding it for Moss to follow, she gave him the kind of look a pious schoolmarm might bestow on a tardy pupil.

The air inside was fogged with cigarette smoke. The din of the crowd made his head spin. Murmurings rich with self-congratulation rose and fell like an oceanic tide. Here and there, peals of laughter rang out from those at the top of the pecking order. Moss's world. The world he knew best. He felt marooned.

He hadn't been back inside for two minutes before he spotted Boo Tice holding forth amid a gaggle of Grosse Pointe matrons. For the swanky opening, Tice had chosen plaid Bermuda shorts topped by a colorful Hawaiian-print shirt. On his feet were bright-yellow plastic boots with elliptical springs attached to their soles. Moss watched as the little man bounced up and down like a pogo stick, gesticulating to the gathering of ladies.

Having navigated a path to where the group stood, Moss gave a half-hearted gesture of benediction. Glancing pointedly at the yellow boots, he said, "You've grown, Boo, at least six inches."

Tice gave him a self-satisfied smile. "Moss! I'm in training," he bellowed, causing the gray heads to retreat a step. "I'm climbing Mt. Kenya at the end of August."

"Africa?" Moss tried hard not to sound surprised.

The little man gave a triumphant bounce that reverberated through his whole body. "That's where the mountain is, or so I'm told. I'll be gone six weeks or more. Got to *acclimatize*." He let the last word dangle in the humid air for maximum effect.

Instead of laughing, Moss found himself dismayed. It appeared even Tice was doing something cool—something beyond the pale—while he, Fairchild Moss, was stalled in neutral. "I suppose congratulations are in order, Boo. I had no idea you'd taken to mountaineering."

The Grosse Pointers twittered. Tice snatched at Moss's elbow to draw him closer. "I've even got a pickax! The point is so sharp it has a rubber guard on it—like a condom. Bethany thinks it's hot." He gave Moss a sly wink.

Moss tilted his head to one side. "Can I assume you've been practicing?"

"Practicing what?"

"You know, the walking uphill part of it."

Tice gave him a dismissive waggle of the head as he lifted a shiny, yellow boot in reproof. "No need." He squeezed Moss's arm conspiratorially. "I got these at a shop in Royal Oak. They build up your muscles. Plus, it's Africa, Moss. They have people for the hard parts. Everybody on the tour has a personal guide. They strap you in. It's like a ski tow."

This explanation elicited excited nods from the ladies.

Moss shivered as if from a chill. His eyes ranged over the room, searching for someone, anyone who could offer conversational relief. No savior appeared. Sally was expressly avoiding eye contact. He was lost.

"Seems like I never see you at your gallery anymore," Tice said, bouncing a little less than before. "I brought you a check last time, but you were gone. I've cleared a spot in storage for that Bainbridge piece."

"Storage?" Moss said, aghast.

"The little woman is on a Moroccan kick these days." Tice nodded despairingly. "She's got these rugs hanging on the walls everywhere at home. Brass tables, potted palms, the whole she-bang. It's just a phase. Maybe I'll put that landscape somewhere in my office—there's still a little space left in the reception area."

So it was to be storage or an office hallway for the Bainbridge? Moss fought back a wave of nausea. Beads of sweat broke out on his forehead. Moss swallowed hard. He was clearly off-kilter. Without a word of farewell, he headed for the door.

7

Outside the gallery, the air smelled cleaner than the breath-clotted atmosphere inside. Moss bent over, hands resting on the knees of his seersucker slacks. Slowly, he regained his equilibrium. Small groups of gallerygoers had started to depart, their cheery voices mingling with the sounds of automobile engines turning over. Darting in the blackness above the streetlights, a pair of nighthawks carved arcs in the sky. He looked at his watch, and it was nearly midnight. A few people on the sidewalk nodded to him. He gave a feeble wave in return.

He took five steps in the direction of the Midtown and then abruptly reversed course. He wasn't ready to make his apologies to Claudine. He needed a script—something at once glib and sincere. He couldn't afford to lose his only friend, not now. Then and there, he resolved to do something nice for a change. He vowed to make it up to her.

By the time he'd walked as far as the edge of Shain Park, his head had cleared some. He cursed himself for not having secretly snagged that bottle of Ardbeg. Donald Morris would never miss it in a million years. Now that he was freed from the press of overheated bodies and the insufferable banter, he was exhausted but too keyed up to sleep.

He plopped down on a park bench and threw his head back in relief. Stars winked down. A sliver of moon hung low on the horizon. On the far side of the park, a few figures walked along the sidewalk in shadow. Keys fitted into locks, doors slammed, headlights cut the darkness.

Moss closed his eyes. He was working himself up over nothing. A hunch? A barb of dissatisfaction that had accidentally hooked into his psyche?

Every fiber told him to accept Tice's offer and be done with it. Why not?

He decided then that he would call Tice the following morning. Given the little man's lust for acquisition, it might be possible for Moss to squeeze loose an extra dollar or two. The industrialist couldn't spend himself poor even if he tried.

Moss was about to set off when he detected an odd odor—a hint of loamy fragrance, freshly dug earth. Something about the scent made him yearn for the cottage up north.

He took another deep breath and was nearly overcome by the earthy scent. Truffle like, so fertile with decay that his eyes shot open, expecting to see someone or something nearby. There was nothing. When he stood to leave, his scalp prickled. Looking back over his shoulder, he saw only the night.

As quickly as the scent had come to him it was gone, erased by a breath of wind ruffling the leaves overhead. He took a few tentative steps, then he lengthened his stride. There was nothing going on; he was just feeling the weight of his own boredom, that was all. Taking a deep breath, he headed toward the familiar silhouette of his town house, two blocks from the park.

• • •

The two-story town house was as he had left it, neatly ordered, dark, and quiet. His mind was another thing. He couldn't recall feeling less settled. The strange smell had disturbed his equipoise.

Olfactory hallucinations were said to be an early signal of schizophrenia. Perhaps he was unwittingly drifting toward the looney bin? Struggling to right his thoughts, he whistled a bar or two of "Waltzing Matilda."

Hearing a voice of reason would be good, but calling Claudine was out of the question after that crack about Paris. Surely she resented him now. Their habitual teasing was one thing, but he'd inadvertently made fun of her. She wouldn't forgive that easily.

He tested the air. All clear. No stench of rot. The foreign smell was gone.

Over the past decade, his life had been pared down to what passed for essentials. He had not taken a lover in more than seven years. Given the scientifically acknowledged rate of cell replacement in the human body, he should be close to becoming a wholly different person by now—a new person. That would come as a relief, to him and to everyone else.

Except for Kaye and Sally, Claudine was his only actual friend—a category that adamantly excluded artists and clients. Now he'd managed to fuck that up.

He went to the bookcase and rifled through a shelf of vinyl albums, fingers trailing along the top of a long row. He wanted something, but he was clueless as to what that something might be. His hand finally landed on an old favorite—Gabriel Fauré, "Élégie for Cello." Turning the sound down low, he poured himself a glass of Chartreuse and stepped outside for a smoke.

In a few weeks he would head north. Most of his clients would be at their lake properties or visiting their horse farms or mountain cabins. Throughout the years, Moss had looked forward to his time of solitude on his rocky, secluded shoreline. This year was no different. Maybe he'd get back to painting or try to write something. If his Gran could pull off writing novels, perhaps he could as well.

Did he have anything to say?

He thought not.

Moss settled on the edge of a low wall that separated the terrace from his garden. The placid surface of his existence had been momentarily ruffled by an unfamiliar scent. So what? If he was on the verge of coming unhinged, there had to be a reason. There was nothing bothering him other than the Bainbridge question. Except for that, his life was ticking on as usual.

He got up and stretched out a kink in the small of his back. The night was turning cooler. Few sounds came from Woodward Avenue. Only the occasional piping of tree frogs punctuated the silence. Taking a step across the flagstones, he walked among the bamboo plants—some more than ten feet tall. He loved the feel of being nestled in the exotic foliage.

Finally, an hour before dawn, Moss stumbled off to bed. He slept a heavy, dreamless sleep, awaking midafternoon tangled in damp and sour sheets.

8

A few days after the July Fourth holiday, Moss secured an audience with Marylou Bigelow, head of drawing and watercolor at Wayne State University. He'd known Marylou off and on over the decades. She was a fixture in the Department of Art and Art History, and she was the longest-tenured member of the art faculty. He had carried her splashy, floral watercolors in the gallery for a time. She rarely sold a piece. Eventually she'd moved her endeavors farther north to a third-declension gallery in the city of Rochester, where her paintings once again gathered dust.

Marylou was an old-school academician in the truest sense. Her brand of professorship populated most college departments in the fifties and sixties. An outspoken adherent to Gurdjieff's Fourth Way, she nonetheless drank hard, regularly took younger lovers, and cursed at students, colleagues, and members of the administration with equal impunity. She wantonly offended anyone and everyone. It was said only Father Death possessed the requisite clout to roust her from the university rolls.

Approaching the red-lacquered door of her modest bungalow in Rosedale Park, Moss felt the tiniest prickle of anxiety. These days, his confidence had fallen to a low ebb, and he knew from extensive experience that dealing with Marylou Bigelow required boatloads of energy in addition to balls of shiny brass. Once she caught the scent of intellectual laxity, moral confusion, or artistic indifference, she could be merciless. It was common for undergraduates to flee her studio critiques in tears. More than one budding art career had broken on the reef of Marylou's profane and acerbic wit. She was legend.

Ditching his cigarette among the begonias, Moss pressed the buzzer, and after an interminable hiatus the door opened a crack.

"Moss?" A voice croaked. A pair of puffy, heavily mascaraed eyes peered out at him.

"None other."

"The fuck? Until you called me, I thought you were dead." The door opened wider. He could make out the colorful print of a voluminous, caftan-like garment.

Shifting nervously, he mumbled, "It's a process."

Her generous figure filled the doorframe. A heavy layer of makeup was caked and cracked on her features. "What's a process?"

"Death . . . I guess."

"Christ in heaven! What *are* you babbling about?" She fixed him with a look of imperious disdain. "Why are you here?"

"I need help." He'd been cryptic about his mission on the telephone, fearing she would rebuff him outright.

"The famous Fairchild Moss needs my help?" She squinted at him. "Well fuck me with a fire hydrant. Why in Christ's good name would I want to help you?"

"Because you like me?"

"Do I, Moss? Apparently, I've forgotten. Do I like you?"

Giving her his best, most ingenuous smile, he said, "Yes, I believe you do—you opened the door. *N'est-ce pas?*"

Marylou nudged the door a trifle wider. "Don't get all Frenchy with me, young man." She took a half step forward, to the edge of the sill. A belated smile broke the crust of her features. "Come give momma a hug." She drew him into a breathy, bosomy embrace saturated with the fumes of lavender-scented soap.

Moss could only tolerate proximity to so much pillowlike flesh for a few smothering seconds. When he was able to pry himself free, he said, "Can I come in?"

Marylou took his face in her hands and turned it from side to side, squinting as if through a dense fog. "Still handsome—handsome and ruined." She nodded to herself, ushering him inside with a sweeping gesture. "I'm in the atelier. Working."

She led him toward the rear of the house. Trailing after her majestic beam, he cast a surreptitious glance around the place. The interior was surprisingly ordinary. Heavy, prewar furniture crowded the small rooms. Dusty surfaces held collections of enamelware, and a pair of blue-and-white china urns stood on the mantel. Every inch of wall space was devoted to her own work—flowers in vases, flowers without vases, flowers swirling in amorphous atmospheres of pastel pink and blue. Shelves overladen with books. A Tibetan Tonka hung like a funeral flag above a battered rolltop desk. Her middle-aged children would have quite the time clearing her goods out once the old gal kicked the bucket.

Marylou had a glass-walled addition where she painted her watercolors. Pots holding every kind of flower lined the sills. Plaster drawing mannequins peeked out from under the jungle-like foliage. In one corner, a huge, brindle-colored cat lay on a red corduroy cushion. Large as a bobcat, it eyed Moss with undisguised venom.

"So, how's Kafka doing?" He nodded toward the feline now busying itself by licking its anus.

Marylou shrugged. "Filled with destructive energy as always. He killed a rabbit two nights ago. Poor thing. Left it on my doorstep. I took it for a sign."

"A sign of what?" Moss asked, instantly sorry he'd opened his mouth.

"Perhaps a sign of your impending arrival, Moss," she grumped. "I don't know. What the fuck?" With both hands on his shoulders, she steered him over to a tiny stool and sat him down. "You stay put. I'll make us some tea."

Left alone, Moss and Kafka engaged in a stare down of epic duration. It was only when Marylou returned with a tray laden with a teapot, cups, and a plate of pastries that the giant creature bestowed a heartfelt yawn on Moss—displaying yellowed fangs and a pink, rasp-like tongue.

"You've turned into quite the pudge ball, Moss," she said. "Have a piece of scone, it'll lighten your mood."

Straightening his spine, Moss said, "I walk to work on most days." He glanced down at his paunch. "I'm too busy to do much exercising." He had no excuses—not for anything.

Marylou let out a long, dismissive sigh. "Shit. You've always been a lazy fuck. I hope you realize your looks will go now that you're turning to fat." Her three chins nodded in confirmation.

Trying to deflect the subject away from his waistline, he said, "I'm hoping to track down a model—posed for Haller. Last winter."

Marylou poured them both a cup of tea and sat down in a canvas sling-back chair opposite Moss. "Model? For Maurice Haller?" She looked at him as she might an especially untalented drawing student. "That covers a lot of ground."

"This past winter," he said. "During the big snowstorm."

"Why do you want to find this woman? Can one assume it is a woman?"

Moss filled her in on the details—the Bainbridge connection, the obvious greatness of the ancient artist's final piece. He even confessed his reluctance to let the painting out of his possession.

"I liked Bainbridge," she mused. "He was a true believer. One of the few."

"Believer?"

She shifted on her seat. A pained expression flashed across her face. "My new hip is killing me." She took a thoughtful pause. "Bainbridge was loyal to his vision for over half a century. Not like these careerist scumbags driving their Maserati sports cars and fucking all the young girls. I despise every one of those vapid posers. Tragically, they're the ascendant species in the art world now. And the academic world, Lord help us." She crossed herself and sipped at her tea.

"We're of one mind in that regard. The seventies will be looked back on as the Epoch of Emptiness." He finished his tea, looking for some place to set his cup. "I hear Haller's gone back to London. I can't very well ask him about the model. He never touches the phone. Apparently, these days he has a lackey whose sole function on earth is to tell the masses that Maurice Haller can't be disturbed."

"I do love your jealousy. So quick on the trigger." Marylou laughed a gelatinous laugh. "Did you ask Sally Bright? She flogs his work for Donald Morris."

"She can't or won't help. Haller has made the gallery too much money for her to cross him. To make matters worse, he's gone incognito." Resting the cup and saucer on his knee, he shifted his weight from one bottom cheek to the other. The tiny stool was intent on crippling him. "Kaye heard a rumor that he's holed up in the Lake District with one of Lucian Freud's castoffs—a teenager from one of those old British families. At least he stays true to his origins."

"God, I hope she cuts that Limey bastard's dick off," she said, making a scissors motion with two chubby fingers. "He's a miserable, womanizing little shit."

Moss waggled his head in agreement. "Amen," He wiped at a

droplet of tea from his mustache. "You wouldn't have hired this Welsh model for one of your classes, by chance? Gerome Nahni claimed she had a distinctive facial tattoo."

"I'm tired, Moss." She gave him a dramatic yawn. "Figure models come and go. They all seem to have some sort of weirdness about them—tattoos, piercings, shaved heads, or unexpected appendages. I can't pay attention anymore. What does she look like? Aside from the tattoo?"

"Dark hair," he said. "That's all Nahni could provide."

Marylou broke off a piece of pastry and stuffed it into her mouth. She narrowed her eyes. "Let me conjure on it, consult my list. Dark hair, a Welsh lassie, you say?"

"Yup."

"You know, figure models are mostly more trouble than they're worth. I'll telephone you if anything comes to mind." She stood up and stretched—inadvertently thrusting her ample bosom in his direction. "I'm having a *thing* later in the week."

"Oh?"

"A séance—more like a kind of party. Just a few initiates." She ushered him toward the door. "Your pal, Claudine, will be in attendance."

Moss tried to fight down a ripple of interest. "We've had a falling out, I'm afraid."

Marylou pushed him through the threshold and into the bright, afternoon sunlight. "So, fix it. We'll commence the proceedings around eleven at night. If you decide to join us, bring a bottle or three. Seancing is thirsty work. By the by, lover boy, I received a package in the mail the other day—from friends in Laos."

Sensing the portent of that bit of news, Moss turned just as the door shut with a thud.

9

Late morning, the day of the séance, Moss received a call from Marylou. He was upstairs in the gallery trying to look busy. A few browsers were strolling through the rooms. They entered, wandered, and left without a ripple. Moss rarely answered the phones upstairs—that was Kaye's turf—but today she was shepherding a couple from out of town, hoping against hope for an impromptu sale.

"I've got something for you, lamb." Marylou's voice registered an octave lower and a beat slower than usual, as if each of her words were suspended in machine oil.

Moss, ever secure in his doubt regarding good tidings, nodded to himself. "Yeah?"

"Indeed, you ungrateful schmuck. I inquired among the drawing faculty on your behalf and came up with some tangible evidence. Don't bother to thank me. Bring some booze—good booze—tonight, and I may show you what I've got." She chuckled. "At least in regard to your phantom model."

"Do tell."

"Not a chance. Not until tonight, bubby." She gave out with a resonant wheeze. "By the way, my Laotian friends say hello. See you tonight."

"Okay." Moss returned the receiver to its cradle. He had little to do over the weekend anyway. If eleven o'clock sounded a little late in the day for the rhythms of his middle-aged lifestyle, he'd make an exception simply to stave off the legions of ennui.

• • •

Moss drove the Buick Estate Wagon down to Rosedale Park. Technically the car was registered to the gallery. It was supposed to be used for the cartage of artworks and other official errands. The tax depreciation paid for the station wagon over time and allowed him to keep Athena in reserve for all the important stuff.

Parked at the curb in front of Marylou's house were a couple of nondescript sedans and a choice little white Mercedes 190SL with a dark-blue soft-top. He gave the sleek roadster a walk-around, noting an unseemly dent in the right-rear fender and a piece of tape covering a cracked taillight. Sighing his disapproval of shoddy upkeep, he headed up the walk. Before he could knock, he heard the heavy thump of music echoing through the walls.

He rang the bell to no avail before giving up and pushing the door open. The entryway was deserted, but he could hear music and the murmur of voices coming from deep in the house. Before he had taken three steps inside, his eyes began to tear from an exotic confluence of warring odors—incense, cigarette smoke, and cologne engaged in a desperate battle for dominance against some strange, acrid scent. There was the smell of ganja to be sure, but there was also something else—something he didn't recognize. Not that he considered himself an expert in such matters.

On his way into the city, he'd stopped at the liquor store and picked up two bottles of Ardbeg as his entrance tariff in addition to a bottle of yellow Chartreuse and a pack of Chesterfields for himself. Marylou would appreciate his choice of whisky even if none of the other guests did. Sobriety was a condition of innumerable degrees and inflections for his hostess. Little in this world could deter her from being herself. She was old, she was fearless, and she had money in the bank.

Carrying his offering into the tiny kitchen, he found the red Formica counters crowded with bottles both tall and short. Scanning the phalanx, Moss concluded that most of the guests were academics of some stripe. Reluctant to leave his pricey offering in less-than-august company, he stowed one bottle on top of the refrigerator, poured himself a glass of Chartreuse on the rocks, and toted the second bottle of whisky to the doorway of the sitting room.

Marylou was enthroned on a divan of brilliant carmine beside the frail personage of Birdie Entwistle. Dressed in his signature vested suit, the old coot appeared busy whispering secrets into her ear. The two ancient heads were bent in close conversation. If Marylou was the old guard, then Birdie, now well into his nineties, was part of the *original* guard. Never a large man, nine decades had shrunk the former museum director to sparrow-size proportions. His knobby hands caged the head of a narrow, black cane that served as a last, tenuous contact with the earthly plane.

Marylou, dressed in one of her colorful caftans, was rocking back and forth in her seat as she whispered her own arcane mysteries into Birdie's pendulous ear. Drink in one hand, bottle in the other, Moss leaned against the doorjamb and waited for someone to acknowledge his existence. Eventually Marylou hissed at him, motioning him over to where she and Birdie were seated.

Seeing Moss's approach, Birdie levered halfway out of his seat, using the cane as a prop. "Dear boy," he said, settling back down after Moss had suffered the obligatory European greeting of cheek kissing. "How good it is to see you. It's been an age." The frail head nodded. "You're older now. I suppose you've noticed?"

Moss ignored the comment on his age and made a gesture of

polite obeisance before surrendering the bottle of whisky to his hostess. He settled on the divan.

"Birdie has some interesting news for us, lambie-pie." She brushed Moss's cheek with her lips, draping her arms around the shoulders of the two men. After a quick glance at Birdie, she asked, "May I?" The old fellow nodded, and she swiveled around to face Moss.

"Birdie heard the most delicious rumor at last Saturday's meeting of the board." She cocked an expectant eyebrow in Moss's direction.

"Do tell." He'd assumed Birdie had left the board of directors of the Detroit Institute of Art many decades ago.

"Apparently," she said, leaning in, trying to be heard above the thump of music, "apparently, several people who are in a position to know say that Boo Tice is in negotiations with the Building and Acquisitions Committee to fund a new wing of the DIA."

"Oh?" That was news to Moss. He felt a little put off—he should've had access to that information long before Marylou. "A new wing?"

"It's to be called the Michigan Artists Gallery. Birdie says there are architects working on the plans as we speak." Marylou lifted her eyebrows in Moss's direction. "Boo wanted to name it after his daddy, but the regents rebelled. The Faustus Xavier Tice Memorial Wing didn't have quite the right ring to it."

Moss looked at Birdie, who nodded. "Millions upon millions of auto-parts dollars finally put to good use. Once the board ratifies it, the newspapers will be full of the story. I would have guessed you'd heard." A skein of geriatric spittle loosened itself from his rubbery lips and hung suspended for a moment before descending to the plush carpet underfoot.

"I've been out of touch. I haven't seen Boo for a week or two,"

Moss said, giving Marylou a look. He preferred to disseminate a rumor, not receive it.

Marylou chuckled. "That's not the best part."

"No?" He asked, wondering what tidal wave of horrors would be unleashed next.

"No," she said, giving Birdie a wink. "Part of the bequest will be the installation of the Bainbridge landscape as a centerpiece for the new gallery. Birdie says Boo plans to donate the Bainbridge along with twenty or so first-rank works by other Michigan artists."

Moss was taken aback. "My Bainbridge landscape?"

"*The* Bainbridge landscape." Birdie gave Moss a careful glance.

Moss turned to Marylou. "What the fuck?"

"Exactly, snookum. Exactly." She pulled Moss close and planted a loud, motherly kiss on his cheek. "I knew you'd be surprised."

Head spinning, Moss struggled to disengage himself. Had he finally become one of the last-to-know crowd? Was his fall from grace so utterly complete? So public? Bracing against the divan's cushions, he cast a forlorn glance at the assembled throng, wondering how many of the others had beat him to the punch.

Devastated by the mention of the Bainbridge painting, he wavered unsteadily to his feet. The room spun. Knocking back what was left of his Chartreuse, he mumbled to no one, "I need another drink."

Both Birdie and Marylou giggled, their expressions alert to Moss's discomfiture.

How was it that Boo Tice was making plans for the Bainbridge, and he had heard nothing? Just how was that possible? "Christ on a fucking crutch," he muttered, stumbling through the doorway into the kitchen.

When he looked up, he found himself bathed in the eyes-wide-open, no-time-for-your-bullshit stare of one Claudine Boatwright.

A fulsome hip planted against the edge of the sink, she appeared to have been in mid-conversation with a bony redheaded woman who was busy opening a bottle of wine.

"Er . . . hullo," Moss managed. "How's it going?" He winced at his own lameness. There were things he wanted to say to Claudine in private.

Claudine twisted her lips. Glancing at the redhead, she said, "Moss, this is my friend Larissa—Larissa, this sad creature is the once-famous art dealer Fairchild Moss."

The woman looked up for a split second and said, "Hey there." She turned her shoulder to Moss and took a lengthy swig from the bottle.

"Can I assume the cute little 190SL outside belongs to you?"

The lanky woman refrained from gracing him with a reply—confirming his suspicion about the Mercedes. Butch lesbians were notoriously casual about the condition of their cars.

Feeling dismissed, Moss turned to Claudine. "You know I'm sorry about that whole thing at the Scarab Club. I don't know what I was thinking."

Claudine shrugged. "Don't worry about it."

"But I *have* been worried about it."

"Sugar, I've known you were an asshole for years." She took the wine bottle from her companion and upended it. "What I can't figure out is why you feel compelled to prove the fact over and over. Don't you realize everybody gets it by now?"

That last comment drew a cackle from the redhead.

Claudine's expression didn't look quite as harsh as her words sounded, but she refused to give him the all-clear sign. For Marylou's party, she had donned a summer-weight celadon shift made from a silky material. The dress fell from neck to ankle, the color contrasting with the rich, red undertones of her skin. The snakelike dreadlocks were swept back, tied with a crimson scarf. He didn't get the presence of the redheaded dyke—not one bit.

He felt a lurch in his gut. He'd missed seeing Claudine. In many ways, she served as the little sister he'd never had. Well, if not his sister, then maybe a distant cousin.

Before he was able to settle things—or perhaps make matters worse—Marylou poked her head in the kitchen and announced that the séance would begin shortly in the living room. Claudine followed Marylou, glancing over her shoulder and giving Moss one last, theatrical stink eye and a heartfelt finger.

At least she'd graced him with a reaction.

Perhaps Marylou's party wouldn't disappoint after all.

10

Badly hungover from the night's circus, Moss stumbled groggily into his host's kitchen.

Marylou eyed him over the rim of her cup, smoke from her cigarette funneling upward around the motionless blades of a ceiling fan. "Lord in heaven, you're a mess." The antiquated kitchen was jumbled with the detritus of last night's party—empty bottles, ashtrays overflowing with cigarette butts, and wine, beer, and whisky spills. In one corner was a cadre of broken glassware. She had cleared a small space for herself at the dinette table and was nursing a cup of black coffee.

"I must have fallen asleep," Moss mumbled sheepishly as he wandered into the kitchen. "Did I have fun?"

"I guess you fucking well did, buckaroo. It's four o'clock in the afternoon."

"You're kidding."

"Not one bit." She took a long, loud sip of her coffee.

"I feel like I've lost a whole day."

"That's what you get for partaking of Laotian delicacies." Marylou set down her cup and fetched another from the cupboard. Filling it to the brim from a scarred percolator, she handed it to Moss.

"What was in that stuff?" Moss liberated a red vinyl–upholstered kitchen chair from under the table and plopped down.

"Not much," she said, cocking an ironic eyebrow in his direction. "Only the best pure opium this side of the Golden Triangle."

"I didn't know."

"I guessed that." Marylou snickered. "Your paramour left early with her current . . . whatever."

"You mean Claudine? We're just friends."

"God's hooks, Moss. Call it whatever you like." She laughed, shaking her graying curls and causing the loose flesh of her face to jiggle. "You're as blind as a bat about women, you silly fuck. That girl has had a crush on you for years." She paused for a moment to light another cigarette. "Worst of all, you haven't even thanked me for inviting you to my séance."

Moss stared at the checkerboard linoleum floor. His head still buzzed. He wasn't fully able to grasp what the old bat was rattling on about, but there was a ring of truth to it. "Did I manage to miss the séance part? I don't remember." In fact, he had been visited by ghosts—in his dreams after he'd passed out. The séance had been accomplished, just not in the way he'd imagined.

"I don't remember either," she cackled. "But it was quite a jolly time, wasn't it?"

"Must've been." His hands were shaky, his tongue thick and furry. "Did Claudine say anything about me?"

"Guess not. She departed while you were comatose. We're the only two left."

Moss nodded. He took a swallow of coffee and felt instantly queasy. "Those were some nasty joints."

Marylou shook her head. "All the way from Vientiane."

"I thought I was going to die."

"Small mercies," she said. "But here you are, Moss. Here you are." She shifted her attention to the window over the sink. Moss followed her gaze outside. Lush greenery swayed in the breeze. "I believe I found what you were looking for regarding the Bainbridge model. A drawing teacher at WSU, one Harold Percy, had a remainders portfolio in his office filled with student work left from past semesters. I told him you were asking about some figure model with dark hair. He let me leaf through his student's sketches. Lo and behold, I found a couple that might depict your girl."

The watch spring in Moss's brain coiled inward. There was hope. "You possess this sketch?"

"Not just one, Moss, three—all done during this past winter term by the same drawing student. Brice Godwin."

"General Motors Godwin?" Moss raised his eyebrows. "I know the mother. She's a regular visitor at the gallery."

"One and the same. I got the impression from Percy that there was something going on between the model and the boy."

Marylou crooked a finger and led him back toward the studio portion of the house. Once in the atelier, she shooed Kafka from a drawing table dusted with cat hair. "I have to admit, these sketches are a little bit odd. Anyone can see that." She busied herself opening a flat cardboard portfolio then removed three large sheets of newsprint. Ceremoniously, she laid the drawings side by side on the worktable, stepping to the side to allow him full vantage.

Moss peered at the charcoal sketches as if they were an augury. In some areas, the smeared charcoal distorted details, but the gist was clear enough. Two sheets displayed the upper half of a nude female figure—the face turned slightly away from the viewer. The third depicted a three-quarter frontal view of the face. It was this last sketch that made Moss's insides quicken. There was a furious mane of thick, dark hair coursing in heavy curls around a woman's vaguely indistinct features. The drawing revealed a sense of both eerie stillness and stroboscopic movement—one contour line deemed insufficient to delineate the physiography of the model.

What was not lost was the depiction of a vertical line bisecting the face from hairline to chin. Moss stared, palms wet. "There's something here alright," he said after a long silence. "Something about this girl."

Marylou said nothing, her ancient eyes observing his reaction.

"I'd like to talk to the youngster who made these sketches." The thread of his quest was once more within his grasp. "Did the instructor say anything more?"

Marylou shrugged a fatalistic shrug. "He hired the model on Haller's recommendation, not through the usual channels. Claimed Haller was adamant with his endorsement."

"Doesn't sound like the Haller we all know and love. He dislikes women on a fundamental level. That's why he dismembers them on canvas."

"Haller is a prick—on a fundamental level."

"No argument from me on that point," Moss said. "What about the model?"

"Percy claimed she unsettled the dynamic of the classroom. Said he'd think twice before hiring her again."

Moss could not suppress the feeling that he was on to something. "How so?"

"How so what?"

"Unsettled, as Percy said?"

"Apparently, this Godwin boy was agreeably gifted. Percy thought the lad manifested a kind of genius. Said the model homed in on it right away."

"And?" Moss fidgeted with the dusty sheets in front of him. "And?"

"And Percy told me the kid left school at the end of the term and never returned. There was an accident, I guess. It was in the papers."

"Accident?"

"Suicide," Marylou said.

Moss took a deep breath and stepped back from the table, whistling a bar or two from "Matilda" between his teeth. From a greater distance he was able to detect a distinct asymmetry to the model's face. Large eyes surmounting prominent cheekbones, the nose narrow and fine, the lips lush. Somehow, the smudged quality of the charcoal imparted an antique effect. Except for the tattoo, the woman in the drawings could've been mistaken for one of the famous Pre-Raphaelite models—Lizzie Siddal, Jane Morris.

He shifted from one foot to the other. "Did he give you a name to go with the sketches?"

"Seren is her given name," Marylou said. "He didn't remember the surname, but if she got paid for the modeling session, then her full name must be on the department's roles. Somebody would've cut her a check."

"Odd name." Lost in thought, Moss tapped the side of his nose with a finger. "This is a help, Marylou. I owe you one."

Marylou placed a meaty hand on his shoulder. "Go home, Moss. You look ghastly."

He waved his hand in a hazy benediction above the charcoal drawings. "May I take these? I need to look a little longer."

"Be my guest, bubby." She led him to the door. "Let me know if you get any closer to whatever the fuck it is you're looking for."

11

On Monday, when Moss got back to the gallery, he gave Kaye the rest of the day off. She was the cornerstone of the business, and he was smart enough to try to keep her happy. Foot traffic on Townsend Street was slow that afternoon, and he felt confident he could handle any passersby that might stop in. July sales were usually light.

On her way out, Kaye asked, "Any closer to finding this model?"

"Not much," he said.

"If you're really intent on locating her, why not hire someone? Track her down? There are detective agencies, you know."

"Hmmm," Moss murmured. "I guess that's a thought." Inwardly disappointed in Kaye's lack of appreciation for the true nature of a mythic quest, he retreated to the gallery's interior. Couldn't she tell he liked having a mission?

Ensconced behind the front desk, he began to consider his annual migration to the cottage up north. Because of the myriad questions surrounding the Bainbridge landscape, his eagerness to flee the city was mitigated by his fear of losing the big painting. He couldn't allow the piece to leave his possession before solving the mystery of its origins. He'd been present at its birthing. He had some rights. On that point, he felt certain.

He was surprised when Sally Bright popped in from next door. "Lover, you're home! You've been making yourself scarce of late. What's up?" She was wearing a beige sweater and skirt set from

Chanel. With her perfectly coifed blonde bob, she reminded Moss of a 1950s movie star. Perching on the corner of his desk, she blew him an air-kiss.

"Too few clients. We seem to have entered the summertime swale," he said. "How is it over at your place?"

"Lazy. I do love days when nothing at all happens." She reached over and stubbed out the cigarette he'd left burning in the ashtray. "Is it true what they're saying about Boo Tice and the Bainbridge?"

"A rumor, nothing more. Boo made some offers on it, but that painting is off the market," he said with an air of finality.

Sally's eyes widened in mock astonishment. "My God!" She let out a discreet, girlish squeal. "So, it is true? What did he finally pay for it?"

"Not a penny," Moss said, lighting another Chesterfield and sounding more confident than he felt. "I'm not parting with it. Simple as that."

"I've heard there's going to be an article in the Free Press on Sunday, by Joy Colby no less. They're announcing plans for the new wing at the DIA. According to my source, Tice and the Bainbridge painting figure prominently in the piece."

Moss shrugged, beleaguered on all sides. More than anything, he needed a drink. "I hadn't heard. Birdie Entwistle mentioned something. I didn't pay much attention."

"Liar," she said, laughing. "You always pay attention, and Birdie is always full of gossip. Why is this painting so special to you?"

He took a long pause.

"The simple answer is—I don't know, but it is," he said. "I need to delve into a few things. That's it in a nutshell."

Sally gave him a cautious look. "Be careful what you wish for."

He breezed on, oblivious. "It's the one and only Bainbridge piece that's inarguably great. It doesn't fit with all the rest—or maybe it's the culmination, a synthesis of all the rest. There's something going on with that painting, and I'm determined to find the answer."

"What about Boo?" she asked. "You two have known each other since forever. Is that piece worth falling out over?"

Moss rubbed his eyes. He was tired. Being patronized about his quest exhausted his spirit. Nowadays it seemed the whole world was questioning his motives, and, to make matters worse, he didn't have a plausible answer. What was he really trying to track down? A bit of riddle, or something more?

He needed his August getaway. He needed solitude and time to think. Problem was, he couldn't reconcile leaving the painting at the gallery. He couldn't stand to have it out of sight—certainly not six hundred miles out of sight. He stood up and stretched out his back.

"Let's take a look," he said, slipping past Sally and locking the front door. "Why don't you tell me what you think?"

He led her down the stairs to the private viewing room. When the spotlights were switched on, the big painting glowed like a beacon from another world. Moss motioned for Sally to sit down and went to the sideboard to pour them drinks.

Knowing she liked her whisky, he found a decanter of Scotch and poured three fingers into a crystal rocks glass. After fixing his own glass of Chartreuse on ice, he sat in the vacant Eames and swiveled around to face her. "Early on, right after the exhibition, whenever I spent time down here it felt like the old guy's spirit was present, you know? I could feel him. Now, I'm not so sure. Anymore, I'm feeling something else."

"Did you know him well? Bainbridge?"

"Nobody really knew him well," he said. "Maybe Gerome Nahni. Bainbridge was a hard one to figure."

"Did you like him?"

Moss laughed ruefully. "He had an abrasive manner."

"How, exactly, did he die?"

"Heart," Moss said.

She took a long sip from her whisky. Staring at the painting, she said, "There you have it."

He liked sitting in this cozy, wood-paneled cave. He enjoyed being with the Bainbridge painting. If he sat with it long enough, he could smell the trees, the ice, the portent of storm.

"Did he title it?" Sally asked.

"He never titled his work. This one is Number 313."

"Lucky."

"Not for Bainbridge." Moss brushed his hair off his forehead. The third presence in the room—the silent painting—drew their eyes. "So?" he said, elevating his eyebrows, awaiting her reaction.

She read the painting like the expert she was. "It's got some rough spots. There's a lot of underpainting showing through—looks as if he changed his direction at some point."

"I know."

"Those smudges just above the tree line. They're odd."

"Fingerprints," Moss said in a distracted voice. "They look like fingerprints to me."

"Bainbridge's?"

"Yes. I think they must be. They're the right size—he had thick fingers, a brick mason's hands."

Sally had a sharp eye. "There are other stray elements that make it feel a tiny bit unfinished, don't you think?"

"It's finished," Moss said too quickly. "I think it's the roughness that makes it so good. It stands apart from his other work. In a strange way, it reminds me of something."

"Contemporary?"

"No. Old." He smoothed his mustache with one finger. "It's the irresolution that gives it energy."

She reached over and took his cigarette, tapped the elongated ash in an ashtray, and returned it to him. After a while she said, "I'm guessing, but I think he started off in one direction, changed his mind, then overpainted the original image. The crazy surface application distracts the eye, but I think there's an image that's been painted over. I know for a fact that Donald Morris would buy it in a heartbeat if Tice doesn't. Name your price."

Moss swiveled around to face the painting. The yellow sky was filled with discordant, crepuscular movement—swirls and ridges of heavy impasto. Sally was right. Underneath lay the suggestion of another image. As always, Moss found himself drawn into the painting. It was not merely a picture—it was a place. But not anywhere in this world.

For a long time, they sat in silence.

Abruptly, Moss rose from his seat and crossed the room. Squinting, his eyes traveled down the left-hand side of the canvas. He turned to Sally and crooked a finger. "Take a look at this."

Sally set her drink on the table and moved to Moss's side.

"See that little depression in the impasto? What do you make of that?"

Her nose inches from the surface, she studied the faint impression in the thick paint. "Nipple?"

"Yup." Moss nodded.

"Bainbridge's?"

"Nope . . . at least I don't think so. Female?"

"That's interesting," Sally said. She leaned in.

"My thoughts precisely." Moss led her back to their seats. They both reached for their drinks in movements so synchronized it made Sally laugh.

She said, "Maybe the DIA is the place for it after all. You can't keep it hidden—it's too good."

Moss lit another cigarette. "I need to sort it out before I think about selling it."

"With Bainbridge dead, the provenance is open to interpretation." Sally eyed Moss. "Does your contract specify what happens to unsold lots after his death?"

"Nope. We never discussed it." Moss stubbed out his half-smoked cigarette. "As far as anyone knows, there are no heirs. If push comes to shove, his estate could be tied up in probate for years and years."

"But you have *possession*."

"Yes, I have possession," Moss said, nodding. "And an exclusive contract to sell his work. That's it."

"Why don't you just buy it?" she said. "Buy it from the gallery, backdate the receipt, then you'd have it for as long as you want."

Moss hissed between his teeth. "I don't have that kind of cash, not on hand." But that wasn't it. He didn't merely want to own the landscape, he wanted to possess it. In order to possess it, he needed to *know*.

"Boo wants it, and he has lawyers—a shit ton of lawyers."

"Don't remind me," Moss said grumpily.

"Maybe you should talk to him," Sally said, standing to leave. "Catch him before he heads off to Africa."

Moss took a breath. "I guess I could visit him." Confronting Tice was the very last thing he wanted to do.

"Honey, can you make yourself free for dinner at my place next Thursday? Grace Hartigan is coming into town. She adores you." Sally blew him a kiss and headed upstairs. "Give a call if you can't make it. Cheery-bye."

12

The steel-and-glass box that housed the headquarters of Tice Manufacturing was located on a lushly treed plot in the Detroit suburb of Southfield. Once inside the polished-brass elevator, Moss pushed the button for the executive level, and with a barely audible whoosh he was whisked skyward.

When the heavy doors slid open, he found himself facing a vast, glass-walled entry alcove a good forty feet away from the long, mahogany reception desk. He had dressed for the occasion in an off-white linen suit with a narrow, navy pinstripe running through and a pale-blue shirt accompanied by a navy, polka-dot bowtie. On his feet were brown and white spectators from Edward Greene in London.

The receptionist recognized him instantly and buzzed him in. By the time he had crossed the entryway, a different assistant appeared, ready to guide him into the glossy depths of Tice-dom. Moss bestowed a barely discernable nod on the receptionist, spun on a polished heel, and followed the swaying hips of his escort in the direction of the high clover. The hallway leading to the executive office was carpeted in gray Berber. On the walls were the showpieces from the Tice corporate collection.

Once announced, Moss passed through one of the large double doors and was greeted by the sight of the industrialist doing leg exercises on a coffee table. Up-down, up-down, up-down—each step eliciting a surprised gasp from the would-be mountaineer. Moss's host sported a neon-pink polo shirt and a pair of lime-green Bermuda shorts. For some unknown reason, the CEO was barefoot. Moss stood inside the doorway and observed the routine until Tice deigned to acknowledge his presence.

Sweat dripping from the tip of his nose, Tice eventually looked up. "*Unakuwagi!* Moss. You hate the city of Southfield," he gasped. "To what do I owe the pleasure?"

Moss grimaced, vowing to maintain his equipoise—he was on a mission. "Hate may be too strong a word. Every suburb has its uses, I suppose."

"This is where the money's made," Tice said, his face florid from exertion.

"True, but that same money chooses to live in the northern burbs. You ought to know; you live in Bloomfield."

"Two weeks until I take off for the dark continent, Moss," Tice wheezed, pausing to grab a towel from the arm of a chair. Blotting sweat from his brow, he gave Moss a once-over. "You look as if you drove straight from the clubhouse at the DRC. Come on, have a seat and I'll pour us a drink."

Moss took a chair next to an antique sideboard. The magnate's office was paneled in pale-blond ash wood that reflected light streaming in from an exterior wall of tinted glass. Campus photos, ZBT mementos, and athletic memorabilia in the color scheme of Tulane green and blue were emblazoned everywhere.

Handing Moss a tumbler of Chartreuse and ice, Tice flopped down in a chair opposite his guest. "Fairchild Moss, what's happening, old buddy?" When Tice elected to use Moss's Christian name, it came out in three drawn-out syllables—Far-uh-chuld, or something to that effect.

Moss waved his hand dismissively. "Not a thing. I couldn't face going in to work, so here I am."

"Good deal!" Tice momentarily examined his vodka on ice, nodded to himself, and took a long, good-natured swallow. "I'm bored as spit on shine. What say we go out on the boat? I'm useless here—way over my head. These frigging Ivy Leaguers, you know? All they think about is numbers. Profit and loss . . . well, profit anyway. That's not real life, Moss. That's not the Tice way."

Not if you're lucky enough to have inherited everything, Moss said to himself bitterly, ignoring the fact he'd done just that himself, albeit to a lesser degree. The tycoon occupied a world Moss could barely imagine.

"Come on, let's grab us some fresh air."

Moss swirled the ice in his drink. "What about dinner?"

"Sarnia," Tice replied, rubbing his face with the towel. "We'll pop in at the marina up there. Let me jump in the shower, and I'll call Captain Bob and see if it's okay to take the skiff out today."

After Moss availed himself of another Chartreuse, they headed down to the Detroit Yacht Club on Belle Isle in Tice's Corvette. The trip south on Telegraph Road was a harrowing whirlwind; Tice drove with cavalier abandon. Traffic laws, intended to keep other motorists from carnage, were treated as benign suggestions, open to an array of interpretations. When they finally arrived at the marina, Moss was a jangle of sparking nerves.

The skiff turned out to be a classic thirty-five-foot Chris Craft Commander. By the time they had parked the car, Captain Bob was dockside and awaiting their pleasure.

"Ahoy, Cap," Tice boomed out as soon as the boat's pilot was in earshot. "What say we take a spin up to Sarnia for happy hour?"

Captain Bob, a deeply tanned fellow with blunt features and a gruff manner, gave Moss a scowl. Turning briefly toward his employer, he said, "Could be some chop later."

"Chop?" Moss raised his eyebrows.

Bob nodded toward the northwest, where a line of dumpling-shaped clouds lay on the horizon. "Shouldn't be much," he shrugged, giving Moss's attire a skeptical up-and-down. "You gentlemen ready to board?"

"Call me Ishmael," Moss chimed in good-naturedly.

Bob responded by hawking up a gob of phlegm that he spat into the turgid green water of the boat slip.

Tice, who'd changed into tan Bermuda shorts, a white polo shirt, and rope sandals, led Moss and the Captain down a long wharf to the boat's slip. The Faustus II was a slim, white beauty with fifteen feet of flying bridge and an open transom. It was considered the baby of the fleet—the big boats were all docked in Key West.

While most of Tice's business associates assumed that the boat's name was a literary reference, Moss knew it was a nod to the industrialist's now-deceased father—Faustus Xavier Tice II. The father's spirit hung like a somber cloud over his son's efforts. While shipping out on the big ore boats on the Great Lakes, the senior Tice had made his reputation as a bare-knuckle fighter. Rumor had it the old man was loathe to bequeath Tice Enterprises—cotton land, bottling plants, boatyards, and automotive assembly lines—to his son. There was no love lost between the generations of Tice males. Moss guessed that the current Tice was the most tractable member of the family, frittering his years at the corporate helm pursuing a variety of expensive distractions.

Big-time art was one such diversion.

Once aboard, lines cast off, Tice and Moss went below while the captain climbed the ladder to the bridge. Searching around in the boat's compact fridge, Tice extracted a couple of cans of Stroh's beer and handed one to Moss, who eyed the offering with a mixture of curiosity and disdain. "Stroh's?"

"It's the only thing Bob drinks. Nothing else comes aboard unless I make a huge fuss." Tice popped the top on his beer, took a sip, and made a face. "It's just not worth the tussle. Captain Bob's set in his ways."

Moss groaned inwardly.

From his perch high above the cabin, the skipper steered them out onto the diesel-slicked waters of the Detroit River, heading north toward the lake. Moss surveyed the panorama as glass towers lining the waterfront slid past in a sun-glittered stream of corporate architecture. They made desultory small talk above the drone of the motors. Leaving the flat and crowded confines of the river, the lake greeted them with a dazzling sheen of blue-green freshwater, gleaming in the brilliant sunlight. Moss smelled the difference in the air as soon as they moved out onto the open water of the Great Lake. The boat, with its twin 427-cubic-inch marine engines, rose up on plane as soon as Bob thrust the throttles forward, and the steady *slap, slap, slap* of the waves against the hull lulled Moss into a kind of contentment. Tice pulled two plastic deck chairs out onto the transom, and they settled in, sipping beer and feeling the cooling breeze.

"Canada," Boo said, nodding vaguely eastward. "I like it."

"The country?"

"The whole shebang," Tice said, lapsing into his Tulane dialect.

Moss said nothing. He knew very well that his friend only affected a southern drawl when his purpose was obfuscation. There was no telling where the conversation might lead, but at some point Moss was determined to confront the industrialist about the Bainbridge.

They sat for a long pause. Moss opened his mouth, the landscape painting poised on the tip of his tongue, when Tice spread his arms and exhaled a loud sigh of maritime contentment.

How exactly to broach the question of the Bainbridge? Acutely aware of the vagaries of provenance, and the very real limitations of his decade-old contract with the grumpy painter, he felt at a disadvantage. Moss could *sell* every Bainbridge at the gallery on a split commission, but he didn't actually *own* any of the works. He guessed Tice's pack of attorneys were aware of this fact. The businessman could force his hand at any time—force him to sell, or take him to court. Moss could stall the inevitable, but he couldn't win in the end. He knew it. Tice knew it.

The longer he delayed, the less likely he would be to tackle the subject at all. He gulped in a breath of air and began. "Boo, we need to talk."

Unperturbed, Tice waved him off. "I was wondering."

"Wondering what exactly?" Moss said, retying his ponytail, undone by the wind.

"Wondering when you planned to ask me about the Bainbridge painting," Tice said. "Surely you've heard the news about the new wing at the DIA?"

"I've heard."

"Well?"

"I was working up to it." Moss fidgeted.

"You were taking your sweet time."

Moss flipped the tycoon a half-hearted bird. "That's my nature. You should know by now. What about the painting, Boo? What about the Bainbridge?"

"What about it?"

"I can't sell it. Not yet." Despite himself, Moss babbled on. "I'm convinced he had help finishing the piece." He gave a hapless shrug. "Something strange went on in that studio. I need to get to the bottom of it. I need to know."

Tice eyed him placidly. "Sure it's not your imagination talking? You seem pretty bored lately."

"No," he said, not sure of anything other than the painful fact that he had misplaced his imagination twenty years ago and hadn't had much use for it since.

"Let's you and I un-worry ourselves about it." Tice relaxed his features, letting his face go smooth and blank. "Construction on the new wing is projected to take at least thirty months—maybe more. We have plenty of time to consider the details."

"Why not donate another Bainbridge painting? Or a handful of his smaller works?"

"You like this one, the big one, don't you?"

"Of course."

"Well then, that's your answer." Tice smiled guilelessly. "You know your art. If you like it, then I like it. Simple as that."

Moss's features slumped into a glum frown.

"Stop fretting, buddy. There'll be plenty of time to barter," Tice said in a chipper voice. "Looks like the weather is clearing." He nodded to the sunlight now breaking through the gray cloud cover. "Things have a way of resolving themselves. You worry too much, my friend."

Listening to his host's reassurances, Moss knew two things. First, the industrialist was lying about everything. Second, he, Moss, would have to act, and act fast, if he wanted to preserve his hegemony over the Bainbridge landscape.

PREDELLA

II

Lake District—Late Summer 1978

"*Stay quite still or this won't work. Another hook or two and we'll be finished.*" *Seren wrestles the red silk organza into submission and threads the last two hooks through their respective eyelets. Haller lets out a loud, exasperated fart. Small as he is, it's a tight fit. The gown wasn't cut for a man's body. The little potbelly he's so proud of almost prevents her from cinching the bodice closed.*

She steps back to admire her work. He looks ridiculous, but somehow it all fits together. Below the hem of the full skirt, the round yellow toes of his work boots protrude obscenely. Behind the mirror and a little off to the side sits an old double easel and a tabouret on wheels holding a lavish array of oil paints and brushes. On the easel's shelf is a canvas, six feet tall and white with a fresh coating of gesso.

The air is ripe with the scent of turpentine and sex. He turns for her—turns for the mirror. "I like it."

She loops her finger in a circle, and he twirls again. She can see the shadow of his erection lengthening beneath the thin material. His big ears turn pink. The air around him sparks with color. When he rubs himself and dances comically toward her, she laughs and twists away. On the stereo, a Kate Bush tune. He swivels closer, knowing he looks absurd, but he's the sort of man who doesn't care about appearances as long as he gets everything he wants.

When the doorbell chimes, she snatches her coat from a nearby stool and dodges around him, beyond his grasp. Peering out a narrow window next to the door, she turns back to the room and announces, "Curry."

Their stone hut—one room with an outside privy—is half-hidden behind the old Leathes-Head Hotel and has a view of Derwentwater and the fells beyond. It's a short distance from the hotel's kitchen, but these days it's always a wet walk. The kitchen boy must place a plastic bag over the parcels of food he ferries to the croft. By the time he reaches their door, his slicker is dripping.

In a corner of the room, by a large, multipaned window, sits Daisy Lytton dressed in a robin's-egg-blue robe. Meticulously hand-painted in days before the turn of the century, pink and white chrysanthemums decorate the entire length of the silk fabric. Daisy's great grandmother once wore this robe, but the twenty-year-old doesn't care about history. One bare leg, bent slightly at the knee, extends beyond the opening.

Carrying a stack of white cardboard containers, Seren shakes drops of water from her hair. It has been raining for days. The eaves drip ceaselessly. Mold sprouts under the rugs. After setting down most of her burden, she carries a bowl heaped with rice and yellow curry to where Daisy is reading. Aromatic steam fills the air. The girl looks up, her face brightening. "Food," she says.

Clearing a side table of books and papers, charcoal sketches smudged and torn, overflowing ashtrays, and three empty bottles of beer, Seren sits, stirs rice into the soupy chicken curry, and offers the younger woman a spoonful. Pausing a beat, glancing out the window toward the sodden garden, Daisy eventually turns, gives her a knowing smile, and opens her pink cupid's lips to receive the spicy mouthful. Seren watches Daisy chew. Once the girl swallows, she opens her mouth again like a baby bird waiting for a worm. Spooning up another morsel, Seren repeats the gesture again and again, wiping the young woman's chin with a rumpled linen napkin.

Behind her, the sounds of Haller ratting through the food containers, banging utensils, slurping. "Fucking-aye," he says. His dress is stained. Curry spatters on the table, drips on the floor.

While Daisy consumes the last bite, Seren bends down and opens the chrysanthemum robe, pulling it wide. Examining the young flesh, she lets out a long sigh and begins to hum an old Celtic tune.

"Your mark, Mouse," Daisy says dreamily, drawing the tip of an index finger from her own hairline to the end of her nose. "I want one too."

"Oh Daisy," Seren laughs. "You're such a silly thing."

13

Moss watched Claudine hover at the opposite end of the Midtown's bar, engaged in a lively back-and-forth with a pair of white-haired matrons. Both women sported tennis tans that had baked their skin the color of strong tea. He couldn't divine the content of their banter, but the saucy cadence of Claudine's voice told him she was cultivating a sizable tip.

She was good at people when she wanted to be.

Advancing toward his end of the bar with a metronomic sway of hips, she bestowed on Moss a look of benign indifference. "Moss, to what do we owe the pleasure of this visitation?"

"Heading north in a day or two," he said, withholding inflection. The nautical outing with Boo Tice had unsettled him. Nights without sleep, days of restless inaction. He was grumpy. Now that he knew the Bainbridge was in jeopardy, the chat with Sally had stirred a plan. He would abduct the landscape. Squirrel it away. Buy himself some time.

She took his empty glass and refilled it. "I envy the vacation. You're lucky."

"You could come with," he said in a moment of inspiration. "I'm on a mission—a real one this time."

"Fat chance, old thing. Besides, I've got better offers." She cocked a sculpted eyebrow. "What's the vision quest this time?"

"I'm installing the Bainbridge up north at the cottage. Out of harm's way."

"This is new."

"This is hush-hush. I'm doing it on the sly."

"Not so hush-hush if you're announcing the fact in a public tavern." Claudine twisted her lips. "Why not take out an ad in the *Birmingham Eccentric*?"

Moss scowled good-naturedly.

She wiped the bar in front of him. "So, how's your love life, Moss? You never come in here with anybody anymore. Haven't in years."

Moss took a swallow of Chartreuse. This subject reared its head from time to time. Lately, there was nothing to say. "Pleasantly absent. As you might've guessed."

"Well, if it's any consolation, you've got a fan club down there." She tilted her head toward the matrons sipping martinis and shooting him covert glances from the opposite end of the bar. "I told them you were a movie actor of middling repute."

"Thanks for nothing." Moss grimaced. He could see the shadow of a future he preferred not to acknowledge. The gravitational tug of life's downslope began to erode the edges of his newfound resolution.

"I bet you could cadge a free drink or two," Claudine smirked. "Auto money, I'm guessing."

Moss grunted. "Not my type."

"Are you sure you still have a type?"

He ruminated for a second. It was not a question he wished to entertain while on the cusp of escaping the city. He needed to focus on the quest. He'd hoped for reassurance, but Claudine was pricking holes. He heard air escaping from his psyche every time she opened her lips. Maybe she was still mad at him.

Pushing up from his stool, he said, "I've got to run."

"Boo came in the other day," Claudine said. It sounded like an afterthought, but he knew it wasn't.

"Oh?"

"He was his usual chatty self."

"Yes?"

"Offered to take me to Africa with him for some kind of mountaineering escapade," she said, removing Moss's empty glass. "Said I might enjoy a return to the 'auld sod' as it were." She carved quotation marks in the air with nails painted bubblegum pink.

"That comment is just wrong—wrong in every way. That man was ruined from the minute he popped out of the chute. If I were you, I wouldn't give him the time of day."

Claudine let out a rueful laugh. "Hard to know who to listen to these days."

Moss said nothing. He wasn't certain if that last remark was aimed at him or not. Clearly something was going on with Claudine. Oh well. Everybody had problems. At the moment, he had more than his share.

"He said something I didn't quite catch. Something about Haller."

"Haller?" Moss's sonar pinged.

"Maybe you should talk to Sally. Boo got it from her."

Extracting two crisp twenties from his wallet, he placed them on the bar.

Claudine swept the bills up with the deftness of a casino croupier at the end of a shift.

Turning on his heel, Moss said, "See ya."

"Moss," Claudine said as he reached the door. "You could at least pretend to care. Pals do that sometimes." She turned away.

• • •

Only through force of will did Moss refrain from breaking into a trot on his way to the Donald Morris Gallery. Sally had heard something new. A rush of blood flooded his face. He'd told no one of his intention to attend Haller's opening at the Tate Gallery in London, a plan so new he'd barely considered the logistics himself. The beginning of autumn was a busy time for his gallery. Could he afford to be abroad during the weeks when buyers were most hungry? He'd said nothing about this planned trip to Kaye. She would be left to shoulder the burden of his absence. She was a brick. She'd kill him when he gave her the news.

In the cool interior of the gallery, the air smelled of sandalwood. Sally was seated at the front desk. On the walls were a series of austere Ad Reinhardt paintings. The rows of black squares gave the place the feel of a nihilist cathedral.

He immediately noticed that Sally sported an amethyst ring on her right hand. The stone, roughly the size of a robin's egg, was set in antique gold. The jewelry spoke of something, but he wasn't quite sure what.

"Blood of Christ," he remarked.

"It was my mother's." She scrunched her face into a wistful smile.

"Looks heavy."

"Heavier than you can imagine, lamb." Shuffling the exhibition announcements she was addressing, she squared the edges and set the pile aside.

Somehow, he'd never given a thought to the fact that Sally might've had a mother—perhaps because he hadn't had one himself. He'd never bothered to ask about her family. That kind of small talk didn't appear on his radar. When he was a boy, his world consisted of his Gran—that was it.

Come to think of it, Kaye, Claudine, even Marylou must have

had parents at one time. The idea made him a little dizzy. He'd never guessed they all might have hidden histories. Who knew?

Then he did something he'd rarely done with anyone. He asked, "What was she like, your mother?"

Sally paused for a beat or two, absently retrieving her pen and placing it in a drawer. On the walls, somber black icons looked on. "She cooked beautifully. Ate with gusto. She sang songs. Happiness was her great disguise."

Moss nodded sagely—just as cynicism was his own. He wondered how another person would describe him when he was gone. What could be said? That he drank to excess and dressed well? Was that it? Good hair. Good teeth. Good cars.

Sally broke into his train of thought. "Have you heard about Haller?"

"No. What?"

Leaning forward, she said, "He's gone missing." She extended her hand for one of his Chesterfields. "Somewhere in the countryside. It's all very sotto voce. A girl is involved, of course."

Moss lit her cigarette with a gold lighter on the desk. "Tell me what you know."

"Not much." She exhaled a plume of blue smoke. "He was scheduled for a publicity shoot for the exhibition—Haller and the other artists. He never showed up. Word has it his girlfriend's family has money. They're upset. The gallery people tried to track him down without any luck. Sounds like he's on the lam."

Moss nodded. "That's news."

"Nobody from the Tate is saying anything. It's all rumor as far as I know." She leaned back in her chair and crossed her legs, giving Moss a speculative look. Today, Sally was all in gray silk, the amethyst sat poised on her finger like an unanswered question.

"I'm heading north in a couple of days. Early this year," he said.

She didn't respond to his non sequitur. "You remember Haller slept with one of Lucian Freud's daughters, don't you? Everyone was furious." She tapped a bit of cigarette ash into the ashtray. "If they catch him with an underage girl again, he's going to jail."

"High time."

She gave him a wave of her hand and returned to her cards. "More money for Donald." She was alluding to the gallery's eventual benefit from any kind of unflattering publicity for its artists. Profits accrued in direct proportion to notoriety. It was axiomatic, pure and simple.

"Who's got the scoop? Anyone we know?"

"Birdie Entwistle comes to mind." Sally leaned forward and gave him a conspiratorial smile. Pure Grace Kelly. "It's nice to see you finally interested in something, sweetie, if only for the moment."

"Haller knew Bainbridge. There's a connection somewhere. I can feel it."

"Mmmm," Sally murmured, tilting her head to the side.

"What's going on with Claudine?" he asked. "Do you know anything?"

"Lady troubles. That's what I've heard. Jilted."

That too was news.

He blew Sally an air-kiss as he headed for the door. The bit about Haller was promising. At last, Moss was back on the trail of his very own private mystery.

14

The next day, Moss phoned the Scarab Club to find out if Birdie Entwistle had made a reservation for lunch that day. Proximity to the DIA ensured the club a steady clientele, mostly curatorial and office staff. Birdie was a fixture, even though he'd been retired from the institute's roster for decades.

Assured by management that Birdie would be at his usual table during the noontime rush, Moss sacrificed his personal preference and drove the station wagon down into the heart of a metropolis he distrusted with every fiber of his being. In late summer, the city took on a dingy, overheated quality that made his stomach lurch. The people of Detroit were pissed off most of the time, and as August approached with its heat and humidity, the collective angst wound itself tight.

By the time he'd wrestled with unruly traffic and rolled into the club's parking lot, his native misanthropy was in full bloom. Proceeding past the host station, he spied Birdie seated at the far end of the dining room.

"Your dear-departed grandmother made an appearance in my dreams recently," Birdie said as soon as Moss arrived tableside.

"No."

"Yes. Indeed. Not more than three nights ago. We were dancing as I recall. Nell was a rather marvelous dancer in her youth. That was long before your time."

Moss had only a vague notion of how well his Gran knew Birdie. Years ago she had mentioned editing several of his monographs—back in the day when he still wrote monographs. Beyond that, he couldn't guess.

"Dear boy," Birdie said when Moss sat down, "you've put on weight."

Moss winced. He could see how this was going to go. "I don't think so. I'm about the same."

"A gorgeous boy like you wouldn't realize. How could you?" Birdie chuckled. "But the trousers don't lie . . . at least not about that." The former museum director was wearing an elegant white shirt with a navy-blue velvet bowtie knotted carelessly at his throat. Draped over his boney shoulders was a lightweight cotton sweater in the palest of mauves.

Moss immediately envied both the tie and the sweater.

Horace, the club's longtime maître d', set a double Chartreuse on the rocks and a tall glass of ice water in front of Moss. "Thank you, Horace." Moss raised his glass in salute. When the tall and solemn figure had retreated, he cleared his throat. "What's this I hear about Maurice Haller disappearing?"

No response. Watery eyes fixed him with a prolonged stare. The old fellow's lips pursed. After an eternity, he spoke. "I don't know much." He dabbed at the corner of his mouth with a napkin. "Rumors cling to Haller like maggots on a corpse," he said, glancing down at his unfinished plate.

"You know more than I do."

"Why do you care about that horrid ruffian?" He deposited his utensils on his plate in disgust. "The very thought of that man has ruined my repast. He's a dreadful creature."

"I just do," Moss growled. "Spill the beans."

The dining room was less than crowded. Lofty ceiling fans

rotated lazily above the drone of voices. A few white-jacketed waiters stood serenely in the corners. Moss pictured himself twenty years hence, perched at his own table for one. He imagined his future self, wearing an old tattersall hacking jacket spotted with soup stains. A palsied hand. Like Birdie—a long, useless life done and dusted.

The old man cast his gaze to the signatures on the overhead beams. "The curator for Asian art, Morgan Eliot, has an ex working at the Tate. He had two yummy bits on Haller—strictly need-to-know." Birdie clutched at the cane he held pinched between his knees. "First, the Tate exhibition is going to be a very big thing for Haller. It's the kind of show that makes a fellow's career. Critics are saying his new work is spectacular. He's destined to be the star.

"Second, when he failed to appear for some publicity function, people started speculating. The current rumor suggests that when he returned to England he holed up in a Lake District cottage with the daughter of an MP—old family, good family. You know the Brits. They have a talent for scandal and an appetite for unseemly liaisons. Evidently the girl is young—not yet twenty. That's the word on the street."

"There's more than a month before the exhibition is scheduled to open in London. Plenty of time for Haller to show his face," Moss said.

"I suppose so." Birdie dabbed at his lips with a linen napkin. "You seem agitated, sweet boy. Why all this bother about a person we both loathe?"

"Curious," Moss said. "That's all."

"Curious enough to drive all the way downtown from your lair in Birmingham? Hmmm. You know what they say about curiosity, don't you, puss?"

Moss dropped his napkin on the table and scooted his chair

back.

"There's a gala tonight at the Remuda Lounge," Birdie said, referencing a seedy leather bar located downriver. The Remuda was an establishment favored by the sexually adventurous.

"I've retired from all that." Moss squirmed. "I have other fish to fry."

"You can't remain celibate forever. You're simply too pretty."

"Celibacy's a choice—like being a Catholic or a Rotarian," Moss said. "One less decision to make."

"What is it that's distracting you? This Haller thing?"

"Yup."

"That's sad. He's a genius, you know—Haller." Birdie tapped the tip of his cane on the wooden floorboards for emphasis. "Another horrid genius."

Moss grumbled at the very idea. Haller was a hack, nothing more. "Haller's no genius, Birdie. Trust me."

"After the Tate exhibition he'll be bigger than Francis Bacon. Mark my words." Birdie tapped again. "They say the new work is ferocious. Original. It's the talk of the art world."

"Haller is a boil on the ass of the art world," Moss said through gritted teeth.

Birdie chuckled. "My sentiments exactly, but he can paint."

Moss tossed his napkin on the table. "Bye-bye, Birdie."

"Beware of ghosts, dear boy," the old man said. "Like the poor, they are with us always."

"Bah!" was all he could muster for a Parthian shot. Flushed with irritation, Moss headed across the dining room toward the exit. His ears rang with the cackle of reedy laughter.

15

On a muggy Sunday afternoon, a couple of days after his encounter with Birdie Entwistle, Moss toted the Bainbridge landscape to the storage room. Once he'd stopped wheezing, he began wrapping it for transport north. Swaddling the canvas with acid-free paper, front and back, he sandwiched it with sheets of archival foam-core board, then a layer of double-ply cardboard, before he secured it all around with packaging tape. He had neither the skill with tools, the time, nor the patience to fabricate a respectable wooden crate. Instead, he wrapped the entire package in a dark-green, waterproof tarpaulin. It looked unworthy of the painting, but it would have to do.

His plan for departing was simple: lock the door to the private viewing room, close up shop, and head north—exactly as he did the first week of every August. The gallery would be shuttered until his return in September. No one would be the wiser. That was the idea.

He had phoned ahead to give Mrs. Numennin, his housekeeper in the Keweenaw, time to open the cottage, dispose of the cobwebs, and air the place out. She would stock the fridge, put fresh bedclothes on the bed, wash the windows, and rid the house of any spiders that had taken up residence in his absence. Her family had lived on the peninsula for generations. Of solid, Finnish stock, she was meticulous in her work and discreet in her revelations about her employer. He felt confident that the cottage would be in fit condition for his arrival.

He would depart Birmingham shortly after the morning rush. I-75 should be manageable on the northbound lanes. The station wagon was packed with a month's worth of necessities—a case of Chartreuse, country clothes, two pairs of L.L. Bean boots, a nifty yellow rain slicker he'd purchased after his adventure out on Lake Ontario, and, on a whim, the last pair of dungarees he could manage to fit into. Birdie was right—he'd gained a pound or two. He attributed the extra lard to his concern over the Bainbridge.

• • •

July in southern Michigan had been a steam bath. Moss spent his final afternoon in the suburbs relaxing in his bamboo garden. Barefoot, dressed only in seersucker Bermuda shorts in a bright lemon color and a white linen shirt, Moss was prepared to spend his last hours in town doing a little reading, a little smoking, and a lot of drinking. Originally he had intended to wait until dusk before he started in on the Chartreuse. Now he questioned the wisdom of delay.

He was restless, eager to be away.

From the west came a faint rumble of thunder. Lately, the heavens had been opening up in the afternoons with torrential downpours worthy of Thailand or Cambodia. His bamboo loved it. They must have imagined that they were back home. The shrubbery had grown a foot in the last month.

"Phuket," he intoned, walking among his plants, trailing his hand over the fronds. "Nha Trang, Phnom Penh." He repeated this Southeast Asian mantra in a singsong voice. Repeating the exotic place-names over and over with as much musical rhythm as he could muster, he two-stepped down the walk and back. Plants loved the sound of a human voice. Maybe they would be reminded of their homeland. Uprooted from the ancestral soil of Indochina, they might be sad without him knowing. At any rate, he liked the sound of foreign words. Taking a pause, he went inside and poured himself a glass of Chartreuse on ice.

Outside once more, his drink in one hand and a Chesterfield in the other, he wandered deep in reverie along the stone path into the depths of his garden, humming to himself. The mossy flagstones of the walkway cooled the soles of his feet. Birds flitted in and out of the trees overhead. One part of him was itching to get on the move while the other part was lulled into a pleasant torpor by the rich scent of foliage and humus in the garden. Recent rains had unleashed a heady smell of moist earth. The loamy effluence conjured the ache of itinerant memory—sadness for no reason.

At the center of his thoughts loomed the specter of the dead man and his mysterious painting: the ice-curdled river, the dark, inscrutable forest overtopped by a sky of incandescent yellow. The picture itself seemed drenched in unfocused longing. Also there was the unseen presence, the female hand that shaped the masterwork—the one ingredient he couldn't account for. The nipple. The muse.

From out of nowhere an old Ray Charles tune invaded his consciousness. Secure in the privacy of his walled garden, Moss began to sing "Come Rain or Come Shine" to his plants in his best imitation of the great singer's voice.

Crooning to the spiky foliage, he assayed a graceful spin, then another—a subtle sidestep left, a hip waggle. He danced to the sound of his own voice. Never confident in his musical ability, he nonetheless swayed and twirled in the shadowed safety of the garden. The very idea of liberating himself from southern Michigan for a month buoyed his mood. Once he'd properly hung the Bainbridge in the cottage, he'd be a free man. He could walk the shoreline looking for agates or sea glass. He could build a fire in the fireplace and stare at the painting. Perhaps he would unearth his paints and brushes from storage in the shed.

"The fuck, Moss?" Claudine materialized on the veranda.

He stopped so suddenly he splashed Chartreuse on the walkway. "Hey," he stuttered. "I was entertaining my bamboo." He'd forgotten that she had agreed to look after his houseplants in his absence. Apparently she'd come to retrieve a key to the condo.

"I don't know about your botanicals, but you sure as shit were entertaining me." Standing just outside the sliding-glass doors, she continued, "I rang the bell—no answer. You left your front door unlocked."

Struggling to regain his composure, Moss said, "Um . . . how about a drink?"

"Vodka over ice will work." Dressed in a short black skirt and a white blouse—one version of her Midtown uniform—she plopped down in a chair and let out a long sigh. "It's cooler here. You should feel the heat downtown—brutal."

"The city is a hellhole." He went into the kitchen and brought back a tumbler filled with vodka and ice.

"I'm wondering." She took a sip and closed her eyes.

"Yes?" He pulled a chair next to hers and sat down. Claudine had never visited him at home before. Several times in the past he'd thought of asking her, but it hadn't happened. Her sudden appearance made him feel a little shy. In his mind, they were both accustomed to being separated by the literal and metaphorical presence of the Midtown's long, polished bar. Now, here she was on his terrace, eyeing him with barely suppressed amusement. It was unnerving.

"I'm wondering whether you actually live here, Moss." She

jerked a thumb toward the interior of the town house. "It's too clean in there."

"I have help. A service comes in twice a week."

"No, I mean like photo-shoot clean. There's not a single thing out of place." She frowned. "It's not normal."

Over the years, others had made similar observations about his fetish for order, but coming from Claudine it made him a little defensive. "I'm not here that much—I'm mostly at the gallery."

"Shit," she laughed. "Everybody leaves tracks of some sort, but not you. You're one weird dude."

He flushed. "I believe we established the extent of my weirdness years ago."

Claudine shifted in her seat, kicked off her sandals, and crossed her legs. Rummaging in her purse, she pulled out a tube of lotion and moisturized her hands. "Just an observation, dude. Men who live alone are the first ones to go off their rockers. In their isolation, they collect unseemly oddments from the sidewalk or become serial killers."

"That's a lot to look forward to." The faint fragrance of coconut entered his nostrils. Suddenly he became aware of his bare legs in comparison to hers. His flesh looked pale and soft—sickly—next to the sleek cinnamon skin of his companion. "What's happening in your world, Claudine?"

"I'm sad."

"How so?"

"Larissa dumped me. Can you imagine?"

He thought for a moment. No, he couldn't imagine. His memory of the redhead gave off a foul odor in his brain. Some of Claudine's girlfriends had made sense over the years, but this last one hadn't. Moss was surprised at his relief over the news. Of course, he couldn't let on. Claudine could have her pick. She was out of Larissa's league by a long way. She was out of his league as well.

"What happened?" he said, trying to keep his voice neutral until she revealed the depth of her feelings about the whole dumping thing. "Do we care? What's the upshot?"

"She developed an unhealthy interest in another woman."

"Ouch," Moss commiserated. "Someone you knew?"

"Yeah." Claudine leaned back in her chair and surveyed the foliage. "She said she needed to be involved with the *authentic me*." This last was framed with pink-nailed air quotes. "I told her I had no interest in such a person."

"How did that go over?"

"Here I am."

"How're you handling it?"

"Blue," she murmured. "Something is better than nothing—mostly." She stared off into the garden. The light had gone from gold to gray in a matter of minutes. The air tasted of metal. Another low growl of thunder came from the west—closer this time.

"I don't know about that. Nothing has worked for me for a while now."

She gave him a look that said she wasn't buying it. "Yeah? Well look at you." After a theatrical pause, she said, "You do realize that your comment can be read a couple of different ways?"

He tried to imagine the pair of women in bed. He couldn't. There wasn't a thing about Larissa that appealed to Moss. Over the years there had been a few males sprinkled into her menu of lovers, but mostly Claudine seemed to like the ladies.

"I don't know anymore. This kind of thing keeps happening. Am I the problem? Is it me or them?"

"Perhaps we should pour another drink," he said. "Are you coming or going? The Midtown that is."

"Going—I finished my shift early."

Just then the first spatters of raindrops hit the terrace. They both jumped to their feet, startled. Claudine helped Moss haul the chairs and side table under the deep, protective eaves. They sat in silence as the clouds burst open. Warm rain fell in vertical sheets, obscuring the surrounding neighborhood, bowing the bamboo plants, and erupting from overfilled gutters. Stray droplets splashed everywhere. Claudine giggled like a girl, stretching out her legs and wiggling her toes in the spray.

Moss worried about getting damp.

Lighting the last Chesterfield in his pack, he held it out for Claudine. She cupped the cigarette in her palm and took a long, thoughtful pull. "So, what's *wrong*, Moss?" She handed back the smoke. "You're not your usual irritating self."

"Out of sorts, that's all."

"Shit. I've seen out of sorts. This is something else."

"I think I may have accidently wasted my life."

"You still have your quest, don't you?" She put air quotes around the word "quest."

He sputtered, then shrugged elaborately. "Maybe I'm just tired of being a middle-aged fart selling other people's art. I dunno." The truth of it was that he was both embarrassed and flattered by her questions—embarrassed because he'd secretly hoped his current emotional state was invisible, flattered because she had bothered to inquire.

"Middle-aged?" Claudine poked him with her elbow. "You'll be fifty in a couple of years. You're a fossil."

"Ouch!" Moss stabbed at his heart. "Dare I ask what brings you here? Other than to increase my misery quotient exponentially?" Rain bounced off the flagstone walk, bent the heads of the bamboo, and formed dancing puddles at the foot of the terrace. He gave a fake grumble. The truth was, he enjoyed the camaraderie of sitting under the eaves and watching the rain.

"I was wandering the galleries in the DIA the other day before heading to the Midtown, and I stumbled onto a painting that made me think of you—the Gentileschi." She absently twirled a dreadlock around her index finger. "I liked the yellow, and I remembered you liked yellow too."

He cocked an eyebrow, waiting.

"So, I was in the gift shop, and I saw a catalog of her work. I bought it for you as a going-away present kind of thing. Something to amuse you while you're up north."

"I admire her work," he said, trying to conceal the fact that he was touched by her gesture. They'd never done presents. It wasn't like that.

"I picked up one on Guido Reni as well. He does a gorgeous yellow," she said, naming the sixteenth-century Bolognese painter whose work straddled a tenuous line between High Renaissance and Mannerism. Moss was a longtime fan of both painters.

"You shouldn't have," he said, thinking she probably didn't have a lot of money to spend on expensive art books. "I have books at the cottage."

Claudine groaned. "I left them inside, on the console next to the front door." She retrieved her sandals from under the chair. "When you look at them . . ." She paused. "Give a thought to those left behind?"

He struggled to get out of his chair. "Of course," he sputtered, following her through the house to the front hallway.

"Happy travels." She retrieved the spare set of keys from a bowl on the console and was through the front door in an instant, heedless of the downpour.

16

The next day, Moss made the drive north in a trance punctuated by the passing of familiar landmarks. It was a journey he'd known from childhood. Making the six-hundred-mile trip in Gran's turquois Studebaker Commander was a seasonal rite etched on his consciousness. His favorite memories came from a time before the interstate was completed in 1973—stopping in small towns for a hamburger, Gran allowing him to help the gas-station attendant clean the car's windows, listening to her plans for the next novel. The interior of the Studebaker smelled of dust, lavender powder, and oil residue. Each adventure played to the slow cadence of his Gran's voice. She spoke of anything and everything: the life cycle of insects, the best apples for pie, conventional plot twists, German poets. He could ask whatever questions were rattling around inside his head, knowing he would receive an answer so circuitous and filled with arcane allusion that he'd forget what he'd asked. The joys of heading north were embedded in his soul.

The litany of names escaping Gran's lips rolled through his head whenever thoughts of the cottage arose: P. D. James, Dorothy Sayers, and Ruth Rendell. Honorable protagonists, useful thematic devices, and blind-alley subplots were intoned in his ear as the Michigan landscape breezed past the Studebaker's window.

Literature wasn't the only subject they covered in the confines of the Commander. Moss couldn't predict when Gran's thoughts would suddenly swerve into new territory. The glossy green of a chard leaf might remind her of the background in a Bronzino painting. Painters were a frequent topic, beginning with American Regionalists like Tom Benton and Grant Wood then moving on to figures like Ed Hopper, John Marin, Morris Graves, and Mark Toby. Most of the time he loved listening to his grandmother's voice, barely aware that his education was in progress. It was all served cold—road-trip chat. By the time he was approaching his teens, it never crossed his mind to think like other kids.

Nowadays the twin lanes of the interstate highway snaked through birch forests, bypassing small towns and reducing the driving time by half.

He hummed to himself. The Estate Wagon ate through the miles with ease. Quiet, rural towns he remembered—Roscommon, Pere Cheney, Grayling, Otsego—were tolled off like beads on a rosary. The farther he got from the city, the more his spirits lifted. Lowering the windows of the Buick, he bathed in the rustic air.

By the time he'd closed in on the topmost tip of the mitten, the outside temperature had dropped. The constant threat of rain that plagued the south abated as he drove north. Blue sky stretched overhead, scored by streaks of thin, white cloud. Cutting through the clutter of touristy Mackinaw City without pausing, he crossed the big bridge and entered another world. Michigan's Upper Peninsula bore little relation to the lower regions of the state—it felt more like Canada, the northern provinces, a lost country.

The wind on the strait was brisk. He could feel the huge spans swaying, and a lighted traffic sign advised drivers to hug the inside lanes, just in case. From time to time he glanced down at the white-caps chasing each other across the surface of the water. The sense of precarious height reinforced his feeling of moving from one thing to another. He needed a change. Maybe the month away from the gallery would adjust his attitude. Humming the refrain from "Waltzing Matilda," he draped an arm over the seatback and experienced an unfamiliar stirring of optimism.

On the long downslope toward dry land, he ruminated on Claudine. She was the one person in his life who invariably gave him shit, who saw through his poses. She deserved some appreciation, didn't she?

Flawed as his character might be, he hoped it was still redeemable. He just needed to figure out how to get there.

• • •

In the humble village of St. Ignace he found a no-frills motel that looked out on the water. The room assigned to him, paneled in knotty pine and upholstered in red-and-black plaid, confirmed every tourist expectation. He was indeed in the UP. The spartan furnishings consisted of two narrow single beds, a Mission-style rocker, and a small writing desk. The bathroom was perfunctory—a sink, a commode, and a metal-walled shower stall. His first thought was to change into his dungarees, a green-checked flannel shirt, and his tall L.L. Bean boots. In August, high temperatures in the Keweenaw rarely rose above seventy degrees. In the evenings, a jacket or down vest was favored by even the hardiest souls.

After a prolonged struggle buttoning his jeans, he was ready to head to the Country Girl Diner for something to fill his stomach. It was only four-thirty in the afternoon, but already the restaurant's parking lot was flush with pick-up trucks and boxy Winnebago RVs.

Inside, he found an empty booth and ordered supper. A waitress brought him a bowl of homemade bean soup, thick broth flecked with bits of onion, celery, and ham. Along with the soup came a side of thick slices of brown bread accompanied by a slab of golden butter. Moss ordered a Molson's Lager in deference to his proximity to Canada.

Above the table hung a framed newspaper clipping. Dating from 1947, the article detailed the passing of the Spanish matador, Manolete. Embedded within the story was a grainy photograph of a man, dressed in a suit of lights, lying face down on the sand of a bullfight arena. Hovering above him was the hazy silhouette of a black bull.

Scanning the adjacent walls, the clipping was an outlier. Other booths were decorated with photos of iceboats in full flight, deer carcasses hung from tree limbs, and luminaries from the Detroit Redwing hockey team. The bullfighting article didn't fit in with the rest. Getting to his knees on the seat, he squinted at the irregular-shaped cutout in its cheap dime-store frame. The text was in Spanish.

When the waitress brought his bill, he asked her, "What's with the bullfight article?"

"Beats me," she shrugged, slapping his check on the table. "That thing has been here since I started working."

"Maybe the owner likes bullfights?"

"Nah. The current guy is new. I heard the previous owner liked snowmobiles—racing them." She gave Moss a frown. "That guy died one winter crossing over the ice on his way to the big island. Drowned—dead as a mackerel. Dead as that bullfight guy." She nodded toward the clipping. "Went through the ice. Never did find his body, not even after the thaw."

"That's a hard way to die."

She grunted. "You know an easy way?"

Moss had no answer, but he thought maybe a warm, cozy bed might be preferable to black water under a sheet of ice. He glanced up at the wall. "Weird," he said.

The waitress tucked a stray strand of gray behind her ear. "You say so." She let out a defeated sigh. "I can tell from the way you talk you're not from here." With that she turned on her heel and wandered back to the kitchen.

Moss sat and contemplated the bullfight article. That sort of anomaly was the kind of literary element Nell Moss would've used to signify a hidden truth—a clue to meaning in one of her mystery novels. She might have woven its arcane significance into her concluding chapters, disinterring an unexpected connection to some thematic seed planted at the beginning of the book. She had been famous for that kind of flourish.

He paid the restaurant bill and returned to his room. Uncapping a bottle from his store of Chartreuse, he began his evening ritual of drinking. With the bottle at his elbow, he pondered the recent trajectory of his life. Had he been cut adrift by the presence of the Bainbridge painting? Or had he been adrift for years and just found a beacon in the painting? He didn't know. What he did know was that he was tired of dragging his past along behind.

That night, creatures from his unconscious brushed against the fabric of his dreams. He tossed and turned on the narrow mattress until he finally fell into a deep, exhausted slumber in the early morning. A few hours later bright sunshine cut through the blinds of his motel room. He had overslept. It took a good forty minutes to force his body upright, and it was another half hour before he'd showered and dressed. There was still half a day of driving before he reached the cottage.

By the time he returned to the diner for his morning eggs, the buoyant mood from the previous day had evaporated. He worried some mishap would delay the transport truck or damage the big painting. The closer he got to his goal of securing the Bainbridge, the more he imagined unforeseen pitfalls along the way.

Inside, the same waitress from the night before led him to the same booth with the clipping of the dead matador mounted on the wall. Nothing about the newspaper article suggested it was worthy of note except for the fact that it was completely at odds with its surroundings.

The waitress appeared with his plate of scrambled eggs smothered in gravy. "I asked Roy," she said, nodding her head toward the kitchen. "He didn't know about the bullfight picture, other than he remembered it being there since he was in high school."

"It's a mystery." There was something about the antique picture that nagged at his subconscious.

"Nah," she said, shaking her head. "No mystery. Just that folks who might know are either dead or moved away. There's always some rhyme or reason to things."

"Do you think the owner would sell it?"

"Shit. He doesn't likely know it's there—rarely comes around. Roy manages the place."

"How about I buy it from you?" Moss said, surprising himself. "You could put whatever you like in its place. No one would be the wiser."

She considered his offer for a split second. "Ten bucks?"

"Done." Moss wrestled his wallet from a back pocket and forked over a ten-dollar bill.

She stared at him through narrowed eyes. "I mean ten for me, and another ten for Roy. He's the boss man."

Moss pulled out a second ten. "It's a deal?"

"Bet on it." She turned and headed back to the kitchen.

17

Departing St. Ignace, Moss took Route 2 as far as the town of Rapid River. From there he turned generally northward on Route 41, another two-lane blacktop that would take him all the way to his destination on the Keweenaw Peninsula. The first part of the drive hugged the northern shoreline of Lake Michigan. The road offered him a slow-paced, scenic ramble peppered with tourist motels, fudge shops, and knickknack emporiums. The morning had turned bright, but the wind off the lake carried the first chilly hint of impending fall.

The Manolete rode shotgun next to him—the ghost of the dead toreador sharing space in Moss's consciousness with the old painter and the canny spirit of his departed grandmother. The fact that the spectral trinity bore little connection to each other bothered him less than the realization that creatures of his unconscious ruled the day. In his current state, reason seemed to have taken a powder.

At lunch in the quaint college town of Marquette, Moss began to formulate a plan that would take him to London for the Tate Gallery opening and, with luck, a long chat with Maurice Haller. Haller might be a false trail, but his gut told him otherwise. It seemed the painter was the best link to the model. Moss would have to play detective.

Gran would be proud.

By the time he'd reached the turnoff to Five Mile Road, a provisional itinerary in the United Kingdom had coalesced in his mind. Brown's Hotel on Albemarle Street in Mayfair would suit him fine—it was his grandmother's favorite. The storied hotel appeared in several of her books, and it was close enough to the Tate Gallery for his purposes.

• • •

Nosing the Buick up the steep gravel drive that led to the cottage's garage, Moss was filled with the sweet syrup of nostalgia. He was finally *up north*. The air, redolent with the scent of pine trees and the eternal chill of the great lake, was heaven after the humidity of Detroit. Lurching to a stop, he sat and breathed in the vegetal scent of freshly mowed grass, the lake, and the pine trees. The place seemed just as he'd left it the previous year.

Low and long, the remodeled structure boasted a steeply pitched roofline of gray slate with pavilions of glass radiating at right angles from the central axis. The only hint of the building's rustic patrimony was in the fieldstone foundation visible at the westernmost corner. To the east, partially hidden behind a stand of trees, was the old shed—a humble edifice unchanged since his boyhood. Gran's ill-fortuned vegetable garden had long been replaced by a redwood deck with a metal fire pit.

Once inside, he found that Mrs. Numennin had left a round of her homemade rye bread. On the counter along with the loaf was a double-crust blueberry pie wrapped in waxed paper and a fresh packet of mild Finnish coffee. Moss paid her well to take care of him, and it was worth it. Once he'd off-loaded the case of Chartreuse from the station wagon, he would be set for the duration.

He brought the Manolete inside and left it on his desk in

the library, carefully cleaning the grimy glass with Windex and a paper towel. He propped the picture on a shelf against the spines of a couple of books. Dressed in his gaudy costume, the matador seemed forlorn and vulnerable in the shadow of the over-looming bull. The grainy image reminded Moss of a kind of ritual double suicide. Both the man and the beast seemed to have fulfilled their sacrifice—their macabre dance come to an end.

Moss knew from his boyhood reading that Manolete had been killed by bad blood—not a bull. A transfusion of a mismatched blood type after his goring had been the actual cause of the matador's death. For a second, he contemplated the historical anticlimax and its implications. Reality only served to diminish the romantic legend. Art was the same—myth was always more satisfying than the truth.

Per her habit, his loyal housekeeper had stocked the fridge with essentials. Eggs, milk, bread, and butter were neatly ranked on the shelves. There might still be a few provisions in the freezer left over from the previous year, and there was a good quantity of bottles in the wine pantry to supplement the case of Chartreuse he'd brought from home. Truth be told, the liquor cabinet was embarrassingly flush. There was little else that needed doing other than clearing a space for the Bainbridge landscape on the main wall of the living room.

Outside, a stiff, offshore wind ruffled the pines surrounding the cottage, slewing the white gulls that hung over the shoreline into precarious, sideways drift. Buffered by a windbreak, the lake itself was barely visible from the house. Only an occasional sliver of light winking through the trees gave evidence of the huge volume of water that lay less than a hundred yards from the front door.

Once the car was emptied and his supplies unpacked, he boiled a pot of water for coffee. Cutting a generous slice of pie to eat on the deck, he took a rest. The cartage boys weren't due to arrive until the next day. For the first time in a long while, he was truly on his own.

Mrs. Numennin's pie boosted his spirits in more ways than one. Packed full of sweet, juicy berries encased in a rich, buttery crust, it tasted of the wilds of upper Michigan and reminded him of life when Gran still occupied the earthly plane. He lit a Chesterfield. The old glider was built for rumination, and he settled back to consider his next moves. England was on the horizon for September, but the month of August stretched out like a calendar of blank squares.

The notion of wandering the shoreline collecting agates and sea glass paled. The beach would be chilly and windy. Hoarding found objects seemed too reminiscent of Claudine's comment about lonely bachelors and serial killers.

Half a pack of Chesterfields later, Moss unfolded from the glider and roamed down the path toward the old shed. During the remodeling of the cottage, he had ignored the structure and its contents. A residue of failures—birthed in his graduate school days—had shied him away.

As his hand searched the ledge above the door for a key, a white van edged up the driveway and ground to a halt, inches from the station wagon's rear bumper. Panicked, Moss retreated along the path. Stopping at the edge of the gravel, he waited for something to happen. After what seemed like a long time, the door opened, and Ari Numennin, his housekeeper's husband, emerged carrying a wicker basket draped in a blue-and-white tea cloth.

"You've arrived, eh, Mister Moss?" The man was dressed in brown Carhartt overalls and a gray sweatshirt. Adorning his sunburnt face was a monumental walrus moustache that dwarfed Moss's own facial adornment.

Moss gave the Finn a lordly wave. Inwardly he groaned at the prospect of dealing with the handyman. The familiarity he enjoyed with his housekeeper evaporated when it came to her husband. Ari Numennin had maintained the cottage and its surrounding land for nearly half a century. The groundskeeper had adored Nell, but his feelings about her grandson were less favorably distilled. Moss's remodeling of the original structure had caused a rift between the two men that had yet to be bridged. In truth, many of Moss's neighbors eyed the new place with suspicion. The blinding exterior walls of cedar stained to look like whitewash, the miles of Thermopane-glass panels, and the fancy slate roof with copper gutters all went cross grain to the area's rustic verities. The new cottage screamed modernity. Ari Numennin believed in the old ways.

"Leena thought you'd like some of her biscuits," the man said, holding out the basket at arm's length. "There's a jar of her thimbleberry jam as well. She knows you favor that."

Moss couldn't suppress a grin. Wild thimbleberry jam was a rarity, and it was one of his favorite memories of boyhood. The red berries grew in the shady woodlands surrounding Lake Superior. Tart and perfect for jam making, harvesting the reclusive berries required lots of luck—and hours of labor. "Tell your wife I'm grateful."

"Sure. I'll be back to cut the grass again and hog out the forest road, eh?" He gingerly handed the basket to Moss. "I've done some thinking."

"Oh? What sort of thinking?"

"Things," he said. "Regarding yourself, Mister Moss."

"And what sort of things might these be?" Moss resisted the urge to lift the tea cloth and peek at his jam. Wasps darted among the quince blossoms that lined the edge of the deck. A car passed on the road below them.

Numennin rocked back on his heels. "You've got a visitor." He lifted his chin in the direction behind Moss. "Something's there behind you."

Moss turned to look over his right shoulder. He could see nothing. He shot the older man a quizzical look.

"Just there." The old man spat. "A visitor for you."

Moss turned again. In the bushes beside the shed path a large, sleek-feathered crow picked at something shiny hidden in the underbrush. He watched the bird until it unearthed a pop-top ring tab and flew off, disappearing in a stand of dark pines. When Moss returned his attention to the Finn, Numennin was already rounding the rear of the truck. The door slammed closed, and the van rolled down the driveway's incline without so much as a toot from its horn.

18

The art movers arrived the next day. Moss guessed from their furtive glances that both young men harbored doubts as to his crating abilities. They had added numerous strategic pieces of tape to his clumsy job of wrapping.

Using the deck as a staging area, they removed the layers of protective materials and gently dusted the painting's surface with cheesecloth, careful to avoid the areas of impasto, which were still wet under a dried crust. The fabric of the canvas was discernably slack on its sturdy stretcher. The boys carefully keyed-out the wooden corner joints to tighten the surface. Wielding small, specialized hammers like orthopedic surgeons, they carefully tapped the wedges deeper into each corner until the canvas's surface was taut.

When the big painting was ready, Moss ushered them into the living room. Earlier that day he had cleared a spot for the piece on a south-facing wall directly opposite the copper-clad fireplace.

Eschewing the sixty-inch midpoint standard for residential hanging, Moss had his helpers install the Bainbridge high on the wall like a devotional altarpiece. Once the heavy-duty mounting hardware was secured, he stepped back and let out a deep breath of relief. The painting was finally home. It would take a major effort for anyone to dismount the masterpiece. Climbing high on his ten-foot stepladder, he positioned the six spotlights that would illuminate the winter scene.

The Bainbridge breathed a breath of immortality into Moss's life. Better off with him than Boo Tice and his ilk.

• • •

For three days after mounting the landscape, Moss shuffled around the house in pajamas, robe, and slippers. If he missed a shower or two, or failed to comb his hair, there was no one to care. He was incognito, and it felt good.

On the fourth day, Ari Numennin brought over a scarred brush hog. The Finn set about clearing the two-track road that snaked through Nell Moss's one hundred forty-odd acres of brambles, hardwood, and pine. In the late afternoon, when the day's work was finished, the handyman loaded the fierce-looking machine back on the trailer behind his van and took off again with nary a wave to Moss, who was lounging on the deck.

Afternoon of the fifth day, while napping on the chaise, he was visited by a montage of dreams filled with eerie locales at once familiar and utterly foreign. He wandered down streets and through labyrinthine structures searching for a thing he couldn't quite name. When he managed to drag himself up through the depths of his unconscious, the only thing he was able to recall was the image of a woman wearing horns, naked and green with rain.

Stiff-legged, he made his way inside. Moss rarely dreamed of women—unless you counted his Gran, which he didn't. He lit a Chesterfield. Cinching the robe around his girth, he plopped down at the kitchen table. The wind had picked up. There was a front coming in; he could feel it in his sinuses. Leena Numennin's blueberry pie, breakfast biscuits, and thimbleberry jam had somehow disappeared over the course of three days. There was a little of the rye loaf left, but not much. At some point he'd have to dress and drive into town for supplies.

He could always ask Mrs. Numennin to shop for him, but that would conceivably entail him having to deal with her husband—something he was eager to avoid. Sighing, he found a tablet of notepaper and a pencil in a kitchen drawer and padded into the living room to make a roster of needed provisions.

Whistling under his breath, he stood for a moment to take in the recently reconfigured room. It was good. The big painting served as the focus of the room's décor. Despite the concupiscent impasto strokes dominating the upper portion of the canvas, the painting exuded the timeless hush of an icon.

He retrieved the Manolete photo from the bookshelf and leaned it on a ledge directly under the massive painting—a votive offering of sorts. What drew him to the grainy, yellowed image was the composition of the supine matador and the shadowy form of the bull looming over the man's body. The figures in the tableaux were contained by the shallow arc of the bullring's barrier fence. That compositional curve served to delimit and isolate the action in the arena. Islero, the Miura bull, was frozen in furious motion—sword hilt protruding from the animal's shoulders. When the photograph was snapped, the bull was already dying, a dark mass above the wounded man. The contrast between man and animal imbued the simple black-and-white photo with a classic dichotomy. Culture versus nature. The scene evoked Goya—man and animal locked in a mythic struggle. Sally had asked about duende earlier. Here it was—black sounds emanating from the vicinity of the soul.

Staring hard at the two pieces, he was able to detect one major compositional difference—other than the obvious. In the photograph the gentle arc of the wooden barrier both confined and defined the space of the arena, as in Francis Bacon's cruel portraiture. In the painting, however, the concave curve of ice along the Platte River's far shore was nearly the reverse effect. The ice-rimmed river in the foreground formed a boundary, or a kind of bridge, between the observation point and the true world of the painting. The river functioned to separate two quintessentially different spaces. In the near ground was the physical plane where the viewer stood. In the middle and far ground lay the metaphysical plane beyond the river, with its impenetrable primal forest and tortured yellow sky. Was this what the old painter was trying to get at in the hours before he died? Two worlds, one physical, the other numinous?

A spasm of epiphany.

He recalled feeling something similar years before, on viewing a *Pieta* painted by Jose de Ribera in the 1630s. The large work hung in a rotunda gallery at the Museo del Prado. He'd never been a religious man, but he could see duende there—the glowing body of the perished Christ, the lamenting Magdalene, the substance and sadness of the world caught in one hushed emblematic moment. The Bainbridge had more than a bit of that feeling. Looking at it, he became conscious of his own ephemeral existence.

Yellow pencil in hand, he began parsing his grocery list.

19

The interior of Gran's old shed looked like an attic scene from an Alfred Hitchcock movie. The air was filled with motes of dust, midges darting in beams of sunlight angling in from windows. Discarded furniture, boxes, and old filing cabinets huddled in a back corner with Gran's Underwood typewriter. Moss's dusty painting tables and tabourets from graduate school were stacked one on top of another beside the skeleton of a broken captain's chair, its legs akimbo. At one end of the space, near the doorway, stood ranks of his MFA canvases covered with a stained drop cloth to protect them from the years. On the north side a bank of windows dominated one wall, while overhead rows of fluorescent lights hung empty. Moss sneezed. There was barely room to walk.

Years past, he had rescued a carton of manuscripts from this very shed. Early drafts of novels in brightly colored paper folios, all bearing editorial marks in blue pencil, shared space with a plethora of short stories—slices of novels that never saw the light of day.

Moss felt a pang of remorse that in his youth he'd paid so little attention to his Gran's career. Perhaps his reluctance was rooted in her public quip that her initials, NR, stood for "No Relation" whenever she was queried about his existence.

He'd understood it was just a joke for her fans. But still it wounded him. A reminder of his detachment from all things.

As the August sun rose, the temperature inside the shed became uncomfortably warm. Moss propped open the door using a stone from the now-defunct vegetable garden. The place smelled of disuse, the windowsills littered with the bodies of dead flies, cobwebs festooning the ceiling's rafters. He opened the lid of a large chest. Inside were sealed metal containers filled with tubes of oil paint and glass bottles holding various kinds of oils, varnishes, and solvents. Boxes holding his paintbrushes crowded one corner of the chest. Small tins containing expensive tubes of watercolors resided in another box—colors from London, Germany, Amsterdam. A heavy coffee-table book about color theory written by Johannes Itten sat gathering grime on one of the shelves.

He took out a small bottle of stand oil and tussled with the gummy cap. Wresting it open, he poured an offering onto the filthy floorboards.

The seal on the turpentine jug gave him even more problems—stuck tight. Finding a rusty pair of pliers, he managed to wrench the top free by brute force, splashing a generous libation of spirit on the pigment-caked glass palette. He breathed in the familiar fumes. The room filled with the scent of pine distillate.

He loved that smell.

It took nearly an hour to loosen the cranks on the big windows. When they finally creaked open, platoons of long-bodied mud wasps swarmed inside. The window screens had disappeared along with the decades. He'd steered clear of the shed all these years. He was embarrassed by his neglect.

Removing the drop cloth from his graduate school projects, he pulled a few of the larger canvases from the stack. He winced in shame. Fuzzy shapes in muted colors so faint as to be barely discernable, a contour fading to nothing, careless outlines that hinted at form but remained immaterial. No wonder he'd stopped painting. These were the aimless jottings of a boy. Had he really been that big a fool? The evidence was in front of him.

He had wanted it so badly in those days. First had come pride, then later came doubt. When the doubt gave way to realization, the fall had wrecked him. He'd lost all faith. The loss rocked him to his boots.

Consumed with despair at the memory, Moss flew into a fit of rage. He kicked at the canvas nearest him, and bottles crashed to the floor, his palette and Tabouret tumbling after. A bottle of stand oil was next. He hurled it against the wall with all the might of his anguish. Glass shattered with a bang. He grabbed canvases from the stack and threw them into the weeds outside. Stumbling against the edge of the deck, Moss tripped, barking his shin. Blood oozed from his leg.

Finally, hands on his knees, breath coming in ragged sobs, he wept at the unfairness of it all.

20

The next morning, Moss awoke still feeling the poisonous after effects of the previous day's temper tantrum. A residue of shame forced him from his bed. Dressed only in his pajama bottoms, he padded grumpily into the kitchen and was startled to see the hunched form of Ari Numennin sitting on the edge of the deck out back. The septuagenarian was dressed in his usual Carhartts and gray sweatshirt. This morning he'd added a denim barn coat and a navy watch cap to ward against the chill.

Flustered by this unwanted apparition, Moss retreated to his bedroom and dragged on his seersucker shorts and a cotton button-down shirt. Barefoot, he returned to the kitchen and began heating coffee. Once brewed, he poured two cups and approached his unexpected guest.

"Early," he said in as cheery a voice as he could muster. "Can I offer you a cup?"

"You can offer, Mister Moss, and I'll say thankee." The man turned his head and bestowed the slightest of smiles on Moss. "Still chilly. Come sunup, the growl in my joints eases off a bit." He glanced upward to where light was just about to break through the branches.

The deck was frosted with droplets from the night's dew. Even during the mildness of August, night's dark hours tended to be cold in the Keweenaw. Moss's bare feet were already turning pink.

He thought about fetching his slippers but was concerned that such a retreat might lose him a portion of manly ground with the old Finn. Taking a meaningful breath, he said, "I love it here. Slept like a rock."

"That a fact?" Numennin blew loudly over the surface of his steaming coffee. He glanced over at Moss's wounded shin but said nothing.

"Fresh air. Sleep of the just." Moss made sure to punctuate his comment with a chuckle, letting the dour rustic know he was being facetious.

"I'm glad you're adapting." He eyed Moss's attire. "See you been clearing out." The old man nodded toward the wreckage from the shed strewn among the weeds. Door ajar, windows cranked wide, the structure looked to have suffered an explosion.

Chagrined at the evidence of his childish fit, Moss said, "Lost my temper."

"You got as much right as any man."

"Maybe, but breaking things is not my usual habit."

"You own all this, Mister Moss," the handyman said. "I reckon you can do as you see fit."

Moss clambered down to sit near the Finn, immediately regretting the move as icy wetness saturated the backside of his shorts. Goosebumps pebbled his flesh. Rocking on his broad buttocks, trying to avoid the worst of the freezing-cold dew, Moss ransacked the file boxes of his memory, rifling through categories of *backwoods small talk* for a chummy tidbit. He came up empty.

Numennin withdrew a small metal canister from his coat pocket. Inside were small paper sachets arranged carefully in a spiral pattern. "*Snus?*" The man held the tin out to Moss.

"No. Not for me." He dug a crumpled pack of Chesterfields from his shirt. "Smoke?"

That elicited a hoarse laugh. "Best not fire up no *bacci* in there," he said, lifting his chin toward the surrounding woodland. He tucked a packet of snuff under his lower lip. "Got to watch your flames. This season trees go *poof*!"

"Oh, right." Moss lit up anyway, sucking a massive draught of smoke into his lungs and exhaling the entirety through his nostrils. What the fuck was it with these people?

Numennin spit a line of juice into the lawn. "Old trees," he said in a low voice. "You know? These old trees, they get into your thoughts." His voice sounded wistful.

Moss was growing aggravated. "Yeah?" The trees the Finn was referring to were *his* trees after all.

Silence stretched between them. Both men sipped their coffee. The sun had risen. There was movement in the treetops as a pair of crows swooped down and over the grey slate of the cottage roof. In the back of his mind, Moss considered the various dance steps that would lead him to a graceful exit. His butt was wet. He was beginning to shiver.

"You know, the Great Northern Forest stretches right across the top of the world?"

"I suppose it does," Moss said doubtfully. "Except where there's water—oceans. Then it stops."

"Right across the top." Numennin dumped the remains of his coffee over the grass, careful not to splash any on the quinces. "Had a thought."

Oh God. Moss fought down the urge to flee.

"About you."

"Oh?"

"Yup."

"Do tell." Moss bit his lower lip.

"I can feel something scratching."

Here it was. Moss girded himself for a pronouncement of wisdom from the fellow who cut his grass, who groomed his property's trails, who tended the circuit breakers in the cottage, whose wife baked pies. Was there no end? "Scratching?" he intoned meekly.

"Saw it. Like a shape in a dark room."

"A dream?"

"No—Leena calls it *sight*." He paused, rubbing the bristly skin of his jaw. "A thing scratching in your tracks, Mister Moss. A good way off, but there all the same."

Moss gave a shrug. What could one say to something like that? He feared runestones or some mystic Nordic offering might come next.

"Some weather coming." He spat again.

"What sort of weather?" Moss asked.

Instead of responding, the Finn fumbled at the bib of his Carhartts. After much effort, he pulled forth a large toggle made of whittled bone. The ivory-colored object was shaped like a canine tooth—perhaps from one of the large cats. Two inches long and clean as a whistle, there was a frayed strand of green thread caught in a hole that had been drilled into the side. Setting it on the deck between them, he said, "Found this on the two-track yesterday when I was on your acreage with the hog. Don't guess it's yours? Mayhap you've had another visitor?"

Moss stared blankly at the object, unable to frame a response. He hadn't ventured more than a few hundred yards into the woods in years. The old man cleared the trail because it was his job, not because Moss wanted to take a walk. The entire property was posted, and the circumference of the acreage was fenced with box wire. Hunters and hikers were unwelcome. Moss thought of them as a kind of pollution. Even the possibility of their presence interrupted his thoughts in unpleasant ways.

The Finn adjusted his overalls. "I'll bring the hog over again tomorrow. Get you a path cut. See what else I find in there while I'm at it."

"You'll tell me if you see anything unusual?"

"Oh, I will, Mister Moss. I will. You can count on that." The handyman limped off in the direction of his van. Over his shoulder he said, "Best get them windows closed. You'll have raccoons for boarders quick as you can say Ritz Hotel." He walked a little farther then turned. "I'm glad you left your grandmother's shed the way it was, Mister Moss. She'd have wanted that." The Finn paused, then glanced in the direction of the lake. "Be aware, Mister Moss. I feel a change in weather coming."

Moss watched as the van rolled down the driveway's incline. He heard birds in the trees and waves lapping on the rocks along Lake Superior's shoreline.

After the old man had gone, Moss returned to the kitchen and sat at the table, deep in a funk. Breaking things hadn't made him feel any better. He felt acutely the impotence of his earlier actions. He wasn't six years old, after all. He'd clean up later. Perhaps he just needed some good news. He vowed to call Kaye that very morning to check on things.

The deck had gouged a chunk of flesh from his leg. He'd managed to stop the bleeding with three bandages, but he'd taken nothing for the pain. Maybe he deserved to hurt a little after his fuss. So, what the fuck was wrong? Was he going off the rails?

Of course, he knew the answer. It was in the painting hanging on his living room wall. It was coded into the Manolete article, in his Gran's famous novels that could be found everywhere, three deep on the shelves at Books & Company. Royalty checks arrived like clockwork from publishers around the globe. He still fielded occasional fan letters from readers who'd somehow missed the news of her passing. Bainbridge. Manolete. His Gran was dead, but she wasn't. How could that be?

21

A couple of days after his visitation from Ari Numennin, Moss once again heard the staccato exhaust from the brush hog—this time from deep in the bowels of his woods. Ever the uninitiate when it came to power tools, the battered machine sounded like an industrial chainsaw hyped-up on crank. With one ear he listened to the rhythmic rise and fall of the engine as the machine ate through any weeds, brush, or saplings that had the temerity to sprout up in the two-track over the course of the summer season.

He made a happy discovery one morning when he was straightening out the mess from the shed: a patch of volunteer rhubarb sheltering at the rear of the structure. The broad leaves shone dark green and glossy with neglect, the stems a deep and promising ruby color. Cutting a dozen stalks with his paring knife, he trimmed and washed the delicacy and stored it in a plastic bag in the fridge. Perhaps Mrs. Numennin would do him the honor of making a pie. Sucking on one sour stem brought back an endless string of fond images from his youth and time with his Gran. He didn't know how much he would be willing to trade for one of her pies nowadays, but it was a lot.

It took a couple of hours to put the old shed to rights, but when he was finished some of the regret he'd felt earlier began to evaporate. Some. Not all. It was torture to look at his graduate work. Vapid, vacant, empty of, well, everything. One small solace was the condition of the canvases themselves. He had constructed them well, and they were as fit for endeavor as they had been some twenty-odd years before. Half a dozen appeared nearly pristine. Each square, fifty inches on a side, beckoned to him in ways that surprised and frightened him.

As soon as the hasp of the shed's lock clicked in his hand, he felt better. His graduate school failure had not been an accident. Unlike his Gran, unlike the cranky coot Bainbridge or, worse, that gnome Haller, Moss simply possessed no creative juice. He didn't have the goods. He might know a lot of shit about art, but when it came down to making it, he couldn't manage to get off the ground.

Moss knew stuff. Sadly, he couldn't *do* stuff.

He'd been fighting a black funk for days. If he let himself dwell on his failures, he'd return to Detroit in worse shape than he'd left. There was still the prospect of a trip to England—ferreting out Maurice Haller, searching for the trail of this Seren creature. There were things to do. He still had some vacation left. He needed to make use of his time. Perhaps an omelet would help. He recalled a cooking program he had seen once on TV. The host, whoever it was, demonstrated the making of a perfect omelet—with water added to the eggs no less. He had liked the visuals of the TV show. It looked easy.

A glass of wine would help the process. Uncorking a bottle, he poured a glass of Spanish Monastrell. One or two manly sips later, and he was ready to commence cooking.

Whipping the eggs and a bit of water in a bowl, he dumped the mixture in a saucepan with some butter. Once the eggs had set, he flipped one third of the omelet over, then he flipped the opposite side, and voilà! Against all odds, he had fashioned a meal of sorts. Too bad there was no one around to witness this triumph. He wondered what Claudine would say.

After enjoying a leisurely meal, he reached for one of his Gran's heralded mystery novels with which to season the prospect of a long and empty afternoon. Alone, again.

Galley Slaves, so named after a famous literary quote from Nabokov, detailed the case of a small-time publisher whose gruesome death may have come at the hands of one of his several overworked and underpaid female employees. Moss enjoyed the double entendre in the book's title.

Henrietta Bloodworth, the grandmotherly detective tasked with uncovering the novel's culprit, required a total of 236 pages of densely packed text to determine the identity of the murderer. Moss had tried this novel twice before, each time finding himself unable to winnow much wheat from what felt like a lot of dialogue-driven chaff. Perhaps too much of his Gran appeared underneath Henrietta's facade. Diffident, demure, yet wily, the detective was always two steps ahead of everyone else. Far too polite to let on—until the end.

That was his Gran all right.

The triumph of gray-haired ladies was altogether too familiar to elicit much enthusiasm. Nevertheless, he plodded through for much of the afternoon. Frequent helpings of Spanish Red lubricated his reading mechanisms, and the occasional short nap helped him endure the hours until dinnertime.

The fall of evening found him feeling a little wistful. His inability to access his Gran's writing felt like a betrayal of sorts. She had always claimed that her writing voice revealed her best self—her true self. If that was so, then his failure to finish her mystery novels seemed like a rejection. Trouble was, he just couldn't force himself to care who had murdered whom—or who hadn't. Most of the action in her books occurred off-stage, the plot carried more by conversation than deeds. Something about that rubbed Moss the wrong way. Coziness revealed a critical absence. He felt sure it was better to see the mortal blow struck. Wasn't it? The coup de grace? Curiously, the sound of the words made him think of Bainbridge and the mysterious model.

At the end of the day, the forest at the back of the cottage turned dark. The spaces between tree trunks became impenetrable shadows. In all his years visiting the Keweenaw, Moss had never gotten used to the shift in character night brought to his woods. Owls hooting and rustlings in the underbrush seemed to amplify once the sun disappeared. A great gray owl swooped low over the deck, its huge wings silent, like a visitor from another world.

His thoughts shuttled from one blind alley in his life to another, always circling back to that patch of dimpled paint on the yellow sky where some unknown female had pressed her breast into the thick oils. He tried to picture the occasion but was unable to do so. Everything was wrong with the image. The old man had been deep into the process of dying—must've been. The idea of a naked female inhabiting Bainbridge's studio went contrary to everything Moss knew about the reclusive painter. Yet there it was.

He went to bed determined not to dream, and for once he got his way.

PREDELLA

III

Detroit—Spring 1978

The boy stands looking out of the high windows of the WSU drawing studio. Despite the cool weather, three louvers are canted open to let the night air inside.

From across the room, she examines his smooth buttocks, lean thighs, and strong calves. His back is a wonder of young muscle—swimmer's muscle. From the slope of his shoulders, she knows he's sad. He always feels empty after she lets him have her. For him, her body is the taste of a promise never quite granted.

Stretching her arms above her head, she turns and stares up at the dusty rafters, barely visible in the gloom. At this time of night the huge old building is silent. They've blocked the doors, just in case. It's not the right time of day for the cleaning staff, but you never know. Rising on one elbow, she wants to get a better look at him. The yellow glow from streetlights outside the room casts stark shadows. Empty easels are stationed in concentric rings like the tall masts of boats or a phalanx of spears surrounding the bare pallet on which she lies—the pad on which they both lay until a few moments ago.

After a minute, the boy returns and stretches out his long frame beside her. Six hours earlier the room was filled with students, all eyes on her. Now there is only one. Her focus is on him. He's not yet ready to give her what she needs, but perhaps soon. Time will tell. The night ticks by. She allows him to handle her body again, smells the blood surging, can hear the red cells jostling each other in their haste to flow through the dark tubes of his veins—so easily aroused. She can tell from his smug expression he thinks he is choosing her—in control. That is never true with any of them. One day, she will savor his last remaining dollop of hope. Roll it on her tongue like a sugar drop— swallow his sweetness. With this young one it won't take long.

As he moves inside her she hums a tune in his ear, something she devised for him alone—hinting at all the wondrous things that will open to him. The language she knows is beyond him. Even so, he is desperate to believe in her.

When he's finished, she lets him sleep for an hour. His mouth curls into a self-reflexive smile—his long lashes, his slow breathing. Slabs of smooth muscle rise and fall as he dreams of genius to come.

Wrapping her shawl around her body, she moves languidly among the easels, letting her hand trail along the cool metal. The air smells of chalk dust, oil from pastels, and the astringency of spray fix- ative. She catches a furtive scent left by one of the female students—it curls her lip.

The outside air is ripe with a thousand odors—the dampness of spring reminds her of home.

She hears him stirring. When she turns, he is sitting up, watching her. A ripple of interest rises from the vicinity of her belly. His eyes are wide and wondering. Even in the shadows of the drawing studio she can see the aquiline nose, the long-fingered hands, the russet hair. He's a sculpture come to life.

"You are light," he says in a voice filled with wonder. "You have a halo all around you, like a Madonna."

She lets the shawl fall to the floor. Allows him to look at her. She sees what he is seeing with the eyes of the Spotted Man—a fugitive aura of gold and pink pulsing around her body. Earlier, before they made love, she brewed him tea. Now he sees with the eyesight of mira- cles. She envies him his newness. She envies his innocence, the one gift he can give her.

"Time to leave," she says, gathering her shift and her coat from where they hang on a chair. "Your girlfriend will be missing you, and I have a place to be."

He pouts a little and pulls on his jeans, facing her just so she can observe how hard and erect his young penis sprouts up below his flat belly. "We could manage one more time," he smirks.

"Not tonight." She shoulders her satchel and unblocks the doors. "I'll walk with you as far as your car. That's all."

He grumbles as they leave the building and walk into the deep, blue night. Beside him, her head barely reaches his shoulder. She must scurry to keep pace as they climb to the third story of the parking garage. When they reach his car, he tosses his portfolio and kit into the back seat and takes her in his long arms.

"Please," he croons in a child's voice, kissing the top of her head. "One more time. We can do it right here. There is no one around. No one can see."

Ignoring his pleas, she pushes him away. "Not now. Another day."

A few blocks away, Haller is at his studio, waiting, smoking, drinking whisky, getting mean. She has a fair picture of what awaits her on Cass Avenue. He will refuse to let her in unless she has a story to excite him—something that will subtly flatter him. Haller is a bottomless pit of carnal appetite. Knowing that one thing is how she survives.

"You'll miss me if I drive off." The boy spins around, his arms outstretched. "The night is unbelievable. All the lights are dancing in unison. Fucking you is magic. Another world."

"Go home." She backs away.

"Show me," he says. "Let me have one last look." He skips around the nose of the car and hops up on the concrete restraining wall. "You are so beautiful. You are perfection."

Laughing dismissively, she drops her satchel and raises the hem of her shift, feeling the cool air of early morning on her skin. "Satisfied?"

"Show me everything, and then I'll go." He glances around, down to the street far below. "Seren," he says. "Sweet Seren. I think I might be God." A look of rapture fills his face.

At the instant her shift is pulled up over her breasts, the silly boy floats backward into the empty air.

22

Moss had just lit a modest fire in the fire pit when the sound of a throaty downshift echoed from the road below his cottage. The tinny vibrato of a European four-cylinder engine linked to an Abarth exhaust lingered in his ears for a few seconds before he detected the crunch of tires on the gravel of his driveway.

He was expecting no one. It had been years since he'd enjoyed visitors at his retreat. When an orange and white Karmann Ghia coupe rolled into view, Moss experienced a moment of panic. It could only be tourists who had lost their bearings. Perhaps a mom and pop from Ohio, disoriented on a family outing. Or worse, some poor wretch trying to sell him something. The entrance to his property was intentionally uninviting, a narrow access marked by a solitary silver mailbox bearing his Gran's name—nothing more. Seen from the road, everything suggested a condition of incognito.

Pushing up from his seat on the glider like a freighter easing from its berth, he admired the diminutive car's design. Late of Studebaker, by way of the Chrysler Corporation, Virgil Exner's creative influence on the Karmann Ghia's bodywork was unmistakable. Though he had little affection for Volkswagens in general, Moss approved of the little sports car. On the other hand, he knew fitting his frame into its skimpy cockpit would necessitate more effort than he was inclined to exercise.

Whistling the refrain from "Waltzing Matilda," he stopped

midstride when he saw none other than Claudine Boatwright egress from the driver's door.

"Hey, Moss," she said, pausing to stretch.

Why hadn't he known the make of Claudine's car? He'd perched on one side of the Midtown's bar for years. She needed to drive up to Birmingham from Detroit for her job. He never bothered to ask how she accomplished her travels. Now he knew.

Before he could stifle his surprise, the passenger-side door swung open, revealing the brightly dressed personage of Marylou Bigelow, who appeared to be wedged tight within the confines of the German auto.

"For the love of God," she gasped. "Get me out of this iron maiden before I suffocate!" Her pudgy hands fought for some leverage to extricate her body from the low-slung carriage. Moss moved in to help, searching his memory for the locations of Marylou's various joint replacements. Gripping both her wrists, he gave a tug—with no result. He shot a glance in Claudine's direction, signaling that he would need assistance in extracting the matronly figure.

Claudine appeared to be busy looking around. After what he considered an unnecessarily prolonged examination of the cottage grounds, she ambled to the passenger side of the car, and together they managed to unwedge Marylou from the Ghia's interior. "Jesus-H-Fucking-Christ," Marylou bellowed once she was freed. "That car is tighter than a whore's pussy on her way to church." She completed a stately 360-degree reconnoiter. "Nice digs, honeybun. Come give momma a kiss."

She engulfed him in a pillowlike embrace. When he was finally able to wriggle free, Moss gave Claudine a long, questioning look. Their sudden appearance up north contradicted every assumption about his state of anonymity. No one ever visited anymore. Period.

And yet, somewhere in the caverns of his psyche, he felt an undeniable twinge of pleasure at seeing the pair of longtime chums. He simply couldn't guess why they had driven two days to the wilds of upper Michigan to find him.

Claudine wandered a few steps toward the deck, then she turned back to Moss. "So, this is the cottage? Really? You could open a hotel." She gave Moss the full frontal. "What the fuck?"

"I remodeled to make room for clients." The lie sat comfortably on his lips.

"Since when?" Claudine scoffed. "Since when do you have clients up here?"

The truth pricked him. "It's been a few years."

"A few?" She was dressed in a pair of faded Levi's, a black T-shirt, and dun-colored Ronnie Stewart cowboy boots. He admired the boots' pointy toes and undershot heels. Her dreadlocks were pulled up on top of her head and tied with a red bandana.

"Maybe ten. Ten years, give or take." Maybe never.

"Jesus." She sent Marylou a wide-eyed look. When she finally returned her attention to Moss, she gave him a prolonged and meaningful up-and-down. "Nice getup."

He had forgotten he was still wearing his robe, undershirt, and pajama bottoms. A pair of monogramed house slippers finished off his regalia. It was four o'clock in the afternoon.

"Somebody had better find me a drink, pronto. My new hip is killing me," Marylou said. She gave Moss the side-eye as she limped toward the turquoise glider. "I hope you have something other than that Frenchy piss you drink all the time."

Moss found a bottle of Spanish Red in the pantry. He brought the wine and glasses outside. Now that his solitude had been interrupted, he felt a little off-center. He had counted on weeks of nothingness, and now he was faced with something—two somethings in point of fact. He wasn't prepared.

Marylou settled down on the glider. She was wearing a muu-muu in a tropical print—Hibiscus flowers in white and yellow against a black background. A pair of broken-down flats graced her feet. Moss dragged over two Bertoia wire chairs, one for Claudine and one for himself.

"Well, here we are," Claudine said. She offered no explanation for their presence in the Keweenaw.

"So it appears," Moss agreed. He hadn't thought to tie the belt on his robe until a look from Claudine made him aware of his relaxed condition.

"Hotter than fuck in Detroit," Marylou said. "This weather is nice by comparison."

After a long sip of her wine, Claudine said, "We decided to come see you—a road trip. Neither of us counted on how long a drive it was. Jesus, Moss, this gives a whole new meaning to the word remote."

He remained silent for as long as he could. Both ladies knew the story of his Gran's retreat. He'd been friends with them for years. He felt embarrassed by the fact he'd never once invited either of them to visit him up north. In truth, he'd never even considered it.

Marylou poured herself another glass. "We did bring a smidge of news."

"Oh?" Moss turned to face her.

"Two smidges, to be accurate," Claudine said.

"Brice Godwin's parents are making trouble at Wayne State," Marylou said, giving Moss a knowing look. "They've got their law-yers involved. The boy's death was suspicious—so they say."

Moss pondered this bit of information. The Godwin boy had done the drawings of Seren. "So?"

"The Godwin parents happen to be big-time donors, and they are convinced their precious baby boy was doing just fine until he got involved with a model in his drawing class. Questions are being asked. An ad hoc committee has been formed to investigate whether there is any connection to the Art Department. Some of the upper-uppers at WSU are uncomfortable." Marylou gave a dramatic pause. "I thought you might be interested."

"Maybe, yes." Moss waved his hand noncommittally. It was news alright, but only a tangent. Bainbridge, and now the boy? "What else?"

"Your buddy Maurice Haller has apparently taken a powder. He's nowhere to be found. Curators at the Tate are in a tizzy."

"He won't miss the opening," Moss said. "He's a publicity whore. The thought of that smug, limey shit having a success makes me want to retch."

Marylou chuckled and clapped her beringed hands. "I do love it so when jealousy takes wing. Your vehemence is somehow reassuring. I don't know why."

"Never liked that asshole." Moss got up to replenish the wood in the fire pit.

Marylou downed the last of her wine. "Lambkins, I'm in desperate need of a long nap. I truly thought the drive from St. Ignace would be the end of me."

Inwardly, Moss grimaced. He had no idea whether Mrs. Numennin had thought to make up the beds in the guest wing. It certainly appeared that his friends were intent on staying the night. He thanked providence the quarters in the addition were spacious—and that they were far from his own suite.

He showed the two ladies to the guest wing. Claudine chose a small bedroom two doors down the hall from Marylou. She'd taken it upon herself to ferry in the two overnight cases from the

Karmann Ghia. Moss was relieved to see they had both packed light. He hoped they weren't staying long.

A half hour later, Claudine joined him out on the deck. The sun was disappearing into the grey waters of Superior. As it usually did around dusk, the wind picked up, causing the fire to flare and sputter. Moss threw on another log and replaced the metal screen cover—he remembered Ari Numennin's warning about stray sparks.

"Are you sure you don't mind putting us up?" she asked. "We could probably find a motel in Houghton."

Moss grumbled. "Not at all. It's a nice surprise. Strange, but nice."

"You should've seen the look on your face when we drove in—I thought you might hightail it into the woods." She poured the last of the bottle into her glass. "I guess we could've called you from somewhere on the road."

"I hardly ever answer my phone. Telephones rarely signal good news." He quickly rethought his answer. "It's good to see you."

She eyed him. "You look better."

"Huh?"

"Better than you did the last time I saw you." She nudged his leg with the toe of her boot. "You can dance all you want up here. No witnesses." She was wearing her belt with the cowgirl buckle and had slipped on a mustard-colored wool shirt with a violet windowpane pattern.

"I see you dressed for the part." He would never let on how much he approved of her choice of apparel.

"I aim to fit in."

"No, you don't," he replied, brushing a tangled lock of hair from his forehead. "There couldn't be two people less able to assimilate . . . three if you count Marylou. Speaking of which,

146

what's she doing?"

"Dead to the world," Claudine said, giving him a wink. "Snoring like a sailor. My guess is she's down for the count. The drive was hard on her. She pissed and moaned the whole way. At her age, she's not really built to ride in my car."

"You're right about that," Moss said. "I'm surprised she made it this far."

"She's worried about you." Claudine finished her wine and stared meaningfully into the bottom of the empty glass until Moss took the hint. "By the way, Sally says hello. I stopped in at Donald Morris before we left—thought I'd see if she knew anything about this Haller business. She seemed uncommunicative."

Moss topped off her glass with a dram from a fresh bottle. "Donald Morris Gallery makes a ton of money selling Haller's work. They're probably holding their breath about this new scandal. Biding their time until they can jack up his prices."

"She asked after you."

Moss cocked an eyebrow. "As you can plainly see, all's well here in the Keweenaw."

"Shit, Moss." She rolled her eyes heavenward. "You're still in your PJs and bathrobe. Looks to me like there's a long way to go before 'all's well in the Keweenaw.'"

Changing the subject, he said, "Fancy a bite to eat?"

She ignored his query. "Radio said there's supposed to be a blow starting tomorrow afternoon. Cold front coming in—straight down from the Arctic."

"Nonsense," Moss said. He paused a full beat to emphasize the delivery of his big news. "I found out how to make an omelet."

"Yeah?" She looked skeptical.

"Absolutely. I can show you how it's done."

She grabbed the wine bottle by its neck and followed him into the kitchen. Surveying the expanse, she whistled. "So, what's the story? You own stock in stainless steel?"

Moss smiled and reached for a sauté pan he'd never used before. "I have chutney."

Claudine laughed. "Moss, you're such a schmuck. Where did you get this butter? Not around here, I'll wager."

"Imported."

"I'll bet the fuck it's imported." She shook her head in mock dismay. "Where do you keep your eggs?"

23

The promised blow couldn't wait for the afternoon. The following day, Moss awoke to grey, turbulent skies and the sound of water crashing hard on the rocks of the shoreline. Wind twisted in the tops of the tall pines that grew around the cottage, buffeting the long glass panels that served as walls for the structure. He was glad the construction was solid and that he had thought to install an emergency generator. The power line supplying the house had never gone down, but there was a first time for everything.

Marylou, fresh from a twelve-hour siesta, had beaten him to the kitchen. Coffee was already made. She greeted him from the table dressed in a flannel nightshirt with a red Hudson Bay blanket wrapped around her shoulders.

"It felt like summer when we drove in," she said. "Now it's winter. What the fuck, Moss?"

"Welcome to the north country." He shrugged. On the counter she had set out two Fiestaware mugs—one yellow, one pink. He looked at the clock over the stove. It was nearly eight o'clock. Claudine was nowhere in sight.

"How're you doing, bubby?"

"I may have had one glass too many." He poured himself a cup and sat down across from Marylou.

"I slept like a baby," Marylou said. "Did you ever think maybe this place is altogether too spiffy for the north woods?"

He was on his second cup of coffee when the kitchen door swung open and Claudine appeared. She had donned a hooded WSU sweatshirt, tights, and fancy orange running shoes. She was breathing hard.

"Cold outside," she said once the door was shut tight against the wind. "Looks like there's some kind of atmospheric mischief about to happen—the sky is crazy looking."

Before Moss could say a word, she went to the French press and poured a cup of coffee. Turning one of the kitchen chairs around, she straddled it and smiled. "Guess you know there's an old guy with a cool-looking mustache cutting brush out in the woods?" She slurped her coffee. "He was surprised to see me, but other than that, he seemed like a friendly old coot."

"Numennin," Moss said. "He's the groundskeeper."

"Fuck me blind!" Marylou exploded in laughter. "You never once mentioned that your cottage came with servants. Who are you—Richie Rich?"

Moss was chagrinned. He didn't like to think about how his life looked from the outside. "They came with the place."

"The mustache guy said you'd better check the firewood." Pushing back the hood of her sweatshirt, she unleashed a flurry of dreadlocks. "This territory isn't much like downtown Detroit. I saw an actual deer when I was coming back to the house."

Miffed to have his handlebar moustache demoted to second rank by inference, Moss pushed away from the table and went to check the supply of firewood. He was relieved to find the lidded storage bin stacked full.

Claudine set about making pancakes. She found a bottle of maple syrup in the refrigerator and set it in a bowl of hot water to warm. The batter she mixed and ladled onto the griddle turned into perfect discs of fluffy amber pancakes. The bacon was crisp and the coffee hot. When they had eaten, even Moss had to admit the breakfast was the best he'd had since his Gran had died.

Hearing the distant clang of a metal grate, he went outside to find Ari Numennin loading the brush hog onto the small trailer he hauled behind his van. The sky had taken on an ominous cast, with clouds roiling violently. The smell of ice rode on a wind holding steady out of the north. When the caretaker saw him, he lifted a hand in greeting.

"Going to blow soon, Mister Moss," the old Finn said. "My joints tell me we'll remember this one for some many years."

"We're okay for firewood—I checked."

Numennin glanced at the cottage's chimney with its wire raccoon cage on top. "Good thing. Weatherman says it's likely to huff and puff for two or three days. Maybe more."

Moss nodded, buttoning up his wool shirt. Nothing had prepared him for a change in the weather. His summer vacation was veering into uncharted territory.

"Your houseguest," the caretaker said, lifting his chin toward the cottage. "The one I saw out on the two-track?"

"Mmmm," Moss said, suddenly wary. Claudine didn't fit the local mold.

"She seems a friendly lass." The old Finn paused a beat. "A beauty—no doubt about that."

24

As the day wore on, the weather remained as threatening as it had been at daybreak—clouds and wind, with an occasional fleeting glimpse of blue sky. After they finished breakfast and stacked the dishes in the dishwasher, Marylou poked around in the pantry until she stumbled onto a cache of alcoholic beverages. Selecting an interesting bottle, she disappeared to her bedroom.

Claudine was standing in front of the Bainbridge painting. "Is this what I think it is?" she said.

"That's it." Moss swiveled in his chair to face both Claudine and the landscape.

"I've never seen it before now, you know—only heard you talk about it." Folding her arms, she took a step back. She remained silent for a long time. Finally, she said over her shoulder, "This is some shit, Moss. Now I see what all the fuss is about. If I had a dick, it would be hard right now. This painting makes me want to join a monastery or something."

"Nunnery." Moss smiled absently. "I doubt a passel of monks would fit your particular bill."

"I might surprise you."

"Please don't surprise me," he said, wrestling down the images that erupted in the back of his brain.

He'd known for years that Claudine was smart, but he felt somehow validated that she also possessed a good eye. Lots of people he knew had a brain, but not many could detect the real goods in a painting without having to think it through. At bottom, he was glad she liked the Bainbridge. "Yes," he said, "maybe so. It's got a touch of that Van Der Weyden feel," he added, referencing the famous *Escorial Deposition*.

"I guess," she said. "In spite of all the fancy brushwork, it feels a lot like old-time religion to me."

25

The two visitors settled in at the cottage as if they'd accomplished the long pilgrimage north many times. Moss was unsure whether to take their evident ease in his hereditary digs as a compliment or an imposition. He didn't quite know how to navigate the terrain.

Claudine browsed the tall bookcases that flanked the copper-clad fireplace until she found a title on Holbein that interested her. Flipping through a few pages, she paused to examine one of the plates then returned it to its slot. Restless, she pulled another book before quickly rejecting it. She was mimicking the same dance of indecision he'd done two nights before. The bookshelves were packed. The range of subjects was wide. She would find something she liked eventually. The shelves devoted to his Gran's works were ignored. He'd never pictured Claudine as a mystery buff.

He observed the ever-adventurous Marylou ferry two wool blankets and a bottle of wine out to the deck. There, she cocooned herself on the glider, glass in hand, and watched the weather blow in. The creaking sound coming from the swing made Moss nostalgic for other times.

With the ladies otherwise occupied, he paced and fidgeted. He moved an ashtray from one side of the coffee table to the other. There wasn't a speck of dust to be found on any surface—Mrs. Numennin had seen to that. There was nothing constructive left to do.

Hanging on the wall near the left-hand bookcase was the recent addition of Brice Godwin's sketch. Moss had had his Detroit framer slip it into an old frame that had been lying around the gallery. Every now and then, Claudine glanced briefly at the smudged drawing out of the corner of her eye. Once, she bestowed a cautious look on Moss. He thought she might offer a comment. Over recent days, he'd examined the drawing more often than he cared to admit. But Claudine kept her thoughts to herself. The charcoal portrait clearly looked to be the work of an amateur, or in this case, a student. The subject was another matter. The face depicted was plain enough but arresting: sharp, slightly vulpine, with features that didn't quite fit with each other, as if the components were pieced together from separate sources by a clumsy taxidermist.

He went to the window, considering his two visitors. At first he'd anticipated wanting them gone as soon as the Ghia rolled to a stop, but in truth their company was a welcome distraction. Maybe he wasn't the hermit he'd always thought he was.

He meandered into the kitchen and stationed himself at the table where he could keep an eye on things. Every ten minutes or so, he poked his head outside to check on the approaching storm. After three-quarters of an hour of his intrusions, Marylou threatened to brain him with her wine bottle if he ventured out onto the deck one more time. Reluctantly, he returned to the kitchen, where he drank, fidgeted, and smoked away a good bit of the afternoon.

At some point Marylou beat a retreat from her chilly outpost and joined Claudine in the living room. Soon both were curled on the couches, fast asleep. Moss completed a desultory tour of the cottage, did a quick check on the grounds, and was satisfied to find all to be shipshape. In the many years he'd been visiting the cottage, not once had he experienced one of Superior's rare summertime storms. A cap of cold air created by the frigid waters of the lake warded off the barometric conditions that led to the advent of such storms farther inland.

True, he'd heard tales from the locals, the old-timers—recollections of huge cold cells descending from the Canadian tundra and erupting over the big lake. But until now his summer vacations had proven uneventful in the meteorological sense. In fact, both he and Gran had enjoyed the few rare thunderstorms—watching the line of clouds scudding landward, lightning crackling between the dark, roiling masses.

The original cottage had been weathertight and time-tested. In bouts of bad weather, his Gran would boil a pot of tea and unearth her stash of shortbread cookies. Without need of words, they'd sit happily and listen to nature—safe in their cozy self-sufficiency.

• • •

At the hour just before dusk, the forest surrounding the cottage was lit with an eerie half-light. The shapes of the black pines shifted with crosscurrents of wind that came and went sporadically from all directions. At one point, noting the sound of the elements had been reduced to a whisper, Moss cast a wary eye toward the kitchen window. There was something about the enveloping stillness that made him uneasy. The plummeting barometric pressure, the refracted light of a sun hidden by storm clouds, the sudden drop in temperature—none of it felt usual for late summer.

He stood at the sink, staring out the window, smoking and flicking ashes into the drain. An old memory rose from his gut, reminding him of the embarrassing panic he'd felt long ago when he'd visited Gran's patch of timberland in Ontario. Misguided by curiosity, he'd ventured beyond his comfort zone and into a world beyond his control. That was the way he felt now, with the unexpected weather. He knew there was little need to worry, but worry he did. Still, there was solace in the presence of Claudine and Marylou. Even if they were both snoozing in the living room, at least now he didn't feel quite so alone as he had back then among the numberless trees.

Wandering into the pantry, he was reassured by the quantities of food Mrs. Numennin had the foresight to lay in the previous year—boxes and canned goods were stacked high on the shelves. No matter the size of the approaching storm, they wouldn't starve, and thanks to his fondness for booze, they wouldn't have to remain sober—not for one second. This last came as a relief.

When he found his way back into the kitchen, Marylou was seated at the table swaddled in her red-and-black Hudson's Bay blanket. She glanced up when he entered the room and gave him a crinkly smile, her weary old eyes puffy from sleep.

"Hello there, bubby." She cradled her chin in one hand. "If I didn't say so before, this is some swell place you've got here. Grim weather or no."

Secretly pleased by her acknowledgement, Moss gave a humble shrug. "Good architects," he mumbled. He took a chair opposite. "Claudine still napping?"

"No, she wanted to see if there was any news about the weather conditions. She had to go out to the Ghia to find a radio. You do realize there isn't a radio or TV on the premises? It's a good thing you at least installed a telephone."

"The cottage is a rustic getaway. I never thought of a TV. At least there's a record player."

Marylou raised her eyebrows, creating a dozen creases on her forehead. "I'll say this, it may be isolated up here, but it's anything but rustic. Those purple couches in the other room are to die for. You're probably unaware, but I knew Florence Knoll when we were both still students at Cranbrook before the war. Sweet kid.

She knew what she wanted, and she got it, one way or another. You know what clever girls are like."

He didn't. Nevertheless, Moss beamed inwardly. Remodeling the cottage had taken him lots of time and boatloads of money. Once the structure was complete, he'd been secretly wounded when the neighbors evidenced their disapproval. Like Moss himself, the fancy house just didn't fit in. He was an outsider. He would always be.

Claudine's return from the outside interrupted Moss's reverie.

"We're fucked," she exclaimed happily as soon as the door slammed shut. "What little radio reception I could get said there's a major storm headed this way. They say it's a big one. The entire Upper Peninsula will get blasted."

Marylou laughed and threw up her hands. "It's this poor lad's worst nightmare, trapped in a house with two women. He may never recover."

Claudine frowned. "I believe you're correct." She stole a cigarette from Moss's pack on the table. "It's likely none of us will escape this storm with our psyches intact. Cooped up with a couple of raving loonies and whatnot."

Moss winced. "A lobotomy might be a blessing right about now."

"Time to open a bottle, buster," Marylou said. "If we're going to be marooned, we might as well avail ourselves of some social lubricant."

"Amen," Moss said. He went to the wine closet and reached for the highest, least-accessible shelf. Tucked away behind more popular varietals were two bottles left from a case Boo Tice had given him long ago. The wines, from vineyards in the Canary Islands, were dark and savage reds fashioned from the Baboso Negro grape on the tiny island of El Hierro. The vintage tasted of fruit and spices but finished with a strong note of turned earth that lingered. The wine's finish reminded Moss of a kind of *memento mori*—a reminder of life's inevitable end. He decided this would be suitable accompaniment to the oncoming weather.

Outside, the light was beginning to fade, giving the kitchen an insulated feel. He placed both bottles on the table where Claudine and Marylou were sitting, sharing a cigarette, and chatting. Finding two balloon goblets for his guests and a Duralex juice glass for himself, Moss cut through the wax collar and uncorked one of the bottles. At first he thought it prudent to let the wine breathe for a few minutes, but he quickly decided he couldn't wait and poured healthy portions into the glasses.

Raising his glass, he said, "Here's to departed comrades." For luck, he poured a tiny splash on the polished stone floor. The toast was an old favorite of his Gran's. When he offered it, he was thinking of no one in particular—certainly not Bainbridge.

"Karl Wallenda," Claudine smirked. The famous aerialist had met his doom a few months earlier. "A man who knew up from down."

Marylou glanced from one to the other as they waited for her to join in. "Oh, fuck it . . ." She let her voice trail off.

Claudine covered her mouth with a hand. "Glad you saved the best for last—could anything be less apropos of the moment?" She shook her head.

Smoothing the curve of his mustache, Moss remained silent. He recalled the solitary crow digging around in the brush by the shed the other day. The bird Ari Numennin had pointed out. *Something's scratching in your tracks, Mr. Moss.* The comment rang in his head. The old bugger had a way with words.

Marylou smacked her lips. "Is it me, or does this wine taste a little like dirt?"

"Mmmm," Claudine said. "Yup. Dirt. Still not too bad, all things considered. Let's go into the other room. I want to look at the Bainbridge again."

26

Taking her wine into the great room, Claudine approached the painting and began scrutinizing the giant canvas. Marylou and Moss followed from the kitchen—Moss with the foresight to bring both bottles.

"Remind me, what about this sent you into a tizzy?" Claudine raised her eyebrows. Wind buffeted the house, whipping a few water droplets against the glass walls. The quince bushes blew one way then the other with the gusts.

Moss pointed out the declivity in the thick impasto. "What does that look like to you?"

She squinted at the faint depression. "Could be a nipple." She shrugged, twisting her lips. "Could be a fingertip. Could be a pencil eraser. Could be the end of a paintbrush."

"Nipple," Moss said with an air of finality. "I'm pretty sure I'd know a nipple if I saw one."

"The jury's out on that one, lambkins," Marylou chuckled.

Claudine said to Moss, "I do recall you liked my green dress well enough. The night of Marylou's party—the eyes don't lie."

"Mmmm." He tried to quell a faint flush of embarrassment. There was quite a lot about that night Moss would prefer to ignore, Claudine's silk shift not the least of it. Nothing about his quest rested easy in his thoughts. Some days the origins of those anomalous markings in the paint consumed him. Other days he felt like an idiot for obsessing about it. Then, there was the dead student. What to make of that?

"My hip tells me there's a shit ton of weather headed our way." Marylou eased herself down on one of the couches. "Are we still talking about the nipple quest?"

"We are," Moss said, slightly irritated at having his foibles be the focus of conversation. "Shall I enumerate all the vexing inconsistencies present in this particular specimen?"

"No!" the women spoke in unison, then they burst out laughing at their evident and unified lack of enthusiasm.

Moss harrumphed and sat down next to Marylou. "Suit yourselves, but there's something going on. I'm sure of it. I just need to track down that asshole, Haller. He knows who owns that nipple. I'd bet the farm on it."

Marylou poured another glass for herself. "I hate to break it to you, bubby, but those nipple things you're so upset about are common commodities. They're all very much similar." She patted his knee. "It's a broad category—pun intended. No need to get so worked up."

Claudine stooped to retrieve the Manolete clipping. She held it up to her face, then out at arm's length. "This is weird," she said. "Where did you find this little treasure?"

"St. Ignace," Moss replied, feeling grumpier by the minute about their making fun of the whole quest thing.

"This photo reminds me of something. I can't quite pin it down." She walked over to Marylou and handed her the framed clipping. "What do you see? You're the history expert."

Marylou gave the quickest of glances. "Manet," she said without missing a beat. Just then a deafening peal of thunder overhead shook the house.

"Yikes!" Claudine exclaimed, startled. "That was close. Not

good." She looked from Moss to Marylou. "Thunder spooks me, always has."

Moss went to the window. After a moment, Claudine joined him, peering fearfully into the descending gloom. As if on cue, the musty tasting wine, with its set of oblique contradictions, seemed comforting. In unison, they emptied their glasses.

The question of Manet and the bullfighter was forgotten with the ping of hail hitting the glider and the metal fire pit. In less than ten seconds, the sporadic clink of mothball-sized pellets turned into a roaring torrent. Suddenly the deck and the vegetation surrounding it went white. Moss stared at the onslaught, his mind a blank.

Almost as quickly as it had arrived, the hail gave way to sleet, then a short time later to a grainy snow that coated the pines with rime-like crystals. Visibility shrank to nearly zero as the fine particles fell in successive, horizontal sheets. A filigree of frost formed on the tall sheets of glass in the sliding doors.

Marylou twisted in her seat, a look of mild concern on her face as August turned itself into January. "What in fuck's name is going on out there, Moss?"

"Snow" was all he could manage to say before a deafening clap of thunder made them all cringe. Claudine grabbed his arm with both hands. Marylou steadied the wine bottles that quivered on the table.

When the thunder subsided, Claudine relaxed her grip on Moss's arm. "Well, this is some strange shit. Does this happen often?"

"I've never seen anything like it," Moss answered. "It's mid-August for Christ's sake."

The snow fell like a monsoon. It soon blurred the outlines of the deck furniture and coated the branches of the pines. Claudine poured another glass of wine while Moss remained transfixed as white obscured his familiar summer world. The roof of the shed and the brush surrounding the old building soon disappeared.

Suddenly Moss bolted for the kitchen. "My rhubarb!" he croaked. Snatching a kitchen knife from a drawer and a colander from the pots-and-pans rack, he scurried out the door and directly into the teeth of the blizzard. Forgetting he was wearing his flat-soled house slippers, he came to a skidding halt at the terminus of the deck, nearly toppling into the quince bushes now turned to puffy white mounds. Easing over the edge, he forged a path toward the far end of the shed. There he found the rhubarb clusters flattened under a drift.

Shaking loose the wet snow, he methodically sliced through each of the plant's red stalks at their base. Moss gathered them into the colander, brushing the deep-green leaves clean. He had no plan, but somehow it seemed important to save what he could from destruction. The air tasted of the Arctic. By the time he'd made it back to the deck, he was soaked—a cold, sodden mess. His long hair hung dripping on his shoulders, moisture clung to his drooping handlebar moustache, and he was beginning to shiver.

Claudine and Marylou were waiting for him in the kitchen, holding bath towels. He made a show of laboriously drying off in hopes of accentuating his heroic rescue of the rhubarb. Claudine ignored him and took the vegetables into the kitchen, where she trimmed off the big leaves and washed the handful of thick, red stalks. When he had finished with the towels, she said, "You'd better change into something suitable, Moss. You're going to need some better footwear."

Moss tromped off toward his quarters, secretly hoping one of his guests would come up with a sweet and delicious solution to the rhubarb problem. A pie might be too much to ask. Certainly a crumble of sorts would be within their collective capacity.

Once changed into garb suited to the Klondike, he returned to find both Claudine and Marylou poking around in the pantry, looking for something to fix for dinner. Aside from a few massive venison roasts and other unidentifiable frozen-meat boulders from years past, the chest freezer turned up a few slices of leftover ham donated by Leena Numennin.

"Hard to stretch this for the three of us," Marylou said, cocking one heavily penciled eyebrow and handing the paper-wrapped packet to Claudine.

Moss was silent, but to him the amount of ham looked barely big enough for a snack, much less a meal for three.

"Soup." Claudine tossed the frozen chunk into the air with one hand like a baseball pitcher contemplating his next strike. "Pea soup. We have enough of the ingredients."

Moss groaned aloud. He couldn't help himself. Pea soup?

Claudine cast a squint-eye in his general direction. "Whatever you're thinking, keep it to yourself, Moss. You've never tasted my pea soup." She located two bags of dried peas on a shelf nearby. "I saw a pressure cooker in a cabinet next to the stove. That ought to do the trick."

Marylou clapped her hands in approval. "You are a clever child, Claudine. Who knew?"

Claudine executed an ironic curtsy. "My daddy likes pea soup."

Before he could stop himself, Moss blurted out, "Daddy?" Until this summer, it had never once crossed his mind that his Claudine, Claudine of the Midtown Café, Claudine the model, dispenser of Chartreuse—had a father. The fact had not come up in conversation, not once. Not ever. Somehow, this revelation cast his old pal in a new light. Exactly what sort of light, he wasn't sure.

"You mean Big Claude?" Marylou gave Claudine a broad,

theatrical wink.

"Big Claude? Your Father?" Moss said, missing the wink entirely.

"One and the same," Claudine said, shooting Moss a serious look. "When Daddy's not sporting with the horses or gaming dice, he likes his pea soup. Why, he'd sooner cut a man gullet to groin than miss out on my pea soup."

Marylou turned to Moss. "Big Claude Boatwright is a man of renown on the west side. Handsome. All the ladies say he's plagued with an unpredictable temper." She fixed Moss with a long, ominous look. "Best behave, bubby."

"Really?" was all Moss could muster.

Claudine and Marylou both burst out laughing.

"No, you idiot, not really." Claudine wiped away tears of laughter. "My father's an orthodontist in Harper Woods! You should've seen your face, Moss."

It took Moss some time to recover. "How was I to know?" he said, feeling vexed. He'd never been comfortable as the butt of a joke. "Big Claude?"

"You could've asked," Claudine said. "You're quite the piece of work, you know." Her eyes told him she wasn't mad. "In point of fact, Daddy's name is Winthrop, but don't let reality intrude on your ghetto fantasies."

"On a more serious note," Marylou said, "I doubt those split peas are going to soften in time for dinner. Even in a pressure cooker." She tapped the face of a demure Bulova wristwatch hidden in the folds of flesh on her wrist. "We may need to improvise."

Sensing his moment of opportunity, Moss offered, "We probably have enough rhubarb for a crisp of some sort. It shouldn't take too long. Plus, there's a gallon of vanilla ice cream in the freezer. We could have a party."

Claudine looked dubious. "I'm from Detroit. Not a crisp-making kind of girl."

"Step aside, my children," Marylou said. "Crisps, crumbles, cobblers, and buckles of all sorts are my middle name. You may recall I have sixteen grandchildren. My kids all turned out to be ferocious breeders." She scanned the shelves, seeking out ingredients. Glancing at Claudine, she said, "Start those peas, honey. Soup will be welcome tomorrow. Weather's coming."

"Bingo!" Moss interjected brightly. "We have a plan. Now that I know where we keep the apron, I can supervise this whole process."

The women looked at him and shook their heads.

27

Moss tried to help in the kitchen where he could, but Marylou and Claudine soon wearied of his constant commentary and shooed him into the living room. With little else to distract him, he turned to the darkened hearth. It was time to build a fire. The long, sloping copper fireplace hood came with a sliding chainmail screen at its bottom edge. He liked the twelfth-century appearance of the thing—it looked like a Viking helmet. He amused himself by opening and closing it a few times before setting to work. There was plenty of dry wood and kindling stored in a large basket on the flagstone hearth. Soon he had a tidy but eager blaze going.

Stepping back, he surveyed the room, pleased with the look of the big space, with the fireplace anchoring one end and the Bainbridge landscape the other. The rugged surface of the painting glowed, reflecting the warm light from the fire opposite. Returning the Manolete to its original location on a shelf above the desk, he shook his head at his own foolishness. The clipping was a minor oddity—a momentary distraction. Sometimes his romantic impulses were out of step with reality.

The record collection Moss kept at the cottage was a smaller version of what was stored at the condo in Birmingham. Flipping through the albums, he found a Patsy Cline record his Gran had favored when she was writing a novel set in the south. He remembered her playing the album over and over as she tried to get in the mood to create certain scenes. The songs would filter through the open window in the shed, barely noticed on a conscious level, and embed themselves into his subconscious until he could recite the lyrics by heart.

Placing the record on the turntable, he gently set the needle in the groove. Soon, the song "Crazy" filled the room. Moss hummed along, gazing at his painting, swaying a little. Just as he was about to sing along, the music was drowned out by a crack of lightning followed by a loud rumble. The house lights flickered—dimming, returning to their usual brightness, then dimming again. Glancing over his shoulder, Moss saw only cascading snow through the windows. There was another crash, and then the lights of the cottage went out. The room was lit only by the glow from the fireplace. Patsy Cline's voice wound down and was stilled. Claudine poked her head around the corner. "Is this normal?"

"No, not remotely," he grumbled. It felt odd having people around, asking questions. "There's a generator in the basement if the lights don't come back on."

"The stove is gas, so we're okay in that department. Still, it would help if we could see what we're doing." She disappeared into the darkened kitchen.

Moss waited. He fed a few more logs into the fire. The tumult of atmospheric upheaval died out for a while, replaced by silence. He heard Claudine and Marylou whispering in the kitchen. Lighting a cigarette, he paced to the windows and back. Still no lights. He flipped a switch, then another. Nothing. A tree branch must have downed a wire, knocked out a transformer. Were there any candles? He couldn't think where they might be hidden. Mrs. Numennin would know.

Finishing one cigarette, he lit another. Thank God the furnace ran on gas. There was a small fireplace in his bedroom that could be used for heat, but the ladies had nothing. If worse came to worst they could snooze by the large fireplace in the living room. No worries—at least not yet.

With electric service restored, walking into the twilight of the kitchen, he found Claudine and Marylou, heads together at the table, a fresh bottle at hand. "I'm going to check the generator," he said, sounding more workmanlike than he felt. Neither woman acknowledged his comment. In a cupboard, he found a tiny tin flashlight. Opening a door next to the pantry, he stared into a black abyss. The basement steps, a remnant from the original cottage, were treacherous at the best of times. Moss regretted discarding the wobbly handrail during the remodel. Now there was only a support beam halfway down to hold onto. He tried to think of another solution but drew a blank.

In the gloom, he could just make out the humped shape of the generator covered by a blue tarp. He'd never had occasion to use the machine before. Ari Numennin had installed it during the rebuilding process. The hulk sat ignored for years and years. Now he needed it to work.

Step by cautious step, Moss made his way down, somehow reassured by the creaking sound each board made under his weight. At the bottom he paused. "Fuck," he said to no one.

After the remodeling project, the basement had become a temporary repository for castoffs from the original cottage. Somewhere along the line, temporary had metamorphosed into permanent, and he'd failed to notice the change. In every available corner were stored items of no use, but too good to throw away. Interior and exterior doors, solid wood and built to last, a few window frames, some century-old floorboards of first-cut pine. A box of shoes. Stuff he couldn't bear to trash—not with Gran's voice whispering in his ear. Hoarding junk went deeply against his grain.

He'd kept the condo neat and ordered, devoid of relics. The cottage was a different story. Even with the rebuild, it was still Gran's.

Removing the tarp, he examined the generator, casting his beam up and down, side-to- side, trying to remember how the thing worked. A clever-looking system of silver ductwork vented the engine's exhaust to the outside via a narrow window located at head height. Without this, they'd all be dead from carbon monoxide. Yooper ingenuity. Recollection said you had to fiddle with some switches before you pulled the starter cord. Try as he might, Moss couldn't remember which switch required fiddling. Dubiously, he scanned the arcane arrangement of tubes, levers, wires, and caps. Surely the operation of such an ordinary object must yield to common sense? In the past he'd left this kind of task to men like Ari Numennin. Those who possessed an innate understanding of mechanical devices. He suspected that kind of knowledge formed a part of their genetic code.

Finally Moss discovered a small silver lever with a painted arrow pointing to the right. With a sigh of relief, he moved the lever rightward then gave the starter cord a manly tug. Nothing. The only response was a sound like a dry cough. "Drat," he sputtered, a word favored by his Gran.

Moving to the other side of the hulking mass, he searched for anything that might bring the contraption to life. Under the bright-red gas tank was a black rubber dome and some clear plastic tubing. Of course! He needed to prime the doohickey. How could he not have remembered? After all, Athena had an engine, and he was able work her. Depressing the rubber dome a couple of times in rapid succession, he heard a squishing sound of liquid moving in the bowels of the machine. He pulled the cord again, and this time he was greeted with a promising sputter. Another mighty pull and the engine caught. After a few breathless moments, the basement was illuminated with a dim light that slowly grew brighter as the engine chugged away. Success. He dusted his hands. Mission accomplished. The silhouette of Marylou darkened the doorway at the top of the stairs. "You can come up now. The lights are back on," she said.

Moss trudged back up the stairs, his being flooded with gaudy delusions of adequacy. The sweet smell of pastry filled the kitchen, and he was much in a mood to reward himself for bestowing the gift of light upon his guests. Just as he was about to proclaim this Promethean feat, the lights flickered and died before a single self-congratulatory syllable could issue forth. "Uh-oh" was all he could muster in the darkness.

"Fucked again," Marylou said, removing her fragrant creation with potholder mittens and placing it on the stovetop. "What happened, bubby?"

Moss flicked on his flashlight and shown it around the kitchen forlornly. "Don't know."

"Gas?" Claudine said, shielding her eyes from Moss's beam. Another round of thunder provided emphasis to her question.

"Gas?"

Claudine shrugged. She was holding a long-handled spoon. "There's probably a gas can in the basement. The peas are getting soft. We'll have soup tomorrow."

"If you don't get the motor started, we'll have to eat all the ice cream before it melts," Marylou said. She dipped a fork into the crisp.

• • •

The gas can was hidden under the old workbench that had served, since he was a boy, as a haphazard repository for miscellaneous hand tools, nails, woodscrews, gardening implements, and stray lengths of wire. He sloshed the contents around, happy to hear liquid in motion. A funnel was attached to the can's handle by a section of greasy twine, almost as if some clever being had anticipated a need such as his. Filling the generator's tank emptied the remains of the can but would provide enough fuel to see Moss and the ladies through the night—at least that's what he hoped. He climbed the lighted staircase to the purring sound of a well-fed internal-combustion motor. He made a mental note to have Numennin procure several extra petrol cans—just in case.

"We're saved," Moss announced as soon as he'd cleared the last stair tread. "You're welcome, ladies."

28

That night, Moss tossed and turned under the covers, dozing fitfully as he listened to the spiteful wind buffeting against the walls of the cottage. He glanced periodically at the clock as the minutes tolled by. He'd eaten two helpings of Marylou's crisp, heaped with melting gobbets of ice cream. They'd washed dessert down with a bottle or two from his stash of white. He was pretty sure Sancerre was an appropriate pairing for rhubarb. True to form, Marylou had insisted on a dusty Merlot for herself.

In the living room, with Patsy Cline once again on the stereo, Marylou produced one of her Laotian cigarettes for the three to share. The jocular mood turned contemplative, then pensive. Moss retrieved the Manolete article from its shelf and stared at it for a while. Claudine closed her eyes and rested her head on the back of the couch.

The evening wore on. Moss returned the photographic relic to its shelf, bade the ladies good night, and trundled off to his own wing of the cottage. The flashing lights of an occasional snowplow reflected on the walls of his bedroom. Drawing the curtains closed, he settled in. Contradictory eddies appeared to be swirling around him lately. He didn't really want things to return to normal.

He wondered how the shed holding his paintings was faring under all the snow.

At last he fell into a shallow sleep. Dream images from the

Country Girl Diner in St. Ignace collided with a nonsensical scene set in what appeared to be a nineteenth-century ballet school. Wearing a suit of lights, he twirled, on point. Somewhere in the distance a bull snorted and pawed at the ground.

A noise brought him back to consciousness.

Before he could open his eyes, he heard music coming through the walls. Competing with the blustering sound of the storm were the low strains of a song coming from beyond his bedroom door.

Tugging on his robe, he padded barefoot into the hallway. The tune had a Jamaican cadence. As quietly as he could, he made his way down the hall, skirting the potted Ficus tree, to the door that led to the living room. It was his long habit to leave that door ajar so that his sleeping quarters wouldn't feel quite so cut off from the rest of the house. Taking in a deep breath, he stealthily pressed his eye to the crack. The overhead lights in the big room were dark; only a single table lamp illuminated the scene.

On the Turkish rug in front of the Bainbridge painting was Claudine. Dressed in socks and an oversized T-shirt, a goblet of wine in hand, she swayed gracefully to the strains of Bob Marley.

Moss knew he shouldn't be spying on her, but he hesitated—reluctant to retreat, afraid to remain. He opened his mouth to say something, but nothing came out. Minutes passed. The song ended. Claudine went to the stereo and queued it again. When she turned in his direction, he stepped back into the deepest shadows. He felt a twinge of guilt at hiding behind the doorjamb but couldn't force himself to break the spell.

He watched for as long as good sense would allow, then he fled back to his bedroom before the second iteration of the song ended. Filled with a mix of conflicting emotions, most of which he didn't care to examine, Moss silently shut his bedroom door and went back to bed, without hope of returning to sleep.

Why hadn't he simply stepped through the doorway, rubbing grit from his eyes? He could've remarked on the music or offered to share a late-night glass of wine. A short, friendly chat, and then both could've gone back to their respective quarters to sleep. He might have teased her about her socks. That would've been okay. The storm was still raging outside. He could have flicked on the exterior lights, examined the buildup of precipitation on the deck, the outdoor furniture. All of that would have been . . . normal.

Instead, he'd peeped on her.

The more he thought about it, the more mortified he became. Thank God she hadn't found him out. What could he have said? "Oh, hi there, don't mind me, I'm just creeping around in the dark, spying on you."

Oh fuck.

He flung himself diagonally across the king-sized bed. Pulling a corner of the cover over his head, he groaned aloud at his imbecility. Thank God he'd escaped unnoticed. He was a grown man, for god's sake. A pudgy, middle-aged man.

He did not hear the door to his bedroom click open, but he was dragged partway toward waking when he felt the mattress shift under the weight of another body. The faint scent of verbena reached his nostrils, the fragrance of Claudine's hand lotion. Cracking one eye, he could just make out the shadow of a figure sitting on the edge of the bed.

"Sorry, Moss," she whispered. "I couldn't sleep. I guess this storm has me a little anxious."

"Okay," he croaked. "Did you want to talk?"

"No. No talk." Silence for what felt like minutes. "Maybe we could cuddle?"

He gave a noncommittal murmur and scooted over to make room, drawing the covers back. She fit herself into the curve of his body, leaving a gap so there wasn't much touching happening. His arm fitted around her, in the deep concavity of her waist. She pulled the duvet up until it warmed them both.

He squirmed, trying to get comfortable, and she stiffened immediately. "Just a cuddle, Moss," she said. "Nothing more." A second later, she arched her back, nesting into him. Now there was contact.

He was afraid to breathe, frozen by the contradictions in the situation. They had both drawn clear and careful lines around their relationship. She was a mostly gay woman. He was—what? He didn't know anymore. Could pals cuddle? He guessed they could, but he was feeling awkward. Was this platonic or something else? He didn't know. He couldn't recall feeling anything remotely similar.

After a few minutes, her breathing leveled out, and he allowed himself a deep breath. She drew his arm closer around her. He felt the weight and warmth of her breast on his forearm. The soft coils of her hair brushed against the skin of his throat. Eventually they slept.

In the wee hours, he was awakened by a sharp elbow delivered with some force to his midsection. "Stop poking me with that thing," Claudine hissed.

His eyes shot open, aware of his arousal. Awkwardly, he squirmed away from the arc of her butt. "Sorry," he muttered. "I was asleep."

Rolling over, she faced him in the darkness. "It's okay. Flesh is blind. That seems to be the cause of half the world's problems."

"What about the other half of the world's problems?" The room was too dim to make out her features.

"I don't know." She rubbed her eyes with her knuckles, like a child. "Probably wanting what you can't have or some such bullshit."

He glanced at the clock sitting on the nightstand. It was four in the morning—too early to get up. He rolled to his other side, and, after a long moment, she pressed against his back.

"Don't poke me," he said with as much irony in his voice as he could summon.

"You'd love that, wouldn't you?" she said.

29

With electric service restored, Moss awoke to an empty bed. Getting showered and dressed, he tried to process what had happened. Every avenue of rationalization dead-ended in the feeling of loss he experienced when he had discovered himself alone. In the light of day, the whole thing felt like no big deal—or worse, maybe a big deal.

The sound of water gushing into the gutters suggested that the storm had dissipated, and the temperature was climbing. Pulling back the curtains, he found his backyard blanketed by two feet of rapidly melting snow. He heard an occasional car on the road. The plows must've been busy during the night.

When he'd gathered his courage to leave the bedroom, he detected the smell of coffee coming from the kitchen. Claudine was standing at the counter buttering toast. She was dressed in her jeans, boots, and a wool shirt. He cleared his throat to announce his presence, but she ignored him. Moss decided that a seat at the table was his safest recourse until he gauged the mood of the room. Marylou was nowhere in sight.

Once she finally turned around, she looked him in the eye and held up the flat of her palm. "Not a word, Moss," she said with no inflection. "Not one word." Sitting across the table, she spread jam on her toast.

"Where's Marylou?"

"Showering. Packing. She needs to get back to town." Claudine's voice was stuck in neutral. "Her school term at WSU starts soon. I guess there are meetings and the like."

"What about the roads?" He was unprepared for this development.

"Clear by noon, so they say on the radio."

"It's a long drive to Detroit."

"Houghton." Claudine went to the counter and poured them both cups of fresh coffee. "She booked a flight when we passed through there on the way here—before the storm."

Moss gave her a confused look.

"She never planned to stay long. I'll head back on my own." She nodded her head in the direction of the stove. "Soup's ready. It's good. I tried some earlier. Think of us when you have lunch today."

"You're missing lunch?"

She shrugged. "Marylou has a plane to catch."

This was all new. No one had mentioned a flight back to Detroit. How could the roads clear so fast? Torrents were pouring out of the gutter. The storm had passed. It was August, after all. He went to the window. The cloud cover was breaking up, and the deck furniture was regaining its form. Clumps of snow dropped from tree branches like dead birds.

He turned to discover Claudine watching him. Was she waiting for him to say something? Without planning to, he said, "You could stay another couple of days."

She looked down at her nails. "I have a job, Moss."

"Call Helmut, tell him about the snow." Helmut was her manager at the Midtown.

"Let me think about it."

Marylou burst into the kitchen, frizzy hair damp from the

shower. "*Hola*, my children. Let us rejoice in this new day." She spread her arms. As she spoke, the sun broke through the overcast, sending yellow light streaming through the kitchen window. Tossing a fresh pack of Viceroys onto the table, she poured herself a cup of coffee.

"Jesus," Claudine said, shaking her head. "What's with you? It's too early for chipper."

Marylou gave Claudine a condescending grin. "Truth be told, I may have freshened my spirits with the tiniest bit of a smoke before I showered." She gave Claudine a motherly pat on the shoulder. "A little good cheer wouldn't do you any harm, precious."

"Some of us have to drive, remember?"

"I could drive us all," Moss said. "The Buick is indifferent to bad roads."

Marylou glanced from Moss to Claudine then back again. She looked like she was about to say something but thought better of it.

"I'll drop Marylou off at the airport," Claudine said. "That was the original plan. Best stick to it."

Moss shrugged. He could take a hint. It was settled. Soon he'd be back to a flat and featureless normal. "When's your flight?" he asked Marylou.

She told him her flight was scheduled to depart at two o'clock. Claudine cleared the table and started back to her bedroom. "We'll leave some extra time in case the roads aren't completely clear."

"Good idea," Moss nodded. It didn't feel like a good idea. It felt like he was being abandoned.

By noon they were saying their good-byes in the driveway. Rapidly shrinking patches of snow and meltwater puddles made it hard to find a dry place to stand. Claudine tossed the luggage behind the seats. The sun was bright. She adjusted her sunglasses and started the engine. Moss did what he could to help ease Marylou into the passenger compartment. It was tight, but they managed without inflicting injury.

"Thanks for putting us up, gumdrop." Marylou gave him a long, thoughtful look directed mostly toward his midsection. "Don't eat the leftover crisp all at once."

Claudine rolled down her window and waved to him across the roof of the Ghia. "See ya!" she said.

He watched the little orange-and-white car descend the driveway and heard the plaintive whine of the engine as she pulled onto the road. He followed their progress down the shore road by the sound of the gears changing.

PREDELLA

IV

Lake District, Summer 1978

From the top of her forehead sprouts a foot with an ankle and a portion of shin attached. A relic from a charnel coronation. Red toenails, shreds of skin, splintered bone. Pairs of lips—hers and Daisy's—protrude from each breast where nipples usually sit. In this portrait, her belly is swollen with an imaginary fetus—an unhatched bird extricated from its shell. The creature lies curled below her rib cage, encased in a sack of transparent skin, its huge eyes covered by bluish lids. He's painted Seren with her legs spread wide and rendered a large and shockingly realistic birds' nest in the juncture of her thighs. The rest of her is singed, flayed, and boned—laid out like a butcher's carcass. Blue veins twist in pink flesh.

Once completed, this new series of paintings will be crated in London and shipped off to Chalky Wilkes's gallery in Hong Kong, where the taste for such work is widely cultivated. Haller will likely never see the paintings again.

Seren steps in to examine the brushwork. The canvas dwarfs her, eight feet tall and seven feet wide. Up close, the surface feels as if it's on fire. The work is horrific but good. Haller has always possessed a deft touch. The negative space surrounding her mangled flesh is a brilliant yellow—the work glows with an exquisite depravity.

She looks at him and nods. "You are truly a beast."

The gnome laughs. He's sitting with one leg over the arm of the chair, playing idly with his erection. "Who would know better than you?"

She returns her gaze to the canvas. "I see some problems." Pointing toward the lower right quadrant. "Your edges are careless. The rendering flaccid. Impotent. Hackwork."

He jumps up from the chair as she knew he would. "Liar! Show me." He hurls a brush in her direction. She dodges it easily. Pointing to a pair of veins embedded in raw flesh that require attention, she executes an ironic curtsy.

"Fuck!" he screams the word to the rafters. Whirling around, face flushed red, he looks for something to smash. He cannot see his own work. Seren is his eye. Without her, he is blind.

She smiles, takes a step to the side, watching his fury subside little by little until he reaches for a brush, a drop of linseed oil, a rag. He wipes the offending section away, muttering angrily.

On the couch, Daisy emerges from under Seren's old green overcoat and stretches. "What's wrong?"

"Nothing, sweet." She sends the girl a reassuring smile. "Mo seems to be losing what little remains of his talent."

Without turning from his work repairing the offending vascular anatomy, Haller shouts, "Shut up, cunt!"

Daisy laughs a child's laugh. "Mumsy, you're so mean to Uncle Mo." She has started calling Seren "mumsy" in reference to the fictitious fetus Haller has bestowed upon her belly in the most recent painting. Daisy's attempt at humor irritates both Seren and Haller. Comedy is not required from the artist's fuck puppy.

Behind the silver bars of a tall cage set well away from the windows, a large black bird observes the theatrical displays of the humans. Silent and ever watchful, it dreams only of the eternal forest, the sky, and escape.

30

After their departure, Moss straightened the living room and kitchen as best he could. Mrs. Numennin was scheduled to clean the next day, so he would leave the heavy lifting to her. He moped from room to room. Meltwater sloshed down the panes of the glass doors from overflowing gutters. He removed the lid of the pressure cooker and peered in. Claudine's pea soup was sprinkled with onions, carrots, and flecks of ham. Droplets of olive oil floated on the surface. He sampled a spoonful and smacked his lips. It was just what he needed to commemorate the visit.

He filled a bowl and sat at the table. Before he could summon a coherent thought, the bowl was empty. Getting a refill, Moss went to the fridge and snagged the remains of Marylou's rhubarb crisp and set it on the table with his soup. Mulling the future, he finished everything without really noticing.

Lighting a Chesterfield, he got up and paced for a minute or two. When he glanced out the window, he saw the last slab of snow detach itself from the shed's roof, slide to the edge, and plop onto the bushes below. Remnants of the storm were disappearing fast. It was almost as if it had never happened. Patches of green grass were spreading over the lawn. The quince bushes were struggling to right themselves under the diminishing weight of snow.

He flopped down on one of the iris-colored sofas. Ten days to England—he'd better check in with his travel agent. It seemed important not to leave anything to chance. Funny how after his night with Claudine, the whole quest thing felt diminished. He couldn't allow that.

It was all he had.

Kicking off his slippers, he stretched out, glancing at the charcoal portrait fashioned by the Godwin kid. There was something off-kilter about the model's features. It was a face no one could forget.

He settled in for a much-needed nap. He hadn't slept well. He wasn't a kid. His life was more than half over. He certainly wasn't eager to engage in any romantic foolishness. Despite the fact that last night's visit by Claudine felt so good.

Eventually he dozed off on the couch, and he did not hear knocking, or the kitchen door opening. But he did hear the unmistakable click of bootheels on the stone floor. A shadow moved across his eyelids. He cracked one eye open. Looming over him was the figure of one Claudine Boatwright, who, as far as he knew, was supposed to be driving the Ghia south toward civilization.

"I seem to be making a habit of waking you up, Moss. Why are you always sleeping when I pop in?"

"It's afternoon," he said, as if it explained everything about his existence. "You came back?"

"It would appear so." Her expression provided no clue to her mood. Sunglasses pushed up on her forehead, she'd shed the wool shirt from the morning. "Earlier, you said I could stay a while longer. Is that still okay?"

He blinked. "Yes."

"Good." Bracing a hand on the back of the couch, she swung a leg over and straddled him. "I don't want to talk about this. Words tend to fuck everything up."

"All right."

Tossing her sunglasses on the coffee table, she eased down, her body settling onto his. Reflexively, he placed his hands on her hips.

"Last night," she said, lips an inch from his ear. "Was very different than I thought. I can't get it out of my mind."

Silence. He scrolled for the correct response. "Better or worse?"

"Better. Strange but ... okay," she said. "I guess my boundaries are more permeable than I thought."

"Good" was all he could muster.

They lay still. She relaxed, let her body conform to his. Moss glanced down to where the toes of her boots dug into the fabric of the couch's upholstery. He opened his mouth.

Placing two fingers against his lips, she said, "One word about your sofa, and I'm gone."

31

Later, they made their way to his bedroom.

Slightly after six in the morning, sunlight filtered through a gap in the curtains. Again, he awoke alone. For a second he wondered if he'd dreamt her, but the night-tossed sheets suggested otherwise. He guessed he should get up, but he was reluctant to leave the bed. He'd forgotten the feeling of sharing a bed with someone he actually liked.

Sounds of movement emanated from inside the house. Throwing on his robe, he followed the smell of coffee into the kitchen. Claudine had apparently located her T-shirt and socks but nothing else. He took a breath and admired her.

"Sleep well?" She greeted his appearance in the kitchen with a nonchalance he found disconcerting.

He nodded—his expression as neutral as he could make it.

Sensing his uncertainty, she gave him a quick, impartial hug. "God, Moss. Can you please stop overthinking? Just this once? Nothing happened last night that we can't take back. It's all good."

"Okay." He looked down at the floor. Something had surely happened—at least to him.

"I think it's a smart plan if I move my stuff into the guest bedroom. Simpler that way." She held him at arm's length, saw his deflated reaction. "Don't worry. We can still sleep together."

He did his best to smile.

Then she did something that took him off guard. She moved one of his hands to her breast and guided the other to the firm swell of her butt. "Let's face it," she said, looking up at him. "You've wanted to do that for a long time. The eyes never lie."

He could feel her heart beating.

"We can try to do this." She pecked him on the cheek and poured him a cup of coffee.

• • •

Thinking back, what surprised him was how easy it all was—and how quickly he became accustomed to having her around. After they'd both showered and dressed, Claudine retrieved her duffle and installed herself back in the guest room.

Later in the morning, they walked down to look at the lake. Recently melted snow made the footing treacherous, so they contented themselves by standing on the top steps of the short stairway that led from the elevated road to the strand. The sky was clear, washed fresh by the storm. Greenish waves pounded the shore with white-capped fury as far as they could see. Wind carried the reminder of snow and the fresh smell of the arctic. White gulls wheeled on the air currents.

"This is a gorgeous spot," Claudine said. The breeze whipped her hair around her face. "It makes me feel twitchy in a weird way."

When Moss gave her a look, she just shook her head no. "I know what you're thinking, but no."

He felt sure he was going to need an interpreter. Maybe that was okay, because he couldn't manage to interpret his own thoughts. He recalled her reaction to thunder a few nights before.

Back at the cottage, he asked, "Is it too early for a glass of Chartreuse?"

Claudine shot him a serious look. "Way too early, Moss. Let's you take it easy on that stuff. I'm feeling the need to keep some clarity right about now."

"Wine?"

She laughed. "Now you're talking. The timing might not be right for going cold turkey on the alcohol."

He broke open a bottle of Spanish red, and they sat and smoked his Chesterfields. Claudine went to the living room briefly and returned with the massive book on Edouard Manet. She flipped it open to a page showing *The Dead Toreador* and set it on the table in front of Moss.

"I think this is what Marylou was referring to the other night. It's not exact, but the spirit is like the Manolete photo." She watched for his reaction.

He studied the image.

Claudine ran her tongue over her lips. "Marylou told me to come back. She's old. She knows everything."

Confused, Moss said nothing. He tried to focus on the artwork. From his schooling, he was aware that it depicted the bottom half of an original, larger composition that the artist decided to split horizontally. The work contained all of Manet's fabled elegance in both form and color. The dead man, supine, with his head pointing in a shallow diagonal toward the viewer, lay in repose. The violent act that brought on his demise was indicated only by the smallish splotch of blood emanating from beneath the bullfighter's left shoulder. The muleta lay useless beside his leg, which was encased in silvery white stockings. The original top half of the canvas had become a separate painting, now housed at the Fricke Museum.

The bottom half was famous.

The Manolete photo revealed what was missing from the Manet painting: the blurry shadow of Islero, the bull hovering above the matador. The visual dynamic of the scene was dominated by the furious mass of the animal. There was no question as to what had happened moments before. The Manet implied. The photograph described.

Two things—the same but different. He could now relate.

After a lunch of soup, they drove the Estate Wagon into town. They weren't short on food, but both felt the urge to get out of the cottage for a while. The familiar drive didn't feel that way. Claudine gazed out the passenger-side window, let him rest a hand on her denim-covered thigh.

Inside the store, they wandered the aisles, making impromptu additions to their cart. She favored vegetables—lots of vegetables. He let her guide him safely past his old habits. On the way back to the car, he tried to take her hand. She gently pulled away and shook her head. "Don't be a dweeb, Moss."

They remained mostly silent on the return drive.

Back at the cottage, Moss automatically reached for his cigarettes and Chartreuse. Her disapproving look made him hesitate and rethink. Did he know how to get through even one evening without his standard pleasures? He couldn't imagine it.

"Grab one of your reds, Moss. Any red." Standing at the sink, washing lettuce, she glanced over her shoulder. "Wine is good."

He brought a bottle to the table and uncorked it. He felt obligated to help with the groceries, but truthfully he just wanted to watch. The context wasn't the same, but her actions in his kitchen mimicked those familiar gestures he loved so well from the Midtown Café. He poured her a goblet. She gave him a nod, then resumed washing and trimming the produce.

A twinge of dread bloomed in his chest. He liked this familiarity, but could it persist when they returned to their real lives only six hundred miles to the south? The prospect of going back to the gallery made his stomach churn. Questions from Boo Tice regarding the Bainbridge were inevitable. Perhaps the little industrialist would somehow fail to return from Africa and his adventure on the mountain.

And what about the others? Kaye didn't need him, but carrying the weight of the gallery on her own was a lot to ask. Sally would only be amused. Away from the Donald Morris Gallery, she lived in a bubble of patrician serenity.

Marylou was Marylou—she'd require details.

The broad belt with its cowgirl buckle hung at an angle on Claudine's hips. When she bent down to retrieve a container from a low cupboard, he glimpsed a band of perfect brown skin between her shirt and jeans.

"My head is feeling a little goofy right now," he announced.

"Aftereffects of a jolt of dopamine, I'm guessing," she said, turning to face him, leaning against the edge of the counter. "Don't worry, it passes."

He frowned. It wasn't what he was thinking—not at all. He had no interest in a chemical analysis—he wanted emotional reassurances. Off-balance, he groped for another tack. "I've had an original idea," he said.

She crossed her arms. "Evidently a number of them lately."

"What would you think about coming to London with me? I'm due to leave in ten days or so."

"God, Moss, you're as bad as Boo Tice! Do you really think ordinary people can just pick up and fly off to Europe on a whim?"

She was right, of course. Once more, he hadn't considered the obvious. "My dime," he said. "I'm going to need a rational person to keep me pointed in the right direction in this quest."

"Seems spur-of-the-moment."

"Absolutely. Would you consider it? Money aside?"

"In a heartbeat."

Any doubt he might have entertained lifted in an instant. The look on her face told him all he needed to know. He couldn't keep himself from asking, "Paris later?"

She lit up. With a big smile, she spun around and gave a wiggle of her hips. "Paris? Yessiree."

"I'll call the travel agency tomorrow."

"I'll call Helmut and see if I can take the time off." She took a long, loving sip from her glass. A line of deep red limned her full upper lip.

"Will it be a problem?" he asked.

"Not likely." She executed a happy little flamenco on the stone floor. "Paris! You're a genius, Moss."

32

The next day they made telephone calls—Claudine to clear her absence at the Midtown, Moss to his travel person. She assured Moss it would be easy to add one more person to the flights and that a little jaunt to Paris for the two of them could be arranged as well.

He experienced a slight sensation of vertigo contemplating Claudine's recent effect on his life. There was now a feeling of hope he hadn't felt in years. Her presence put a different spin on everything—as if his native myopia had suddenly been corrected by new glasses.

They'd spent the next night trying to get used to each other in bed. No sex, but some closeness. A little like teenagers on a blind date, bets were small, and they were playing with house money. Whenever an inflection point approached, Claudine pulled them back from the edge with a word or gesture. Moss was fine with that. Acutely aware of his extra poundage, he knew he was far outmatched physically. There was no mistaking how out of shape he was.

As for Claudine, she appeared comfortable with having him nearby, so his ego was left intact.

By the time he hung up the phone, they'd been booked. Their agent said she was searching her lists for something fun in Paris for the week after the Tate opening.

"Done," he said, smugly dusting his palms.

Claudine looked up from where she was seated at the kitchen table. She'd been bubbly earlier, but her mood now appeared to have turned pensive. "Am I going to need fancy clothes for the trip, for the Tate?"

"Nothing to worry about," he said too quickly, realizing that for her it might be something to worry about. He didn't want to repeat the careless slight he'd committed at the Scarab Club. They'd need a day just to pack. "It's the seventies; nobody dresses up to travel anymore. Jeans and a jacket are good."

She gave him the squint-eye. "Bullshit, Moss. You're the man with a special closet reserved just for suits, and another one for shoes. I'm going to need some time to plan for this little outing."

He shrugged. She liked finery as much as he did. Finding ensembles wouldn't be much of a problem for her. "Bring as much or as little as you like."

"Who even are you?" She screwed up her face at him. "Where'd you hide the real Fairchild Moss? You know, the guy who changes outfits at midday just for fun?" Snakelets of hair bobbed and weaved around her features.

"I trust you," he said. She had changed his entire feel of things. Everything she did made his home seem more real. He found her earrings left on the nightstand, a towel kicked into a corner of the bathroom, lipstick stains on the rim of a coffee cup, a tube of hand cream on the kitchen counter. Reminders he was no longer solitary.

After lunch, when her jeans had come out of the dryer, she made him show her his boyhood studio—the shed. The puddles left from melting snow had long since disappeared. The sun had returned to the Keweenaw with renewed vigor. The afternoon temperatures were nearly too warm for the north country. Dressed in his lemon-colored Bermuda shorts, a long-sleeved shirt, and slippers, he snapped the lock open with a mix of nostalgia and dread. He never escaped a visit to that haunted interior without reliving some psychic wound or other. The scrape on his shin still hurt. Graduate school failures had slept with him his whole life. He wasn't sure he wanted to share those memories with Claudine.

Flipping the light switch and opening the bank of tilt-out windows, he spread his arms. "Here we are. Nowadays, it's just used for storage."

Claudine said nothing. She floated around the cluttered space with her usual economical grace, surveying the scene. Here and there she paused to pick up an object, spent some time studying his Gran's old Underwood, the jars of pencils and charcoal. Once, she held an old paint rag to her nose to smell the oil and turpentine. She paid attention to things. It reminded him of her actions at Gerome Nahni's studio on Cass Avenue. He guessed she'd spent a good bit of time in artist's spaces when she modeled. The tiniest twinge of jealousy pricked him.

When he started to point out something obvious, she held up her hand to silence him. Lifting an old sheet used as a dust cover, she dragged out a few of his old canvases. Moss felt increasingly uncomfortable. Her sleuthing around was like picking scabs.

"So, there you have it," he said, ready for the tour to end. "Why don't we have something to drink on the deck and talk about Paris?"

She paused midstride and turned to him, hands on her hips. "Good idea. Maybe you could break out a bottle. I'll meet you out there in a second."

Moss fidgeted. "I should lock up."

"Gimme the lock. I'll handle it."

He hesitated for a long second, then shrugged and handed her the padlock.

An hour later, she was still inside poking about. He waited on the glider, drank one glass then another. He amused himself by humming "Waltzing Matilda" over and over. Varying the tempo of the tune, he was able to alter the mood from an upbeat traveling song to a dirge-like iteration that felt more in keeping with his anxiety. He hummed and whistled, smoked and drank, trying to ignore the sounds issuing from inside the shed. Like so much else in his life, things in the studio were being shifted around.

Waiting for Claudine felt like being prepped for involuntary surgery. When he heard the windows being closed, he sighed with relief. She approached the deck, dusty and disheveled, looking happy. A dark stain of perspiration rimmed the neck of her T-shirt, and a streak of cerulean-blue paint graced one cheek.

He handed her a glass. "You look like the cat and the canary both."

"That's a nice little space you've got there," she said, patting his knee. "I've been formulating a plan."

"Dare I ask?"

"Not yet." She stretched her legs and waggled her cowboy boots. "I'm going to do some research before I commit."

Interrupting their respite, Ari Numennin's white van pulled up the slope of the drive, towing a trailer with the brush hog. Before Moss could levitate himself from the glider, Claudine had bounced down from the deck to greet the old Finn. Moss was more than a little surprised to see her give the caretaker a quick hug before he rounded the back end of the contraption and lowered the tailgate.

How exactly did that happen? As far as Moss knew, she'd only seen the geezer one time out in the woods. Now she was hugging him? Moss was pretty sure he didn't approve. His acceptance needle for old Numennin remained stuck on undecided. The groundskeeper was a tough nut, but Claudine had apparently made more headway in a day than Moss had in three decades.

The hog sputtered, died, and sputtered again. Eventually the motor caught, and the bulky machine was guided down to ground level. Claudine made her way back to the deck while the brush hog rumbled slowly toward the forest road. The Finn sent a short wave in Moss's direction, a bright-orange bulldog pipe tucked into one corner of his mouth.

"Numennin is here," she announced.

"Hmmm," Moss said, looking anywhere but at her.

The blustery cough of the machine was buffered by the trees and foliage. Soon, it was nothing more than a distant hum.

Claudine went inside and returned wearing her running shoes. "Come on, pudge ball. Let's go for a walk on the beach."

Moss groaned. In the afternoons he was generally disinclined toward much physical movement. Drinking and smoking suited him. Snoozing was okay. Walking to the fridge was okay. Anything more? Not so okay.

"Come," Claudine said, taking his wrist. "Change into those spiffy guide boots of yours and take me to the water."

Moss disliked effort. Even so, he laced up the many eyehooks of his L.L. Bean boots and dragged the yellow rubber rain slicker he'd procured after his maritime adventure with Boo Tice out of the closet. Handing the coat to Claudine, he helped her roll the sleeves. Sized for him, it hung on her smaller frame like a cape. When all was said and done, he thought she looked rather fetching draped in jaune brilliant.

"Seeing that raincoat reminds me," he said. "Did I tell you about my excursion onto Lake St. Claire with Boo?"

"You did."

"Do you want to hear about it again?"

"Nope, no way." She shook her dreads. "Let's go walk."

Walk they did.

As the sun began to sink, the wind off the water turned sharp. The summerlike warmth from earlier was now chilled. The air was filled with spray. Boulders along the strand dripped moisture.

A hundred yards north of the road and the access stairway, they came upon a tumbled block of concrete, five feet square. A fragment of the foundation of an old dock, it was a remnant from sometime in the early years of the century. Embedded into one side was a heavy iron ring, coated with rust. The artifact had always puzzled Moss. It seemed too close to the shore to be used as a boat mooring, yet there it was. The ancient cube, stained and chipped, had long been a fixture of this stretch of shoreline.

Another hundred yards up the beach, they located a boulder large enough to accommodate them both and shared a Chesterfield. Battered by the elements, they hunkered down, huddling together for warmth. They smoked in silence. The pressure of Claudine's shoulder pressed against him was enough to alter the way he felt about the big lake. He experienced a slight tumescence.

Claudine observed his predicament with an amused expression. After a moment's hesitation, she reached down and rendered him a friendly squeeze. "Will miracles never cease?" She planted a peck on his cheek.

When they returned to the cottage, Numennin's white van was gone, and they were left with each other.

33

As evening came on, they migrated into the kitchen and concocted a pasta sauce with ingredients plucked from the grocery aisles in Houghton. Claudine was her usual efficient self—humming softly while she pared, chopped, and minced. There was wine, but no Chartreuse.

From the stereo in the living room came sounds of the Wailers. Moss remembered spying on her a few nights earlier. "I have something of a confession," he ventured.

"Oh?"

"I saw you dancing the night of the big storm."

She didn't turn from her duties at the stove. "I know."

"You knew?"

"I knew."

He was befuddled, certain he had escaped detection when he'd crept away in the shadows. He felt his face color. "How?"

"You're not as sneaky as you think, Moss."

"You didn't say anything."

"No." She tasted the sauce, smacked her lips, and held the spoon coated with red for him to try.

He took a taste. How many other things about her had he managed to miscalculate? "I thought I was invisible. I'm going to have to think about that."

"Oh Lord!" She playfully poked at him with the spoon. "Don't think. Please don't think."

· · ·

After dinner Claudine gathered an armful of art books from
the bookshelves and spread them, open-faced, on the couch and
coffee table in the living room. What she assembled was an odd
assortment of painters—Gauguin, Hans Holbein, Manet, Matisse,
Bonnard, and more. Her gifts of Gentileschi and Guido Reni were
also featured among the cache.

Moss watched from his seat at the end of the sofa, Chesterfield
in hand. Picking a bit of tobacco leaf from the tip of his tongue, he
wondered what she was up to. Reining in his curiosity wasn't easy,
but he was determined to remain silent. Art was his gig.

He lit a fire in the copper-hooded fireplace and tried to quell
the unfamiliar feeling of contentment. Claudine offered no indi-
cation as to her intentions. Leafing through until she located an
image that caught her fancy, she appeared lost in her own world.
Every now and then she took a sip from her glass or paused for a
quick drag from his cigarette.

Relegated to his own devices, he thought about the furtive squeeze on the beach. He wondered if there might be more
squeezes offered in days to come. He hoped so.

Claudine ferried a large tome to where he sat and opened it to
a Gauguin nude—*The Spirit of the Dead Watching*. He knew the
painting—not a favorite, but important in the artist's oeuvre.

Next came *Olympia*, Manet's great reclining nude. Hans
Holbein's *The Dead Christ*, made notorious by Dostoyevsky in *The
Idiot*, was then positioned next to the Gauguin.

"Am I sensing a theme?" Moss couldn't help smirking. "Naked
people lying down?"

"Moss," she said quietly. "It's imperative that you not be an asshole."

"Okay," he said. "Sorry."

"I'm working something out. Please don't distract me."

He composed his face into a serious mien. So many decades spent talking down to clients had ingrained a snootiness in his manner that was tough to shed. Over the years, he'd found a degree of superciliousness attractive—at least in himself. He quickly realized that such an attitude would not go over well in this situation. Each succeeding day they spent together reinforced the fact that Claudine was scary bright. She knew plenty of stuff he didn't.

He eyed the growing disarray of books splayed about his living room. Maybe she had a handle on what she was trying to accomplish by pulling out these musty tomes. Maybe not. Either way, it offered a pleasant opportunity for him to bask in her company.

She extracted more giant volumes, moved the Manolete photo next to the Holbein Christ, then flipped the pages of the Gauguin text until they stood open to *Te Tamari No Atua*, the famous nativity. Bending over for a closer look, she returned to the page depicting *Manao Tupapau*—the prostrate young girl watched over by the spirit of the dead. Nothing but reclining figures. He tried to find a balance between the Tahitian women and Olympia. Both nudes knocked your socks off with their sensuality, both emanated a sense of inner sanctuary in their remoteness, as if the eyes of an observer could never penetrate their interior selves.

Moss got up, went to the window, and looked out at the dark trees that ringed the cottage. A splinter moon hung low in the sky. Claudine took his spot on the couch and riffled through more pages. She sat carelessly, one knee cocked out at an angle. He cracked the sliding door, letting the night filter through the screen. A gust of air from outside chased a swarm of orange sparks up the flue in the fireplace.

Claudine looked up. "Brrr." She was wearing only a T-shirt, socks, and underwear.

Moss closed the door. In the background, the Bainbridge landscape hovered on its altar-wall. Its visual power stood up well against the immortal paintings in the books spread out on his couch. Funny how great art worked its magic without appearing to exert much effort.

He thought about the names scribbled on the ceiling beams at the Scarab Club. Haller was up there, Bainbridge too. Birdie Entwistle was wrong. Haller was no genius. The limey fuck was just a pervert who knew how to paint. He sliced and diced his models until they became nothing more than lumps of meat on a butcher tray, then constructed totems made of human body parts. That wasn't art. It was vivisection.

He turned back to the room. Claudine had a hand draped over the back of the couch. She kept rearranging the position of her fingers. It took him a second to realize she was mimicking Christ's hand in the Holbein painting. Try as she might, she couldn't seem to replicate the boney claw of the defunct deity.

He opened his mouth to comment but was stopped short by a glimpse of white underwear. Just then she glanced up and met his gaze. "Are you freaking out, Moss?"

"Maybe a little."

"Have you had a woman up at the cottage before?" She twisted one dreadlock around her finger.

"Never." No answer could be the correct answer.

"It's weird for me too," she said. "It's probably going to take some getting used to—on both our ends."

He nodded.

"I'm feeling totally unsettled. I honestly don't know why

getting dumped by Larissa bothered me so much. But it did. I don't think I even wanted *her* exactly, I just wanted someone." She pushed the pile of books to the end of the couch with a sock-covered foot. "She was a steady horizon—something I needed. Losing that part felt like another failure, I suppose."

"That makes sense, I guess." Personal feelings were not his gig. He left his spot by the glass door and joined her on the couch. Not wanting to hear about her previous lovers, he needed to stem the tide. "Are you glad you decided to stay? Up here?"

She knuckled his shoulder in a chummy way. "I am. I like it." She folded one corner of a page in the Holbein book, leaving it open to the great portrait of death. "It feels like we're on the verge of something."

He searched for a cigarette in a crumpled pack. He knew better than to make a joke, but the mushy alternative seemed like dangerous ground. Instead, he settled for their itinerary. "Nine or ten days until we fly to London."

With a lacquered fingertip, she traced the arm of the dead Christ on the page next to her. "When was the last time you used that shed for painting?"

Moss cleared his throat. That was the last thing he expected to come out of her mouth. "More than twenty years." More like twenty-five, truth be told.

"Haven't you ever wanted to get back at it?"

"No. Not ever," he said too quickly. She didn't need to know the gory details of his stint in graduate school.

"I'm wondering if you'd do something for me, in the days we have left up here," she said. "A favor, if you like."

"Anything." He meant it. "Ask away."

Eyes serious, she said, "What if I told you I want to model for you? I want you to paint me—something more permanent than a photograph. I know you can do it."

Just then, an owl hooted loudly from the eaves of the house. Moss ducked his head on reflex. "Don't be stupid."

34

He slept alone that night. More accurately, he didn't sleep at all, but he lay awake on his own. Claudine had nudged a toe across some invisible line. She had no way of knowing he'd react the way he did. In return, he'd stomped on the line with combat boots. He would never forget the look on her face. He would've hurt her less if he had slapped her. *Don't be stupid?* She'd proven time and again that she was the farthest thing from stupid.

Idiot, he told himself.

He'd thought a thousand times he should go to her room and apologize. But he didn't. He was a coward. She'd offered him something, and he'd kicked it back in her face. He expected to hear the Ghia fire up and head south in the middle of the night. What would he do then? Events had occurred. He couldn't bear to go back to the way he had been before. Another opportunity to change his life had been left for dead by the side of the road thanks to his stupidity. Squeezing his eyes shut, a solitary tear rolled down his temple and onto the pillowcase.

In the morning, he woke early, showered, and dressed, determined to make amends. Peering through the window, he was relieved to see the little orange Ghia still parked in the driveway. His hands shook as he poured hot water into the French press. When Claudine finally appeared, he was on his second cup of coffee, his apprehension ratcheting through the roof.

She was fully dressed and had slung his yellow rain slicker over her shoulder. Hanging the rubber garment over the back of a chair, she got herself a cup of coffee and sat opposite Moss at the table. "I warned you to stop being an asshole," she said. "I guess you missed the point." Her voice was devoid of inflection.

"I'm sorry, Claudine."

She waved him off. "You have to stop."

"I don't think I know how." He couldn't bring himself to tell her about his graduate failures. How his grandmother had been forced to buy him an art gallery because he couldn't paint. People knew. Marylou, Birdie, Sally, even Boo. He guessed it was an old joke by now—but a joke, nonetheless. His successes, even Athena—they didn't make a bit of difference. He could fool strangers, but he couldn't fool himself. He couldn't fool Claudine.

"I heard all the stories about your troubles at Cranbrook." She wafted her hand in the air between them. "How could I not, working at the Midtown and all. I heard the talk. I'm pretty sure they got it wrong. My gut tells me."

Moss looked up morosely and shook his head. "Maybe they got it right."

"No," she said. "I don't buy it." She took a sip from her cup. "But, for some unknown reason, you seem intent on proving me wrong."

"It's too late."

"First off, you can try not to be such a jerk," she said with finality. "We're at a tipping point. Either you're going to paint me, or I'm going to leave. Two choices, Moss. Pick one and do it now."

He couldn't face either prospect. He hadn't held a brush in half a lifetime. It was an ultimatum he would never be ready for. His whole life, he had managed to disappoint his grandmother in nearly every way. Now he would botch it with Claudine.

209

When he looked up, she was staring down at her hands resting on the table, examining the varnished nails. Was there the slightest tremor of her lower lip? He realized in that instant he could hurt her.

"Okay," he said. "You win." Knowing perfectly well that it wasn't Claudine who'd won, but him.

She didn't crack a smile. "Good. We'll have breakfast and get to work."

The thought of trying to paint again terrified him. "I need some time to contemplate. Plan my moves."

"You've had twenty years to think, Moss. Something needs to happen, and now's the time."

• • •

Work on the painting didn't start immediately after breakfast. Claudine insisted they move one of the Knoll couches into the shed. He was about to protest but checked himself. The day prior, she'd cleared a space for it, tight but just enough. The sofa looked at odds with everything else in the dusty interior. Moss knew better than to grumble over a scuff on the legs or a smear of dirt on the iris-colored fabric.

Washing the windows brightened the inside with natural light. Around noon, Numennin showed up with his trailer hitched behind the old white van. Desks, chairs, file cases, and boxes were loaded for storage at the Finn's farm. How this was arranged, Moss could only guess. When they had finished, the shed had been turned into a serviceable painting studio. There was light, there was a makeshift easel, bottles of solvents and mediums were un-stoppered and wiped free of grime, a tabouret had been cleaned and scraped free of dried paint. Cobwebs were dusted, old hornet nests dislodged from the rafters and discarded. As the afternoon wore on, Moss required more frequent breathers and cigarette breaks. He tried not to think about what would come next.

Numennin exited the driveway with the last load as the sun began to touch the tops of the pines between the cottage and the lake. Finally, Claudine called a halt. "Tomorrow, you paint," she said.

Once the shed had been closed tight, they sat with their legs dangling off the edge of the deck, smoking and sharing a glass of wine. As the final gesture, she had ferried an armload of books out to the shed—the same ones she'd pulled from the shelves in the living room earlier. The Manolete photograph was propped on a shelf next to Gran's Underwood.

"That was some good job of work we did today," she said. A kerchief was wrapped around her dreadlocks. Despite the sweat and dust, she appeared to have fared better than he had.

Moss grunted. His hair hung in damp straggles on his shoulders, his forehead coated with grime, a shirt ruined. He wondered what Gran would say. She might approve.

Claudine poured another glass while he lay back and rested on the planking of the deck. Once he had recouped some energy, they made a fire in the fire pit and watched the twilight stars appear overhead. Sharing leftover pasta, they finished the bottle in a state of numb exhaustion.

Inside the cottage, the telephone rang and rang.

When full darkness fell, Claudine retreated to the guest room for a shower, leaving Moss to his own devices. He expected her to join him for sleep, but she never appeared. He spent an hour waiting, expecting the door to click open. Finally, he fell asleep and dreamt of a thin girl dripping water.

• • •

Cryptic at breakfast, Claudine sipped her coffee and nibbled on a slice of apple. Moss, distracted by what he feared would come next, drank cup after cup until he was forced to make a visit to the bathroom. When he returned to the kitchen, she was nowhere in sight. He wondered if, sensing his reticence, she had decided to call the whole thing off. Relief flooded into him. Perhaps he could escape humiliation for at least one more day? They could explore the trails Numennin had cut through the back one-forty. They could drive to Copper Harbor and eat lunch at a café he knew. They could plan the trip to Paris—talk with the travel agent about possible hotels, pensions, the left bank. Whatever.

As he was about to light a celebratory cigarette, Claudine appeared wearing his robe and her running shoes. She carried his yellow rain slicker folded across her arm. Tossing him a pillow from the bedroom, she said, "Time to saddle up, bucko." She breezed through the kitchen door, heading toward the shed.

Filled with dread, he followed her.

Inside, he watched as she opened the windows as far as they would go. Still cool from the nighttime temperatures, the interior looked vastly different than it had a day ago. She had organized his palette and brushes as best she could when he was resting on the deck the previous afternoon. Three four-foot square canvases were propped on crates end to end along the wall. Two of his big picture books, Gauguin and Holbein, were laid out on a worktable.

Moss went to the tabouret and tried to buy himself some time by squeezing out colors. Most of the tubes were usable because he had stored them for their long hibernation in air-tight canisters. A few had dried out, but these he slit down the length of the tube and added a healthy amount of stand oil, hoping to resuscitate their workability. His brushes, untouched for decades in a metal box, were in good shape. They too had been stored to prevent the incursion of either light or oxygen.

Positioning the yellow slicker on the purple couch, Claudine fiddled until the arrangement suited her. *Manao Tupapau, The Spirit of the Dead Keeps Watch*—she dropped the robe and lay face-down on the yellow slicker, resting her cheek on the pillow. "Move me however you need to," she said. "Look at the Holbein hand—do something like that, but in reverse."

Without a thought in his head, he adjusted her right arm at an oblique angle to her torso, letting the hand trail off the edge of the couch. As gently as he could, Moss shifted her head until she was gazing at him, at the viewer. He was astonished at how she'd thought it all out. What he didn't know was how the two similar but dissimilar paintings could be resolved into one unified composition—the dead and decaying Christ, and the young Polynesian girl just past puberty. It represented a confluence of opposites.

The paradoxical amalgam revealed a kind of genius.

"I'll need to do some sketches," he said.

"Paint, Moss." She stretched out her legs, rotating her ankles and wiggling her toes. "When it warms up outside, this rubber coat is going to get sticky."

"What about the background?" he asked.

"You'll figure it out once you get going. Just paint."

He hesitated, dawdled, finally gave in. Mixing a dab of burnt umber into a smear of French ultramarine blue, he worked the color into the bristles of his brush. Where to start? With a few desultory marks, he blocked in the dorsal contour, the bend of the left arm.

He transferred the brush to his off hand and clenched and unclenched his left, trying to loosen up, trying to remember what dexterity felt like. Everything felt alien. He put it aside and fiddled with the bottle of turpentine. Soaking a rag, he wiped down his initial attempt, obliterating the lines until there was nothing but a fog of thin paint.

Maybe the feet? They should prove within his capacity. He had done well in his anatomical-drawing classes, years before. Working fast, he sketched in the geometry of the couch, her lower limbs. It wasn't right. Wiping everything he'd done away, Moss let out an exasperated sigh.

Claudine's eyes tracked him as he moved from one unsuccessful gesture to the next. She lay as still as a human being could. Her nostrils flared every now and then, but her body remained immobile. Her hair stood out around her face like spikes—a crown of thorns. Below her waist were two identical dimples above the swell of her rump. He tried not to let his eyes linger too long in any one place, feeling a little like an interloper. Painting was half-remembered territory. He would proceed cautiously while he worked out twenty years' worth of kinks.

Claudine ignored everything. He could imagine her in a college art studio, the focus of twenty pairs of eyes—observed but invulnerable.

He shifted his efforts to the third panel, the frame that would contain the head and shoulders, and the critical right arm and hand. That panel would form the crux of the painting and represent a large proportion of the visual focus. Reading left to right, the last panel would fashion the concluding argument for the entire work—and it would represent a major diversion from *Manao Tupapau*. Claudine's right arm would stretch away and below the axis of her body, the hand extending out from the picture plane, gesturing toward the viewer. The concept was stolen entirely from Holbein—who stole it from Caravaggio, who likely stole it from someone else.

If he could get the hand, then maybe the rest would follow.

He began again, only to pause after a minute or two. Nothing he tried seemed to work. He went to the couch and moved her hand, then her arm. Her skin was slick with sweat.

He returned to the canvas, squeezed out more paint, and blocked in some of the underpainting around her arm and shoulders. Colors that would form the substrate for the final coat of yellow surrounding her body were tints of blue-green and blue-violet—cool colors diluted with white to lighten the natural darkness of the tertiary hues. Roughing in the negative space helped. It provided something to work against when he returned to the hand and arm.

She watched him out of the corner of an eye half-closed.

The slope of her back barely moved with her shallow breathing. "I'm afraid you're going to melt," he said. "Let's take a pause and grab a sheet from the guest room to use instead of the slicker?"

"Work a little longer," she said. "There's no rush. It's been a long time since you did this kind of thing."

Moss made a few more marks then tossed the brush down on the glass palette that covered the top of the tabouret. "I need a break." The interior of the shed was warming. He was sweating now and had been for a while. Once the sun crested the tops of the pines, the interior space resembled a sauna.

She rolled onto her side, one hand cradling her head. Her facial expression reminded him of Manet's Olympia. The frontality of it all unnerved him.

"Don't be afraid. Use your eyes." She cocked one leg until her foot was resting on the opposite knee. "It's just flesh."

He dragged a stool next to where she lay and sat with his elbows on his knees, taking her in. Five uncomfortable minutes passed. He fished a Chesterfield from his shirt pocket, lighting one for himself and one for Claudine. They smoked in silence. When her cigarette had burned halfway down, she handed it to Moss, who stubbed it out on the floorboards. Lying back against the pillow, she closed her eyes.

"Why bother, Claudine? Why all this?" He spread his arms to encompass the shed even though her eyes remained closed. "Why did you suddenly decide to choose me?"

Her lips creased into a wry smile. "Well, for one thing, you're not the sort of man who ends up dead in a ditch. That's probably a plus."

He had only the slimmest idea what she meant, but he laughed anyway. "Well, at least you've set the bar at an all-time low."

"Your hands are good, Moss. I've known that for a long time. You have the hands of a painter, not a businessman."

"That's something," he said, pleased to hear that she'd noticed him at all in the old days.

"Mmmm." Her breathing deepened as she fell into a doze.

Shadows of birds in flight were caught on the canted panes of the windows. Outside, sounds of insects buzzing in the Quinces, of traffic passing on the road below. Wind off the lake ruffled the tops of the pines.

35

They worked until midafternoon. Moss needed to pause frequently. His shoulder muscles throbbed. His neck developed a kink. It was hard to imagine how she was able to hold her pose without complaint. As the day wore on, the temperature climbed inside the shed, making their work increasingly difficult. Moss's shirt was soaked. Claudine's body glistened under the lights.

When it was time to call a halt, they sought refuge in the shade of the deck with a chilled bottle of Chenin Blanc. Claudine wore Moss's bathrobe belted loosely around her waist; blotches of dark perspiration stains dotted the fabric.

"So, how was it?" she asked after they'd both downed their first glass.

Moss shook his head. He knew nothing of merit had been accomplished. He'd painted like the amateur he was. The deftness he'd hoped for had not returned. Everything felt clumsy.

She watched his reaction. Pushing a stray dreadlock from her forehead, she said, "Don't fret, it will all come back. Give it some time." Standing up, she headed into the house. "I'm in need of a bath."

Moss sat, trying to process this futile attempt. A deep-seated irritation with Claudine for putting him in a position to fail clawed up inside him. He hadn't asked for this. He was perfectly happy—or, at least, reasonably content—with things as they were.

He'd been blindsided by the changes visited upon him in recent days. Two weeks ago, Claudine had been a pal from the Midtown Café. She watered his houseplants when he was away. She poured him Chartreuse.

Now she was . . . what?

He couldn't answer that question. Under his shirt, beads of perspiration rolled down his chest and pooled at the waistband of his shorts. A splash of alizarin crimson bloomed on his thigh just above the knee. He flipped the last of his Chesterfield into the bushes and went inside for a drink.

After a quick shower in one of the guest rooms, and a change of clothes, he padded into the living room and opened the sliding door to let in the evening air. Rifling through the stack of record albums, he chanced upon Tom Waits' new album, *Small Change*, and put it on the turntable. He was less cranky now that he'd washed and had a chance to catch his emotional breath. The painting part hadn't been all that bad, and the looking part had been downright pleasurable.

There was no sign of Claudine. He decided to take a risk and search her out. From the pantry he selected a smoky red from the Cahors region and carried two glasses and an ashtray into the guest quarters. Empty. Where could she have gone?

When he entered the master suite, he heard water running in the bathroom. There was light coming from under the door. He tried a timid knock. No response. Knocking a little louder than before, the sound from the faucet ceased.

Easing the door open, he found Claudine mostly submerged in the tub—the level of the water just lapping at the rim. "I was looking for you," he said, feeling more than a little like an intruder. She had propped a rolled towel under her head and was stretched out. Only her head and the tips of her toes broke the surface of the water.

She opened her eyes. "Lo and behold, you found me."

"I brought you some wine and a smoke."

"Okay." She made no move to cover herself.

Moss poured two glasses, perched a hip on the broad rim of the tub, and lit a cigarette for them to share. Claudine twisted around and rested one arm above the water's surface. He had never felt comfortable with his own body, particularly after turning forty when he'd started to put on weight. He wanted to admire Claudine's nonchalance, but he couldn't conceive of anyone indifferent to being naked.

"It was good to watch you paint," she said. "Everything is sexier with art."

He couldn't imagine it, so he said nothing.

They sat together in silence for what seemed like a long time, listening to the music coming from the other room. After their prolonged stint in the studio, he no longer had to train his eyes to avoid her, but his upbringing wouldn't allow him to stare for too long. A crescent-shaped scar high up on the inside of her left thigh caught his attention. Slightly more than an inch long, it scribed a pale glyph on her brown skin. He couldn't guess what mishap could have created such a cut, but he was willing to spend time trying. He was contemplating a closer look when she splashed a handful of water on him, nearly dousing his Chesterfield.

"Snap out of it, Ahab," she laughed. "I fell off my bike when I was little. That's where the scar you're so fascinated with came from."

Moss reeled himself back into awareness. Embarrassed, he mumbled an excuse.

"Are you sure you're okay with all of this?" She cadged a drag from his cigarette. Her bubblegum-colored nails glowed brightly against her damp skin.

"The last couple of days have been a lot to assimilate."

"They have," she nodded. "Are you sorry? About any of it?"

He raised his eyebrows and took a deep breath. Too much was contained in that question for any reasonable man to answer. "No," he said. "I don't think so."

"Good," she said. Without further preamble, she kissed him. This time there was nothing sisterly about it.

• • •

The next day, work in the studio improved. Once he surrendered to the inevitable, and stopped fighting, his touch with the paintbrush regained some lost dexterity. Mixing colors, working up surfaces, began to feel natural again. Claudine spoke less and less, retreating into her figure-model mind-set—letting him work without commentary.

During breaks he referred to the texts on Gauguin, Holbein, and Manet, adjusting the composition and trying to find a balance between the three. He thought of different objects that might be appropriate for her right hand to hold—finally settling on nothing, merely the replication of the gesture of the Holbein Christ. Gauguin's fondness for the Olympia was well-known to historians—the artist even made a copy in order to understand Manet's work.

By the end of the day, half the art books from the shelves in his living room had migrated to the dusty confines of the shed. They lay open and dog-eared on every available surface, pages smeared with paint and fingerprints.

Stepping back to examine his work, Moss's gut twisted with disappointment. His touch had returned. The technique was good, but there still wasn't a coherent painting connecting the three canvases. He'd blocked in some areas, left others vague and amorphous. When he compared his figure to Gauguin's, it was clear from the differences in anatomy that Claudine's body was that of a woman in her prime, whereas the subject of Gauguin's masterpiece was painted when she was just fourteen years old. That difference alone provided Moss's painting with a distinctive spin—as much Olympia as *Manao Tupapau*. The dramatic curves possessed by Claudine also diverged radically from those of the figures in *The Dead Toreador* and Holbein's Christ. He was building a stew of references and hadn't yet found the ingredient to tie everything together.

Periodically, when they were in the shed, the telephone in the house would ring for prolonged bouts. Moss was in the habit of ignoring incoming calls. If people needed him, they could drive up to the Keweenaw.

At noon on the third day of their project, Moss thought to call his travel agent to inquire about their planned stay in Paris. Earlier, she had promised to book something on the Left Bank near the river. He hadn't heard a word since.

When he was able to get through, she informed him that their flights and ground transportation had been reserved, but she was still searching for a satisfactory place to stay. After he'd hung up, Moss thumbed through his Michelin travel guide for Paris and located a hostelry he felt might work. The Hotel Académie, in Saint Germain des Pres, sounded promising. It was close enough to walk to the Sorbonne and the Luxembourg Gardens. Small and quaint, he felt sure it would suit Claudine's romantic vision of the city—circa 1925.

Once he'd set his travel agent on task, Moss joined Claudine on the deck. The wind, calm early on, had picked up during the morning and was now blowing relentlessly in from the west. The breeze was good for painting as it cooled the temperature inside the shed and made Claudine's job of modeling more bearable. Clear blue August skies meant they'd be spared a repeat of the freak snowsquall of a few days before.

"Can you give me an hour in the shed—alone?"

"Sure," she said. "Why not?"

"I need to look. That's all." He shifted uneasily on his seat. "It's not right, the painting. But I think maybe I can fix it."

• • •

He sat for an hour, then another, trying to make some sense of what he had created. Not that the painting before him was bad. It was not. It was competent—just not good enough. The figure was okay—the edges, the modeling of volumes and proportions, were correct. But her expression, looking obliquely at the viewer, one hand partially covering the lower portion of her face, was missing something—an element of character. Unlike Manet's Olympia, she was missing a covert, female quality. He needed to make her features register some feeling that still eluded him. As for the background, the sheet, and the cushions of the couch, it was too dense, too turgid with paint. The negative space outweighed the figure. The balance was off.

With a sigh of disgust, he grabbed his largest painting knife and began to scrape away most of what he had applied during the preceding days. After half an hour had passed, he felt as if he was getting somewhere. In between bouts of erasure, he added new colors to his palette—rusty English red, manganese violet, cobalt green, Naples yellow. On the lower right-hand side of the first panel, he slashed in an arc of burnt sienna and laid in a shadow of Windsor violet. When he stepped back, the iron ring embedded in the old concrete block along the shoreline had appeared below Claudine's foot. It was an artifact from his boyhood memory, but now it was given a new context in paint, and a new meaning.

He tackled the scene anew, alternating bouts of application with periods of removal, letting earlier passages remain as hints, as residual scars of the initial brushstrokes. He barely noticed when Claudine entered the shed, doffed her robe, and assumed her pose. Her cheek pressed onto the fabric of the pillow, she gave him a secretive smile—at once knowing and expectant. As soon as Moss saw her, he knew he'd found the expression that had been missing.

Working with a kind of conviction he'd never experienced before, he altered her features to reflect what he'd just seen. Once satisfied with the face, he blocked in the surrounding yellow sheet with smears of cadmium yellow overlaid with thin washes of zinc white.

Mixing some white into rose madder, he etched in a pattern of pink flower blossoms along the hem of the yellow sheet. Above Claudine's head, a thicket of yellow-green bamboo fronds appeared, echoing the spikey disarray of her dreadlocks.

She watched out of the corner of her eye.

The light began to fade. A soft rain fell, pinging on the glass panes of the open windows, dampening the doorway. Claudine switched on the bank of overhead lights then fetched a pack of cigarettes and an unopened bottle of Chartreuse. Moss painted on into the night. The direction the work needed to take was now clear to him. There was no more reason for hesitation. For the first time in ages, he felt he knew what he was doing.

After midnight they both fell into his bed, exhausted, smelling of turpentine and sweat. When they finally slept, tangled in each other, it was only because there was no resistance left in either of them.

The following day, after loading up with coffee, they began again. This time Moss's gestures were filled with intention.

Claudine spoke less and less as the day wore on. She allowed him to place her limbs where he wanted them, to move a tendril of hair, to shift the position of her feet.

When he rested, she stretched the kinks out of her body, shared a cigarette. She never once allowed herself to look at his work. She knew enough about figure modeling to know what he needed from her. He was in another place where no one could reach him.

That night, Moss tossed on the bed, roamed the cottage, flipped through the pages of history books, art magazines. When morning came he was haggard, with blue circles under his eyes. Claudine offered to make some waffles, but he shook his head no.

The telephone in the hallway rang and rang. They ignored it.

As evening fell on the following day, Moss sat slumped on a stool, hands clasped between his knees, head bowed. His hair hung undone in long, damp strands. A dozen colors stained his clothing, his face, his hands. All the fire that had possessed him on the two previous days had fled, leaving him empty.

His painting was a mishmash of starts and stops, of thinking, rethinking, and finally not thinking. Old, discarded contour lines intersected the newest edges. Passages scraped down to nothing, drawn and redrawn until the concrete figure became abstract—a schema for his process. Claudine was there. Powerful. Sexual. Like her actual self, the painted figure was a composite of charged and seductively contradictory elements.

When she could stand the suspense no longer, Claudine got up from her pose and, without bothering with her robe, stood next to him. Her eyes took in the long painting—all twelve feet of it. Moss observed her warily. The canvas was drenched in vaporous color. A figure, at once evocative and timorous, reflected erotic ambivalence. The pattern of leaves above her head glowed in brilliant light, yellow-green and red-orange. Her right hand hung in a languorous gesture, beckoning the viewer to approach . . . but not too close.

He heard Claudine's sharp intake of breath. "It's something," she whispered. Stepping closer, she drew his head to her naked belly, pressing his face into the soft flesh. "Oh, baby, it's me."

• • •

Moss was in the shed packing up the painting, carefully wrapping it for the trip back to Detroit. The Buick could easily accommodate the square panels in its cavernous rear compartment. Far from eager to start the journey, he wished their time up north was just beginning. The long drive back to his former life seemed a cruel punishment. The only good thing—Claudine would follow in the Ghia.

Numennin received last-minute instructions with his usual stoicism. The cottage would be closed tight, awaiting their arrival the following August. The old Finn joked a little with Claudine.

Inside the cottage, the telephone rang and rang.

Claudine detached from the men and went to answer. When she returned, her face was clouded. "Haller's dead," she said. "Sally just called with the news."

PENUMBRA

V

Lake District, Summer 1978

Daisy sings in her little pink voice, sitting astride Haller in a shallow eddy of the River Derwent just downstream from Grange Bridge. "Swishy-swoshy, swishy-swoshy, washing out the clothes. Swishy-swoshy, swishy-swoshy, humping with the whores." Haller laughs and snorts, swigging happily from a bottle of Jameson while the girl's bare thighs clasp his midsection. His red gown billows under his arms in the turbid currents of the stream, now flush from the recent rains.

Seren sits on the grassy bank, chewing on long stems of greenery, musing on the shapes of passing clouds, wondering if returning to America will erase the hunger that plagues her these days. Haller is all but used up. His gnome-like features remain twisted in a sour scowl from morning until night. He complains of her presence in the studio. When she's gone, he curses her absence. The level of his malaise has even broken through Daisy's limited awareness. The air of their cottage is filled with bitter invective and hurled objects.

He finished the last of the canvases this very morning. Now they will celebrate for as long as they are able to remain upright.

"Up a ladder, down a ladder, swishing paint around, up a ladder, down a ladder, dancing round the town." Daisy posts up and down as if she were mounted on one of her favorite jumping ponies. The blue robe is soaked through, nearly transparent, revealing her rosy body. The painter mauls her flesh from time to time between swallows of Irish whisky.

Seren removes a cigarette from her coat, which lies bundled on the river's edge. She's long grown weary of Haller and his paramour, but there's still the exhibition at the Tate Gallery in a few days' time. Haller has vowed to boycott the show, claiming the London press have unfairly defamed him. She knows the real reason is his fear of Daisy's family and their deep-rooted societal influence. He feigns indifference to the rumors and speculation but searches the newspapers for any hint of mention. If Daisy were younger by a year or two, he'd go to prison.

None of that matters to Seren. Hypocrisy in English mores is a well-worn path. She knows young Daisy is capable of matching Haller's depravity any day, any night. The young socialite's appetites are a chasm of perversity.

Seren has long planned to travel south in time for the Tate's opening. The envelope bearing Haller's invitation card resides in a pocket of her coat. She's a ghost. No one will notice her haunting the galleries. Mayhap she'll cross paths with another hungry painter? A sculptor? Some wary stick of a filmmaker? A poet? The prospect of something new courses through her—the tingle of desire. Her anticipation tastes vaguely of copper, a little like blood in the lungs.

A startled yelp from the river alerts her that the pair of lovers has entered the penultimate stage of their coupling. On his knees in the riverbed, Haller has mounted his filly—now obscured from view by the voluminous skirts of the red ball gown—and is pounding into the home stretch. Water drips from his eyebrows, his nose, his lips curled in a snarl of passion. Beneath her red veil, Daisy wails piteously.

Lying on the grassy verge, Seren considers that Daisy's hidden form is somehow more enticing than when she was openly riding the supine painter. Cloaked in wet silk, the young woman's figure suggests a libidinous ambiguity that offers a whiff of fresh intrigue. Anyone could be crouched beneath the gown's skirts—girl, boy, fish, or fowl.

She's certain that the identity of his partner doesn't matter to Haller at this point.

On the road following the far bank of the river, a lone car pauses to survey the primitive spectacle. At climax, Haller lifts his head to the blue heavens and howls.

36

Brown's Hotel was everything Moss remembered from boyhood trips with his Gran. The venerable white building, set on the soft curve of Albemarle Street, evinced not a single sign of modernity. London was changing, even Mayfair, but Brown's was not. Their agent had booked them into the Kipling Suite, with a view onto genteel neighborhoods. The suite's heavy furniture and its broad bed were a testament to a particular version of timelessness. The emerald-colored paisley wallpaper provided an Indian flavor to the bedroom, but the rest of the suite was pure England, down to its massive leather chesterfield chairs and gray stone fireplace.

The British art world was abuzz with talk of Maurice Haller's demise. Tabloid writers gushed about the notorious painter, found floating face down along the grassy banks of River Derwent in the Lake District. His corpse, it was reported, had been dressed in a woman's ball gown. He had recently completed a new group of paintings in a cottage nearby.

No foul play was suspected—the matter was deemed an accidental death. A swirl of gossip among the London gallery set hyped the coming Tate Exhibition to the rafters.

Moss pored over the newspapers in hope of some actual enlightenment. There was little to be found.

The morning of the opening saw Moss and Claudine picking at a tray of tea and scones in front of a pair of French doors leading to their narrow balcony. Wads of wrapping tissue were strewn haphazardly on the carpet. Heavy glass ashtrays sat swollen with cigarette butts. A gray drizzle glazed wrought-iron railings and the leaves of potted geraniums. Moss sat at a small table sipping a milk tea heaped with cubes of sugar, a pile of newspapers scattered in front of him. Claudine, propped on a half-dozen pillows, was reading from the Michelin guide. She wore a blue, black, and yellow checked robe, sewn from a bolt of Thai silk, her cup and saucer balanced delicately on one knee.

Moss glanced over and was filled with astonishment. How had he arrived at this happy place in his life? It was both improbable and gratifying. The drive south from the cottage in Michigan remained hazy in his memory, steeped in a jumble of emotions. Surprisingly, the painting was quite good—all twelve feet of it. Once back in Detroit, he had ferried it to his framer, who would assemble the panels and fashion a slim, modern frame for it. On seeing the artwork for the first time, Kaye seemed dumb struck. When she could tear her eyes away from the canvases, she gave Moss a long, lingering look.

"The painting's a beauty, my friend," she nodded to herself. "You've accomplished something here."

Moss was pleased. He had always respected Kaye's taste, and now she saw him in an entirely new light. Then, a second later, his heart sank. She gave him a lopsided smile and a discreet head-waggle. He knew that response. He'd seen it a million times when she dealt with other artists. It said, *Good work, not great work.*

Good, yes. Genius, no. He went numb. He'd created something fine, but it wasn't the Bainbridge. Competence doesn't equate to greatness. He was lacking an ingredient—the singular thing the old painter had found before he died.

They agreed to hang Claudine's portrait in the gallery's front room once the canvas returned from the framer. Kaye said she was eager to gauge reaction from the public once it was on display. There was some discussion as to how the painting should be priced. Finally, they agreed on a sum so lofty that Moss was certain the piece would never sell.

Their trip from Detroit to London proved uneventful. A car was waiting for them when they landed at Heathrow, and the ride into the city offered few surprises for Moss. Claudine was mostly silent. Her eyes darted here and there, taking in the newness, eager to absorb everything.

The days after landing had been spent on Jermyn Street and Savile Row, for him, and at Harrods and Marks and Spencer for Claudine. She appeared to enjoy the bespoke shops as much as the department stores and was happy to assist Moss on his choice of shirting. For the Tate opening, she picked a narrow black skirt and a black satin tuxedo jacket with brilliant turquoise piping on the peaked lapels. For his part, Moss selected a charcoal pinstripe suit with double vents and slash pockets.

Moss spent some mental energy sorting out his emotions over Haller's demise. He thought a world absent of Haller would be a far better place. On the downside, though, his last link to the model, Seren, seemed to have been submerged along with the little man.

There had been a good bit of chatter in the media surrounding the exhibition—mostly focusing on the group of paintings Haller had produced during his time in America. Recent events only whetted the public's hunger to view the new work. Voices hinted that every piece had been gobbled up sight unseen before the last label had been affixed to the wall. Critics were universal in their awe of the canvases. Those in the know whispered that the Lytton family had whisked Daisy into a secluded rehabilitation center located on the banks of Lake Lucerne.

In a taxi back to the hotel, Claudine said, "Now that we're here, what exactly is the plan?"

"Reconnaissance," Moss chuckled. He liked the sound of the word. "If we can locate this model at the opening, we'll corner her and get to the bottom of the whole Bainbridge issue."

"And if she doesn't show?"

"We'll ask around. See what we can find out."

Claudine glanced out at the passing cityscape. Traffic was congested around Piccadilly, the air dense with diesel smell and raucous sounds of automobile horns. "We've come a long way on a hunch, Moss. I hope you know what you're doing."

Moss shrugged. "Have I ever? The whole thing with Bainbridge seemed to make sense back in Michigan. Now that we've traveled all this way, it appears more farfetched."

"When has farfetched ever mattered to you?"

"Never," Moss said. "But the quest appears to be on thin ice."

"What are you going to do?"

"Play it by ear, I guess."

"Oh God," Claudine groaned.

37

Hours later, a taxi dropped them off a block short of the Tate. The drizzle had abated. They followed the swarms of glittery guests into the brilliant light of the main salon, already packed too tight to breathe. As soon as they crossed the threshold, Moss began to perspire mightily.

From a far corner came the strains of a string quartet, its members dressed in black velvet outfits. Opposite the musicians was a long drinks table manned by servers in white jackets. It was, he thought, the right way to handle an opening. Leave it to the Brits.

The crowd was a mixture of patricians and posh punks. Denizens of the English upper crust bumped elbows with leather-clad, spike-haired musicians, lithe fashion models, film stars, and various other iterations of the art demimonde. Through a phalanx of bodies, they caught a glimpse of the American wunderkind, Bobby Mapplethorpe.

Claudine snatched at his elbow. "I heard someone say David Bowie is coming. Keep an eye peeled, Moss."

Glowing from one wall of the main salon was Bacon's famous double portrait—Lucian Freud and Frank Auerbach—on loan from Sweden. Moss began a slow approach to the painting, weaving through throngs of bodies alive with chatter. Claudine followed in his wake. By the time he'd made it halfway, streaks of sweat were lining his face. He regretted choosing a wool suit so early in September. Many of the other guests seemed to be suffering as he was—folded programs waved in front of flushed faces.

Once he'd made it within thirty feet of the Bacon portrait, Clarence Wilkes, London gallery owner, appeared at Moss's side. Lanky, with coatrack shoulders and a sunken chest, Wilkes's sleek suit jacket hung loose as a scarecrow's vestment. "I see you decided to grace us with your presence, FM." In the time-honored fashion of the British, Wilkes had coined the abbreviation of Moss's full name as a sobriquet. Contained in the appellation was a class chumminess combined with a blithe dismissal in the same breath. Every sentence the sallow Brit issued seemed congested by a jumble of unnecessary syllables jammed together without apparent reason.

"Hey there, Chalky." Moss returned the nickname favor, calling Wilkes by his schoolboy nom de guerre.

The Englishman greeted Claudine's arrival with a toothy grin that exposed his lifelong nicotine habit. "This is a welcome development." His eyes traced a zigzag between Moss and Claudine. "Can I assume this devastatingly lovely creature is your . . . ?"

"Friend," Claudine said, giving Moss a nudge with her elbow.

"Ah." Wilkes's mouth twisted into a smirk of disbelief.

Moss waved a hand to encompass the throng. "Where'd they stash the Haller paintings? You know, the ones people are talking about?"

"Next room over," Wilkes said. "You'll have to fight your way through the mob." He gave Claudine another long look, unburdened by ambiguity. "See you at the Black Dog, after?"

Moss knew of the pub but had never visited. "Of course, Chalky." He made a mental note to round back and query Wilkes about Haller's model later.

As Moss was about to turn away, Wilkes caught his elbow.

"Went mad, you know, Haller. Completely bonkers." Wilkes tapped his temple with a forefinger.

"How so?"

"Pulled an Ophelia, so they say. Facedown in the River Derwent, dressed up like a trollop." The sentence was a slurry of vowels.

"Mad?" Moss tried not to smile at the image of Haller in a woman's gown. These Brits. "How's his new work?" Moss was eager to see what the fuss was about.

"Deranged . . . genius . . . everyone says so." Wilkes grinned a wide, deeply dimpled grin. "Brilliant . . . the whole dying thing. We've tripled his prices since the news. I'm sending six new pieces to Hong Kong. The chinks have developed quite a taste for Haller." With a nod to Claudine, he turned on a well-polished heel. "Toodles. See you at the pub."

Rocking back on his heels, Moss digested the conversation. The heat in the salon was insufferable. Part of him envied Haller, being dead and all.

• • •

In the second room, ranked side by side, were three tall canvases depicting a woman in various stages of crucifixion. Against a background of florid rose color, the figure hung naked from a Petrine cross. Each panel depicted ascending degrees of romantic agony in the subject. On the third and last panel, legs splayed open, the facial expression captured was one of extreme pain—pain touched by a kind of erotic ecstasy, eyes rolled back, mouth frozen in a snarl of savage orgasm. A thick, mottled creature like a giant salamander curled between the model's legs, as if emerging from her womb. The muddy color, vestigial eyes, thick tail, and wide, shovel-like mouth made Moss recoil. Folds of loose skin and stubby-appendaged, webbed hands gave the amphibian the taste of nightmare.

What struck Moss was the look of ambiguity etched on the woman's features—features bisected by a vertical black line, hairline to chin. It was the same face that hung framed on his living room wall in northern Michigan, this time captured by a master painter, not an undergraduate. There was the same tangled storm of black hair, pale skin, full breasts. An expression of intense pain mingled with equally intense pleasure so raw and exposed it made him wish to avert his eyes.

Moss became aware of Claudine gripping his arm. Around them, whispered mutterings issued from a crowd packed five deep around the grotesque triptych.

"This whole place stinks of misogyny," Claudine said. "Can't you smell it?"

He said nothing, trying to keep his balance amid the swirling eddies of humanity.

She narrowed her eyes.

"What?"

"I'm troubled that you seem so untroubled."

Moss scanned the walls. Haller's loathing of females was everywhere in evidence. Added to Freud and Bacon's famous misanthropy, the entire atmosphere felt toxic. "Inventive," he said, intending to add to his comment, but Claudine cut him off.

"He took that facial expression from Breughel, or something medieval," Claudine whispered. "I'd bet the farm."

"Or Goya's witches," Moss replied.

"Horrific, yet strangely sexy at the same time."

Moss nodded. What troubled him most was how good Haller's paintings were. Despite the content, they were unforgettable. They made his own efforts in the Keweenaw studio look amateurish. A trickle of sweat rolled down across his rib cage. Out of the corner of his eye, he saw the patrician profile of Lucian Freud. The British painter, whose own work graced the wall opposite Haller, was staring at his former colleague's work with an expression of distaste. Dressed in a shabby cardigan and chinos, the famous artist stood motionless in front of what could only be, in his eyes, an abomination. At Freud's side, next to a pair of minor royals, stood the Irish portraitist Reginald Gray. Both artists appeared at once captivated and repulsed by the debauchery depicted on the canvas. Gray whispered something to Freud, words that brought the hint of a tight-lipped smile to the older man's face.

Moss glanced around the room, looking for the model. No one in the assembly matched the otherworldly woman birthing a giant Chinese salamander.

"My God," Claudine said, nudging Moss in the ribs. "That's Sloane Ellis, from Detroit, standing over by the Freud painting. She's a photographer I knew from way back. I modeled for her in days of yore. Before she moved to England."

Moss turned to see a slightly built woman with short, salt-and-pepper hair standing by herself. Displaying the caustic look of a self-righteous academic, with horn-rimmed glasses and battered, black, high-topped tennis shoes, she was staring at Lucian Freud with an intense air of dislike.

"I'm going to scoot over there and say hi. Come along?"

Moss rejected the idea. There was nothing welcoming about the austere woman. A hive-like buzz among the gallerygoers was gradually increasing in volume as more and more people were drawn to the Haller triptych. The undercurrent of outrage was beginning to build. "I think I'll wander through the adjoining rooms. See what I can see," he said.

Claudine nodded and floated away with a backward glance.

Moss sidled through the crowd, heading toward one of the

other rooms. Here, he found fewer people circulating in front of works by lesser-known artists. In one space, the last of five, Moss came upon a portrait by Haller that appeared to have gone unnoticed. In the painting, the model was posed in a more conventional fashion. Reclining on a black-and-white striped coverlet, she stared brazenly out at the viewer a la Goya's *Naked Maja*. The painting and pose seemed conventional, particularly for an artist so wedded to shock value as Haller. A second look revealed something more chilling. The model's face had an out-of-focus quality. It reminded Moss of the hazy sketches of Brice Godwin hanging at his cottage. A subtly disturbing aspect to the painting was the suggestion of pale spatters of milky semen on the woman's belly. A juvenile cliché in pornographic photography, it startled Moss more than it should have. He found it hard to tear his eyes away from the aftermath of fornication—a point in time often redacted from any lover's memory.

The figure's pale skin was slit with a long, thin incision from gullet to groin, showing just a hint of red where blood was starting to seep from the lower abdomen. Circular cuts around her wrists and ankles indicated a kind of ritual. It was, Moss realized, meant to reference the initial gestures of a flensing knife, in preparation for flaying the victim. The implication of what was to come for the model.

Just then, he felt something brush against him. Turning, he found himself face to face with the subject of the painting. His breath caught. For a moment, he had to fight to keep his balance. The air between them reeked with the scent of freshly turned earth.

"Hellish hot. Whyn't we get out of here? Go for a smoke?" she said with no preamble, her voice low and musical. The words located themselves more in his head than his ears.

She looked something like the picture he'd formed in his head—but also not. Heavy, unwashed black hair falling in waves to the small of her back. Skin so pale it seemed translucent, laced with a webbing of bluish veins. A simple, earth-colored shift fell to her ankles. On her feet, just visible poking from the hem of her dress, were a pair of light-blue ballet flats. The shoes alone were enough to set her apart from the glitz and grunge of the opening-night crowd, most of whom favored heels as lofty as they could manage. Small of stature, the top of her head came barely to chest level.

Without hesitation, he followed her to a doorway in one corner of the room. The door led to a service hallway that led to a second door opening onto a narrow back alley. A light mist fell from the gray sky. Paving stones glistened. The smell of dampness and diesel fumes hung between the walls.

Leaning against the building, she pulled a pack of menthol cigarettes from a hidden pocket. Moss accepted one and let her light it from a box of matches. "Yer likin' my pictures in there. I could tell."

Moss nodded. Her proximity dazed him. The tiny figure radiated a kind of glimmer, like a mirage waiting to evaporate. Moss puffed manically on his cigarette. The menthol opened his sinuses. Her scent flooded in like a drug.

"I know who you are," she said, tilting her head back. "I've seen you a time or two in America."

"Oh?"

"You're the art dealer." She eyed him. "The old man's shill, in Detroit?"

He acknowledged the words with a waggle of his head. "I was. He's dead now." She couldn't mean anyone but Bainbridge.

"Dead but not gone, I'm thinking."

"No," he said. "Not gone."

She smirked.

It was nearly impossible for Moss to meet her eyes. Everything about her felt alien yet strangely familiar.

Lighting a second cigarette from the coal of the first, she observed him observing her. Her hands were small, lightly fleshed, and efficient looking, with blunt nails and a hint of metacarpal bone across the backs. When her smoke caught, she flicked the old butt across the alley with a practiced finality. Sparks flew briefly then died on the wet brick wall.

Keeping his voice neutral, he said, "What happened to Haller?"

She lifted her eyebrows, as if the question were irrelevant. "Not my worry."

"You were his favorite model. Your likeness is on every wall in there." He inclined his head toward the gallery.

She shrugged.

Moss was at a loss. He found her nonchalance irritating. At the same time, something about her appealed powerfully to some part deep inside.

Flaring her nostrils like an animal, she tasted the air for molecules of scent. She gripped his forearm with surprising strength. He felt an electric tingle. "Yer wanting me, but I shan't be in London long." Head tilted to the side, she smiled more to herself than at Moss. "Tomorrow, I travel to Paris for work." That said, she turned on her heel to depart. "If you hope to fuck me, you'll need to find me in France, Mister Moss."

Blindsided, Moss stuttered, "How will I know where to look?"

"You won't," she said, disappearing through the doorway, leaving him standing alone in the drizzle.

After what felt like a long time, Moss exhaled. To his mystification, he discovered he was sporting an enormous erection. Buttoning his jacket, he hoped no one in the gallery would notice.

38

Later, when he found Claudine, it seemed as if everything had changed. She was standing by herself in the middle of the main gallery, looking uncomfortable. "You're sweaty, Moss," she said when he approached. "Did you find anything of interest?"

"No," he lied. "More of the same. How about you?"

Her eyes traveled past him, scanned the faces in the crowd. "I'll tell you later. Once we get out of this bedlam."

Bedlam it was. Angry voices spilled over the general hum of the opening-night horde. He gave Claudine a questioning look.

"Some asshole tossed their drink at one of the panels of Haller's triptych. White wine—not much harm done as far as I could see, but it caused a stir. Security ushered him out. That set off someone else, and there was another bit of hubbub. Freud took off. I'm guessing dustups aren't his thing." Claudine gave him a look. "Let's get out of here."

"The pub?" The prospect of finding a bar cheered him some. He needed a Chartreuse.

"Anywhere," she shrugged. "You're looking weirder than usual."

"I'm not feeling myself at the moment." Taking her elbow, he looked for an exit.

"That's putting it mildly." She glanced at his trousers. "What happened to you?"

"Nothing," he lied again.

"That doesn't look a lot like nothing to me."

Beads of sweat glistened on his cheeks. Moss fled the exhibition hall, bulling his way through the press of bodies, Claudine following.

• • •

Safely ensconced in a taxi, Moss settled down. A cold, damp breeze from the open window reduced the urgency of his fever but did little to diminish the magnitude of his swollen appendage. Claudine leaned back against the seat cushions and rested her head on his shoulder.

"I don't know about you, but I could use a drink . . . or five."

"Ditto," Moss said, squirming. His newfound libido was a bother. He'd never been that sort of man. Over the years, he'd grown secure in of the absence of a sex drive. Now he found himself wriggling on the car seat like some frustrated teenager.

"What's going on, Moss?"

"I'm in need of relief," he pleaded. His trouser front tented.

Ever practical, she said, "Let's take a look."

Undoing his zipper, he exposed a protuberance so red and insistent he barely recognized it as his own. For a moment, he wondered if he'd contracted some European virus.

"Oh, my," Claudine said. "This is new for you. We'll need to fix that."

"How?" Moss moaned.

"Let's see if this will help. Give me your handkerchief."

39

By the time they stepped from the taxi in front of the Black Dog, Moss's problem had noticeably diminished. The old pub was alive with clusters of drinkers, standing in chummy pods. In a back corner, they located Chalky Wilkes, holding forth in a small group of well-dressed folks from the Tate opening.

An elderly couple stood to leave just as Moss and Claudine arrived, yielding their seats beside a bookcase stacked to the top with well-thumbed tomes. Once seated, Moss regained some of his composure.

"Never in my life did I imagine myself doing that in a London cab, or anywhere else for that matter," Claudine whispered. "At least we provided some entertainment for the cabbie. What the fuck has gotten into you, Moss?"

"I don't know," he said, chagrined.

"No offense, but I've never associated you with random hard-ons."

"No offense taken," he said, a bit more grouchily than he'd intended. There was no plausible excuse. It wasn't something he felt like discussing with Claudine. Not yet. It was stupid not to tell her about the model, but he couldn't think how to justify an unsolicited erection that simply refused to go away. He guessed she would be amused.

Spying Moss and Claudine, Chalky Wilkes detached from a

conversation and ambled over. "What a night," he said. "Somehow, I didn't expect you to make an appearance, FM."

"Need a drink." It was all Moss could manage.

Claudine patted his shoulder and said, "You stay put. I'll grab whatever I can at the bar. Do you have any cash?"

Moss nodded numbly and handed her a wad of sterling.

"Forgive me for saying, but you're looking somewhat frayed." Wilkes propped himself on the arm of a nearby chair. "Any thoughts on the exhibition?"

"The Tate was a steam bath," Moss said. He was sweating again. "What do you know about Haller's model?"

Wilkes eyed Moss for a long moment, then his gaze traveled around the room and lazily returned to Moss. "Curious, your curiosity." Sucking on a tooth, he continued, "What do I know? Nothing really. A little maybe." A shaggy eyebrow cocked skyward. "Seems to be a free electron of sorts. What exactly is your interest, FM? Provide me some *context*."

Moss considered his response. The supercilious Brit might be his last chance at inside information. "I'm thinking she might have some insight on an American painter I know—or rather, knew. He's dead now."

Wilkes grinned an ironic grin. "Dead painters seem to be the rage these days, eh?"

Moss nodded. "Geriatric landscape painter—good but not great—miraculously paints a masterpiece right before he dies. It's the stuff of fiction. I think this Welsh model might know more. I'm hoping you can shed some light."

"*Manus Dei?*" Wilkes leaned forward. "I've seen this model, of course. A bit of the old will-o'-the-wisp, that one. Haller was enamored of her—in ways one can only imagine. Her name pops up here and there among a certain group of artists."

"His muse?"

"If a wraith can be a muse. Apparently, she has a nose for genius. Haller liked having her around."

"How so?"

"He thought he painted better when she was nearby. You know these artists."

Moss raised his eyebrows expectantly. "Go on." For the first time in a long time, he experienced a twinge of validation for his quest.

Wilkes emptied his glass and glanced around the room. "Bohemian. Frankly, she's always seemed *off* to me. Deviant blood. Some such thing."

"Deviant blood . . . that's an odd way of putting it. Was there any talk of the artists she worked with coming to a bad end?"

Wilkes smirked. "Is there ever a good end with these chaps? What with the drinking, the drugs, and the sex."

Claudine returned, balancing three glasses of Scotch. She handed one to Moss and another to Wilkes. "No Chartreuse, Moss. Sorry." She edged in next to him and clinked glasses. "To artists and their models," she said, giving both men an ambiguous look.

"What's the deal with her do you think?" Moss asked Wilkes.

"Who can know? There's myth, and then there's truth. Never the twain shall meet. As I said, she's more rumor than fact."

Leaning back in his chair, He tried to collate what Wilkes said with his own recent encounter. "I'd like to talk to her. Any idea where I could find her?"

"None at all," Wilkes said, turning his attention to Claudine. "I'd love to hear your first impressions of London. Hoary old place, but it has its moments."

Claudine swiveled in her seat to face the Brit, but before she could open her mouth, Wilkes cut her off. "I spoke with Sloane Ellis earlier, at the reception. She told me you're a talented model. Any truth to it?"

"Mostly myth." Claudine winked at Moss.

40

It was well past three in the morning when they made it back to Brown's. Before leaving the Black Dog, Wilkes searched his memory files and provided the name of a Parisian painter, Alexis Dufy, who had worked with Seren in the past. It wasn't much, but it was something. Privately, Moss planned to track down this French artist when they traveled to Paris in a few days' time.

By midmorning, the rain had cleared and given way to brilliant blue skies. When tea and scones arrived at their rooms, Moss and Claudine settled in at the table by the French doors. It was warm enough to leave all the windows open, admitting breezes of freshly washed air. Moss was in a mood to ruminate. The events of the night before had left him feeling out of sorts. His recent tendency to tumescence had waned overnight, but instead of welcoming a return to normalcy, he was experiencing a mild sense of loss.

For her part, Claudine seemed lost in her own thoughts. Moss looked for an occasion to mention his strange meeting with Seren, but Claudine's silence forestalled broaching the subject. Finishing her tea, she retreated to the bathroom for a soak, taking with her their only map of Paris. They had a day and a half to kill before their flight. Meandering to the couch, he succumbed, per his habit, to the temptation of inaction. His thoughts drifted across the ocean to Birmingham and the gallery. Was he still connected to the gallery that bore his name? Evidence suggested not—or at least not much.

An armful of newspapers was delivered by one of the bellmen. Reviews of the exhibition were in. Assessments of the art were mixed, but there was universal outrage over the subject matter. The *Telegraph*'s headline blared: "Tate Steps In It!" while the *Mail* was content to ask: "Art or Porn?" Everyone had an opinion. One thing seemed clear to Moss: Chalky Wilkes would be getting rich off Haller's death.

Squeezing his eyes shut, he listened to the sounds of occasional traffic on Albemarle Street. He could hear Claudine singing softly to herself in the bath. Instead of contentment, he was washed with guilt. His conversation with Seren felt like a kind of betrayal. How could that be? He'd done nothing beyond what he'd set out to do—track down the muse and grill her about Bainbridge. He'd had a perfect opportunity at the Tate. He'd muffed it. He might get another chance in Paris. It was a long shot, but it was his best shot.

Moss cracked an eye as Claudine emerged from the bathroom. "You're unusually quiet this morning."

She sat on the edge of the couch next to him. "Mulling. Last night was passing strange . . . in so many ways. I'm feeling disoriented."

"Me too," he said. "The Tate thing would have been much less manageable if you hadn't been there."

She didn't reply at first. Indistinct voices rose from the street below. From somewhere came the sound of a clock striking the hour—reminding them they were in London. A faint streak of white bath powder was sprinkled on one brown shoulder. She turned away from the window. "I don't think I'll be good for much today. I'm feeling pretty wiped out."

"We'll stay in and catch the car to the airport tomorrow." He was done with London, eager to depart for France.

"There's something we need to talk about."

"Okay." He didn't like the sound of that. He wondered if he'd been found out and she somehow knew he'd spoken with the Welsh model. Why hadn't he told her right away?

"Sloane Ellis asked me to work with her—to model for her. She's putting together a book of photographs. Said she wanted me to be in it. What do you think?"

A sigh of relief escaped. "What sort of book?"

"She said it would be a kind of feminist allegory—great art from history, except with females instead of males as the subject. Art about art. She's a pretty big deal."

"I think that's fabulous," he said. "Has she decided what she wants you to do?"

"She has a couple of things in mind. One for sure is going to be a recreation of *The Raft of the Medusa*. I'll be the one in front, just hauled out of the sea—or about to be dumped into it."

Moss pictured the Gericault painting. "Sloane Ellis is going to need a huge studio. There must be twenty figures on that raft."

"She has a space already." A light came into her eyes. "Get ready." She laughed. "She's rented an atelier in Paris. I can do the shoot when we're there. Isn't that great?"

"That is great," he said, getting up to pour himself a half glass of Chartreuse. "When does she want to start this enterprise?"

"Soon. Midweek if it suits our plans." She gave him a questioning look.

"Swell," he said. The urgency to tell her about meeting the model diminished substantially. The throaty rumble of a lorry drifted through the open window. He would have free time in Paris to find Seren. Was there really any need to bring the whole thing up to Claudine? The model was *his* quest, after all. Paris was something she had been looking forward to since their travel plans were made.

"I'm getting the urge to buy something," he said, turning from the street. "There's a shop around the corner with some nice-looking scarves in the window. Let's prowl the neighborhood. I think a scarf or two would be a proper way to celebrate your new assignment."

"You read my mind," she said.

41

The trip into the city from Orly Airport was fraught with minor impediments, including traffic delays and a suffocating humidity that made everything seem grim and shabby. The lunch-hour congestion soured Moss's mood. Heedless pedestrians, bicyclists, delivery vans, and tourist buses made it impossible to make good time through the city streets. Despite the heavy air, Claudine rolled the window of the Citroen partway down. Diesel fumes filled the taxi. While his companion was busy inhaling the smells of Paris, Moss was lost in a maze of his own thoughts.

Their Parisian hotel turned out to be less grand than Brown's. Its location on the left bank, with convenient access to the Musee D'Orsay, was a plus, but the rooms were on the small side, and their view was truncated by neighboring buildings. Claudine seemed untroubled by any disadvantage in the locale. She immediately found a nearby bookstore and purchased several prints of Gericault's famous painting. Initially, Moss was ambivalent about her project, but her enthusiasm eventually drew him in. The huge painting itself was housed in the Louvre, a short taxi ride across the Seine.

Around the corner from their hotel they found a bar, Café Louise, that was to their liking. The ground floor was a typical French bistro, while down a flight of spiral stairs was a cavern-like formal dining room. After their trip to the bookstores, Moss found Café Louise a perfect place to relax with a glass of wine and a smoke. He still hadn't brought up his meeting with the model, and as Claudine's preoccupation with the Medusa project grew, his need to come clean diminished proportionately.

A day or two after they'd arrived in France, they found themselves standing in front of the giant shipwreck. More than twenty feet wide, the painting dominated the wall on which it was hung. The turbulence of action made Moss dizzy, even though he'd studied the painting in graduate school. Seen in real life, the actual painting was hugely impressive. The torment and agony of the castaways, huddled on the battered raft. Their despair contrasted with a glimmer of hope depicted in the upper right-hand quadrant, where a lookout spotted the rescue ship, Argos, on the distant horizon.

After minutes lost in thought, Moss blurted, "That's some shit."

Claudine nudged up against the velvet rope meant to keep viewers at bay. "You said it, buster. Sloane said I'm going to pose for the figure in the lower left." She tilted her chin toward the nearly naked corpse being wrestled out of the sea.

Taking a deep breath, Moss studied the larger-than-life-sized figure sprawled at a diagonal stretching from the lower left toward the upper right. "That's an interesting pose. Nude?"

Claudine nodded. "No big deal. You've seen me without clothes plenty of times."

Moss remained silent. The full-frontal nudity required to emulate the figure in the composition would likely make Claudine famous. Sloane Ellis was important. Her work ended up in museums as a matter of course. It was art, after all. He wondered whether he would be allowed entry into the process—if there was a process. He guessed an all-female photo shoot might not welcome his presence. Too bad, because Sloane Ellis's concept echoed his Gauguin-like portrait of Claudine. He suspected comparisons between the two works wouldn't flatter his sophomoric attempt. More and more, events seemed to shunt him and his quest to the periphery.

He became conscious of the monumental scale of Gericault's masterpiece looming over them. The artist had been in his early twenties when he painted it. Moss was closing in on fifty. He was too late. A sour taste welled up from his stomach.

Moving quietly to the center of the salon, Moss found a bench and took a seat—turning partly away from the big painting. Claudine remained transfixed. To Moss, she appeared to be studying the painted figure lying half on and half off the timbers at the rear of the raft. He contented himself in studying her. With her snakelet dreadlocks bound in a new scarf and wearing a tweed jacket over her Levi's and boots, she looked like a native Parisian, in a fashion model sort of way. Despite it being her first time in France, she belonged. Through his uneasiness, he tried to feel happy for her.

• • •

Sloane Ellis's atelier was located a few blocks south and west of Necker Hospital, in the Fifteenth Arrondissement. A nondescript commercial building found only after a dozen wrong turns, it held little promise when viewed from the outside. The large carriageway entrance was barred by a well-battered metal gate. They pressed all the buttons on a worn keypad and were buzzed through into a raddled courtyard littered with bicycle parts, rundown wicker furniture, and high stacks of wooden pallets. Claudine checked notes taken during a telephone call to Sloane and led Moss to a timber staircase coated in flaking green paint.

"She's on the top floor," she said, gazing up at the four-story structure.

"Of course." Moss took a deep breath, and they started their climb. The sound of hammering drifted down from an open window. The stairway smelled of urine.

The photographer's studio was a revelation—a large open space that reached up to the rafters of the gabled seventeenth-century building. Jutting from three of the walls, high above their heads, ran a curved wooden balcony spanning three-quarters of the room. Studying the configuration, Moss concluded that he was seeing the remnants of a running track, like what you might find in an ancient college gymnasium. Clearly the building had been repurposed numerous times. At some point the space had been divided into two. A tall extension ladder was propped on one railing, indicating that the original access stairway had been lost in the remodeling process. Ranked along the balcony at regular intervals were large klieg lights directed down toward a jumble of lumber in the center of the floor.

In that area, several women in coveralls hammered and sawed, rigged ropes and plaster-stiffened sails, marked off stations on the concrete floor with masking tape. On one whitewashed wall was a schematic drawn on brown butcher's paper detailing the components of the raft. Moss observed their progress with only minor interest. Hammering and such was not his forte. Opposite, Sloane Ellis stood in rapt conversation with two other women. Everyone, including the photographer, was dressed in work clothes. The sporadic din of construction echoed off the walls.

When she recognized Claudine, Sloane Ellis broke away and made her way across a tangle of electrical cables toward them. Claudine briefly embraced the other woman in a quick hug-and-kiss. Moss waited patiently for his turn at greeting, but it never came. Instead, he was left twiddling his thumbs while the two women talked. After what seemed like an interminable time, Claudine motioned him over and introduced him to the photographer.

"I've blown a fuse in one of the kliegs. How are you with electrical stuff?" were the first words from the famous artist's mouth.

Moss gave her a blank look so uncomprehending that she burst out laughing.

"Never mind," she said. "I know your name from when I lived in Detroit. Welcome to the circus." She waved her arm expansively. "We're going to be ready for mock-up shots in a day or two, if I can find an electrical contractor in Paris that is willing to do some work. I'll need Claudine starting tomorrow for a couple of hours."

Moss nodded. "Okay." While the two women walked around the circumference of the raft. Moss ambled around the studio. A door to the darkroom was emblazoned with a hand-scrawled sign—Keep Out!!! Another door led to what he took to be a dressing room. Workers hammered and heaved, and a blue haze of cigarette smoke clouded the air, filtering light from a skylight far overhead. Underneath the hubbub, he felt the crackling current of art being birthed.

After a lengthy discussion with the photographer, Claudine ambled over to where he was standing. "Sloane has decided she needs me for the afternoon," she said. "Can you make it back to the hotel alone?"

He gave her an ironic look. "I'll try." She was the Paris neophyte, not him.

She caught him off guard by bestowing a kiss to his cheek, then she returned to her conversation with Sloane.

Smarting from his summary dismissal, Moss retreated down the long flights of stairs and made his way through the courtyard and into the street. In that neighborhood, taxis were few and far between. He was forced to walk a good distance before one deigned to stop for him.

42

Back at the hotel, Moss found an overnight post waiting for him at the front desk. The return address on the large envelope was Fairchild Moss Gallery, Birmingham, Michigan. When he opened it in the room, he discovered that it contained a rather slim stack of papers held together by a large, black clip. The cover sheet was a handwritten note from Kaye.

> *Hello Sweetie! I hope you and Claudine are enjoying your trip.*
>
> *All well here in the Midwest.*
>
> *Kisses,*
> *Kaye*

Something about the packet didn't sit right with Moss. Kaye knew better than to bother him when he was out of town. She could manage his affairs perfectly well without him. He was expendable. He liked it that way. Ordering a baguette and a bottle of wine from room service, he flipped through the pages Kaye had sent. On the first two pages was a list of artists applying for representation—he was pleased to note some well-known names that had previously shunned him. Several were already represented in New York and Chicago galleries, and their applications meant his gallery was going strong. Beneath the list of applications was a three-page roster of recent sales. The balance sheet looked good—better than good, really.

He noted several midsize Gerome Nahni sculptures had made the list. He smiled, secretly pleased for the gawky revenant. If anyone needed the reassurance of money, it was Nahni. An entry farther down the list caught his eye. Two small landscapes by Norris Bainbridge had been sold to Tice Enterprises. That made him pause. Those two paintings were certainly good pieces, but their relatively small scale placed them beneath Boo Tice's notice. The auto-parts tycoon liked big.

Moss's puzzlement increased as he scanned the rest of the list. At the bottom of the last page was a sale to Tice Enterprises marked with an asterisk. Moss squinted at the entry. The title of the painting was *Untitled Portrait of a Woman*. The price listed was larger than the rest. Moss had to sit down. The painting could only be the portrait of Claudine he'd painted up at the cottage. Tice had purchased it for an impressive sum. Whistling the chorus from "Matilda" under his breath, he scanned the list again. Yes, there it was. It was typical of Kaye to have said nothing in her letter. It was considered bad form to make much of a to-do about sales—they were what was expected of the gallery. But this was different. Before he'd left, they had intentionally overpriced the work, never expecting it to sell. Neither he nor Kaye had taken Boo Tice into account.

After the rush of gratification passed, the letdown ensued. Why would the businessman spend that kind of money on the painting of a failure—an amateur? He and Claudine both liked the piece when it was finished, but it was understood—at least by him—as a one-off. He was too old to start a new career. Wasn't he? Too old, too fat, too lazy? He'd hesitated even hanging the work in his gallery. How would Claudine feel? Would she be pleased?

Opening the window, he stared out at the buildings across the street. This unexpected news was disorienting. He thought he should write an aerogram to Kaye but didn't know what to say. Part of him felt twenty years old again. Another part was suspicious of Tice's motives. Was it a ploy to soften Moss's resolve to hold on to the Bainbridge? Here it was nearing the middle of September. Somehow the sale of Claudine's portrait made finding the model more pressing, not less.

He glanced at the clock on the mantel. There was still time. With a glass of wine and a cigarette in hand, he pored over his city map looking for the address he'd found for Alexis Dufy. Eventually he located a street that matched his search, huddled in the shadow of Sacre-Coeur Basilica in the Montmartre district. Considerably farther from the hotel than he had hoped, nonetheless he decided to do a reconnaissance that very day.

Leaving his bottle half finished, he hailed a cab outside the hotel and spent most of the half-hour drive formulating a plan. Moss found himself in a neighborhood of narrow cobbled lanes and undistinguished four- and five-story buildings of stucco or yellow sandstone construction. The lower stories of most were occupied by brightly painted shops and cafés so similar in size and ornament that Moss quickly lost track of where he was.

The building he sought was in a narrow alley off the Rue Andre Barsacq. A plaque near the doorway indicated that Alexis Dufy's atelier was located on the third floor. Unsure of his welcome, he walked around the corner and found a bar with tables outside. From his seat, he could observe any comings or goings without being noticed himself. From this vantage, he hoped to spy the model en route to her assignment. After ordering a double Chartreuse and a fresh pack of Gitanes, he settled down for a civilized stakeout.

An hour passed, and he realized his vigil might take longer than he hoped. There was plenty of automobile and pedestrian traffic on the Rue Andre Barsacq, but little action going in or out of the alley. Ordering a second Chartreuse and an espresso, he contented himself to drink and smoke the afternoon away.

It didn't take long for his thoughts to turn to Claudine. He felt her absence. The new project was exciting, but it was sure to take her away for long periods of time. He hadn't expected Paris to turn out this way. He recalled her initial enthusiasm for the trip—for joining his quest. A mission on his own wasn't appealing.

Finally, he summoned the courage to ring the bell for Alexis Dufy's studio. The loudness of the buzzing startled him back into rationality, and he fled back to his perch at the café. What could he say? Would Seren be there at all? Minutes passed. Admitting defeat, Moss hailed a passing cab to the hotel.

Claudine was in their room when he arrived. Clearly pleased by what had transpired with Sloane Ellis, she bubbled away, outlining the plans for the photo shoot, detailing the nuances of the composition, and rattling off the names of the other models who were also scheduled for the session.

"How about you? What did you do with your afternoon?"

"Not much. Went for a stroll," he said with as much nonchalance as he could muster. "Bought some Gitanes."

"Blonde?"

"No, *Brunes*. They have quite a kick." He plopped down into the confines of an armchair. "How did you like Sloane Ellis?"

"She an interesting woman, Sloane. Intense." She wandered over to the fireplace and ran her fingers over the old stonework. "She has lots of ideas for her book."

He detected something new in her voice, as if she were holding something back. Moss tried to keep focus. "Oh?"

"I told her about the painting you did up north in Michigan, and about the Manolete photograph you found. It sparked an idea. Said she might steal the concept. She's made a career doing art about art." She examined the Gitanes package, removed one slim yellow cylinder, and lit it.

He was pleased that Claudine had mentioned his painting—their painting—to the photographer. They'd never talked about it after it was hung in the gallery. Other things had gotten in the way. Now that she'd acknowledged its making and its existence, he felt validated somehow. The impulse to tell her about his afternoon stakeout evaporated.

"Kaye wrote."

"Oh? What's up?" She sat on the arm of his chair and passed him the cigarette.

"Boo Tice purchased our painting. Your portrait." There was no other way than to blurt it out. He was still digesting his own feelings.

"Wow!" Claudine turned toward him. Her eyes wide. "Kaye sold it?"

"Just like that."

"Oh my God," she sputtered. "I guess that's good?" She stood and paced to the windows and back. "With everything else going on, I'd forgotten you'd hung it in the gallery."

Moss said nothing. Claudine's expression told him she echoed his own ambivalence. This unexpected development seemed fraught with contradictions. No decent artist desired to collect his own work, yet this sale felt like a loss. The painting was as much her creation as his—maybe more so. He had been a reluctant tool, acting at her urging. In hindsight, he saw the portrait as something like a devotional icon. Without Claudine's belief, it simply wouldn't have come into being.

"Are you happy?" she said. "About the sale?"

"I don't know. It hasn't sunk in quite yet." Moss was honest.

"Me neither," she said. "Somehow, I wish somebody other than Boo had bought the painting. I don't trust him." She lit another cigarette. Kicking off her boots, she gave him a long look. "I'm going to have to digest this piece of information."

"I'll call Kaye in the morning. Get the details." He had already decided that the artist's portion of the commission should go to Claudine. The gallery—his gallery—would keep its half. That's the way it worked. He guessed the money would make a difference to her once they'd returned to the states. He wondered where Tice would hang the twelve-foot-wide painting.

She sat in the chair opposite his and curled her legs under her. "We should celebrate," she said, her voice sounding anything but celebratory.

"Maybe tomorrow night. I'll ask the concierge to reserve a table somewhere nice."

She shook her head. "Let's just go to Louise. It's easy to talk there. Sloane wants me to come over tomorrow around eleven o'clock. I should be done by dinnertime."

"Is she about to shoot already?"

"No, it's just preparatory stuff. Framing the shot, lighting details. Most of the other models will be there."

They sat and smoked. Claudine poured a glass of wine. Eventually Moss's thoughts strayed back to the Rue Andre Barsacq and his quest to find the model, Seren.

43

The next morning, both Moss and Claudine left the hotel shortly after ten o'clock, taking different directions. Claudine headed south, while Moss found a taxi to take him back to his stakeout location in Montmartre.

Instead of returning to the café on Rue Andre Barsacq, Moss directed the driver to drop in at Place Emilie Goudeau, the square across the lane from Bateau-Lavoir, site of the historic building that once housed a pantheon of famous artists from early in the century. Picasso, Modigliani, Matisse, Braque, Derain, and more were connected to the studios that stood on that site until a fire destroyed it in 1970. For Moss, it was a pilgrimage of sorts.

When he arrived at the tiny square, construction was in progress on a replacement structure. He found a seat on a bench near the fountain and mulled over recent events. Before they left the hotel, he had placed a call to Kaye, reaching her at home. The long-distance telephone line was full of static, and there were times he could barely make out a voice. He instructed her to wire a check for Claudine for the big painting and send it to their hotel in Paris. He was able to hear Kaye's acknowledgment through the cracking reception, but not much more.

After a half hour communing with the ghosts of long-dead painters, Moss headed downslope toward the bar he'd discovered the day before. The proprietress greeted him with a pleasant smile, and it wasn't long before he was ensconced at a sidewalk table with a double espresso and a Chartreuse on the rocks. A blustery breeze forced him to turn up the collar on his coat, and he was grateful for the warmth of his coffee and cigarette. He watched and waited, but there was no sign of his quarry.

As the clock approached noon, and the café began to fill up with a lunchtime crowd, he ordered a light repast of chicken and fries. The meal was good, and he tipped more than he needed to—a tariff for keeping his table. Uneventful hours passed, and Moss made a mental note to bring something to read the following day.

He wondered how Claudine was getting along with her modeling stint. Part of him wished he could be there, though it was unlikely his presence would serve any purpose. There was little advice he could offer when it came to a raft full of women.

Lighting the last of his Gitanes, Moss paused mid-match when he caught a brief glimpse of a figure with dark hair, wearing a long green overcoat, turn into the alley leading to Alexis Dufy's atelier. His heart jumped in his chest, and he fought down the urge to dash after her. He marked the time—just after two o'clock—and waited for his nerves to settle. The sight of her gave him goose-bumps. There was nothing much to see—just a flash of color, a thick mane of hair. She moved with the furtive grace of a feral cat. If she was just arriving at the studio, midafternoon, he'd need to alter his lookout schedule.

He bought another pack of Gitanes. Using gestures and a few words, he asked where he could catch a taxi. The woman pointed downslope, away from the basilica. He headed home. There was a feeling of accomplishment at seeing Seren, but he didn't yet have enough of a plan to approach her. The way she glided into the alley gave him a rush of adrenaline.

This time, it took longer to find a cab that was free. Fortunately for Moss, the walking was mostly downhill. At the terminus of Rue Ravignan, near the theater, he found a taxi that would return him to the hotel. Traffic was heavy, and the drive took the better part of forty-five minutes. He let the blur of urban architecture pass by without really seeing anything. Tickling in the back of his mind was the reminder that he'd have to tell Claudine about his movements at some point. He couldn't understand why he dreaded the moment. There was nothing to hide. After all, she had her own interests that didn't include him. He resolved to mention it at dinner that night.

Unlocking the door to their room, he was surprised to find the suite empty. She'd left no note. Evidently she was still at the photographer's studio. Or maybe on her way home. He went to the closet and took out a gray windowpane jacket to wear for dinner at the Louise. The bottle from last night was empty. He lay on the bed waiting for the click of the door announcing Claudine's return. Sounds of late-afternoon traffic drifted in from the street.

When he jerked awake, the room was dark. No Claudine. He glanced at the clock. It was after seven. It was possible her session had run long. He tried to form a picture in his mind of what the preliminaries of a photo shoot entailed. Staging, lighting, angles, he guessed. She'd reminded him that there were a lot of people involved. It was a complex composition. Not easy to organize and arrange all those naked bodies.

Claudine didn't return until ten o'clock. With no explanation, she'd showered and hopped into bed. The next morning, she had gotten dressed and left for the photography studio while he was still rubbing the sleep from his eyes. Before she departed, she'd ordered room service for him.

It was afternoon before he shrugged on his coat and set off for

Montmartre. He'd spent a good part of the morning sorting out his feelings about Boo Tice's purchase. The gesture felt like a tit for tat because Moss had declined to sell the Bainbridge landscape. A reminder from Tice about who could own whom.

• • •

He entered the bar just as the lunch crowd was thinning out. Ordering his usual, Moss waited while the proprietress brought his coffee and Chartreuse. He'd thought to bring a small notebook as well as a paperback copy of Thomas Mann's novella *Death in Venice*—ready for another long wait.

His accustomed table was waiting, the sun shone, and the domes of the great white basilica loomed high above him. He purchased a newspaper from a kiosk outside the bar. Moss had never been much for world news, and there wasn't a lot to report in the middle of September. An article commented on the illness of the new pope, John Paul I. Trouble in Rhodesia, another plane crash somewhere. Folding the paper, Moss scanned the pedestrian traffic on the street. A few shop folk scurrying around, two women pushing prams, a triad of gray-haired tourists out to see the sights. He sighed. Another long vigil seemed in the offing.

Cracking open the Thomas Mann, he soon lost himself in the familiar story—one both quaint and cautionary when viewed through eyes of the '70s. Visconti's film version had made an impression on Moss earlier in the decade, and he fancied his quest after Seren had echoes of Achenbach. Life copies art, or some such thing.

The afternoon wore on with no sign of the model. Occasionally, shadows cast by strangers would give him a start, but once again he was frustrated. Around three o'clock he grew restless. Leaving his reading materials at the table, he went inside to order a sandwich. When he returned, his quarry was sitting at his table. Dressed in a heavy tweed overcoat, she seemed even smaller than he remembered. She failed to look up until he loomed over her.

"Yer a long way from home, Mister Moss." She took a swig from his glass of Chartreuse and made a face. "Ugh."

"An acquired taste—Chartreuse." Moss sat and examined the woman he had sought for so long. Much of her face was hidden by waves of dark hair, and her coat, buttoned to the neck, effectively hid the rest. The hands that removed a pack of Newport cigarettes from her pocket were blunt fingered and looked grimy around the nails and knuckles. He waited while she lit a cigarette. The same inexplicable shyness he'd felt at the Tate filled him. He opened his mouth, but nothing came out.

"So?" She fixed him with large, pale-gray eyes.

Her features were unbalanced. The thin black line that bisected her face from hairline to chin emphasized the appearance of asymmetry. Her lips were slightly twisted. One eye was gentle, the other savage. "You're a hard woman to track down," he said, feeling the heat of her proximity.

"I come and go as I please."

He detected the undercurrent of fresh-cut earth in the air around her. It was not an unpleasant scent. Moss had to shake his head to clear his thoughts. "I'd like to ask you about Bainbridge . . . I own the big painting he did at the end." Was that what he wanted to ask? The tattooed line disoriented him. All the while, she observed him with chilly disinterest. "There was an imprint, an impression . . . of a breast."

"You've traveled all this way because you like my titties?" She laughed, canting her head at him like a bird.

"I'd like to hear what you know about the old guy."

She was silent. His sandwich was placed before him. Once the waitress left them, Seren cut Moss's sandwich in half and proceeded to eat one section. Crumbs and a smear of mustard clung to the side of her mouth.

When she'd swallowed the last bite, she said, "I knew the old man." She wiped the back of her hand across her lips. "What do you care?"

He was forced to think about it. Even to him, his motives now seemed hazy. Was it just the painting, or was it really something else? Was it the truth or was it the magic he wanted to discover?

"I want to know how that painting came about," he said, then stopped. That wasn't it. "What can you tell me about his last days?" His vision seemed off register. Rubbing his eyes with a knuckle, he was suddenly drained.

She narrowed her eyes. "Is it Bainbridge you're interested in, or is it Haller? At the Tate you talked about Haller."

"Both, I guess."

"Guessing, Mister Moss?" she tapped her finger on the table. "You've got to do better. I won't walk uphill on a guess." She lifted her chin toward the steep Montmartre streets.

"During the blizzard, were you there? With Bainbridge?"

Her eyes had shifted to dark, moonlike pupils. Maybe it was just the light changing. He didn't think so. He tried to focus on something other than her face, but there was only her coat, heavy green tweed shot through with skeins of a dozen different colors. One toggle closure was missing. She stood abruptly.

"Meet me tomorrow at the baptismal fountain in Sacre-Coeur. Same time."

His hands were shaking as he watched her depart. Her presence affected him on a molecular level. His earlier expectations went out the window—she was primal in a way he could barely comprehend. She'd said nothing, yet he felt changed.

The preposterousness of his quest came suddenly into focus.

He was a middle-aged fool searching for a key to something that probably didn't exist—chasing after a nipple. Could anything be more ridiculous? But the prospect of returning to the Midwest empty-handed seemed an admission of failure. In the shadow of the Bainbridge landscape his own irrelevance was obvious. And comical.

44

Claudine was in the room when he returned, sitting at the table by the window, drinking a glass of red wine and studying a photographic print of Gericault's painting.

Moss joined her and poured himself a glass. Barefoot, she was wearing jeans and a T-shirt. "You look nice," he said.

"Do I?" she smiled. "You haven't said in a while."

"You've been gone."

"I've spent the entire day mostly naked. I'm tired."

"Oh."

"Naked, except for socks. I get to wear socks for my pose."

"Historical accuracy is important."

"It was cold as fuck in Sloane's studio. I needed some wine just to thaw out." She stretched her arms out and yawned.

He tried to glance away, but she caught him. "You're staring at my boobs, Moss."

"Sorry." He got up and retrieved his pack of Gitanes from his coat pocket. His hand encountered another object, something cold and metallic and unfamiliar. When he withdrew his hand, he found an aluminum ring tab from a soda can. A tingle of electricity shot up his spine. He dropped it back in his pocket.

"They were cannibals, you know, those raft people," he said. "Keep an eye peeled."

"So far, no troubling signs.

"It's still early."

"So, what did you do all afternoon while I was gone?"

"I found the model."

"Seren?"

He nodded. "Who else?" he said, ignoring the fact that several models now populated his existence.

Her expression turned serious. "Was it all you hoped?"

"I'm not sure. We're meeting tomorrow at Sacre-Coeur," he said. "I want to hear about Bainbridge's last days. Would you like to come with? Your presence might change the dynamic. She's hard for me to figure out."

Her face went flat. "I'm working with Sloane all day. You go. See what you can learn."

He noticed the change in her. "What's wrong?"

"It's not easy to share a bed with a man who's obsessed with another woman."

"It isn't like that," he said.

"No," she said quietly. "If it was, I wouldn't be here."

On an impulse, Moss walked around her chair and placed his hands on her shoulders. He buried his face in the nape of her neck, breathed in the mixture of lemon and spice. His pelvis pressed against her shoulder.

She looked up at him. "This is new," she said. "Let's get into bed before it changes its mind."

45

The wide staircase leading to the entrance of Sacre-Coeur Basilica was littered with sightseers basking, taking in the view of the great city. Moss was out of breath by the time he'd reached the top. Bending over, hands on his knees, he fought for air, cursing the absence of an exercise regimen in his life.

Despite it being a weekday, the interior church was filled with tourists. Signs at the doorway recommended silence as well as a donation. Moss dropped a coin in the box and went inside. He was immediately jostled by a large group of German tourists traipsing behind a muscular woman carrying a placard.

Staring up at the image of a white-robed Jesus that dominated the altar vault, Moss noticed the abrupt change in humidity. The air of the interior was cloyed by incense and the exhalations of hundreds of pilgrims. It was a greenhouse—the atmosphere dense with CO_2. Beads of sweat broke out on his forehead, and he dabbed at his face with the square of his pocket handkerchief, wondering what sort of idiocy had prompted him to make the climb.

Bumping his way through the group of Teutons, he plopped down on the polished wood of a pew for a breather. The sunshine outside had given way to a gloomy twilight within. Votive murmurs competed with the drone of tour guides detailing the structure's history and architecture in a dozen languages. High above, under the gray arches supporting the ceiling, hypothetical angels trilled to each other as they battered their huge wings against the cage of cut stone. He was too sweaty and too out of breath to take notice. Living a life in art meant you couldn't avoid the presence of Christianity, not if you bothered with history. The church might be a scam, but for centuries it had served as the primary patron of visual art. That had to be counted as a good deed, take it or leave it.

Myriad candles lit by hopeful souls flared and sputtered in the huge space. Each day, hundreds were drawn to the white architectural confection built at the top of the hill. At least half the population of Paris hated the building, while the other half loved it. Moss was undecided. He'd been to a lot of famous churches in Europe over the years. Most had failed to move him—St. Peter's in Rome as well as Catholic cathedrals in Florence, Milan, and Siena were all okay. Notre Dame was okay. He admired the paintings inside, but religion just wasn't his thing.

To escape notice of the throng, he adopted an attitude of reverence—hands clasped in front of him, eyes closed. In a few seconds he was drifting off to sleep.

Snapping awake after a fifteen-minute nap, he resolved to do something. Making his way toward the altar, someone looped an arm through his. He knew from the scent that it was Seren. Her fingers held a cigarette—much against church rules. Without a word, she tugged him toward the baptismal font. An arc of humanity surrounded the gold, mosaic-tiled basin. Seren slipped between the bodies and pulled him along to the front. He was conscious of hard glances but was surprised at how easily she cut through the press around the sacred alcove.

Releasing her grip on his arm, she stepped up to the pedestaled basin, dipped two fingers in the holy water, and touched her forehead where the tattooed line bisected it. People in the crowd frowned. Dipping her fingers again, she hopped down and made a cross on Moss's forehead. There were angry mutterings—only the faithful could anoint with holy water. With some alacrity, he followed her to the exit. When the two burst into the sunlight, Seren was giggling like a schoolgirl.

"Are you Catholic?" Moss asked.

"Don't be daft," she said, as they headed downslope toward the village of Montmartre. "God's gone, Mister Moss. Best get used to the idea." She said with a finality suggesting she had been present when the door slammed shut.

"Why meet at Sacre-Coeur? At a church?"

"Stone angels seem to suit you. You're not the type who likes to get dirty because of girls," she said, over her shoulder. "To my way of thinking, believers are more fun to fuck with than agnostics. Besides, I thought the church might be big enough and white enough for you to find."

Lumbering behind her as best he could, Moss considered what he'd witnessed. Adolescent hijinks were the last thing he'd expected. Truth be told, he hadn't thought far enough ahead to cobble together a plan for their meet-up.

Skipping down the cobbles, the skirt of her green coat flying, she seemed less a weird-woman than a schoolgirl.

When she slowed at the entrance to a café, Moss was grateful. His heart pounded from the pace of their descent, his quads ached from walking on the cobbles, and he realized that he'd lost the initiative in his quest. Things weren't going as he'd hoped—not at all.

They took a table in the rear, away from the bustle at the bar. Soon a waiter came with a bottle of fizzy water and two glasses of red wine. Placing their drinks on the table, he spoke with Seren at a pace too fast for Moss to follow. Unable to understand a word being said, he paused to light one of his Gitanes and observe the woman he'd crossed an ocean to find.

His eyes lingered too long on the slim, black line that divided her face. She finished with the waiter and turned to him. "Am I not what you thought, Mister Moss?" She flicked the tip of a pink tongue over her upper lip—a reflexive gesture both predatory and sexual. Undoing the toggles on her coat, she pulled it open to reveal the same brown shift he'd seen at the Tate. Now that he was allowed a closer look, he thought the material might be linen—it was coarsely woven and permanently wrinkled. She had the air of a country person, but not one of this century. When she shifted in her seat, her full breasts moved freely under the garment. He noticed a dark smudge at the base of her neck. A webbing of veins visible under her skin. The mark of a thumb, maybe an old bruise, now fading.

Lifting his eyes, he was greeted with an ironic smile. "Go ahead. Look all you want. You're not the first to want a gander." She smirked. "I doubt you'll be the last."

Moss blushed. "Sorry," he said. "I didn't expect to be anointed with holy water this morning." He tried to chuckle, but it came out more like a croak. He may have been destined for something, but he was pretty sure messianic anointment wasn't it.

"Surely you didn't, but now we've joined the elect." She sipped at her wine. "Good thing for you, Cece approves of you."

"Cece?" He'd not heard that name before.

"Me sis." She gave him a long, calculating look. "She fancies you, she does. Why she likes what she likes is a mystery to me, but there you have it."

Moss could find no suitable reply. Every word or glance kept him off-balance.

She lit a Gitanes. A plume of smoke filled the space between them. "You've found me. Now what do you plan to do with me?"

"I'd like you to tell me what occurred with Bainbridge. During his last days."

"Yeah?" She regarded him coolly—like he was a specimen pinned to a board.

"If you know anything about the big landscape he finished right before he died, I'd like to hear it. For instance, were you there? In his studio during the blizzard?"

Seren set down her glass. "I was. The old man—he and me go back some long way. Used to call me his black mouse because of my hair. Why do you want to know?"

"I found an imprint that appears to be an impression of a nipple in the paint." Moss hemmed. "It didn't add up. He was a loner. It got me wondering."

Her mouth twisted. "I knew you liked my titties." One hand hefted a breast through the material of her shift. "I'll show them to you if you like. We can be done with it."

"Bainbridge painted landscapes. What need did he have for a figure model?"

Exhaling a cloud of smoke, she shrugged dismissively. "You decide, Mister Art Dealer."

Moss changed tack to Haller. The little Brit's death was too big of a coincidence. "What happened with Haller?"

"Got the only thing he ever wanted," she said, stubbing out her smoke and fixing him with an impatient look. "You were there—at the Tate. You saw. Now he'll be in all the books, immortal."

"He's dead."

"Let's eat," she said, grabbing up her utensils.

She had ordered steak frites. Moss watched as she ploughed into her food with a fury. He wondered when she'd last eaten. As she ate, she kept one wary eye on Moss, as if he might try to snatch a French fry from her plate. Between forkfuls, she puffed on her cigarette.

He picked at his food. "I'm curious, what was it like to work with Haller?"

Pausing in mid-chew, she waggled her head. "Like the rest. Maybe a little rougher. Maybe a lot rougher."

"Modeling?"

"Fucking."

Of course, that was what Haller was about. Everyone knew. But still . . . "You and he were lovers?"

At that she laughed so hard that bits of partially chewed fries flew from her lips. Once she'd composed herself, she replied, "Are you so much a lamb? Mo Haller had one love and one only—his work. The rest were props or prostitutes, nothing more."

"Were you a prop or a prostitute?"

She gave him a sly look.

Moss mulled this over. There wasn't much that surprised him. "Why bother? Why stick it out?"

"You're a fool like the others, Mister Moss. A fool if you believe I can understand myself. You've been anointed today. Let that be enough." Seren pushed back her chair. "If there's an answer to your question, you'll have to earn it. For better or worse, our threads are crossed, you and me. We'd best untangle them." Lacing her fingers together, she slowly pulled her hands apart, then pushed a lock of hair from her face and gave him a hard stare. "I'll be heading back to Michigan soon."

"Where can I find you?" Moss sputtered, chewing on a piece of chicken. She was here then gone, already rising and heading from the table. His reflexes weren't that quick.

"Ask around," she called back over her shoulder.

• • •

Moss sat in the café. After all the time and effort, he still hadn't gotten any closer to an answer. He'd found her, and she'd ditched him. Among all the other feelings was the very distinct sense that he'd been not merely jilted, but also gypped. He'd made her up.

When he finally made it back to his room, Claudine was absent. Moss lay on the bed smoking for an hour or two. He was angry with himself for staking his hopes on the model. He had failed. Maybe there were no answers other than the obvious— Bainbridge had simply slapped a lot of paint on the big landscape then died. End of story. Anything else was in Moss's head. It wasn't a quest, but rather a ruse. Art was just art; life was just life. Neither of them amounted to more than they seemed.

His funk deepening, Moss put on his jacket and went to Café Louise looking for a glass of Chartreuse. By the time Claudine tracked him down, the streetlights were burning, and Moss was having difficulty focusing on anything other than his own misery. She stood beside the table, watching him for a few beats, then sat down opposite and took a drink from his glass.

"I'm guessing from the look on your face, you found Seren?"

"After a fashion." A crumpled pack of Gitanes and an ashtray full of butts graced his table, along with a half-dozen empty glasses.

"It wasn't a success?"

"That's putting it mildly." He motioned to the waiter for another drink and one for Claudine. "She cadged a lunch and disappeared."

"You asked about Bainbridge?"

He waggled his head glumly. "She was there the night he died, that's all."

Claudine eyed him. "That's it?"

He gave Claudine a hopeless shrug. He'd fired another blank.

"What now?" Their waiter brought drinks, and they ordered a light dinner.

He hadn't considered his next step. Stay in Paris until Claudine had finished her assignment? Return to Detroit? Resuming his ordinary life seemed bleak. Even less appealing was the prospect of the upcoming Detroit winter.

He'd already used up a good portion of his life. He was on the downslope. Recalling Birdie Entwistle at his lonely table in the Scarab Club, he shivered. Oblivious to his surroundings, he rested his head in his hands. "I'm fucked."

A few seconds passed, then Claudine gave him a merciless kick under the table. "You're such a silly dweeb, Moss. Don't be a drama queen."

He raised his head and stared blankly.

"Did you honestly expect this woman to give you all her secrets over lunch? God, you're a moron. Did you even ask the right questions?"

"I don't know." Hope drained from him.

Claudine shook her head. They ate mostly in silence. Moss could sense her irritation giving way to something else. "How about you? Did your session with Sloane and the cannibals go well?"

"She knows what she's doing. Despite the chaos of dozens of models in the studio, she managed to get things together. She has plans, lots of plans."

"How so?" Moss was happy to make small talk to avoid any further discussion of his missed chance with Seren.

"When I told her about us looking at Manet's *Olympia*, she said she'd been thinking about a series of photographs substituting women for men, black people for white people, in famous paintings. She suggested I could pose as Olympia with a white woman as the maid."

"Has that been done already?" Moss wasn't pricking holes in the idea. It sounded familiar, that was all. Art repeated itself endlessly until it got things right . . . and then inevitably wrong.

"What hasn't?" Claudine gave him an ironic look.

"Does she have an idea of when she wants to do this project?"

"She has plans for a whole book, coffee-table size. It might take a year or two. She indicated we could do my part right after the shoot of the *Medusa*."

Moss calculated. "Stay in Paris? For how long?"

"It's just a thought," she said. "Don't fret over it."

Moss swallowed hard. The thought of another couple of weeks in Paris didn't seem unpalatable, but if Seren was headed to Detroit, he had to follow. The image of a pink tongue licking her lip lingered in his brain.

46

When they entered their hotel, the clerk at the front desk hailed them. He handed Claudine an envelope bearing the imprint of Western Union. Up in the room, she tore open the envelope.

"What the fuck, Moss?"

He guessed it was the wire from Kaye. The check. He was suddenly worried about her reaction. He'd intended to show his appreciation. If she read the check as a quid pro quo of some sort, he was truly sunk.

What Claudine had accomplished during those few days up north was invaluable. She had single-handedly turned him around. Or, at the very least, redirected his life. Those moments in the shed had rekindled a hope he'd long thought extinguished. She was the fearless one, not him. Money from the painting would serve as a small thank you—at least that was his intent. Now, observing her expression as she stared at the slip of green paper, he wasn't so sure she was getting his drift.

She widened her eyes. "Is this from selling the painting?"

"Yes, of course," he said as quickly as he could get the words out of his mouth.

"For modeling?" She looked at him incredulously. "For taking off my clothes?"

They were at a cusp. He'd better think fast. "Not just that. For everything about the painting, Claudine. It was your idea, not mine. You practically blackmailed me into trying to paint again. You did all the research, not me. You organized the pose—the composition, the hand like Holbein. Without you, the painting wouldn't exist. We're splitting it fifty-fifty." He tried to keep his voice steady but failed.

"Does this have anything at all to do with your model friend, Seren?"

"Not one single thing," he lied. His own words rang untrue—even to him. He was absolving himself for what was surely to come.

"Bullshit." She examined the dollar amount etched into the green rectangle. "What are you getting from this?"

He refrained from blurting . . . *you*. She wouldn't buy it. She knew him too well. "The gallery kept half. That's the usual deal."

"This is a lot of money."

"Not so much." He sank on the couch while she paced.

"I don't know what to think."

"Be happy," he said. "Take the money and don't second-guess it. Let's be happy for once."

"This coming from Fairchild Moss, the poster child for gloom and doom?"

• • •

Moss and Claudine had a few days of downtime before her work with the photo shoot started in earnest. He welcomed the distraction of wandering around in Paris. Claudine took the lead. On the north side of the river, they discovered a dozen cafés under the roofed colonnades at the edge of the garden of the Royal Palace. They walked along the Seine as far as the Quay d'Orsay, where they could look at Manet's *Olympia* in the flesh.

Along this bank of the river were spots where tourist boats docked. The strand was crowded with sightseers. Claudine seemed happy, and that made Moss happy. "You're in a good mood," he said.

She nodded. "Notice anything?" She gestured toward the groups of passersby.

"Nope. Not really." He looked around. "People."

"No long, hard stares," she said. "Not a one."

It took him a while to get her drift. He'd grown up in the Midwest. She had also. In a very different version. It was unusual to see a Black woman with a white man. "France is different."

"Bingo," she said. "It's like another world. A better world."

He thought about that comment for a long time. In the Musee d'Orsay, standing in front of the Manet, he'd noticed the African maid. For the first time, he understood the magnitude of what Sloan Ellis was attempting. The reversal of societal roles seemed like a small thing. It wasn't. Not to Claudine. Not to a lot of people.

They stood side by side gazing at the masterpiece for nearly half an hour. Claudine took his hand, her fingers interlaced with his. People flowed around them. The air was trancelike, heavy as it had been in Sacre-Coeur. Attendants sat stoically by the doors, periodically moving from one side of the salon to the other. Moss imagined Claudine replacing Olympia—it felt right in a revisionist kind of way. He wanted to put his hand on her bottom. He didn't.

Offhandedly he asked, "Any thoughts on portraying a model portraying a prostitute?"

"Nope. Irony."

"Irony?"

"The real model, Victorine Meurent, later became a painter. She was ambidextrous, sexually that is." She nudged him with her elbow. "Worried about me horning in on your model obsession?"

"It's too late for that, wouldn't you say?" He thought about Seren, with her strangely divided face. He'd never felt farther from home.

"Never too late." Claudine walked a little ways away. He had to force himself not to look at her too long. His eyes had followed her for years. The whole thing about attraction was a mystery in so many ways. He turned his gaze back to *Olympia* and realized the impulse to gaze was nearly the same. To distract himself he glanced around the room. Hush, high-ceilings, votive offerings, uniformed acolytes. Another temple. When you came down to it, the church and art were nearly identical, sometimes inseparable. They both had their histories, their icons, their heretics. Art was older. Older than Christianity anyway. Once, he supposed, art and religion were one and the same. Sex was a game. He thought about the Venus of Willendorf—the paleolithic limestone fertility carving. Humans had been going at it for a long time. There wasn't much of an off-ramp. Celibacy had worked for him for a while. Now what?

He wandered around the gallery, looking at labels and reading some of the text. Every so often, he glanced over to where Claudine was standing to make certain she was still there. After a while he ambled back and put a hand on her hip. She turned as if she were surprised to see him.

"That's not like you," she said. "What do you want?"

"I don't know."

"That's for sure."

"I was thinking it might be nice to see you in that pose."

She paused for a moment, longer than he would've preferred. "How about tonight?"

"Good," he said. "What about the velvet choker?"

"We'll use the small end of one of your many neckties. You won't notice the difference."

She was right about that.

• • •

Later they took a taxi to the Gustave Moreau Museum in the 9th arrondissement. This was one of Moss's favorite artists. Half of the works on display were unfinished. Somehow, he liked those the best. Looking around, Claudine said, "This is some of the kinkiest shit I've ever seen. I get that you like this guy."

There was a bistro near the museum where all the tables were painted blue. They shared a plate of antipasto and ordered rigatoni with red sauce. After looking at art, Moss was hungry for ordinary fare. They ate in silence until it was time for espresso with their wine, then he said, "Do you think Sloane Ellis would mind if I came to her studio for the final shoot? It might be fun to observe the process."

"I'll ask," Claudine said. "She's finicky about her work from what I can tell."

"She seems to like you well enough."

"So far, so good." She downed her coffee in a gulp. Her eyes were bright.

Moss paid the bill, and they searched for a taxi to take them back to the hotel. Claudine hadn't mentioned the check after her initial reticence in accepting the money. He hoped a little extra cash in hand would provide some measure of satisfaction. Part of his brain had already returned to Detroit.

That night, she kept her promise to replicate the Olympia pose for him. He instantly approved of the photographer's plan. Claudine made a phenomenal nineteenth-century courtesan. Part of him wished they had chosen Manet's positioning for his own portrait of her. Wineglass in hand, she practiced the gaze made famous by the painting. The full erotic frontality of Claudine's look was, in his mind, superior to the stare of Victorine Meurent.

The gloss of her rich, cinnamon-hued skin added another layer of sociosexual tension.

After several minutes had passed, she motioned him to her. "Let's try something."

Untying the necktie, she directed Moss to sit next to her on the bed. She blindfolded him with the strip of silk and said, "Look at me with your hands. Let your touch see me." With that, she placed both of his hands on her face and reclined. Her skin was heated, as if she'd been lying out in the afternoon sun. Working blind, Moss discovered things he had previously ignored. Fingertips traced the crescent scar.

"Do you like it?" she said, her voice disembodied, dulcet, alien.

"It's the difference between a road atlas and physical topography. One's a schema, one is an unknown country." A lot of different information was coming at him now that he was blind.

"Don't get all philosophical on me." She cuffed him lightly on the head. "Try using your tongue for something besides talking."

47

Sloane Ellis had no interest in Moss observing her photo shoot. To fill time while Claudine posed, he taxied to Montmartre and walked the steep cobble streets. Returning to the café that Seren had steered him into, he sat and read. Once or twice, he considered climbing the hill to the Basilica of Sacre-Coeur. The effort seemed too much.

He had no idea how long Claudine's *Medusa* shoot was going to last. The work stretched on and on, eating the days. Preying on his mind was the notion that Seren was likely back in the States, and he was spinning his wheels in Paris. When the weekend arrived, Sloane Ellis called for a hiatus. Moss and Claudine ventured to the Gare de Lyon and caught a train south to Aix-en-Provence for three days.

His aim was to flee the city, hers to see the countryside in the south. The train was crowded. After a short search, they found seats in a first-class carriage. The landscape changed from lush farmland to palms and scrub, dotted with steep, rocky escarpments. By the time they'd reached the old station in Aix, the temperature had risen to summertime levels. They had made no reservations. The town was full. By asking around they found room at a quaint hotel within walking distance of the railway. Hotel Le Pigonnet turned out to be a pleasant compound with extensive gravel-walked gardens and many fountains. One corner of the garden revealed a view of Mont Saint Victoire. At one time, Cezanne had painted from the exact same overlook.

For two nights they slept late, ate well at the hotel's restaurant, and walked the ancient streets of Aix. At the Deux Garcons, a restaurant habited at various times by the likes of Hemingway, Cezanne, and Zola, they sat outside and watched the parade of tourists and students on the broad sidewalk of the Cours Mirabeau.

"I think I could live here," Claudine confided. "Paris is too cloudy. The weather in this place is nice."

"Yes," he said. "Warm in winter." Looking up from the guidebook he was reading, he said, "Apparently, the Visigoths liked it here, too."

"When was that? Visigoths?"

"Fourth century AD."

"It's still nice." She watched the flow of pedestrians. "No matter what those gothic fellows thought."

"Yes."

"It could work for us. Staying here." She gave him a dreamy look. "I could tend bar somewhere. You could open an art gallery. We know how to do those things."

"We know how to do those things," he repeated, trying to picture it. A small apartment with a balcony. Potted plants. An oilcloth on the table. Coffee in the morning sun. Claudine singing to herself—happy. He a merchant again.

He returned his attention to the guidebook, wondering how he was going to find the model in Detroit. What did he want from her? He hoped she would change him in the same way she had changed Bainbridge.

• • •

Back in Paris, Moss was once more left to his own devices during the day. He walked north to the river and visited Notre Dame Cathedral, climbing timeworn stairs to the roof and strolling among the gargoyles and gutters. The view of the Seine and the city was spectacular. More and more he was planning his escape back to Detroit.

Claudine was happy in France. He was not. It was a problem.

A solution appeared when she returned to the hotel with a folio of proofs from the *Medusa* shoot. The black-and-white prints were magnificent—even Moss could see that. The centerpiece of the composition, in the foreground of everything, was Claudine, reclining as if having been dragged from the sea, socks loose around her ankles. She eclipsed all the others.

She explained that the museum prints would be forty-two inches wide by thirty-two inches high. Once framed, they would be impressive. The edges of the final image would be vignetted, dissolving into the white of the paper, providing an antique look. There would be sepia prints as well, giving an even older look. He knew he was looking at something important. It gave him a twinge. Once again, he had the feeling of being pushed to the margins.

"Do you think I should've trimmed my bush?"

"No," he said. "You look good."

Examining the image closely, he saw that several of the women in the pyramidal composition were engaging in sexual activity. In fact, the entire central portion of the raft revealed an orgy of carnality—a reference to the rumored cannibalism, he supposed. He had to take a breath. It was a surprise, but it shouldn't have been. He shot a questioning look at Claudine; she shrugged.

Finally, he said, "It's good. Anyone can see that."

"I know." She walked to the window. "Next week we're going to start planning the *Olympia* pose. Sloane has some ideas. Some of them are kind of sexy."

"Oh?"

"It's no big deal," she said. "It's art."

"All right."

They ate dinner in their room. Moss ordered two bottles of wine from a vineyard near Aix, Chateau De La Gardine. On the bottle's label was a papal crest. Despite finishing both bottles, he lay in bed listening to traffic on the street below their window. Getting up after midnight to close the window, he spent some minutes observing Claudine. One bare arm stretched from beneath her pillow, a sculptural thigh curved outside the coverlet, her snakelike hair hidden by a scarf. Her skin possessed the surface tension of a glass full to the brim—just shy of spilling over.

The vision of Claudine on the bed felt like a memory, something seen in a childhood picture book long ago. In a second, the feeling passed. He knew it was nothing more than a brain blink—when the now becomes a figment of the once. A fragment from a past life. Déjà vu. He went to the folio and withdrew the *Medusa* proof, staring at it until his eyes unfocused. The twin pyramids of intertwined flesh, Claudine stretched in the foreground, her legs slightly apart, the intimation of necrophilia—the photograph was disturbing and arousing. The flesh-and-blood person in the image was only a few feet away, sleeping in the bedroom, but this was something else. A corner of the photograph was dog-eared and smudged by careless insertion into the envelope. It was paper and gelatin. It was art. He forced himself to resist the urge to masturbate.

Moss sat with the photograph of Claudine until he was sleepy again, then he returned to bed. The next morning, he sifted through dreams from a restless night and made plans to fly back to the Midwest.

Claudine didn't seem surprised when he told her. He'd

imagined a thousand ways she might respond. If she had asked him not to go, he would have stayed. If she had complained about being deserted in a foreign land, he would have stayed. If she had told him she loved him, he definitely would have stayed. Instead, she merely nodded.

"I know this is hard for you, Moss. But the voice of reason tells me this isn't about the Bainbridge and the nipple—not anymore." Her voice was so neutral it frightened him.

Moss shrugged, not knowing what to say. Not wanting to say anything.

"You're thinking Seren will provide the same bit of magic she gave Bainbridge. Am I right?"

He had known it for a long time, but hearing her say it made it real. "I can't go back to the old me. I simply can't."

"I know," she said.

She rode to Orly Airport with him in a taxi. He hadn't expected her insight on his quest, but then he was never adept at gauging her thoughts. She remained silent for most of the drive. Once they'd arrived outside the departure terminal, she said, "When will you be back?"

"I don't know," he said.

PENTIMENTI

VI

Lake District, Summer 1978

Daisy crawls dripping from the river, long, blonde hair plastered to her skull, her robe sodden, soiled, rucked above her hips. From a seat on the grassy bank, Seren observes the young woman's exhausted features, her labored movements. Fugitive patches of red—the imprint of pebbles from the stream—are embedded in the skin of her knees. Having been submerged for so long in moving water, the painted flowers on her robe have relinquished their hold on the fabric, running in bright smears down the blue silk. The garment would have been an heirloom in any world but this.

"Daisy, naughty lass, you've ruined your robe." Seren rises to her feet.

Daisy stares at her blankly, eyes unfocused. She opens her mouth, but nothing comes out. Her bare breasts are pricked with goosebumps from the water.

Half-submerged in the slow eddies of River Derwent, Haller, dressed in his red ball gown, has rolled onto one side, is staring vacantly at the sky. His fist is clenched the neck of the whisky bottle. His lips are a shade of blue. "Who's next?" he slurs. "Either of you silly cunts up for a go?"

Seren hops down the embankment and into the turbid water. It's shallow, only reaching mid-calf. She feels the sand and grit of the riverbed through the thick callouses on her feet. A few minnows dart around her legs as she wades to where Haller lies.

He glances up when her shadow darkens his vision. "You?" He takes a swig from the bottle. Less than a third of the liquid remains.

"Who else?" she says.

With a bare foot, she rolls him onto his back. The straps of the gown have given way, and a mess of red cloth is bunched around his chest. His little potbelly looks like a pale balloon above his erection, which juts undiminished by either Daisey's efforts or the river.

Deftly, easing onto him, she straddles his midriff, knees pressing against the cage of his ribs. She removes the bottle from his grasp and feeds it into his hungry mouth. When he begins to choke, she takes it from his lips and sets it carefully in the stream. Wiping spills from his chin with a finger, she gazes down at him.

"Does this remind you of the first time, Mo? The place we met?"

He stares up at her dumbly. His eyes begin to close, but she slaps his face gently until they open again. Humming an old tune, she moves her hips to keep his attention.

"It was the beach at Brynmill Park. Grandparents snoring away in their striped beach chairs." Closing her eyes, she croons, "You were a young lad. So fresh. So hungry back then."

He tries to shift position out of the water, but she has him pinned. "Seventeen I was," he mumbles. When his teeth chatter, she feeds him another sip of whisky.

"And me younger still," she says without missing a beat. "That was a rare day. The sun shone brilliant, the waves like horses. We stayed past dark." His expression is puzzled. She can see contradictory thoughts collide. "You were the boy from uni. So careless and sure of yourself."

He sputters, drools, breath reeking of liquor. "Cecily. Cece her name. Not you." His hands, still stained with oil colors, clutch at her. "It was Cece, not you."

"No." She smiles, pressing down on his chest with both hands,

forcing the air from his lungs. "Me, always me. Me. Me. Me."

His eyes close. He drifts away. She slaps his cheeks. "Surely you remember the girl who drowned? Sunday by the sea? The sea." *More whisky sloshes down his gullet.* "Now do you see?"

His mouth goes slack. She presses her knees into his boney chest. "Shall I sing you to sleep?" *she says, but no answer comes.*

48

Speeding through a tunnel of darkness, Athena's headlights cut the gloom, illuminating the edges of the forest flanking the two-lane road. Exhausted, Moss pinched the bridge of his nose, trying to clear his vision. On the drive north, he questioned every choice that had brought him to this juncture. Even the feel of Athena's wood-trimmed steering wheel failed to allay his apprehension. They had traveled part of a day and most of a night. Now the big bridge was behind them, banks of hardwood in yellow and orange foliage giving way to expanses of white pine, fir, and larch. Whitetail deer, singly or in small groups, ambled across the highway. Slowing, he switched on the high beams. A collision would be bad for the Jaguar—much less for the innocent deer.

Moss kept his right foot ready to brake. He hated night driving. The landscape, shrouded in darkness, was no landscape at all. This time the trip to the Keweenaw hadn't elicited any fond memories from his youth. Since returning from France, nearly everything in his life had been turned upside down. His quest hadn't yielded the single thing he'd hoped for. The muse had been found, but she wasn't saying much. Once over the Houghton-Hancock bridge, Moss sighed in relief. They were almost at their destination. Their drive had tired him out. His passenger's strangeness sucked the air from the cockpit of the Jaguar.

Since returning to the States, life had been a blur. He'd

bequeathed the daily operation of the gallery entirely to Kaye. At first, she'd been reluctant, but Moss convinced her that he was no longer capable of doing it. When she finally said yes, his gratitude was so great he hugged her—a thing he'd never done before.

He was free.

He viewed the trip as a stopgap solution until he could clear his head and plot a course to the next thing. The cottage would be in hibernation mode for the winter—the thermostat set to the mid-fifties, the refrigerator emptied of perishables, the furniture shrouded with sheeting. There would be wood in the bin and wine in the pantry—enough to see them through. Old man Numennin checked on the structure twice a month. It would take little effort to get the place running again.

His passenger remained eerily quiet most of the drive. She was the common thread that linked the two dead artists—three if you counted the boy, Brice Godwin. And who knew how many others? She seemed indifferent to his attempts at conversation and disinterested in anything except the passing scenery. At the Phoenix corner, they turned onto Highway 26 and headed downslope toward the big water. At the junction with 5 Mile Point Road, Moss lit up a Chesterfield.

"I'm out of cigs," Seren said, her first utterance in miles.

He handed her his pack. She had brought only a leather shoulder bag. The cash he'd given her as an advance had been stashed between the pages of her passport—secured by a stained rubber band.

He'd gradually become accustomed to her scent. It seemed to fade in and out of his awareness. What he was unable to get used to was the tattooed line. Her face was a divided thing—two halves imperfectly rejoined. He considered the line as the night sped past his window. For some reason, he couldn't bring himself to ask her about its origins. In the dim light of Athena's cockpit, it seemed nearly invisible, yet it somehow tilted the world off-center.

"Almost there." The lake was on their right-hand side as they headed south along the shore. In what was left of the moonlight, breakers rolled in from the deep water—silvery crescents chasing each other toward the land. They were close enough to feel damp in the air and smell the inland sea.

"Jesus," he said when the hard left-hand turn caught him by surprise. He'd almost missed the entry to his own property. Athena took the incline faster than he'd intended, scraping her undercarriage on the steep gravel ramp.

He switched off the ignition, and they sat for a moment. The engine pinged. Athena had not traveled such a distance in years. The spectral whiteness of the building, the black pines hovering in the background, spelled isolation. Seren opened the door and slipped out. She dragged her satchel from behind the seat and stood waiting for Moss. Triggered by their arrival, the security lights flashed on, bathing the structure and its grounds in cold brilliance. The deck furniture had been stacked under the eaves—the place looked well and truly battened down.

Unlocking the door and flipping the light switch in the kitchen, he was relieved to see things in their accustomed order. He reset the thermostat to normal temperatures. Toggling the light switches in the living room, the Bainbridge landscape glowed like a beacon under its bank of spotlights. As he'd anticipated, his housekeeper had placed dust covers over the chairs and sofas, washed all the ashtrays, and returned his record albums to their jackets and shelved them in the proper order. The fireplace was dark and cold, and the Manolete photograph had been misplaced on a bookshelf. When he started to pull the sheeting from the couches, Seren joined him at the task. She made a neat job of folding them, making a stack near the door to the guest wing.

"I'll show you your room," he said. "Actually rooms—you can stay in any of them you like. All of them if you wish."

"One'll do." She followed him down the hallway like a shadow.

The word *gravedigger* popped into his mind from out of nowhere. Maybe it was the earthy smell she wore like a badge. He was home now, and he was not in the mood to cater to her eccentricities.

He led her to a room at the end of the hall. It was the biggest, and it was far away from his quarters. When he opened the door, she glided inside and made an orbital reconnaissance. After a quick look, she said, "Not this one."

She exited and led him down the hall to the room where Claudine had stayed. "This will do me. It smells of girl." Her lip curled, revealing one pointy incisor. Tossing her bag on the bed, she turned toward him. "What now, boss?"

"I need a drink, then some sleep. Would you care for some wine or whisky? Coffee? Tea?" he asked.

"Or me?" she said, a smirk twisting her features. When he stammered, she laughed out loud. "Whisky and a fire. It's fucking cold in here. I need to get warm."

Everything she did contradicted his expectations. After pouring a glass of Ardbeg, she'd built a fire with the few logs left in the caddy while he made himself a tall glass of Chartreuse. Soon, a warm glow emanated from beneath the copper hood. While Moss slumped on the sofa, bone-tired from the long drive, she rummaged in the pantry, locating a box of water crackers and a tin of Moroccan sardines in tomato sauce. Arranging the food on a plate, she brought it into the room and placed it in front of a drowsing Moss.

They ate in a stupor of fatigue. The fire crackled. Gradually, the room warmed. Seren sat cross-legged on a cushion across the coffee table from his place on the sofa. Tossing off one glass of Ardbeg without blinking, she poured another glassful to the rim. Licking the red sauce from her fingers, she opened a second tin and set it between them. He hadn't realized how hungry he was. They had driven a long time—smoking, stopping for coffee occasionally. She'd brought forks but ate with her fingers. Soon the sardines were gone.

Seren possessed an urchin-like quality—a street kid. Nothing like what he'd imagined. But underneath that childlike veneer lurked something savage. Sensing his gaze, she looked up. "Here we are, Mister Moss."

"Let's rest for now. We can go to work in a couple of days." He had no firm plan now that they'd arrived. His mind was scattered. Recollections of Claudine and Paris evaporated before they could coalesce. Now someone different sat across from him in his living room. He had no idea what he should do. He was no longer his true self but some alien iteration, bent on a mission so esoteric it seemed unknowable and unattainable even to its author.

"Yessir, boss man." She affected a southern drawl. "Suit yourself." Her gray eyes were pale and restless, appraising everything around her. In this light, he thought, she could've passed for twenty years old. Every now and then she turned her head and glanced at the big painting behind her.

"I know that spot." She nodded toward the canvas. "As well as you—better maybe."

"Did you first meet Bainbridge in Detroit?"

She shook her head, the black mane of hair swirling around her face. "We go way back. He was as much a farmer as a painter early on. Later, he moved to Detroit."

Moss tried to do the math but couldn't get the numbers to

work in his head. He gave her a questioning look.

She said, "Platte River. He had a farm on the north bank. There was a big garden. We grew everything." Sitting up on her knees, she leaned toward Moss. "It was our spot. That's what I thought."

His head lolled back against the cushions of the couch. He closed his eyes. "There was a garden here. Where the deck is now. Nothing grew there for very long." It was hard to resist slumber. With an effort he raised his head. She had shucked off her coat and was wearing a moss-green tunic with a deep V-shaped neckline.

After a while, she got up and wandered around the room— looking, touching. She examined the charcoal portrait done by Brice Godwin. Minutes went by. Looking over her shoulder at Moss, she said, "You have a peculiar taste in your decorations, Mister Moss. I didn't think to find me likeness hanging on your wall."

"There was some student work at WSU. That drawing was among them."

"Are my old skins so interesting to you?" Turning, she placed her hands on her hips. "Do you like this girl so much?" She tossed her mane of hair toward Brice Godwin's picture.

"I'm wondering what happened to that student. You modeled for him, as I understand."

"Keeping tabs are you?" She gave Moss a long, ambiguous look. "Wasn't me that nudged him off the ledge if that's what you're thinking. He was a pretty boy, that one."

"I'm curious."

"Curiouser and curiouser." She gave a laugh. "You'd have me pinned to a board like a butterfly, Mister Moss?"

49

In the morning, Moss walked down to the road to check the mailbox. Athena's windscreen was beaded with droplets of moisture from the night. He suffered a twinge of guilt for not putting her in the garage. He'd been distracted. He vowed to wipe her down after the trip to Houghton for groceries.

His mailbox was stuffed with fliers, but nobody had bothered to write—nobody being Claudine. Kaye had promised to forward anything interesting that arrived addressed to him at the gallery. When he'd mentioned the possibility of a letter, Kaye had given him a knowing smile and assured him that she'd do her best to keep him current. She was helping him phase out, which was something he'd asked for. Nonetheless, he bristled at the ease with which he had been relegated to back-burner status.

He twiddled the morning away with no sign of life from his guest. Around noontime, he heard water running from the guest wing. It was after two o'clock before she appeared, freshly bathed and looking for a cup of tea. Moss put the kettle on and searched the pantry for food that would serve as breakfast. There wasn't much.

Seren evinced no interest in accompanying him into town, so he made the journey on his own. The absence of a passenger allowed him to stash his purchases on the right-hand seat in addition to the tiny storage compartment that served as a trunk in the

Jaguar. For a short moment, he wished for the greater carrying capacity of the Buick Estate Wagon, but only for a moment. The pleasures of driving Athena outweighed any disadvantage in cargo capacity. The freezer at the cottage still held plenty of roasts and chops, so he limited himself to basics—milk, bread, a few vegetables, and two dozen eggs. He had no idea whether the muse would help with the cooking chores. What did muses do? At any rate, he was confident in his own ability to create a passable omelet. To this end, he purchased some gruyere cheese, tomatoes, spinach, and onions. If worse came to worst, he could always ask Mrs. Numennin to prepare a casserole—and maybe even a pie or two.

Back at the cottage, he ferried the bags of groceries into the kitchen and put everything away. His houseguest was nowhere in sight. He searched the common rooms and eventually the guest quarters to no avail. Her bag was still in a corner of the bedroom, but she had disappeared.

By the time she reappeared, it was going on dusk. Moss was sitting at the table and having his first glass of Chartreuse of the day when she came through the kitchen door carrying something wrapped in a tea cloth.

"I came upon these lovelies in your woods," she said, dumping the contents onto the table. Two dozen mushrooms rolled onto the tabletop. They all looked slightly different to Moss, who had not the slightest interest in botany. Some of the fungi were white discs, some had yellow caps, some were frilly in shape, some looked like old potatoes still covered in dirt. Moss stared uncomprehendingly at the musty pile. He gave Seren a questioning look.

"I'll do us up a supper," she said.

"We could make an omelet."

"Brilliant." There was dirt under her fingernails, a smudge of something grayish on her forehead, a yellow leaf caught in the strands of her hair. "I'll wash these treasures."

Moss brightened only a little. Nothing in her gatherings looked the least bit appetizing—a few of them more than dubious. "Omelets are good," he said. "I'm something of an expert." He extended a hand to touch one of the cleaner-looking specimens—whitish, with a large, flat cap.

She slapped his hand hard enough to make him wince. "Not that, you fool. That's the Death Angel."

Slightly offended, he said in a peeved voice, "I wasn't going to taste it."

"One touch," she tossed her hair, eyes hard. "One touch."

If it was so dangerous, he wondered, how had she managed to pluck it from its lair?

"It helps to know things, Mister Moss." She selected a medium-sized specimen with a bluish-gray cap spotted with white dots. "We'll save the Spotted Man, mister Moss. He will be useful later on. He'll show you another side to this tired old world." Choosing another from the pile, she handed him something that looked for all the world like a rock. "This we'll have with our eggs."

He hefted it warily. The thing was lighter than it looked.

"Truffle," she said. Taking a paring knife from the drawer, she halved the lump and handed it back. "Smell," she said.

He did. The rock-like object smelled like a milder version of the woman standing in front of him. Sweet, earthy, pungent. He recognized the scent as elemental, and he thought for the briefest of moments of Ari Numennin, his groundskeeper, and his pronouncements. "In my woods?" he said.

"Just off the track." She looked at him as if trying to gauge the true depth of his stupidity. "Is there anything you do know about?"

"Not much," he replied. "Maybe art."

She laughed at his glumness. "I guess we'll see about that."

"I'll open a bottle."

• • •

He watched her at the stove. When he offered to help, she laughed him off. She'd removed her coat, leaving it draped over one of the chairs in the kitchen. Underneath, she wore a different dress, a purple shift with a square neckline. Once she had come inside, she'd kicked off her slippers and remained barefoot. Moss figured her outfit was a hippie affectation. He didn't mind. In fact, it gave her a medieval peasant look that he found appealing. So far, her presence had generated zero spontaneous erections.

The supper she prepared was good, eggs sprinkled with slices of truffle and washed down with a middling red from his pantry. After they ate, she left him in the kitchen to clean up while she went into the living room. When he had completed his task, he found her staring at the Bainbridge painting, humming to herself, and swaying to some internal music. He positioned himself on one of the couches and lit a smoke.

The days were growing shorter. Soon winter would smother the cottage with a heavy blanket of snow. If someone had asked how he had gotten to this point in his life, he wouldn't be able to tell them—some unseen current. He was being drawn along, willing or not.

Looking at one side of her face then the other, he received two contrary impressions. One appeared fragile, fey, and ethereal; the other sly, earthy, and feral. When he was around her, he was forced to fight off one irrational thought after another. One minute he was afraid to be alone in the dark with her. The next instant it was all he wanted.

Seren made a fire. When the kindling took, she stood watching the flames grow. Firelight shining through the fabric of her shift outlined the shape of her body. As if sensing his thoughts, she pulled the purple garment over her head and tossed it on the sofa. He wasn't surprised to find her naked underneath.

"Is this what you wanted? Me without my clothes? It's what men like." She turned to face him, backlit by the glow from the fire. Pale skin underlaced with bluish veins. Her breasts were heavy, her nipples rose-colored. She was small in stature but clearly a grown woman. Aside from the line on her face, she bore no other decorative markings.

His eyes must've been wide, because she seemed amused by his reaction. After a few moments she sat on the sofa next to him, curling her legs underneath. "For an old man, you're too easy, Mister Moss," she said. "I'll give you some time to decide about the things you want to do with me, and what you'll give me for the privilege of doing them."

Instinctively, he reached out to touch her knee.

She brushed his hand away. "Look at me for now. I'll decide when you can touch."

50

Midmorning the following day, they walked along the shore, bundled against a cold wind that blew in from the north. Earlier, Moss had discovered a pair of battered Wellingtons stored in a box in the basement. The boots, once worn by his Gran, were a fraction too large, but they sufficed. Seren's ballet flats were not suited to the Keweenaw.

From the stairway leading down from the road, they walked northward in the direction of the hamlet of Eagle River. Moss straggled along, buttoned up in his yellow nor'easter. His companion outpaced him. In her rustic coat and gum boots, hair caught by the wind in a black mare's tail, she looked like a character from a Victorian novel. He had no idea where this woman would lead him or what would change, only that he was now committed. His life was on a trajectory—the arc of which he could not gauge.

When they reached the weathered block of concrete resting near the water, she paused to examine the rusted ring protruding from its side, tugging on it a couple of times to test its strength. "Do you tie your girls to this, Mister Moss? Keep them safe just for you? Wouldn't that suit you?" Her hands were coated with brown stains.

"That thing has been there since I was a boy," he said. "It's a fixture on this part of the shore."

"No doubt," she said, rinsing her palms in the shallow water.

Looking up at him, she said, "Perhaps you'll decide to paint me naked lashed to that ring?"

A chill passed through him. A flash of déjà vu. He knew some part of him would enjoy exactly what she described. He envisioned doing things to her. Things he could barely admit to, even to himself. Moss paced off along the edge of the waves. Spindrift dampened his slicker. A crow followed their progress along the edge of the water, alighting in the top branches of the pines. He tried to light a cigarette, but the wind blew out every match. Seren observed him with an amused look on her face. He could feel her presence in his head.

"Let's try in there," she said, nodding toward a gap in the brush. "The trees will shelter us from the wind." She pushed through the scrub, yellowing foliage barely clinging to gray branches. Twenty yards away from the beach, he was finally able to find a patch of still air. They came upon a narrow trail heading inland, and it led them to the remains of a small building—a stone foundation with a brick chimney at one end. Deeper in lay the white-enameled hull of an old ringer washer, hidden in a stand of red buckthorn. It was a part of the shore he had never visited.

Wandering, Moss found a rusted tricycle, its front wheel missing. Farther on was a large pile of paint-lorn clapboards—a remnant of someone's good intentions now long forgotten. There was no sign of an access road east toward the highway—time had erased any traces. He thought the dwelling must date from his grandmother's era. The landscape felt more deserted because of the existence of the derelict habitation. The place emanated an aura of loss. Leaning on an exposed chunk of masonry, he watched Seren poke around the roots of various trees, prodding in the dirt with a dead twig. Now and then she'd put something in the pocket of her greatcoat. More mushrooms, he guessed. After half an hour she joined him where he sat and pulled out a smoke. From her pocket she withdrew a handful of small brownish fungi, some old and withered, some bluish-gray, a few looking fresh.

"Me mam showed me these darlings. They grow all over Europe in the old woods."

Moss cast a skeptical glance at the slimy-looking things. "You're welcome to them," he said with a wave of his hand.

She blew a cloud of blue smoke into the air. "There are different ways of knowing things."

Moss had already turned toward the path to home.

Making their way back along the shore, he thought about his quest. She'd revealed nothing of value about Bainbridge, the great painting, or even Haller and his ignominious death. She appeared to have no interest in Moss at all.

It was time to press her for information. Fish or cut bait, he thought. He was weary of the whole cryptic-earth-mother schtick. In the back of his mind, he wondered if Maurice Haller had put up with her mumbo jumbo. He surmised Haller would've dunked her in a pond rather than listen to her irritating blather.

"Let's make a pot of something warm," he said, trudging up the steps to road level.

• • •

Moss still had a few packets of English tea from his shopping trip with Claudine, but Seren preferred what she had stashed in her shoulder bag. He didn't care, as long as it was hot enough to cut the chill. She fussed at the kettle for longer than he would've wished, at the end adding a fine, black powder to the brew. Eventually they had tea. After sharing the pot with his guest—liquid so bitter he had to add heaping spoons of sugar and a dollop of cream to the concoction—Moss retired to his room for a much-needed nap.

An hour later he was awake and feeling jumpy. Splashing his face with cold water, he put on his slippers and robe and headed toward the kitchen. When he got there, Seren was arranging slices of her newly acquired fungi on a baking tray. The oven was lit. He could feel the heat warming one side of the room. She greeted his appearance with a nod and went about her business of cutting the mushrooms into small pieces.

Moss sat down at the table. He didn't give a shit about mushrooms. He wanted to know what she knew. "Why did you go to Bainbridge's studio? There was a blizzard. The city was frozen solid."

Seren paused briefly, her knife poised above the final fungus. "What I wonder, Mister Moss, is why it matters to you at all." She finished her task and slid the tray into the oven.

"Something altered Bainbridge, right at the end. His painting style changed," Moss said.

"Maybe he found a thing he had lost."

He gestured toward the living room and his painting. "I don't know. It's like the old man had an epiphany of some kind. His other work is grounded in direct observation. This one isn't."

She turned to face him, leaning against the edge of the counter. "That painting, it's merely a swatch of cloth, covered in color. What good will an answer do you?"

"It's important." Of course, it was more than *an* answer he sought. It was *the* answer. The transformative ingredient that spawned greatness in art. Even as he formed the words in his head, the whole idea seemed embarrassingly naive. "I just don't see the connection . . . you and Bainbridge."

"That's an easy one. Me mam. There was a war. Afterwards, the old man was posted in England." She went to the sink and filled the kettle with water from the tap.

Minutes ticked past. Moss was silent. This was news. He tried to dredge up Bainbridge's resume from his brain. He could recall nothing about the army. "I thought you were from Wales."

"It's a small island." Seren gave him an amused look. "Is that plain enough for you?"

He digested this bit of banal news. "What about Detroit?"

"I traveled with Haller," she said. "It was chance seeing the old man." The teapot boiled, and she poured a cup.

"Just chance?"

"Only chance." Her mouth twisted in a bitter smile.

He could see she was lying about part of it. Or all of it.

Walking over to the table, she pulled a chair next to his. Their knees touching, she said, "Aren't you a bit long in the tooth to be chasing some riddle?" She placed both hands on his face. Her touch was warm and dry. She read the shape of his skull like braille.

He was tempted to remove her hands but didn't. Every word she spoke tasted like a lie.

"The old man's secret? Is that what you traveled to Europe to find?"

"I guess," he said, knowing how flimsy it sounded. "That was the idea."

"You silly man," she said.

He struggled to keep his voice steady. "It's a masterpiece," he said, glancing in the direction of the landscape.

"All this because I pressed my tit into wet paint?"

Moss considered his answer for a moment. "That was a clue."

"What will you do if you get an answer, Mister Moss?"

"I don't know. Not yet."

She thought for a second. "I can tell you a little," she said. "I can show you more. We'll peer through the eyes of the Spotted Man. Just us."

"Okay." This sounded like more witchy gibberish.

Without another word, she crawled onto his lap, agile as a monkey. Her smell filled his senses. The room spun. His initial reaction—powerful and instantaneous—was revulsion, as if something slimy from the depths of the ocean had slithered onto him. His body recoiled. He had to restrain himself to keep from pushing her off his lap.

He was unprepared for what came next. Disgust was replaced by an overwhelming lust. Contradictions flooded through him. Before he could consider what he was doing, he slipped a hand beneath the hem of her garment. The skin he encountered— smooth, cool, and female.

As soon as she felt his touch, she grabbed his wrist.

"Have a care, Mister Moss," she whispered, her face only inches from his. "One step too far, and you'll not find a way back. Be sure of what you want." Her eyes locked onto his.

He withdrew his hand, heart thumping wildly. Her eyes scoured his face. A long pause, and then the moment seemed to have passed. Resting her head on his chest, she took his hand and examined it finger by finger, lines and creases. Never a callus. She tested the tendons and held the palm against her cheek. "These are soft, but they'll do. There's more strength than I would've thought, for a man like you."

Saying nothing, he concentrated on her closeness. Her arms looped around his neck, and she settled against his chest. "You're comfy as an old pillow," she giggled. "I may fall fast asleep."

He liked the feel of her body. When she turned her face to his, the tattooed line appeared to have widened into a black meridian. Her crooked gaze pinwheeled into his. She tasted his breath, breathed him in, ran her tongue from his chin to his temple and back, licking like a cat. A chill went up his spine. He was afraid to make a wrong move, as if a thing mythic and unbridled were now perched on his lap. A sound emanated from somewhere deep in her throat—something like a purr, but not quite.

"Shall I tell you stories, Mister Moss?" She tasted his skin again, tongue rough and wet. "I know all kinds of lovely tales. Would you like to hear about the things Mo Haller liked to do to me? How I pleaded with him, and how he laughed? Would that satisfy your curiosity? Maybe you'd like to kiss my titties, the ones I pressed onto the old man's canvas? Would you like to give them a suckle? You never had a mother, did you, my poor orphan? Will you beg me for a taste?"

"Please," he gasped, not knowing what he was asking for.

She pulled his face to her breasts. "Try to imagine it," she whispered. "She held me down while they tore me apart. Can you picture it, orphan man?" She nipped at his earlobe, nuzzled the skin of his throat. "Do you like the feel of me?"

Blood rushed to his face. He struggled for breath. Around him rose cold, wet walls of fresh-dug clay. Muddy puddles of water climbed over his ankles. Far above winked a few lonely stars, lost in an empty sky.

51

Moss awoke the next morning in the grip of a fever—shuddering, clothes damp, and rank with sweat. His mouth was gummy, the taste of iron lingering on his tongue. His bedroom was dark. Outside, the gusts whipped the branches of the pines surrounding the cottage. The house was silent, with no sound other than the wind off the lake.

His memory of the night was peopled by dark outlines, half-familiar forms shifting like amoebas under a lens. A hideous figure dressed only in a pair of tattered trousers shambled in a dimly lit interior, the upper portion of its body covered with ridges of scar tissue. A smell of burnt flesh. The sound of a female voice humming tunelessly drifted in and out of earshot. Not far from where he lay came the rhythmic crashing of waves and the piteous cries of a child or a small animal.

Before his eyes opened, he knew her presence by her scent.

"I see you're back with us," she said. Her voice sounded unconcerned.

"What happened?" he moaned.

"Don't trouble yourself."

"I nearly died." He remembered the shambling creature in the dark room.

"I'd guess not."

He groaned. "It felt like it."

"Death doesn't feel like anything." She rose and went to the window. "Death is death. It shouldn't come as a surprise to anyone."

Later—he had no sense of how much time had passed—the bed moved when she slipped under the comforter. At first she was content to lie side by side. After a while she pressed her body against him, turned him onto his back, and mounted him. When he entered her, it was a perfect match. He wanted to remain inside her forever. He lasted less than a minute. Soon after, he was starved for more, but she had gone.

• • •

He had no idea how long he'd slept after she'd fucked him. The wind from earlier had died, and around was only silence. The house betrayed no movement, no sign of Seren. He'd staked all his hope on her. Now he didn't know what to think. It all felt like a terrible mistake.

In the bathroom, he washed his face and ran a brush through his hair. Looking in the mirror was a mistake. A haggard stare, dark circles under his eyes, his mustache hanging down at the corners of his mouth. Donning a fresh set of pajamas, his robe, and slippers, he ventured forth from his bedroom on unsteady legs. Most of the house was dark. A single lamp lit the living room. His guest was nowhere to be found. He poured a glass of water and wandered, looking for her. It was only on his second pass through the kitchen and pantry that he noticed the door to the basement was ajar.

Opening it partway, he peered down into the darkness. "Hello?" he called out softly. No response.

He flipped the light switch, and the first thing he saw was a white cup resting on a corner of the workbench. Gingerly he descended the precarious stairs—one hand bracing himself on the wall. The generator sat under its tarp. Three bright-red gas cans, purchased by Numennin, rested next to it. The distillate odor of gasoline overwhelmed all the other basement smells.

He found her curled in a corner. Stepping closer, he detected a miniscule rise and fall of her chest. Her body twitched spasmodically. Whatever she was dreaming, it wasn't a part of this world.

Retrieving the cup, he examined the residue of a brackish liquid in the bottom. The smell was pure tidal effluence, or a raw potato long gone over.

He fled up the stairs.

$$\bullet \ \bullet \ \bullet$$

Moss was sitting at the kitchen table when Seren emerged. She didn't say much. Nothing about her sojourn in the basement. She allowed him to fetch her a glass of whisky, which she downed like water. He made a pot of coffee, avoiding the memory of the tea she had prepared for him the night before.

Without preamble she said, "If we are going to work, we should start now." Her tone was flat, as if she had never visited him in the night.

"All right," he said. "I see no reason for you to take off your clothes."

"You're a liar," she laughed. "You're no monk, Mister Moss, not after last night. Tomorrow, we visit your shed. I want to see what you've been hiding all these years."

"Not much. All the paintings in there are old."

"No worries. We'll make a cage for your past. Strip dead flesh from the bones. Perhaps we can use what's leftover."

He didn't care for the tone of any of it. Half of what she said sounded like it came from a cheap novel. All he wanted was a straight answer—about Bainbridge, about the painting, about her secret.

He missed Claudine and frequently wondered how she was doing in Paris. Okay, he guessed. She hadn't bothered to write. He imagined her working with Sloane Ellis and felt a twinge of jealousy. He pictured her in the Paris studio, naked—dozens of other women, flesh sliding against flesh. It wasn't an image he wished to linger over.

Now here he was with no guarantee he'd be better off after learning what he could from the model. The only thing for sure was that his old life seemed gone for good. He didn't miss it much. He might end up in a Parisian apartment with Claudine—that was her dream. Lately her dreams seemed preferable to his own.

All evidence so far suggested his quest would fizzle out.

Humming "Waltzing Matilda" under his breath, he fumbled with an open pack of Chesterfields. The last remaining cigarette was bent at an angle. He straightened it and lit it with a match.

Moss looked up and found Seren's eyes on him. "You're an odd duck." She spread her arms wide, encompassing her surroundings. "You and all this, your fancy car. Why not leave well enough alone? Most people in your place would be content."

"Contentment," he said, "may not be all it's cracked up to be."

She gave a dismissive shrug. "If you say."

"I saw you in the basement." He returned her stare.

She remained silent for an uncomfortable minute. When she answered, her voice was light and playful. "I'll give you a demonstration, if that's what you wish, Mister Moss. We'll take a wander to places you've never guessed at. But first, you'll need to earn it."

"How do I do that?"

"We'll start in the shed, tomorrow," she said, not answering his question. "For now, I'm starving."

She had thawed a chunk of beef from the freezer, and they set about making a stew using the vegetables he'd purchased in

Houghton. She worked without any wasted motion. He did his best to assist, but she was clearly in control of the process. Soon the kitchen was filled with the smell of browning meat.

Moss brought out a couple of bottles of red wine from the pantry, and for a few hours life in the cottage felt almost normal. Lulled by the smell of cooking, he let himself relax. She was a force like the tide. There was nothing he could do but be swept along.

When the stew was ready, they ate in silence. She consumed twice what he was able to without ever seeming to get full. The absence of talk allowed Moss to examine his thoughts. He was close to a decision to pack her up and drive back to Detroit. Bringing this strange woman to the cottage had been a mistake. She wasn't about to spill the beans about Bainbridge, about anything.

Pushing back from the table, he said, "What part of Wales did you say you were from?" His voice was laden with skepticism.

"I didn't say." She kept chewing.

"But you *are* from Wales? Is that at least true?"

"Near Cemaes, on the northern coast. Not far from Mouse Island." She forked a piece of potato dripping with brown gravy into her mouth. "Have you been?"

"No," he said, shaking his head. "That's a long way from Detroit."

She sent him the blankest of looks. "Where I was born has little to do with anything."

"Did you sleep with Bainbridge? Was that it?" A random shot.

She laughed. "You're daft. He wasn't like that. He called me his *black mouse*." She set down her fork and wiped her mouth with a napkin. "He had *vision*, Mister Moss. That's the thing you lack— for all your money. Art is an old game, and you're new to the table. Best not forget that fact."

Moss was silent. The fondness in Seren's tone when she spoke of Bainbridge made him doubt she had caused his death. The painter was old. That was that. Maybe Kaye had been right. Maybe the old fellow just got lucky with the big painting. Still, Moss had a hunch this woman had something to do with it.

She stood up so suddenly it startled him. "Why don't you wait for me in the other room? I'll join you in a few minutes. We'll look at that painting you love so much."

He couldn't think of a reason to object.

Alone for a half hour in the living room, his mind wandered between the Manolete photograph, the recollection of Paris, and the Bainbridge painting. The image that kept floating up in his head was that of a Minotaur. It came from nowhere. There was no logic to the emergence of that archetype in his consciousness. It must be sourced in the deepest reaches of his brain. Perhaps its origin lay in the configuration of Manolete and the bull, somehow annealed into one creature.

Seren entered the living room carrying a cup of steaming liquid. "Drink this," she said, holding out the mug.

Moss sniffed the contents and recoiled. The smell was the same as what he'd smelled earlier in the cellar—rot. This time he detected a new acridity that singed his nostrils. His instincts told him to run. "I'm not tasting that."

She stepped closer. "You will if you want to learn about your painting, Mister Moss. You need a touch of the Spotted Man."

What choice did he have? If he wanted answers, it was part of the deal. Reluctantly, he took the mug. "What's in it?"

"A brew. Mostly things I find," she said, cocking her head to the side. "And one or two other things."

"It looks like poison, and it smells like sewage."

Letting out an exasperated sigh, she took the cup from his hands, raised it to her lips, and took a swallow, and then another.

Despite the noxious smell, she never winced. "See. No harm," she said, offering the cup to him again.

He was far from medical help if it came to that.

She stood watching. No expression marked her features.

He'd come a long way for this. The Bainbridge quest was all he had left. With a fateful exhalation, Moss drained the container. The stench was horrible, and the taste worse. He gagged and gagged again. His stomach recoiled, bile filling his mouth. Struggling to keep the potion down, he stumbled to the couch.

Seren sat beside him. "The taste is foul, I'll grant you that, but you'll forget the taste in a moment or two."

"Foul is too weak a term." The potion had coated his mouth with grit. The flavor of decaying earth—a freshly dug grave—crowded out his other senses.

Minutes dragged on. "What now?" he asked.

"Patience."

His gut grumbled. He shivered. The room turned arctic cold. Goose bumps rose on his skin. "Good Christ," he said. "It's freezing in here." He ground his teeth, jaw muscles like walnuts under his skin.

Seren stubbed out her cigarette and went to the fireplace. "Never mind. I'll light a fire to keep you warm."

Waves of chills started at the base of his spine and raced to his scalp. Fugitive light pulsed from the wall fixtures in sync with the frantic beating of his heart. His eyes ached, his vision fading in and out, tunneling down to blackness broken only by flashes of lightning. "Help me."

"Indeed I will, Mister Moss." Flames flickered in the copper-hooded hearth. She fed in more wood until the room was bathed in yellow light. Satisfied with her blaze, she joined him on the couch, facing him. Her thick, black mane coiled around her shoulders.

The caldron of his gut tamed a fraction. His mind became restless, agitated. It was impossible to sit still. He rose and paced to the fireplace, catching sight of the charcoal portrait by the dead boy in Detroit. Moss peered at the sketch as if its network of contour lines were a map pointing toward someplace far from home.

"The line. You never told me about the line."

She yawned a deep yawn. "A memento."

"Memento of what?"

"The other half—my sister."

"A twin?"

"Hmmm." Gliding silently across the carpet, she joined him, looking at the portrait. "Two apples from one seed, we are." Taking him by the wrist, she led him back to the sofa. "Cecily was what me mam called her—Cece to me. Gone, but not forgotten." She giggled to herself. A glimmering halo rippled, cloaking her in living light. A pink and gold aura undulated in waves of color.

His hands shook. "Your sister. What happened to her?"

Brushing a curl away from her face, the tattooed line expanded and contracted like a pulse. "Stolen from me."

"She died?"

"Aye. Drowned in shallow water. Two bodies—now only one remains."

"Cecily?" he said, trying to get a grip on himself. He blinked. Seren was engulfed in radiance.

"The drink I gave you will help. A kind of sharing. You for me—me for her. All for the Spotted Man."

"A drug?" Foggy as he was feeling, his suspicions bubbled up to the surface.

"Nothing so easy," she said. "Don't ask for an explanation. You're a bigger fool than you look if you think any of this comes cheap."

"You poisoned me?"

"Hush!" she hissed.

Moving close, she took his face in her hands. She peered into his eyes, their noses almost touching. He felt his moorings give way, pieces of memory breaking off and being bled out of him. Images of his early work, saturated with all his youthful hope, ripped loose. She was emptying him, and he had no way of stopping her. He felt his brain being scourged of all its contents.

Bit by bit the room turned granular and dissolved. Then it all faded to black.

When he was able to open his eyes, Moss found himself lying on rough cement. Drafts of frigid air seeped in through the window frames and swirled around the high-ceilinged loft. Twelve inches of freshly fallen snow had built up on the ledge outside. Along the walls were stacks of canvases. A jumble of plastic milk crates, rags, and twisted hulls of used-up paint tubes littered the floor. Not far away, a tall wooden easel stood, bearing a large canvas with an unfinished winter scene. He recognized the pine forest and the curve of the brown, ice-rimmed river. Above the tree line was a woman's face surrounded by incandescent, red cloud formations. It was a portrait of Seren hovering over elements of landscape. The line bisecting her face was unmistakable. In the painting, the tattoo took the form of a broad stripe, separating two slightly incongruent sets of features.

Moss pushed himself up to a sitting position and looked around. Off to his right was the old painter, slumped in a chair. Seren crouched at his feet, wearing her long, green greatcoat, her dark mane falling past her waist. Puddles of meltwater marked the trail of her bare feet. Moss rubbed his eyes, the overhead lights faded, and the room turned dim as a cave. His focus wavered in and out, making it hard to be sure of what he was seeing and what was a mirage.

The old man's lips moved, but there was no sound. The girl

rested her head on Bainbridge's knees. He stroked her hair from time to time. Eventually, both figures stood and went to the canvas. The painter methodically scraped away the paint using a broad palette knife, wiping the residue on a turpentine rag. When two-thirds of the canvas had been flayed clean, only the barest bones of the original red portrait were left. Here and there, Moss could still make out the trace of a contour line, or the blush of color hovering just above the tops of the trees. Other than those remnants, the model's face had all but disappeared.

Shrugging off her coat, her body was naked under the green plaid. She rifled among the boxes of paint and extracted a dozen metal tubes. Squeezing mounds of yellow and white paint onto a glass palette resting on a tabouret, she emptied them and tossed the husks on the floor. The old man fumbled for a large brush, but it slipped from his grasp. In anger, he kicked an open can of solvent aside and reached for a brush to replace the one he'd dropped. Clumsily taping the second brush into his clawed hand, he spread great, viscous strokes of white and yellow onto the canvas.

Moss watched in fascination as more layers of paint were built up in creamy, opalescent swirls. When the old fellow faltered, Seren took the brush and added more paint until a thick, wet impasto covered the upper portion of the picture-plane. She worked in a frenzy, squeezing great coils of color onto her hands and smearing it across the surface. Soon, Bainbridge collapsed into his chair, head sagging onto his chest. The girl continued to add more paint. Finally, satisfied, she embraced the canvas, imprinting the top portion of her body into the wet paint. When she turned, her breasts were coated with a brilliant, sunflower yellow. Flames sprang from the studio's floor planks, climbing up the walls, engulfing the canvas.

Moss squeezed his eyes shut against the glare.

Around him stirred the past, like a thing disturbed by wind so vagrant and unrepentant its source was unknowable. What he saw was not *his* past, and not wholly *hers*, but a communion shared in a mystic landscape. And the past was not solely past, but reality revised and reworked over again on time's slow wheel.

He was dying—surrounded by impenetrable dark and silence. The cold of deep space. Clinging to his departing senses, he willed them back into his body. Slowly, feeling sprang alive in his limbs. Agonizingly, he recovered his vision. The scene from the studio faded. In its place, a broad shingle beach swept by a strong wind. Grains of sand blew against his skin, into his eyes. He found himself in the lea of a sand dune, covered in sea grass. Beyond, blue ocean stretching to the horizon. Gulls floated on invisible currents.

He was on his hands and knees in a shallow tidal pool. Beneath the surface, an unseen creature struggled in his grip, writhing desperately to escape. The water was too murky for him to guess what sort of thing he wrestled with. It thrashed about with frenetic energy, trying to escape.

Instinct told him his only hope was to hold it under. Everything depended on refusing to let go. Minutes passed. Finally, he was able to get a knee on it, using all his weight to keep the thing submerged. Volleys of air bubbles rose in the brown water. Gradually, he felt the manic power wane.

The pool calmed. He eased his hold. Long strands of dark hair floated up to the surface, followed by the head of a black bull, horns curved and sharp. The beast's head grew from the pale torso of a child dressed in a bathing costume. Moss recoiled in horror. Before his eyes the face of the animal transformed into that of a young girl, delicate features haloed by heavy black hair. Relinquishing his hold, the dead child submerged into the murk.

From somewhere out at sea came the strains of "Waltzing Matilda."

52

Moss awoke to the mother of all hangovers. His head and joints ached so desperately all he could do was curl into a ball of misery and wait for the pain to subside. His sinuses burned as if he had inhaled acid fumes. Finally able to crack an eye, he discovered he was back in his own living room, lying on the Turkish rug. The house was dark, and the fire in the fireplace had died. The smell of stale smoke lingered in the air.

He covered his head with his hands, hoping that would ease the jolts of pain that arced through his brain. Whatever the witch had given him, he was sure it was some sort of poison. Not what he'd expected. His guts felt raw. Helplessly, he fell back into a deep and tortured sleep.

When he woke next, daylight was streaming in through the glass walls, and his constitution seemed improved. He managed to make it into the master suite for a shower and his pajamas and robe. As far as he could tell, he was alone in the house.

By midafternoon Moss was starting to feel better, but he couldn't shake the feeling that what he had experienced was far more than a dream. The fall sunshine had warmed the deck to a point where he felt inclined to sit in the fresh air. He hadn't been outside very long when the white van of Ari Numennin appeared on the gravel drive. Moss groaned at the prospect of dealing with the Finn. Unfortunately, there was nowhere to hide. Besides, he had a task for the old man—a job Moss couldn't manage on his own.

"Checking in, Mister Moss. I see you're getting a late start to the day." The caretaker eyed Moss's getup. "Leena sent me over with a pot of soup."

Moss tried to lighten his voice. His stomach rebelled at the thought of food. "Thanks, Numennin, and thank your wife. Really, you're too kind."

Rocking back on his heels, Numennin said, "No bother. I thought I'd see if there was anything you needed. It's not usual to find you north this time of year."

"Special project. I may be at the cottage for some time." Moss tightened the belt on his robe. "I was thinking it might be smart to make sure the heaters in the shed are in working order."

"You're staying for a while?"

"I may," Moss said. He silently prayed Seren wouldn't appear in the doorway—absent her clothing or riding a broomstick. Moss's credibility was never high in this neck of the woods at the best of times.

Numennin set the soup crock on the deck and made a gesture to depart. "Those heaters are showing their age. I may need to replace a few parts. I'll tackle the job tomorrow if it's all the same to you, Mister Moss."

Moss nodded. He wished the old guy would leave.

Still the Finn lingered.

"Was there anything else, Numennin?"

"There's one thing."

"Oh?"

"Willis Lahti said he saw a person in your outback the other day." Numennin mentioned a neighbor from down the road whose property joined Moss's on the south side. "Didn't get a look. Too far off."

"Hunters?"

"Could be," Numennin said. "A visitor. I thought you'd want to know."

"All right. I'll keep a lookout."

"Do that, Mister Moss. I'll be by with a spare coil for the heaters in the morning." And with that the caretaker retreated to his van without a rearward look.

Seren failed to appear that night. Moss was grateful to be alone; he needed to think about what had happened after he drank the potion.

The caretaker arrived early the next morning and spent an hour or two in the shed. When he had finished the job, the old Finn knocked on the door to inform Moss all was up and running. If the weather turned colder, the shed would be habitable—at least until winter set in.

Seren was nowhere to be found. He checked the basement several times, making sure she wasn't playing Dracula down there. The place was empty. Her shoulder bag was gone from the guest wing, but her few toiletries were still in the bathroom. Ultimately, he decided he'd just have to wait. If she was gone, then she was gone.

His quest had hit a dead end.

Worst, there'd been no word from Claudine in Paris. That could mean she was too involved in the photography project to take time to write, or that there was nothing to say. She had found her dream, and his had come up dry. Things like that happened. He couldn't blame her for not wanting to return to Detroit. She'd been very clear about how she felt about the city. Why not find a new life in France? He wondered if that life would include Sloane Ellis in place of himself. He missed her mightily.

The more he thought about it, the glummer he felt.

• • •

In the late afternoon, long after Numennin had done his work, Seren reappeared. He found her sitting at the kitchen table with a cup of tea in front of her. She didn't seem eager to explain her whereabouts, and Moss was fed up. He was ready to drive back to Detroit the following day, his quest dead and buried.

As soon as he sat down, she said, "Whyn't we look at your studio, Mister Moss? That is, if you're up to it." She gave him a calculating look.

"What's the point?"

"You wanted something from me, innit? More, I'm thinking, than the tale of the old man's death. Did you not see what was shown to you?"

"I don't know what I saw." Moss waved impatiently. "I drank that concoction you gave me. I nearly died."

She smiled to herself. "Yet here you are. In the pink."

"I saw a girl's face in the water. A girl with black hair. Who was she?"

"I know very well what you saw, Mister Moss." She placed a hand on his wrist and pulled it toward her across the table. Her touch sent a tingle up his arm. He fought the urge to snatch his hand away.

"I'm not drinking any more of that tea," he said. "I'm done with that sort of bullshit." Part of him wished he'd never started this quest foolishness. The muse didn't play by any rules he had ever heard of.

"Once is enough," she said.

"Did Haller drink that shit?"

"Mo did whatever he had to do."

Sitting near her, the room seemed inordinately bright. Motes of dust danced in the sunlight. He glanced down at the hand gripping his wrist—the skin was nearly transparent, a webbing of blue veins traced across the back. He could feel the pulse of blood in her veins, the sound of her heart, each beat distinct as beads on a rosary.

Outside, a bird settled in the branches of the pines behind the cottage. The rustle of its feathers was as clear as the sound of its two-chambered heart beating beneath the glossy-black plumage. Moss felt suddenly wide awake. More alert than he had been in years. He started to stand, but she held him immobile with one hand. Hairs on his arm and on the back of his neck bristled. Panic welled up from the pit of his stomach.

"What's happening?" he croaked.

"Breathe," she instructed. She ran the tip of her tongue over her lips, her expression a perfect melding of innocence and violence. A vein squirmed under the skin of her temple like a snake uncoiling.

The muscles in his body were so tense he was shaking.

Suddenly she released her hold on his arm and stood up from the table. "Show me your paintings, Mister Moss. We can have a smoke in your studio." In the blink of an eye, things were back to a version of normal.

The key was in its usual spot above the door. The lock opened easily, smelling of oil. Inside was a stronger smell of lubricant, plus the faint scent of singed dust that had been burned off the coils when the caretaker had tested the large, wall-mounted heaters. The temperature in the shed was comfortable. Seren dropped her heavy coat on one of the stools and sat down. "Let's take a gander at your work." She lit a smoke and kicked off her flats.

Girding himself for derision, he pulled a canvas from the stack. Clouds of mauve and saffron floated over the surface, and here and there a sooty black wash interrupted the vaporous colors. Irregular patches of white canvas appeared to glow from under the dissolved passages of hue like light within a cloud bank. Across the top portion stretched a breath of cerulean blue.

He withdrew another and positioned it next to the first. This one was darker, but just barely. The model said nothing. Stubbing out her smoke, she lit another. Moss wished to flee. "These were all done long, long ago. I was a kid."

She gestured for him to bring out more. When he was done, the evidence of his failure was ranked across the floor of the shed. Seren motioned for him to sit. The whole charade reminded Moss of graduate critiques he'd weathered in school. In those days, the faculty would squat in front of the work and ramble on—more about themselves than the work facing them. When it was over, they'd clap him on the shoulder, or give him a sage nod of the head, and that was it. The teaching, if there was any, was done by osmosis. Only one or two of his advisors ever gave advice. The tips they offered came mostly in the form of other artists' work he should look at. It would have come as a relief to Moss if one of them had suggested adding a patch of red or obliterating some errant passage. But they clearly felt he knew what he was doing. Nothing could've been farther from the truth. A day came when he could pretend no longer. That day had broken his heart.

53

As they were leaving, Seren put a hand on Moss's arm. "I see what you were trying to accomplish back then." Later, over a dinner of potatoes cooked with bacon and onions, she looked up between mouthfuls and said, "Those early paintings aren't as bad as you think. You could turn them into something if you're willing to work. If not, let's drive home. Either you're a painter or you're not. Most people in this world are not."

'I'm not sure I know where to begin."

"Just paint," she said. "You may be fat and lazy, but once you had some ability. That's a rare thing—rarer than even you know. Either you'll find your lost touch, or you won't."

Even after drinking her noxious brews, the hope in her words buoyed him. It was possible he couldn't really see merit in his own work, the worth of it obscured for years and years by the taint of failure.

"Tomorrow we'll look again. Perhaps you'll find a place to begin." She drank a swallow of wine and smiled at him with a child's face. The line had nearly disappeared.

That night she joined him in bed. Her lovemaking was a revelation—she made love in slow motion. Touch, smell, and taste were magnified as in a dream. When they were done, she welded herself to his body, murmuring a wordless, breathy tune in his ear. When it came to making love, there was nothing that she could not do. Afterward, when he slept, he dreamt of alien landscapes and savage colors. The following morning, he felt eager to resume painting.

Back in the shed, he discovered gestures in his old canvases he hadn't seen previously. He was able to divine the underlying structures that had eluded him years before. By noon he had mixed a palette full of fresh colors, and he was ready to begin. Seren sat watching as he restructured the underpainting on one of his old failures, pulling shapes he needed from an incoherent ether of hues. If a painted passage didn't work, he ruthlessly wiped it away and replaced it with something stronger. The process was brutal, but he persisted. Working with Claudine earlier had helped prepare him. Now he was a different creature. When he felt stumped, he did the opposite of what his brain told him. The strategy proved effective nearly every time.

Now and then, Seren wrapped him in her arms, transfusing power into him. By the end of the day, it seemed like they had been doing the same ritual for years. His instinct and intuition were finally in sync—a gnostic synthesis that felt both old and new.

Later, she gave him a glass of wine at the kitchen table and cooked dinner for him. Meat and potatoes were what she favored. They drove Athena to the supermarket in Houghton and rode home with bags of groceries on their laps. She seemed to appreciate turnips, and so they ate turnips with lamb or beef. Each night, when the first bottle of wine was empty, they went to bed. She sang to him as he dozed, exhausted from lovemaking. As soon as he heard her voice in his ear, he began to slip into a place rich in visions. So many ideas for new paintings came to him in his sleep that waking felt like a rude amputation. He couldn't wait to resume working.

By the end of the first week, he had completed three canvases.

He grew stronger—physically and artistically. His acuity increased. The colors worked. Seren said little. Occasionally, she suggested he revisit one area or another. "You know this," she would say, looking hard at the canvas. "You know that passage is weak, the edge misplaced." She had worked with dozens of artists, yet it seemed to Moss that only the two of them mattered. She knew his work better than he did. The days passed, and they constructed a private world in the dingy shed.

At night, there was music on the stereo, and they talked in the shadow of Bainbridge's great painting. She spoke a little of her childhood in Wales, of the sea, of poverty being always a shadow in her life. She grew up knowing she was somehow different from the others. Village dogs grew silent whenever she walked the lanes at night. She had a brother who was very ill and who never left their croft during daylight. Badly burned as an infant, any sudden movement sent him into a murderous rage. As a consequence of his fury, she learned to control her body—to be stealthy, invisible. At fourteen she found work modeling in the city. Her twin sister accompanied her on those trips, but she never posed. It was only Seren who was required to disrobe for aging artists. When she could, she took money home.

Moss asked her how she came to know Bainbridge, though his need for such information had diminished to nearly nothing. She never spoke directly about the old man and their relationship. After her sister died, her mother shipped her off to Nebraska. She remembered the vegetable garden on his farm—rows of tomato plants, pole beans, and clumps of rhubarb. She told him how sweet the nights smelled in the country, and how the old man took her to an overlook above the Platte. She sat while he sketched the curve of the river and the forest beyond. She practiced staying perfectly still so as not to disturb his drawing.

Near Platte River were fields and pastures, but Bainbridge insisted on leaving them out of his compositions, trying for something more magical, more primal. At night, crows roosted in the trees at the edge of the yard. When she was still little, she sat on the old man's lap in the evenings while he rocked in the white rocking chair under the willows.

Her visits ceased when the painter moved to Detroit. He never explained why he chose to leave Nebraska, only that things had changed.

A few years later, Haller found her in London. She'd recognized him, but he never admitted to knowing her in the early days. His brain was already rotting from alcohol. With Haller, there was money. He was famous even then. The relationship was convenient for both of them. Seren became the doorway for his visions, and for his demons.

Moss listened. He guessed he had earned a modicum of honesty—at last. His gut told him she might be Bainbridge's offspring. The numbers made sense. And why else would her mother ship her off to Bainbridge when she was bringing in money at home? When he questioned her about it, she ignored him.

With each revelation from the model, the facts began adding up. In the end it didn't really matter, because he was painting better than he ever imagined. The work demanded everything. Moss's extra pounds melted away. He felt he was closer to what he wanted than ever before.

The month of December would be a trial. In those days, it rained constantly. Moss started dressing in his yellow slicker as a matter of habit. There were leaks in the shed's roof. Seren found buckets to catch most of the water. Moss worried the electric heaters would short out, but they never did.

Most nights, he fell asleep with the sound of her voice in his head. He never questioned how the bedrock of his perception had changed, how color seemed a living thing, how the pattern of waves on the lake determined the rhythm of his brushwork or how a hastily described edge carved out an immaculate space. Seren was a part of everything. At night they made love in a cocoon of desire. Dreams flowed out from his subconscious like pythons—each one perfect, each one deadly.

Hanging over him was the guilt he felt about Claudine. He feared happiness was at the root of her silence. He wanted her to be happy, but happy with him. He never forgot it was Claudine who had started him painting again. Everything he put on canvas carried her imprimatur.

After a month, Moss sent a shipment of six paintings south to the Fairchild Moss Gallery on Townsend Street. He'd spoken with Kaye and agreed that if she didn't think they were worth hanging, she would simply store them in the basement. She loved them. When Sally visited the gallery, she immediately offered to carry them at Donald Morris if Kaye was worried about a conflict of interest. Kaye wouldn't have it. She sold two in the first week. After hearing a rumor, *Free Press* columnist Joy Colby came by the gallery. She was stunned. She had never liked Moss, but she was blown away by the paintings and offered to write a glowing review if Kaye were to mount a show.

Up in the Keweenaw, Moss paid little attention to news from the outside. He could see for himself the work was good, and he knew it was Seren's doing.

Numennin agreed to ferry their groceries from Houghton so Moss could work without distraction. The old Finn even visited the studio occasionally at the end of the day, sitting with his pipe while Seren and Moss shared a cigarette once the work was finished. Every other Sunday, Leena Numennin brought them a casserole and a fruit pie made from the last of the year's harvest. The four of them sometimes ate dinner together while a fire blazed in the next room. Seren got on with Numennin's wife. No one mentioned her otherness.

The Numennins appeared subtly vigilant but eager to help. Moss thought little of their newfound friendliness. It seemed overdue. In their visits, they formed the family he never had. He was a changed man.

His work took on a greater urgency. When a shipment of blank canvases arrived, he was ready. He had started thinking about mounting a show at the gallery in January—in the back salon, not the main room. He wasn't front-room material. Not yet.

One day, Seren brought the Manolete photograph into the studio. Moss started a painting based loosely on the image. Blacks, violets, brilliant yellow. Cadmium red pooled on a ground of alizarin crimson. He recalled the dream he'd had of the tidal pool. The bull's head on the child's body floating out of the water. Sacrificial victims merged into a single entity. His mind formed the image of a Minotaur. Both Goya and Picasso had fixated on the mythical beast. Moss recalled the wet, black muzzle he had seen in his dream, its pink tongue curled to the side. The curved ivory-colored horns, black at their tips. The dead eyes of the animal. The dead eyes of the girl.

He filled one canvas and began another. By the time he was done, the painting spanned four fifty-inch square canvasses lining the studio wall. It was bigger than Claudine's portrait. The creature, swallowed in a matrix of color, was surrounded by a halo of thin lines—spears or arrows—its image reminiscent of paleolithic drawings from the Altamira caves, where art and religion melded into truth. When he had finished, he pressed a handprint into the wet paint as a kind of signature.

"These paintings of yours are something, lover," Kaye said over long-distance wires. "Boo Tice has already put a hold on two of them. People are beginning to talk. Even Birdie Entwistle stopped by the gallery—he never leaves downtown, not ever."

Moss didn't react. Everything except his work seemed incidental and far away. He said nothing about Seren to Kaye. They were two worlds he wanted to keep separate. He had a hard time remembering his previous existence at all. He'd shed a skin, and now everything behind him seemed like an illusion. Except for Claudine. He wished she would write. It didn't occur to him to write to her.

Seren was now so embedded in his consciousness he no longer saw the strange line on her face. They lived as pagans. Without conscience. Without regret. In bed, they did things he had never dreamed of—in the act of love she was boundless. Anything was possible.

Their comfort did not extend, however, to the subject of Haller or her twin sister. Whenever either was mentioned, she shut him down with a finality that made him wince. What he was able to piece together was some relationship between Haller and the dead twin. The specifics were clouded, but his intuition told him something big had occurred. Only a fool would ignore the arrows pointing toward the model. At best, she may have been an accomplice. At worst, what? He didn't press the point. He was addicted to himself. The self she had conjured in the night.

One day Numennin reminded him of the coming winter. The shed lacked insulation for temperatures below freezing. With the old Finn's help, Moss and Seren rolled up the rugs in the living room, pushed pieces of furniture to the edges or carried them to the guest wing, and moved the studio equipment to the cottage. All the art except the Bainbridge painting, the Brice Godwin sketch, and the Manolete photograph were stored in spare bedrooms.

They covered the stone floors with giant tarpaulins, added portable lighting, and a new studio was born. Lining the walls were canvases in various stages of completion. The big easel was positioned near the fireplace. The main portion of the cottage was rededicated to his work. When he wasn't painting, they lived mostly in the kitchen and the master bedroom.

Seren never offered him a hallucinogenic brew from the Spotted Man again, yet their synergistic connection grew. Often it was difficult for Moss to sort out which memory belonged to him and which to her. They communed more and more on a nonverbal level. Food, and especially drink, became an afterthought to Moss. He'd lost enough pounds that his dungarees hung loose at his hips. A trip into Houghton produced a couple of new pairs of jeans he could wear while painting.

Weeks went by, and the temperature dipped below freezing. The first flurries turned to drifts that melted within a few hours.

54

Two or three little things nagged at him. He couldn't ignore the guilt he felt over leaving Claudine in Paris. He'd fostered a fiction in his head that she would return to him at some future point. Occasionally, the two women, Claudine and Seren, merged into a single entity in his mind. Seren shared his brain and his vision. Claudine, however, shared his past and his heart. He missed her. Sleeping with Seren was a betrayal, but he eased his conscience by assuming Claudine was sleeping with Sloane Ellis. He'd seen their emotional connection firsthand in Paris. There were parallels—tit for tat. He allowed that thought to salve his guilt.

Another thing—a lesser thing—was Seren's periodic slippage into the royal plural. It seemed grandiose, as though an angel sat on her shoulder.

One night in bed, she sat astride him, pleasure filling her face. It felt if he were seeing someone else. He was sure this was more than the dichotomy her face displayed. The expression he saw seemed different—softer, younger, without the underlying savagery he'd become familiar with. He opened his mouth to speak, but she placed her hand over his lips. The rhythmic movement of her hips soon distracted him. Nothing was said.

That night a disturbing dream woke him. He was lying on his back, looking upward through a murky lens. Above him a malignant figure straddled his chest, pinning him. His wrists were restrained above his head. Gasping for breath, he fought against the shadowy beings above. As he was about to suffocate, the lens cleared, and Moss saw the faces of Maurice Haller and Seren looming above, laughing. Tearing himself away from the dream, he was covered in a greasy sweat.

A few days later, after dinner, he asked Seren what had happened to her sister.

She set down her glass and gave him a long look. "You know her as well as you know me. Two trees from one seed, I told you. She-me, and me-she."

"Tell me again."

She shook her head and said icily, "This has nothing to do with you."

"No, but it has to do with you," he said. Suddenly it seemed important to know. "You're here. With me. Surely there's an 'us' now?"

She stood up from the table and started to collect the dishes. "Stop," she said, shooting him a black look over her shoulder. "I share your bed. Don't think it means more than it does."

"What if it means something to me?"

"It's your problem then, innit?" She busied herself scraping plates.

"Who was the girl I saw in my dream? Long black hair in a pool of water?" Moss knew he should shut up at that point, but he couldn't. Suspicion lodged in the back of his brain. If Seren was one half of a being, where was the other half?

She threw down the dishcloth and faced him. "These are no dreams, you fool! You asked for all of this, don't forget! Did you believe you'd find a rosy fairytale in the other world?"

"Your sister?"

Seren tossed her hair, the line between her eyes pulsing like a vein. "Leave it alone. I warned you."

"What did Haller have to do with it? Was your sister involved with him?"

"I warned you to leave it alone. You know nothing of Mo or Cece, or me." Her eyes blazed. "You've got what you wanted, Mister Moss."

"You had something to do with Haller's death?" Moss guessed the answer.

"He knew the game from the start," she hissed. "He got what he wanted in the end. He's in the books."

"Was it Haller and your sister?" Threads that had once seemed random now wove together. "It was Haller." He was now convinced.

She surprised him by laughing, a little-girl laugh. "Questions and more questions. Remember what curiosity did for the cat, puss." He heard Birdie Entwistle's voice coming from her mouth. Throwing on her coat, she stepped into her wellies and walked into the night.

55

Haller being involved in Seren's sister's death wouldn't explain everything, but it would explain a lot. It seemed likely she had her revenge. Seren was involved with the Brit's death.

For the first time in weeks, he had a yen for Chartreuse. Pouring himself a tumbler with ice, he took his drink into the living room turned art studio. He studied the big, multipaneled Minotaur painting. It was his best. Filled with a dark energy and foreboding, the sensations it generated reminded him of the vision he'd had—weeks ago—of the girl in the pond. Nearly twenty feet wide, it would be the focal point for his upcoming exhibition. Everything about it was grand and dramatic. The human eye of the black-dappled bull, and the suggestion of a maze shape in the lower portion of the second panel, provided just enough of a bridge to the mythic subject matter. It was an homage to the Neolithic, to Goya and Picasso, but it was more than that. It was an homage to Seren and her dead sister.

By eleven o'clock Seren still had not returned. He ran a bath, determined to read and soak until she showed up. He was dozing off when she appeared in the bathroom's doorway. She said nothing of where she'd been. He scrunched up his legs, making room in the tub. "Come, join me." He turned the tap to warm the water. Seren pulled her shift over her head and climbed in. As soon as she touched him, he became aroused. She lit his cigarettes and hummed a little while stroking him. He knew better than to bring up her sister again. Soon they would ship the new paintings south, and Kaye would mount his first ever solo show. He was finally living the life he wanted—muse or no muse.

He made his voice as normal as he could. "Can we expect to see the Numennins tomorrow?" The following day was Sunday. He was looking forward to a casserole.

"Not tomorrow. Maybe next week," Seren said.

"I've gotten used to them coming over."

"They're pleased to see you with a purpose in life," she said, stubbing her Newport out in the ashtray. "You should be happy, orphan man."

His fingers were pruned, the bathwater cooled. She ran hot water for him. The drink made him sleepy. As his lids drooped, an idea for a new painting came to him. "Will you pose tomorrow? I'd like to try out a composition with your wrists tied to that big iron ring. A girl with horns—what do you think?"

"On the shore?" she said dubiously.

"No, no," he laughed. "In the studio. We'll cobble together a fictive setting."

"One last painting, Mister Moss?" She looked past him to a thing he couldn't see. "Have you not got what you sought?"

Later in bed, he fell into a contented, dreamless sleep.

56

Moss awoke to searing heat scorching the membranes of his nasal passages. At first he was sure it was another dream. He reached to the other side of the bed for Seren. She was gone. He sat up abruptly when he heard crackling sounds coming from outside his door—he smelled fire. His bedroom door was closed, and smoke was seeping under it. Panic rose in his chest. Naked, he flung the door open. Billows of acrid smoke filled the room, choking him. The air scorched his lungs. He fled to the bathroom and grabbed for a towel. Soaking it with water from the bathtub tap, he held the wet cloth over his nose and mouth.

He could sense enormous heat now. His skin prickled. When he entered the red glow of the hallway, the hair on his arms singed to ash. The cottage was engulfed. He must've been deep asleep not to have awoken earlier. Scuttling back into the bathroom, heart racing, he soaked a larger bath towel and wrapped it around his shoulders. Water coursing down his back evaporated in the heat before it could reach the ground. He needed to save his paintings. He was in a panic, desperate to rescue his new work and, more importantly, the Bainbridge. Wrapped in an armor of wet towels, he dashed to the living room. Fire danced along walls, reaching up to the ceiling. The room was clouded with smoke. His eyes watered. Fear wrenched his gut. On one wall, the Bainbridge smoldered. The temperature was so intense Moss could barely breathe.

The surface of the big painting glistened with oil in the light of the flames. The yellow sky started to melt. Its heavy impasto, still wet beneath a dried crust, loosened from the surface of the canvas and began to peel away, revealing the scraped-down portrait of Seren still visible underneath.

For a brief second, he allowed himself to stare at the mismatched features he knew well. A half smile, half smirk graced her lips. Her remote and merciless eyes bore into him, stripping him down to his core. He knew he could never let her go. She had created him.

As he struggled to lift the painting from its moorings, spatters of hot yellow paint rained down and burned into his bare arms, dripped onto his hair. The mounting hangers refused to relinquish their hold. He cursed, tugging and twisting the canvas stretcher, trying to wrench it free. One hook yielded to his efforts at the exact moment he felt his hair ignite. Metal cannisters of turpentine on the tabouret exploded, adding fuel to the inferno.

Moss gave up his grip on the painting. His heart was a trip-hammer. There was no air left to breathe. With one last look at the face of the muse, he slumped to his knees. A heavy beam from the ceiling came crashing down, glancing painfully off his shoulder. A section of the ceiling fell around him, sending a jagged splinter of wood through the back of his hand, taking flesh and sinew with it. Fire shrieked. Hot ash flew into his face. The flesh on his scalp blistered. On instinct, he crawled on hands and knees toward the kitchen just as the entire roof of the living room collapsed. There were no thoughts in his head now—only that he needed to save himself.

Scuttling to the kitchen door, he grabbed at the knob. The flesh of his good hand withered, seared by the glowing metal. He screamed with pain, but the sound of the fire drowned everything.

From the corner of his eye he spied a shadow in the cellar door-way—a ghost, a patch of darkness visible against the inferno.

He heard his skin start to crackle. Vision fading, he was about to lose consciousness. He slammed his shoulder against the door. Nothing. Again, nothing. He was about to try a third time when the door flew open. Through clouds of smoke, he saw the outline of a figure—Numennin! He was dragged from the building by the old Finn just as the cottage exploded with a blast of scorching smoke. Hurled face first on the decking, he scrabbled like a crab onto the surrounding grass.

Numennin knelt beside him, patting out the still-smoldering embers on his skin. "I was driving past, saw the flames."

"Thank God," Moss gasped. He felt nothing of his burns. His mind had detached itself from his body. Two hundred feet away, the shed was a bonfire, flames shooting thirty feet into the air. Perfect kindling, loud cracks filled the night as the structure disap-peared like an offering.

The old Finn guided Moss to the van, opened the back, and helped him sit. "Wait here," he said. "I called 911. Firemen will be here shortly." Numennin turned and wandered back toward the cottage.

From his seat, Moss glimpsed a diminutive figure skirting down the driveway toward the lake. He willed himself up, despite his wounds, and followed. When he arrived at the steps leading down to the shore, he lost sight of her for a moment. His vision was hazy. Something bad had happened to his eyes. Rivulets of blood from a wound on his scalp streaked his face. After a moment, he caught a glimmer of her at the water's edge. She loped along the beach, heading northward toward Eagle River.

Descending the stairs, Moss stumbled on the uneven planking and fell down the final two steps. Every nerve in his body woke up at once—pain shot through his synapses like an electric current. He screamed.

Hobbling after the fleeing Seren, he realized he would never catch her. Sinking to his knees where the waves touched the shore, he bellowed her name. To his surprise, she stopped and turned back. He could just make out the shape of her coat and the whiteness of her skin. Approaching within twenty feet, she looked down at him. The black line dividing her face widened. "Blow me, I surely didn't think to see you alive." She turned to go.

"Wait," he croaked through blistered lips.

"We're quits, you and I." Her voice was distorted by the sound of waves. The sky beyond the pine trees glowed yellow with flames. "Salvage what you can, but do not follow me."

Moss reached out to her. She backed away, disappearing into the dark.

EPILOGUE

Detroit, Spring 1979

Late afternoon at the end of April, Moss made the short walk from his condo to the Midtown Café. He had only been back to his former haunt once or twice since the fire. Hearing from Kaye that Claudine had returned from Paris, he decided to see if she was around. Lately, he'd started to feel a little better—considering. Some days he was able to shake off the events in his life, and other days he chose to stay in bed. Kaye ran the business even better than he'd imagined. When he'd first returned, she had been unable to conceal her astonishment at his gauntness. She said nothing, but her face revealed everything.

At the Midtown, the happy-hour crowd was filtering in. The tables and booths were beginning to fill. Moss found a spot at the end of the bar and swiveled the stool away from the noise. A few patrons cast a wary eye his way. He no longer fit in with the glossy clientele.

Whistling a few bars from "Waltzing Matilda," he ran a hand over the scruffy bristles on his scalp, the ridged surface where stitches had recently been. The hairs on his head were coming in pure white. His beard was better, but it was still a salt-and-pepper gray—leaning more toward salt than pepper. Helmut made his way down the bar from the opposite end, where he'd been phoning in late orders to suppliers. Like everyone in town, he'd heard the story of the fire and Moss's stark transformation. Without a word, he poured a Perrier on ice with a twist of lemon and set it in front of him. Moss lifted his glass in a gesture of appreciation.

Four-thirty came and went. He was feeling increasingly antsy. True to type, Seren had vanished. Once he was released from the hospital in Houghton, he stayed a few days at the Numennin farm. Little was said about the muse. It was as if she'd never been. There was no inquiry as might happen in the movies. The local authorities didn't ask many questions. They blamed the whole incident on the gas cans stored too close to the furnace. Moss was content to let people assume whatever was most convenient.

Ten minutes later, Helmut set another Perrier in front of him and asked if he wanted something else. Moss declined. In the time he was up north, he had dropped more than thirty pounds. His trousers were hanging loose these days, and he was determined to keep it that way. When he'd visited the Donald Morris Gallery, Sally said he looked like a Bohemian and gave him a sympathetic peck on the cheek. The degree of awkwardness forced him out the door sooner than he'd intended.

In the bar, the decibel level had risen steadily as shops and offices set their minions free after a day slaving in the temples of commerce. Everyone looked younger than he remembered. For lack of anything better to do, he examined his hands. A few new brownish spots had made their appearance. On his left palm there was a blotchy-red patch running from the base of his thumb to his knuckles. It would turn into a glassy scar eventually. He had fashioned a simple brace to use when painting.

At a quarter after five, Claudine appeared dressed in the customary black skirt and white shirt. After chatting with Helmut for a few minutes, she made her way down the length of the bar, greeting regulars and spreading the cheer of her smile. When she arrived at Moss's perch, she paused a beat to give him a lingering up-and-down.

"I see you've gone butch on me," she said. Her words hung in the air before she gave him a wink. "Seriously, Moss, the buzz cut works for you." She glanced at his new eyeglasses with their coke-bottle lenses but said nothing.

He decided to ignore the remark about his singed scalp. "You made it back from France?"

"So it would appear." She retrieved a bottle of house vodka from the back bar and poured herself a glass. "Double Chartreuse?"

He shook his head. "I've fallen into the slough of abstinence these days."

"That doesn't sound like you."

He tried for a smile but didn't succeed. "Things are different."

"I can see that." Her voice was guarded. "I heard about the fire. I'm sorry, Moss."

He nodded. It was no secret. The effects were visible to all.

"Athena?" she asked.

"Burnt to a crisp."

"The Bainbridge painting?"

He shook his head. "Gone." He said nothing about the great bull painting that had gone up in flames.

"Oh God, that's a shame," she said. "The painting, the car, the cottage? All of it ashes?"

"An architect is drawing up plans for something new. A work-space. Bare bones, but big." He drained the glass of fizzy water. It was impossible to sort out how seeing her again felt. He hoped she didn't notice his nervous tick. That would be weird.

"That's good," she said. "It's nice up north in summertime."

"The new building will be pretty basic. Numennin seems glad of that."

"I'll bet." She turned on her heel and strolled to the other end of the bar to see if anyone needed refills. He took the interlude to rearrange his thoughts for the ten thousandth time. Claudine looked mostly the same, though she might've added a pound or two. It looked good on her, but it was hard to improve on perfection.

Several minutes later she returned from her circuit and resumed her familiar stance across the bar. He wanted to look into her eyes but was suddenly shy. Instead, he said, "Numennin saved me from the fire."

"Your Gran was a wise woman," she said, leaning a hip against the backbar. "Do you ever wonder about her and him?"

"No. Why?" She was right about his Gran, as with most things.

"Never mind."

His mouth felt dry. He reached for his glass but found it empty. "Congrats on the *Wreck of the Medusa* photo," he said. "It's big. Lots of press."

She shot a smile his way. "Who would've guessed?"

"Maybe everyone?" he said. "I've got a print hanging at the condo." He glanced around the room. The place had filled up. A lot of eyes were on Claudine. A month ago, the *Free Press* had done a four-column piece that included an interview. She was a home-town girl.

"I could've asked Sloane to send you a signed one."

"No need." He detested the way she said Sloane's name. He glanced down at the bar to keep his equilibrium. "How's Sloane?"

"The world is what it is," she said, shrugging her familiar fatalistic shrug. "Marylou says you're working for Boo nowadays."

Moss laughed the first genuine laugh in months. "Not working for—consulting with. There's a difference. He wants to get the collection in shape before the new wing at the DIA opens. You can guess the experience is a tad *unusual*, for lack of a better word."

"Some things never change."

He nodded. Tice had been persistent. Moss couldn't force himself to return to the gallery, but he couldn't stay in bed all day, every day, either. "Maybe you could pour me a Chartreuse? For old time's sake?"

She placed a hand on his arm. "You bet."

When she set the drink in front of him, he asked, "How's the work on the new project going?"

"It's okay. I go back to Paris next month. The book Sloane is putting together goes to press sometime this summer and will come out in late fall."

"That's good," he said, with the ring of a question.

"I guess." She peered into his eyes. "I hear you're painting."

"I rented a place in town until the studio up north is finished. Bainbridge's old attic on Cass Avenue."

"Ironic," she said. "It's like the old guy's ghost is still hanging around."

"Ghosts everywhere," he said with a smile, thinking it was true, thinking it had always been true.

A momentary frown crossed her features. "What about Seren?"

"Disappeared," he said. In the days following the fire, he wondered if he had truly seen her on the beach, or if he had simply blacked out near the water where the rescue team found him. His savior, Numennin, said nothing about the witch.

"Will you try to find her?"

"No." The muse was gone, but she'd left a small something among the wreckage of his life.

"Good," she said.

"I need to paint." He could feel the muse. Out there. Somewhere.

Claudine said, "That's important."

"I've been thinking a lot about what you said when we were in Aix. You know, finding a place in the south of France for the winter."

"I've thought about it too," she said carefully. "Most every day."

He kept his voice as matter-of-fact as he was able. "Maybe we could grab dinner?"

"Okay." A momentary shadow chased across her features, then she brightened. "Sure. That could happen."

END

ACKNOWLEDGEMENTS

When I finished the first draft of *Seren* in 2023, I had no real idea of how complex, collaborative, and energizing the process of getting the narrative into print was going to be. I am fortunate to have an extensive base of writers and readers on which to draw for the early critiquing stage. Many people were willing to look at the initial draft and provide helpful feedback. Among those savvy and highly literate helpers were members of the Corrales Writers Group—Chris Allen, Sandi Hoover, Joe Brown, Pat Walkow, and Maureen Cooke. Additionally, fellow writers Julie Sando, Kristen Keegan, and Jim Tritten, along with Professor Barbara Smith, a longtime colleague from the University of Dayton, provided excellent suggestions. Developmental editing and advice were contributed by authors Shanna McNair (*Soul Retrieval*) and Scott Wolven (*Controlled Burn*) of the Writer's Hotel, Professor Arnold Johnston (*Swept Away*) and Debra Anne Percy (*Invisible Traffic*) of Western Michigan University, and Adam Prince (*The Beautiful Wishes of Ugly Men*) and Phaedra Greenwood (*Those Were the Days*) of the Taos Writer's Circle. Skilled copyediting was performed by James Ayers of the University of New Mexico Press and Becca Thompson of Apprentice House Press. Oversight of the entire publication process was carried out by the director of Apprentice House Press, Professor Kevin Atticks.

Numerous others were involved in the formation of this book, but no one contributed more than my beloved wife, Dr. Sharon A. Ransom, without whose enduring support this work would not have been possible.